"WHAT ARE YOU DRESS?" he asked, the words whisper-sof Not what she expected him to s

His teeth sank into her low.. ... "Focus."

On what? The demon club? The humans dying downstairs? The fact that you're a fucking vampire? Where should I begin?

He sighed, his forehead falling to hers. "Astasiya, we have very little time to sort this before the Conclave. I need you to work with me. Both our lives depend on it. What are you wearing?"

She cleared her throat, her hold on his neck tightening as if needing his support to respond. And maybe she did. This was all a lot to take in. "A, uh, thong," she managed to say. "And a strapless bra."

One of his hands drifted from her hair to her waist, then down to her ass. His palm flattened and forced her to arch up into him. A breath hitched in her throat at the feel of his growing arousal.

He's turned on... here... now?

She trembled, the heat of his body seeping into her cool skin, warming her blood. They were standing rather close. And he smelled amazing, as always.

Anywhere else, in the dark, she'd have kissed him. But here...

"The dress will have to stay, then," he said, the disappointment evident in his voice.

She frowned. "What's wrong with my dress?" It hit her midthigh and clung to her curves. She looked good in it.

He ignored her, his mouth brushing hers in a chaste kiss as his hips pressed firmly into hers.

Definitely aroused.

"You're going to see things tonight that will make you want to scream, but you must remain calm and quiet. Mortals who overreact die, and they die badly."

IMMORTAL CURSE SERIES

BLOOD LAWS

FORBIDDEN BONDS

BLOOD HEART

ELDER BONDS

BLOOD BONDS

ANGEL BONDS

Blood Laws

AN
IMMORTAL CURSE
NOVEL

USA TODAY BESTSELLING AUTHOR
LEXI C. FOSS

Blood Laws

Editing by: Outthink Editing, LLC

Plotting Consultant: Heart Full of Ink

Proofreading By: Barb Jack, Joy Di Biase-Giachino Katie Schmahl, & Laura Schoenfelder

Cover Design: Covers by Julie

Photography: Wander Aguiar Photography

Models: Thom Panto & Tiffany

Published by: Ninja Newt Publishing, LLC

Print Edition

ISBN: 978-0-9985557-7-5

To my parents, for encouraging me to follow my dreams, and to Elaine, for believing in me…

BLOOD LAWS

BOOK ONE

IMMORTAL CURSE SERIES

GLOSSARY

PRETERNATURAL BEINGS

Fledgling (noun): The child of a male Ichorian and a human female, who has not yet been reborn as a Hydraian; they do not typically possess supernatural or psychic gifts until their immortal rebirth.

Hydraian (noun): An immortal offspring of a male Ichorian and a human female, who possesses two supernatural or psychic gifts and does not require human blood to survive.

Ichorian (noun): An immortal being of unknown descent who possesses one supernatural or psychic gift and requires human blood to survive.

Immortal (noun): A general noun designating a being who does not age and is immune to natural human death.

Seraphim (noun): A being who belongs to the highest order of angelic hierarchy.

KEY TERMS

Arcadia: Notorious Ichorian club in New York City that also serves as the primary meeting location for the Ichorian government.

Blood Laws: A series of ordinances created by the Ichorian governing board in response to the Treaty of 1747.

Catastrophic Relief Foundation (CRF): A global humanitarian aid organization headquartered in New York City with a secret paramilitary unit designed to destroy rogue supernaturals.

Conclave: The Ichorian governing board.

Edict: A law or rule issued by the High Council of Seraph.

Elders: The original Hydraians who also serve as the Hydraian governing board.

Fated Line: Seraphim who can foresee the future.

High Council of Seraph: Seraphim governing board.

Nizari: Ancient Ichorian assassins who hunt and kill fledglings.

Nizari Poison: A green substance notorious for killing fledglings and preventing their rebirth.

Sentinel: A soldier in the CRF unit designed to slaughter rogue immortal beings.

Treaty of 1747: An armistice between Hydraians and Ichorians to cease fire and live in their designated areas. Those who opt to cross these boundaries do so at their own risk.

"An unknown power is surfacing. She will possess the strength and will to destroy us all unless certain measures are put in place to curb her inclinations."

—Prophetess Skye

Blood Laws

By order of the Ichorian Conclave, the below behaviors are forbidden:

The intentional creation of fledgling immortals through procreation with human females

Knowingly allowing fledgling immortals or Hydraians to exist on Ichorian soil

Consorting with Hydraians in any capacity, unless otherwise negotiated by birthright and rank

PROLOGUE

"READY?" ASTASIYA'S ANGEL FRIEND ASKED, gesturing to the house before them.

She shook her head, not ready at all. He had told her these new people would be her parents. But she didn't want new parents. She wanted her old ones back. Right now.

"They'll protect you, just like your parents did."

She bit her lip, her focus on the door so unlike the one at home. "But Momma keeps talking to me," she whispered. "She needs help."

So much heartbreak.

Sadness.

Momma's all alone.

Astasiya's lips trembled. The dreams scared her the

1

most. All that water with nowhere to go. She drowned over and over and over.

And it hurt. So, so much. Astasiya woke screaming every time, that madman's eyes fresh in her mind.

They were just supposed to play hide-and-seek. But Daddy never came for her. She tried to find him instead, and she did, but her angel friend appeared and took her to a safe place with lots of trees. He promised to keep her safe, like he always did when he visited.

But Momma isn't safe.

"I'll search for your mom," he said to her now, his voice soft yet stern. "While you live here, okay? And then one day, we'll go find her together."

"Promise?" she asked. 'Cause if he did, then he'd have to see it through. Because that's what Daddy always told her—*a promise can't be broken.*

"I vow it," her angel friend replied, squeezing her hand. "We'll find her."

She nodded. "Together."

"Together," he agreed.

"Gabriel," a soft voice whispered through the cool air, causing the hairs along Astasiya's arms to dance. She couldn't see anyone other than the angel holding her hand, but she could *feel* the new presence.

Another angel. This one was misting like her momma sometimes did when they played hide-and-seek. Technically, it was cheating because Astasiya couldn't see her momma when she did that. Just like the unfamiliar angel who had joined them without revealing herself.

Astasiya's heart gave a big jump in her chest, her lips wobbling again. *Can Momma mist under water? Does she have her wings?*

"Astasiya," her angel friend murmured. "You won't remember me when we meet again, but I will make sure you know the truth when the time is right."

Her eyebrows crinkled. That didn't make sense. "But I know you."

"Yes, but to keep you safe, I need you to forget me. For now." He looked toward the space where the chiming voice originated—at the invisible angel.

Astasiya wished she could see, but she wasn't old enough yet. Had to be a grown-up, her parents always said. But she so badly wanted to see the feathers, especially the blue ones her daddy once described.

"Your mother has the most beautiful wings, little angel. A light blue with traces of white and sapphire. You'll see them one day."

"Everything from this week, including Osiris if she saw him," her angel friend said to the empty space.

"What about the death?" the chiming voice asked.

What color are your wings? Astasiya wanted to ask, but she knew it was rude to interrupt. She'd ask when they finished talking.

"She needs that to grow," he replied. "And Ezekiel needs to be the villain."

"I can do that. Anything else?"

"Yes. Give her doubts about Caro's true nature."

"That's going to be difficult."

"Indeed, that's why I called the best memory manipulator in existence for assistance." His light eyes met Astasiya's again with a sadness in them that reminded her of her dreams. "Consider me your personal Seraphim, Astasiya. I'll always be watching over you." He kissed her on the forehead and straightened. "Now, Vera."

The air tingled with energy. *That feels weird.*

"Already started," the chiming voice whispered.

I don't understand, Astasiya tried to say, but her lips didn't move. Something felt… weird. Like floating. Another dream? But she didn't want to sleep. Not yet.

These people, who were they? Her new parents.

No. She had parents.

They… they died.

No, they didn't!

Momma… water…

Their house went up flames. Her mother and father

inside.

That's not… It didn't… What are you doing?

Black eyes, flickering with gold embers.

Drowning…

She shivered. That face belonged to the devil. He lit a match and watched them burn. Astasiya had been trapped, hiding, watching it all happen. Every scream. Her name from her mother's mouth.

In my dreams, she calls for me. Not de—

There was nothing she could do. Just watched them die. A horrible, painful death. That's what happened when Astasiya persuaded—those around her were hurt.

No! Daddy said it wasn't my fault!

Except, maybe, no. She shouldn't have compelled that man for the ice cream. Her parents were found because of it. She would be found, too, if she ever did it again.

They'd kill her.

Just like her parents.

She had to be good. She had to behave. She had to hide. With her new family. The Davenports.

Astasiya blinked. Her head felt funny. Like she'd fallen down and hit it.

Momma?

She sniffled. No. Her momma was gone. She'd never see her again. And not because of the misting game. Or were those part of her dreams? Astasiya scrunched her nose, confused. It all felt so… *wrong.*

"Goodbye, little sister," a voice whispered in the wind, causing her brow to pucker.

What was that?

The doorbell rang, startling her from a daze. Had she just done that? Her fingers curled at her sides. She must have because no one else stood out here. Someone had just dropped her off.

So fuzzy.

And cloudy.

"Astasiya?" a warm voice greeted, the female before her

unfamiliar, but her eyes were kind. She smiled, holding out a hand. "Welcome home, sweetheart."

Home.

She frowned. *This isn't my home.*

But she belonged here now. Because her parents died.

That's not…

"Oh, Henry! Astasiya is here!" The woman sounded so happy. So welcoming. She even smiled a nice smile.

Trustworthy.

Astasiya felt her lips curl. This could be okay. Maybe she'd stay.

But Momma needs me… She just couldn't remember why. Something about water. No, a fire. It engulfed them, killing them, leaving her here.

With the Davenports.

Her new parents.

My new home.

CHAPTER ONE

Fate Comes Knocking

Seventeen Years Later

"GOOD MORNING," JEFFREY GREETED, SMILE firmly in place.

Stas Davenport didn't know how the elderly man always appeared so cheery. And in New York City, of all places. No one smiled here, especially not at this ungodly morning hour.

"Hi," she replied, forcing her lips upward. "Just here for Owen." *Who couldn't be bothered to meet me at the café for coffee.*

"Of course, miss." He never called her Stas even though he knew her name. "Go on up. I'm sure he's expecting you."

"Thank you." Stas managed another grin before stepping into the waiting elevator.

You better be awake, Stas typed as the doors closed. *And holding a coffee cup with my name on it.*

No reply.

He'd texted her this morning reminding her to come over. If he fell back asleep afterward, she'd kick his ass.

After her coffee, of course.

She selected his floor and narrowed her gaze at the numbers overhead.

"Let's meet Saturday at seven," she mimicked, doing a poor impersonation of her friend's voice. "No interruptions that way." Fuck. Not even her internship at the Catastrophic Relief Foundation (CRF) made her move around this early. Maybe she'd nap on Owen's couch while he practiced his dissertation. The slides for his presentation were all correct. He just needed to follow along.

She glanced at her screen again as she stepped out onto his floor.

Still no reply.

He totally went back to sleep.

Well, he wouldn't be sleeping for long.

She slid the phone back into her pocket, preparing her fists for a beating against his door. Except a man dressed in a tailored suit stood in her way, his focus on his hand.

Stas frowned. *Odd.* Owen usually preferred bulky, blond men, not athletically lean males. This one was much taller than her close friend's usual conquests, and prettier, too, in an aristocratically perfect kind of way.

She could see the appeal, especially in the way his suit pants cut across his strong thighs.

"So, you're why Owen's running late this morning," she said in greeting. "I suppose I can forgive him, as long as there's coffee waiting."

Striking blue eyes met hers, making her heart skip a beat.

Pretty had been too feminine a word.

Gorgeous was the more accurate adjective.

His high cheekbones and chiseled jaw were a deadly combination with those midnight irises. Lizzie would be elbowing her repeatedly right about now, her not-so-subtle way of calling attention to a handsome man. Good thing Stas left her back at the condo.

The elegantly dressed male glanced over her, his gaze exuding indifference before returning his attention to the phone in his hand.

Not even a hello.

Doorman Jeffrey would be so disappointed.

"Right, well, nice to meet you, too." She couldn't help the sarcastic note at the end. Not smiling, she understood. Outright ignoring someone, especially after fucking her friend, qualified as rude.

His alluring gaze shot upward, holding her in place when she would have moved around him for the door. "You're talking to me?"

Stas glanced up and down the empty hallway, her brow furrowing. "Who else would I be talking to?"

He cocked his head to the side, renewed interest flaring in his pupils. "You can see me." Not a question, but a statement.

A tingle crept down her spine, centering at the base and flaring outward across her skin. She almost shivered, her breathing uneven.

Something's not right.

She couldn't tell what. Just an inkling. An instinct. It curdled against her insides, kicking up her pulse.

I should—

The man pushed off the wall, his over-six-foot frame dwarfing her five-foot-eight one.

"You really can see me," he repeated. "How intriguing." His deep voice held a touch of a foreign lilt that she couldn't put her finger on. *English, maybe?* But not exactly. The accent seemed aged somehow.

"Uh, yeah. I can see you." She doubted he escaped much female notice, but his personality left a bit to be desired.

Her lips flattened as the stranger began to circle her, his midnight gaze roaming over her slowly and purposefully, touching on every curve and detail along the way. She swallowed, his blatant appraisal causing the hairs along her arms to dance in warning.

That is not how a gay man looks at a woman.

"Are you one of Jonathan's new toys?" he asked. "Come to review the details before the authorities arrive?"

"Jonathan?" *What the hell is this guy talking about?*

"Hmm, perhaps not, then." His irises finally returned to her own. "I doubt he'd send such a young candidate to survey the scene. Too brutal an introduction, but what is life without death?"

Her blood chilled. *Okay. Owen brought home a crazy person.* A good-looking one, sure, but the man was clearly mad.

"Right." She took a step away from the lunatic and another toward the door. "I'm just going to go in and talk to Owen now. You have a good day, okay?"

She took a third step, her fist raised to knock—

The air whooshed out of her as she was yanked backward into something hard. Her lips parted on a scream, only to be covered by a warm palm. A band of steel came around her middle, holding her arms in place when she tried to squirm.

Stas blinked.

What the fuck just happened?

Owen's door remained closed beside her as she faced the hallway.

The man stood behind her, his chest to her back, his solid arm around her waist, and his hand over her mouth.

How?

"Shh." Warm lips brushed her ear. "I'm not done with you yet."

His tense form held hers with ease, his back brushing the wall behind him.

Oh, hell no. Gorgeous man or not, she was not okay with being held against her will.

She threw her elbow backward just as the door beside them opened.

Thank. Fuck. Her muscles relaxed, relief settling over her shoulders. *Owen would—*

Her nose twitched. *What is that smell?*

So acrid.

So potent.

So *familiar.*

Burning flesh. A distinct scent, one she would never forget, and it was coming from inside her friend's apartment. Vivid memories overwhelmed her, locking her in place.

Her parents screaming in the flames, telling her to hide.

An evil man with eerie gold-flecked eyes.

Laughter.

Death.

"He says to leave it," a deep voice announced, stirring her from her memories, her palms clammy. "Someone will discover it soon."

"Works for me," a second male replied, grunting.

Both stepped through the threshold from Owen's apartment in matching black outfits, their hulking sizes far more intimidating than the male behind her. Not that she trusted him any more than she trusted them.

The one with lighter hair wiped his hands against his dark pants. He looked like the kind of man who went by Hank, while his olive-skinned friend was more of a Brutus.

And neither of them appeared the helpful sort.

They exuded an air of danger and malice, not because of the guns proudly displayed on their belts, but because of the grim satisfaction radiating from their expressions.

Stas froze. *What have you done to Owen?*

Because she knew that scent. It reminded her of death.

No. That's ridiculous. Maybe he burned breakfast, or popcorn, or *something.*

But then who the hell are these guys and why are they here?

A chill skittered down her spine, her heart in her throat. *Don't panic. It could—*

She held her breath as Hank turned to close the door. Why he scared her more than the man behind her did, she didn't know. It was all driven by instinct.

And he would see them in three, two…

He looked right at them.

Nothing.

"All right, let's go." It was directed over her head.

Oh, right. Because they're working together.

Of course they're working together.

Why else would the deranged man be here, holding me against my will? He'd clearly been waiting for these goons in the hallway.

I just need my mouth free, then I can get to Owen.

"Nah, something seems off out here." Brutus searched around them. "You feel it?"

Hank glanced up and down the corridor, his gaze passing over them in the process. "Yeah, I feel it. It's probably a residual from that." He gestured at Owen's door.

Stas shivered, not liking the insinuation or the stench still wafting around them. *What happened? Where's Owen?* she wanted to demand. She started to squirm, only to be held tighter by the man behind her, his palm practically smothering her mouth.

Does he know what I can do?

Are they here for me?

Impossible.

Brutus shuddered. "Yeah, that was bad."

Hank didn't seem as bothered and continued walking. "Let's just go."

Yeah, no thank you.

Stas had played this game of quiet mouse long enough. All she needed was to free her mouth. One demand would solve the problem.

Wiggling hadn't worked.

So she stomped her heel against the man's expensive shoe instead, eliciting a wince from him. She lifted her foot in an attempt to loft a kick backward into his shin and only met air.

Her shoulder blades protested as her captor slammed her into the wall. Hard.

Fuck.

She struggled to move but couldn't. Both of her wrists were in one of his hands above her head. The rest of her was pinned between the wall and his body. Her chest heaved against his at the wasted effort. She would have screamed, but his other hand had never left her mouth.

Blue fire swirled in the depths of his gaze, the intensity of it scattering goose bumps down her arms. Fury poured off of him in waves, intoxicating her, thrilling her, terrifying her.

Who are you? she wanted to ask. *What are you doing to me?*

"What the fuck was that?" Brutus stared right at her, his murky eyes emanating confusion.

Stas waited for her captor to reply, but he didn't. He seemed to be concentrating very hard on holding her against the wall despite her lack of a struggle.

"Probably one of the neighbors waking up. We gotta go, dude." Hank stood at the top of the stairwell. "Now."

"Nah, that was something else…"

"Man, I'm leaving with or without you. Your choice." He went through the door, leaving Brutus in the hallway. His dull eyes passed over them again without focusing. Almost as if they weren't actually there.

Her heart skipped a beat.

He can't see us.

The male's irritated expression said, *Finally.*

Oh…

His earlier statement, *"You can see me,"* suddenly took on a whole new meaning.

Her eyes went wide. *No… That's not possible.*

And yet, entirely plausible.

Stas knew better than anyone that the supernatural existed. Not the kind kids enjoyed reading about or the stuff of fairy tales, but the real kind. The scary kind. The kind that killed.

But she'd been so careful. No one knew about her psychic talents—no one alive, anyway.

12

The door to the stairwell slammed, the finality of it shuddering down her spine.

Blue eyes burned into hers, the intensity stealing her breath away. *He's one of them—a supernatural.* And now he knew she existed.

Her father's smile had been so sad...

"You have to play today, little angel. For me and your mom. Just in case the bad men come, okay?"

"'Cause of the ice cream?" she whispered, her heart breaking. Daddy always said not to use compulsion on strangers. Bad things happened. Now the bad men were coming. Because of her.

"No, darling, not the ice cream. The bad men who might come will be here for me and your mom, not you. So you have to stay hidden and wait for me to find you, just like all the other times we played."

Except it hadn't been anything like the other times. Because a bad man did come—a supernatural one—and he burned her parents alive.

She couldn't blink. Couldn't move. Couldn't think.

It had finally happened.

The supernaturals had found her.

She needed to fight, to flee, but her limbs refused her. There wasn't any point.

Because she stood no chance, just like her parents that day.

This is my ending, not my beginning.

Today is the day I die.

~*~

Issac Wakefield did not like complications.

And the woman he held up against the wall? She definitely qualified as one.

Why he felt the need to hide her from the two Conclave lapdogs was beyond him. He almost let her fall into their sight when she tried to kick him, but instinct forced him in another direction.

She's immune.

Issac could manipulate everyone's vision, including that of Hydraians and Ichorians. Yet, this woman had *seen* him. That implied his gift didn't work on her.

Fascinating.

And from what he could tell, she had no idea.

Her pulse practically sang to him, her fear alluring to his predatory drive. He thought maybe Jonathan had caught wind of the recent assassination and sent a pet out to investigate. It could have explained her immunity, but her poor fighting skills and paling expression suggested a lack of training. And Jonathan would never allow one of his experiments to wander about without defensive skills.

So what are you? he wondered, holding her gaze.

He slowly removed his hand from her mouth, knowing the other Ichorians were no longer in hearing range. "What's your name?" It seemed a solid starting point and an easy enough query to answer.

She gaped at him, her lips moving without sound.

Shock.

Fantastic.

He released her and she nearly fell. Of course, she could be faking it, but his centuries of experience said otherwise. This woman had no idea what world she'd just stumbled into.

Issac almost felt sorry for her. Now that he knew of her existence, everything in her life would change. It already had.

"What are you doing here?" he tried again. The woman had seen right through his glamour, which meant she'd seen his face. He couldn't just leave her in the hallway. Not without understanding who and what she was, and why she'd chosen today to appear. It felt very orchestrated, which again had him thinking about Jonathan. This was exactly the kind of trap he would set.

"I... I..." She shuddered, her arms wrapping around herself.

Well, he supposed this was better than screaming.

He could knock her out and deal with it after he completed his task. It wouldn't take him long to review the scene, unlike the two Conclave minions who had spent over an hour in Owen Angelton's apartment.

Someone had clearly tipped off Osiris. If Issac hadn't shown up in the middle of their investigation, he'd have thought the two idiots killed Owen. But no. The Hydraian died before they arrived. And Lucian, the Hydraian King, wanted to know how it happened. He hadn't even been aware that his immortal was residing in the city until a distress call arrived early this morning.

Jacque had gone in first, the teleporter was good friends with Owen. Alas, he'd arrived too late, the message having been delayed by an unknown cause. Mateo was looking into it now.

And Issac was here to finish the investigation, the location too dangerous for any of Lucian's men to thoroughly review it for themselves. Case in point, the departing Ichorians downstairs.

"Wh-what are you?" she stammered.

His eyebrows rose. "The better question is, what are *you*, darling?" A fledgling, perhaps? It seemed appropriate considering she could *see* him.

Her face paled even more, her lips gaping like a fish again.

Right. They were just wasting time. He'd complete his mission and then deal with the traumatized woman. "Let's go inside," he suggested, opening the door.

She gagged as the acrid air wafted into the hallway.

He grabbed her wrist and tugged her inside, closing the door behind them. This way he could at least hear her if she tried to escape. Because the last thing he wanted to do was have to track her down after this. It would be much easier if she just stayed put until he was ready to deal with her.

"Oh God…" Her eyes clouded with dark embers, taking on a distant gleam, her knees collapsing beneath her and sending her to the ground. A glance into the kitchen confirmed why. Blood and glass littered the tile, indicating the struggle started there. And it seemed to have triggered a memory of some kind from the girl trembling on the floor.

Definitely not moving anytime soon.

Issac took advantage of her collapsing mental state by using the time to visualize the scene in the kitchen.

He pictured the dark-skinned male standing in the kitchen, pouring himself a glass of wine, just as the door burst open. The blood evinced a fight. Natural. Understandable, even. But what prompted the distress call to Lucian? It seemed a bit out of sequence. If Owen knew he was in danger, he wouldn't pour himself a glass of wine while he waited for the inevitable.

No.

Something wasn't quite right here.

Issac followed the light from the windows, down the hall, and into the small living area, his stomach twisting at the scene before him.

Owen's head—or what was left of it—appeared carelessly tossed on top of the coffee table with his charred remains on the recliner beside it.

Blood, innards, and other unmentionables were scattered about, making it bloody difficult to determine a safe walking path. While he adored Lucian and considered him a brother, he was not about to soil his shoes in the name of friendship.

"Wait," the woman called out, the whispering of her jeans suggesting she was trying to stand. "Hold on." She stumbled into the room, her green eyes glowing with the fight he'd witnessed in her earlier. Her mouth fell open at the sight on the table and chair, her palm going to her abdomen. "Oh my God…"

"Not God, darling," he murmured.

But she didn't hear him, her stomach heaving as she ran to the bathroom. She clearly knew her way around because she chose the right door on her first try, the sound of her emptying her insides following soon after.

The ghastly scene had been too much for her. Issac remembered a time when he may have reacted the same, but death had long since lost its impact on him. People died every day. Sometimes naturally, sometimes not.

And Owen definitely fell into the latter category.

Someone had clearly tortured the Hydraian. For information? Not likely. He was too young an immortal to know much. Which meant someone wanted to make a statement. But what?

Issac eyed the remains, searching for evidence or a clue.

The misshapen head on the table didn't resemble the man he once knew—his brown hair and dark skin replaced by a ball of gore with a gaping hole in the center.

The methods were reminiscent of a Conclave assassination, but Osiris didn't order this hit. If he did, he wouldn't have sent his henchmen to investigate this morning. This was either the work of a rogue Ichorian teaching a Hydraian a lesson or something else entirely.

Regardless, the murderer was definitely nonhuman.

"Owen," the woman moaned as she returned, tears trailing down her face. "What the fuck did you do to Owen?"

He gaped at her. "You think I did this?" He nearly snorted. "I had no cause to harm him. I'm merely here as an emissary to find out what happened."

"What?" Her face crumpled, reason not fully registering over her blatant emotions. "Why would someone do this?"

"Why does anyone do anything?" he countered, focusing on a series of photos decorating the fireplace mantle. *Ah, I see.* "You were friends," he surmised. *Definitely not a minion of Jonathan's.* But it also suggested Owen had been in New York for quite a while. *What were you doing in the city?*

"Who are you?" she breathed, her palm against her chest.

His lips twitched. She didn't recognize him? "Well, I may just let you live after all." Lucky day and all that.

A buzzing caught his attention before she could reply.

He navigated through the bloody mess toward the origin, careful not to touch anything crude.

Crouching down, he found the source beneath the couch.

A cell phone. Using a trick Mateo had taught him, he unlocked the main screen and started scanning through the text messages.

"You must be *Sassy Stas*," he guessed, reviewing the most recent text message regarding coffee. She'd mentioned something about it in the hallway as well.

A glance over his shoulder confirmed his suspicions. Her focus had fallen to the item in his hands, her lips trembling at having her name disclosed. Part of him wanted to console her, to tell her he meant her no harm. While the other part of him refused to lie. Because he would most certainly harm her if he needed to.

She gagged at the head on the table, averting her eyes to the ceiling—the only surface of the room not coated in blood splatter. She swallowed visibly, her cheeks taking on a greenish tint again. If he didn't say something to snap her out of it, she was liable to be sick again, perhaps even in the living area. And wouldn't *that* be incriminating.

He stood and read one of the texts from Owen's screen. " '*You better be awake. And holding a coffee cup with my name on it.*' Hmm, no coffee, just a corpse with a cell phone displaying your name. If you don't contact the authorities, I'm guessing you'll be their first house call. Woman deprived of caffeine kills friend—has a nice ring to it for a story, yes?"

Some of that emerald fire he'd witnessed earlier returned to her gaze, a faint blush overcoming the sick pallor of her skin. "Who *are* you?" She winced at the dead body and took a step back. "*God.* I can't." She stumbled into the hallway wall. From the way her nose wrinkled, he gathered the stench and sight were both affecting her.

He left her to console herself and scrolled through the other messages as well as Owen's contacts. Nothing out of the ordinary, but he pocketed the phone anyway. Mateo might see something he couldn't. He could also dust it for prints to find out who messaged Stas this morning since it was clearly sent after the Hydraian's death.

Someone wanted her to find the body.

But that someone couldn't have known Issac would be here, too. Only Lucian knew about this visit, and anyone he would have told would be a trusted confidant.

Issac ventured into the bedroom, finding more photos and other items that confirmed Owen's tenure in the city. The textbooks on his desk were for a journalism or political science degree program, based on the titles. Not a lot of useful information, just a notebook filled with scribbles and a laptop.

"How long have you known Owen?" he asked as he reentered the living area. The blonde had collapsed near the front door, her arms wrapped around her knees.

She eyed him warily. "Why?"

He cocked a brow, not used to repeating himself. "How long?"

"Since freshman year," she mumbled. "Almost six years."

That long? Lucian would not be pleased.

"What was he doing here?" Issac wondered out loud.

"Studying," she whispered. "We were supposed to graduate next weekend."

"Graduate," he repeated, recalling the textbooks from Owen's room. "From?"

She swallowed and shook her head, whether in rejection or because she couldn't speak. From the defiance he'd witnessed early, he guessed the former. While clearly traumatized, a fire still lurked in her gaze, one that screamed challenge.

"Stas," he murmured, cocking his head to the side. "Is that short for something?"

She glowered up at him, confirming his suspicions. Now that the initial shock of her friend's death had faded, her senses were returning, and with them came anger. "Why?"

No sense in lying to her. "So I can find you later."

She snorted and hugged her knees to her chest. "Good luck."

He shrugged. "I'll just find out from the police report, then."

She started, her gaze widening. "What?"

"Well, clearly someone wanted you to find the body. You have, which—"

"Wait?" she interjected. "Someone wanted me to find him?"

Had she not figured that part out yet? "Who do you think sent you a text this morning? Because it wasn't Owen. He's been dead for nearly four hours, give or take." Issac based the math on his senses. The blood was dead for far too long to be viable. Hence the reason he and his brethren could wander the Hydraian's flat. Had the blood been fresh, it could still be toxic. Alas, the lethal properties had died with their owner.

"*What?*" The color drained from her pale cheeks. "You're saying someone texted me from his phone *after* they killed him? *Why?*"

"Best guess? To ensure he was found. It would only take a few glances at his message history to see who he talked to most. You." Which begged the question, why had Owen befriended her? Did he, too, notice her penchant for being immune to Ichorian gifts? Was she resistant to Hydraian abilities as well?

"Which means," he continued, "phoning the authorities is the next step. Feel free to do that now, as I'll be leaving momentarily." And he'd track her down afterward. If he'd learned anything in his long life, it was to involve the cops early, let them draw up their ridiculous conclusions, and work behind the scenes to solve the real crime.

They'd never suspect Stas anyway. The strength required to rip a man's head from his neck and burn a body was nonhuman, and her athletic form didn't possess the necessary strength or mental stamina for such things.

Besides, they were clearly friends. Her presence here wouldn't be abnormal, though they'd likely want to know all about Owen's history.

"The police," she groaned, as if just realizing their importance. Most humans would call right away, but her instincts had led her astray. Why?

"Yes, the police," he said, brow furrowing. "I'm surprised you haven't tried to call them already." He half expected her to when she'd stumbled back into the foyer.

"I was a little busy." She waved a hand toward the apartment, her face paling again. "Damn it."

Right. She'd been sick from the shock.

Still, most would have thought to call. Fascinating that she didn't, or perhaps she thought he would. In that case... "I wouldn't suggest discussing my presence here." Even if she realized who he was, no one would believe her. A renowned billionaire over what appeared to be a college student? She didn't stand a chance in hell.

She didn't acknowledge his request, just stared at him. "How did you know Owen?"

"I didn't." Not well, anyway.

"Then why are you here?"

As if he would tell her that. "We'll catch up after you handle the authorities because, by my calculations, you were seen downstairs entering long enough ago that they will question what took you so long to call." Osiris's minions— Michael and Cain—had graciously left the doorman alive after altering the camera footage. It worked to Issac's benefit as well, leaving absolutely no trace of him in this building. While he could manipulate visual sensors in humans, he could not alter technological proof, such as a video evidence, of his presence.

"God, it's happening all over again," she whispered, her fingers threading through her long blonde hair and tugging harshly. "I can't do this. Not again. Not after..."

She trailed off, leaving him wondering what incident she was referring to. The last Hydraian death in the city had taken place long before she was born. Most of them were smart enough not to venture here, not with it being the heart of Ichorian territory. One could only push the treaty so far.

"Again?" he prompted, curious.

She shook her head as tears gathered behind those beautiful eyes again. Real pain etched into her features, stirring a strange urge to console her. Issac understood that agony far too well, having experienced substantial loss himself. It's what kept him motivated and inflamed his need for revenge.

It was why he resided in this city when he could live anywhere in the world.

And while a part of him wished to impart some wisdom to her, he had none. Only a drive to keep moving, to continue plotting, and to seek justice.

"Call the police," he told her. "I'd not recommend mentioning me," he repeated. "Or the two men from earlier," he added, thinking about how Cain and Michael had covered their tracks. "Your story won't be corroborated by any evidence and will only leave you looking insane."

That seemed to strike a chord in her, because her nostril's flared. "And if I mention you anyway?" she asked, her gaze hardening. "You'll come after me?" she guessed.

He smiled. "I'll be seeing you again regardless of what you say to them, darling." It didn't matter whether she gave him a name or not. Mateo would hack the system to find everything he needed to know. Besides, he had her phone number in Owen's phone. He had all the breadcrumbs he needed to learn more about this mystery woman and her unique ability to see through his glamour.

Stas sighed, her head falling back against the wall, her expression resigned. No fight or argument, just acceptance. She pulled her phone out of her pocket, her eyes locking on his. "If you're going to leave, do it now."

At least she'd managed to pull herself back together, a feat considering their surroundings. But this one familiar with death. He'd bet his life on it.

"I'll see you soon, darling," he murmured, opening the door. His fingerprints were untraceable, making his exit easy.

"Yeah," she muttered after him, her phone already dialing.

He considered staying to listen in on her conversation with the authorities but didn't want to risk her seeing him again this soon. The police report would give him the information he needed.

Then Mateo would work his magic on her background.

Stas.

Hmm, Issac really hoped that was short for something because the name just did not fit the unique woman.

Time would tell.

Until then, he had a call to the Hydraian King to make.

CHAPTER TWO

Caught in the Act

THE WOMAN DIDN'T MENTION ISSAC OR Osiris's lapdogs, stating she found the door slightly ajar when she arrived. Her omissions intrigued him, but not nearly as much as the rest of her portfolio.

Astasiya Davenport.

Adopted seventeen years ago by Susan and Henry Davenport in Havre, Montana. Whereabouts prior to adoption unknown.

Now twenty-four years old. NYU master's degree candidate set to graduate at the end of this semester—in less than two weeks.

CRF intern in the marketing department.

Roommate to Elizabeth Watkins, daughter of renowned

George Watkins—an asshole to the highest degree.

Issac grew more curious with every detail he learned about Astasiya from her dossier. He'd memorized all of it, including her transcripts and familial history. All in preparation for seeing her again.

She had a lot of explaining to do.

And soon.

Issac brushed his thumb across his bottom lip as he eyed Astasiya and Elizabeth from the shadows of the Kimmel Center auditorium.

He'd cloaked his presence from everyone around him but remained conscious of Astasiya's ability to see through his glamour. Hence his position behind her, leaning against the wall. If she turned, she'd see him. Fortunately, the dean of the College of Political Science held her attention as he spoke about Owen Angelton from the podium at the front. There were photos of the Hydraian everywhere, all smiles, most of them including Astasiya.

The phone records confirmed the age of their friendship—nearly six years, just as she'd said.

Lucian had been astonished to learn his immortal had been lurking in renowned Ichorian territory. Issac purposely withheld the details about Astasiya, wishing to learn more about her himself first.

She could prove useful.

Or maybe she'd played him all along.

Her proven ties to Jonathan suggested the latter. The redhead beside her damned her even more. But something about Astasiya felt genuine, innocent in a way that Issac couldn't help but wonder about her true purpose here.

Elizabeth wrapped her slender arms around Astasiya's neck after the dean finished, her hug expressing a firm friendship between them. "Just say the word and we're out of here." The words were faint but clear.

"I'm okay," Astasiya replied, the tension in her body betraying the lie as she pulled back. "It's just all these memories, you know?"

"Like the photo they used from freshman year?" Elizabeth snorted. "I can't believe they chose that one."

"It was a good day. A good week, really."

"Duh. It's when you met me." The redhead smiled, her peculiar genetics fully on display. Issac wondered if she knew about her birthright. Did Astasiya know? Their history extended as far back as the one Astasiya had with Owen. That couldn't be a coincidence. "Seriously, we can go if you need to," Elizabeth added, her expression sobering.

"I'm okay, Liz. Being out is what I need right now. Owen wouldn't want me, or any of us, to sit at home."

Elizabeth nodded. "True, he—"

"Lizzie!" A gaggle of girls had approached, their dyed hair and made-up faces a stark contrast to Astasiya's natural look. They all reached for Elizabeth, pulling her away into their circle and leaving Astasiya staring after them with a sardonic twist of her mouth.

Disapproval, not envy. And a slight touch of humor.

Issac agreed with her entirely, especially as the women begin sobbing over Owen's untimely demise. He suspected the females barely knew the immortal.

Astasiya, however, clearly knew him.

He lifted the program up to hide his features, stepping back into the wall just as she turned. Her sweet scent taunted his nostrils, the lure of her blood exciting his instincts.

Definitely a fledgling.

So who created you? he wondered as he followed her.

The minds of the room were easy to manipulate, his presence here lost in the recesses of their thoughts. He likened it to a room littered with televisions all set to the same channel as he wove through the crowds after Astasiya.

She remained lost in thought, not sensing the predator in her wake—a fatal error. He could snap her pretty little neck with a flick of his wrist. Thankfully, she was of more use to him alive.

A curvy woman with bouncy curls stepped into his

quarry's path, her round face smothered in tears. She sobbed some story about Owen that had Astasiya cringing and taking a step back. The words continued flowing, none of them intelligible.

"Stop crying," Astasiya demanded. Her shoulders seemed to tighten even more with the words, her upper body stiff. "I mean, just, it's going to be okay… It's…"

But the girl had ceased her blubbering, her gaze eerily unfocused. "Sorry," she mumbled, taking her leave.

Issac frowned after her. *How odd.*

"Fuck," Astasiya muttered to herself, her steps faster now.

Until yet another female waylaid her from the side. A reporter with overdone lips and hair bigger than the room.

He nearly snorted.

Tabloids belonged to the devil.

"I heard through the grapevine you and Mr. Angelton were close. What can you tell me about his social activities?"

"Yeah, I'm not interested. Thanks, though." She tried to maneuver around the pushy woman, but a set of manicured nails snagged her arm.

"Is it true he was gay?"

Astasiya winced, causing Issac to take a step forward. It seemed it was time for him to intervene. She'd not be pleased to see him, but it had to be better—

"Let me go," she said, her voice low and steady. A cascade of energy seemed to follow, alerting his senses.

The reporter released her immediately, her expression filled with shock.

Astasiya didn't miss a beat, her legs quickly carrying her out of the room.

Issac stood motionless, shocked at the display of power.

All fledglings were gifted with two supernatural abilities, but they couldn't access them until their resurrection—until their Hydraian rebirth.

Just like Ichorians couldn't access their inherent talent until their own death and reawakening.

But this woman could compel.

How was that even possible?

She wasn't a Hydraian yet. And definitely not an Ichorian. He'd sense it in her blood.

What are you, Miss Davenport?

Or better yet, who *are you really?*

He trailed after her engaging scent, requiring answers. She maintained ties to Jonathan, lived with a renowned experiment, and had befriended the late Owen Angelton. Too many coincidences when wrapped up with her ability to persuade others.

Not a typical human. Far from it.

Issac caught a glimpse of her disappearing into a nearby classroom, her hands fisted at her sides. He entered silently, closing the door behind him without a sound as she stared blankly at the vacant room.

His lips parted, but her rounding shoulders silenced his words.

She reminded him of a broken raven in that black dress, her body curling in on itself as she fought not to cry.

That hint of innocence slammed into him again, confusing his instincts.

She mourned Owen's loss.

A true friend.

Not an act, because she thought she was alone here.

He leaned against the wall, crossing one ankle over the other as he surveyed her long, slender legs—exposed by the dress—and her supple curves. A gorgeous woman, especially with that thick mane of hair.

Time to play this from a different angle.

He waited until her breathing evened, and murmured, "Well, that was enlightening."

Astasiya's hand flew to her chest as she whirled around. "Jesus," she managed on a harsh exhale. "You scared the shit out of me."

Issac slid his hands into his pockets and cocked his head to the side. "I'm curious. How old were you when you

28

realized you could bend others to your will?"

She paled. "What?"

"Oh, come now, Astasiya. Feigning ignorance doesn't suit you. Order me to do something instead. I dare you."

She froze instead, her full lips parting, her slender arms locking at her sides. All signs that confirmed his suspicions. Not only that, but she was very aware of her gift as well.

"I thought the hysterical woman might just be emotionally mad," he said, pushing off the wall to saunter closer to her. "Persuasion is a rare gift, after all." An understatement. Issac knew of only one other with the ability—Osiris.

And wouldn't he be pleased to learn of Astasiya's existence.

A fledgling who could compel without having been turned.

The things Issac's kind would do to her... Correction, the things *he* should do to her...

Alas, no.

Not just yet.

He tucked a stray blonde strand behind her ear, reveling in the way it made her pulse skip a beat. "The scene with the reporter—telling her to let you go—was clear compulsion, Miss Davenport." He'd witnessed it countless times during Conclave meetings. She certainly possessed the power of persuasion, a dangerous ability in the wrong hands, indeed.

She swallowed. "How long have you been watching me?" The steady quality of her voice impressed him, especially with the way her heart thundered in his ears—a calling card to his kind.

"Long enough." He allowed his gaze to roam, admiring the elegant lines of her dress and the way it hugged her curves. Gorgeous. Athletic. The type of woman he'd entertain in his bed before leaving in the morning. Except this one possessed something more, something that piqued his interest in a way few others had throughout the centuries.

Her pupils flared as he met her gaze again, her heightened breaths an indication that his open perusal of her assets had not gone unnoticed. And the subtle hint of interest in her green irises told him the attraction was mutual.

But he doubted she'd be as easy as his usual conquests.

And he liked that about her.

"It's customary for one in my position to kill you on sight," he informed Astasiya, deciding not to lie to her. "Fortunately for you, darling, I'm not an admirer of our archaic laws."

Fear tinged the air, her tongue darting out to lick her lips. Yet her expression hardened, as if she was struggling not to lay a retort at his feet.

Fascinating.

All it would take was a command and he'd back off, yet she remained quiet. Nearly stoic. Unfazed.

"You really have no idea what you are, do you?" The prospect of a fledgling walking about with persuasive abilities intrigued him immensely, so much so that he smiled. "Amazing. You were adopted at age seven, yes? Surely you learned something from your birth parents before that point?"

Her fingers curled at her sides, her shoulders tensing. "I learned not to trust the supernatural world."

"Yes, I'm guessing the house fire was a cover story." He'd read about it in the report. "Very nice of the Davenports to take you in, though." He considered her carefully, searching her features for tells to decipher truth from lies. "Does anyone else know what you can do?"

She folded her arms, her bare skin brushing his suit jacket in the process. If she wanted him to step back, she'd have to try harder.

Astasiya cleared her throat, her pupils narrowing. "It's not something I go around advertising, no."

"Then you clearly want to live."

"Most people do," she replied, her voice flat and emotionless. Too bad for her that he could *hear* the escalated rhythm in her chest.

And it was bloody intoxicating.

"Are you going to get to the point of this visit anytime soon, or do you plan to tell me more things I already know about myself?" she demanded, causing his lips to curl.

Feisty.

He approved.

"Tell me, darling, would you like to know more about your unique talents?" It was a test phrased as a query. What he really meant was, *Do you know what you are?*

The slipping of her bravado answered him immediately.

No. She had no idea.

And now he'd baited her, because curiosity flashed across her features, and a longing that nearly fractured his plans. It wasn't nice to play with fragile toys, and while she exuded a tough exterior, a delicate essence lurked beneath her skin.

One that gleamed with hope as she asked, "You can tell me?"

"I can," he admitted. "For a price."

The hint of hope died, replaced by a flash of annoyance. She glanced over him, her lips flattening into a line of disapproval. Not the usual look women gave him, especially when dressed in an expensive suit.

"You don't look like someone who needs the money."

Ah, right, she's still clueless. He chuckled and considered fondling the strand of hair brushing the side of her breast. It would be soft, addictively so.

"I do love that you have no idea who I am," he confessed. It felt like an eternity had passed since he last hid from humanity. Hopefully, his reasons for being in the city and in the spotlight would diminish soon—something this woman just might be able to assist him in accomplishing. Especially with her connections and otherworldly ability.

"You know, a name would help with that," she snapped.

He smirked. "No, I find I like the anonymity." He leaned into her space, his eyes holding hers. "But do let me know when you figure it out."

"By, what, calling you?" she asked sweetly.

Humor touched his chest. "You could try." But even if she found his name, no one would put her through to his phone without permission. Maybe he'd add her name to the approved list, just for fun. Maybe he wouldn't.

She pursed her lips. "Can you tell me who killed Owen and why?"

Probably not, but... "I can tell you all sorts of things." And he could always work with her to determine the culprit behind Owen's demise. Lucian would benefit from the information as well.

"For a price," she repeated, amusing him more.

"Indeed."

She considered, her brow furrowing. He wondered if she would try to demand some answers out of him. That would spoil his plans, but he knew how to answer evasively, had been doing it for years with Osiris. And once she realized that, she'd hopefully take him up on his offer. Because he *wanted* her to agree, to enable him to have the opportunity to learn more about her unique background and talent.

And to determine if she was yet another product of Jonathan's lab.

Like her roommate.

"What do you want from me?" she asked, her voice holding a touch of uncertainty.

He admired her neckline again and the way her dress stopped at her thighs. Magnificent, long legs ending in a pair of heels that accentuated her calves. "Money is not the only form of payment, darling," he murmured, meaning every word.

Why not mix a little business with pleasure? Assuming she agreed, of course.

And the flush creeping up her neck said she did.

She swallowed, her tongue darting out to lick her lips

32

again as if readying them for his mouth.

Fear, he found, lent well to foreplay. He gave in to his desire to fondle the loose strand of her hair beside her breast, his fingertips purposely brushing her dress along the way. Her nipples beaded beautifully beneath the fabric in response, another tell of her mutual interest.

Something to play with later.

"I'll be in touch when I decide what I desire." He gave her hair a subtle tug, releasing it. "Until then, I strongly suggest you keep that psychic gift of yours under control. You never know who might be watching, darling."

CHAPTER THREE

Demons and Nightmares

SO MUCH PAIN. IT PIERCED STAS'S CHEST, *suffocating her so severely she couldn't help but reach for the source of the agony.*

"I'm okay, little angel," her mom assured. "I'm okay."

"Mom hurts," Stas whispered. "Bad hurt."

"I know, baby. But I'm okay." Her mom pulled her into her arms, holding her tight. "I love you."

"I love you too, Momma."

A game of hide-and-seek.

Go play.

Go hide.

Don't come out.

That's what Daddy had said.

And she listened because he always liked to play. She went to her favorite spot in the trees, waiting, but he never came.

She waited and waited and waited.

But nothing.

"Daddy?" she whispered, peeking through the branches, her forehead marred with a frown. He should have found her by now.

Stas crept out of her spot, quietly. He'd told her not to come out until he found her. She'd promised. Maybe she should stay.

But what if he couldn't find her? She'd chosen a real good spot this time. Her lips twitched to the side. He probably just needed a little help.

She took a few more steps, her nose twitching at the smoke wafting through the trees. A fire.

Oh no!

Her little legs carried her fast toward the flames, her heart beating in her chest. But a hand stopped her, holding her back, caging her as her parents screamed.

Cruel black eyes flecked with gold.

A sinister smile.

Her parents burning, the agony of their deaths ripping Stas in two.

Momma! Daddy! But her voice refused her, a prisoner to her own body, forced to watch their suffering. She could do nothing, not even as Owen joined them, his face contorted on a scream.

The smell…

The heat…

It consumed her, ringing a bell in her head, forcing her to—

Stas threw her phone across the room, her body convulsing violently.

Fuck.

It'd felt so real. Her limbs shook from the exertion of her fight, her shoulder burning as if the hand actually held her now, not just in her nightmare. She shuddered, her knees tucked into her chest.

Not again.

Not now.

But ever since finding Owen in his apartment, she'd been unable to sleep without the night terrors.

So fresh.

So new.

So cruel.

She hadn't saved them. She hadn't saved Owen.

Not that she could have. Not that she'd known. But the torment of it all stole her breath, left her limbs quivering in the bed, her body fighting for air as she, too, burned with her parents and friend.

"I hate this," she whispered. "I fucking hate this."

She pulled a pillow over her head. It felt like a truck was attempting to parallel park on her skull. Forward, backward, crushing every bone. She cursed a blue streak when her alarm continued to sound from the ground.

I'm going crazy.

It had to be the guilt. She should have told the police the truth about the two men in Owen's apartment, about the stranger who held her against the wall. What if they found something? The man said there wouldn't be any evidence, but what if he lied?

She pressed the pillow harder into her head.

If they found out she'd lied, she could be accused of working with the murderer. But her instincts had held her back, an old part of her believing that the cops really would think her insane if she mentioned the men.

Just like they did when her parents died.

They called it a house fire—an accident. Even when she screamed and cried and told them a man had burned her parents alive, no one *listened* to her. The deranged stories of a child, using her imagination to tell an outlandish tale. It left an inherent distrust in her heart, one that she hadn't considered in years but felt rise to the surface when the police arrived at Owen's apartment.

Don't say anything. They'll just think you're crazy.

She couldn't live through it again, so she'd given them a version of the truth—that she'd come over to study with Owen, found his door ajar, and discovered his dead body inside. The shock had rendered her useless, making her sick, before she could finally place the call.

And they believed her.

She showed them the text message.

They confirmed it was sent after his death and asked if she'd seen his phone.

She lied and said she hadn't.

Then *he* found her at the memorial service, the demon with all the answers.

Yes, a fucking demon. That's what she'd decided to call her mystery suit man since he wouldn't give her his fucking name.

She growled into her pillow, her mind fracturing from the lunacy of her life. This did not happen to normal people.

Normal people can't compel.

Not helping!

"Stas?" Lizzie knocked on the door softly, likely having heard whatever screams Stas had let loose during her nightmare. "You all right in there?"

"Yeah." Ugh, her throat felt like sandpaper. "I'm fine."

"Uh, okay. I'm making coffee."

Such magical words. Her roommate knew her way too well. "Thank you, Liz."

Stas removed the pillow and blinked up at the ceiling.

It's Sunday morning.

Graduation day.

She glanced at the clock.

Henry and Susan Davenport were expecting her in less than an hour. And they had an afternoon of activities planned, all meant to take her mind off of Owen and to celebrate her accomplishments.

It sounded like hell.

But her adopted parents had flown in from Montana to celebrate.

Lifting a hand to her aching skull, Stas padded into the bathroom.

Well, didn't she look fantastic. Tangled hair, bloodshot eyes, sunken cheeks with sleep marks etched into her fair skin.

Nothing a good old-fashioned shower can't fix.

* * *

Wishful thinking because the shower didn't fix anything. Not even Stas's makeup could hide the dark marks beneath her eyes, but at least she rocked the dark blue dress and matching heels.

She didn't bother drying her hair, opting for coffee instead. Caffeine worked wonders.

Walking into the kitchen, she found Lizzie dressed in a lavender dress and white heels, holding Stas's favorite mug. "One teaspoon of brown sugar already added."

"I love you." A sentiment meant for her best friend and the liquid gold inside her cup. Stas took a fortifying sip and smiled. *See? Everything's better now.*

Her roommate scanned her with discerning brown eyes, her pink-painted lips scrunching to the side. "Still not sleeping well?"

Stas sat down at the breakfast table, sighing. The coffee seemed to be helping her head heal, but not her soul. "Nightmares," she admitted softly. "I hate them."

"About your birth parents again? Or Owen?" Lizzie knew a little about Stas's history with sleepless nights because they lived together. There were only so many times a woman could wake up screaming before the other demanded an explanation. But they grew less and less common over time.

Now they were back in full force.

"Yeah." Stas shuddered as an image of Owen's head rolled through her mind. Literally. Still on fire and rolling.

"I'm sorry," Lizzie whispered.

Stas's hand tightened around her coffee mug. "I'm sorry, too." For her birth parents. For Owen. For lying to the authorities. For allowing a demon to leave her tongue-tied in a classroom. For—

"Do you want anything besides coffee? There's some quiche in the fridge from yesterday." Most days, Lizzie acted more like a mom than a roommate. Sometimes it drove Stas nuts. This morning, she appreciated it.

"That sounds great." She started to stand, but her best friend beat her to it.

"You keep working on that caffeine binge. Can't have a grumpy Stas today."

She snorted. *Can't argue with that logic.*

Taking another fortifying sip of the liquid heaven left Stas feeling warm and relaxed. She should marry coffee. It'd probably satisfy her more than a man ever could, except maybe a certain blue-eyed demon. Similar to the one smoldering up at her from her roommate's society magazine.

Stas choked on her last sip, snatching the paper from the other side of the table.

Sapphire gaze. Chiseled jaw. Broad shoulders. Tapered waist. Sexy as sin.

A literal male advertisement for men's fashion.

No. An article.

About her demon.

"Holy shit."

Lizzie turned around, her focus falling to the magazine in Stas's hand. "Oh, I know, right? I mean, I guess he's handsome and wealthy, but calling him one of New York's hottest bachelors is a bit of a stretch, isn't it? Just because his dad, like, created the CRF doesn't mean he's going to inherit the company." She huffed as she set a plate in front of Stas and collapsed into the seat across from her. "False advertising, if you ask me."

She gaped at her best friend. "What are you talking about?"

"Tom." She gestured at the tabloid. "And I can't believe they used that picture of him." She shook her head. "That man rocks a suit way better than army garb."

Stas blinked back to the article. Tom Fitzgerald's wide

grin flashed up at her from the opposite page. "Huh." He and her demon were in the same featured article. She read the title on the front.

New York's Ten Hottest Bachelors.

Issac Wakefield was listed at number two. The thirty-four-year-old billionaire was the CEO of Wakefield Pharmaceuticals. Apparently, he inherited the company from his father at the young age of twenty-five. No wonder he expected her to recognize him. Almost everyone would, except Stas rarely followed this gibberish. She preferred business articles, of which she'd read several about his company, but she'd never thought to look for a photo of the CEO.

"This is insane," she marveled. Her demon was a billionaire playboy who masqueraded as a murder scene detective. *Because* that *happened in real life.*

"I know!" Lizzie slammed her coffee cup down. "Did you read the part about how he's ready to settle down?" She forced a laugh. "Yeah, right. That man is married to his job."

Stas focused on the other article so she could see what her best friend was going on about. "It's not a bad picture." He actually looked pretty good in those fatigues, with his muscles on display, his sandy hair windswept, his dimples flashing.

My demon has dimples too.

Not that she cared to think about that.

She refocused on the words, ignoring the temptation to glance at Issac's photo again.

"They captured his personality pretty well, Liz. The article calls him a hero for his time overseas, saying it's admirable that he took a job in the CRF paramilitary unit rather than on a business team." A Sentinel, as the CRF called him. Most of the men recruited for that section had military backgrounds, making Tom a perfect candidate considering he spent several years in the Special Forces. He could have gone into a government agency, but his father owned the CRF. It also paid better since it was privately owned and funded.

Lizzie's snort did not match her housewife appearance. "Yeah, a true humanitarian."

"Come on, Tom's not that bad." Stas pushed the article back across the table before she gave in to the urge to study Issac again. *Not happening.*

"I know. That's exactly the problem." A deep sadness overcame Lizzie as she gazed at Tom's picture. Every other male in this city noticed her feminine charms except the one man she actually wanted. Hell, Lizzie could prance around in a skimpy swimsuit and the former sniper still wouldn't see the supermodel in front of him.

Lizzie closed the magazine, her expression holding a touch of resolve as she met Stas's gaze.

"I don't like that look," Stas started, her quiche uneaten before her.

"Yeah, so, speaking of Tom... he's coming to dinner tonight."

Stas groaned at the mention of the dreaded after-graduation dinner. She would rather gouge her eyes out with a spoon than spend an evening with the Watkins family. It was bad enough she saw them once a month for brunch with the Fitzgeralds—a tradition, which started over twenty years ago, that she was roped into during her first year at Columbia.

"Oh, no, you're not backing out of dinner," Lizzie said before Stas could even suggest it. "Our parents are going to finally meet. They missed each other at our Columbia graduation, something I *know* you orchestrated, but they are meeting this time."

"To be fair, they were busy giving you this condo." A multimillion-dollar property on the Upper West Side. Somehow, they felt giving it to her would make up for all the years they mistreated her growing up. Stas wondered what gift they had in store for their only child tonight as she graduated with her master's degree in education.

"Yeah, a convenient excuse." Her gaze narrowed.

"They're meeting tonight, Stas. You're not bailing on me."

Stas put her head down on the table. Owen was supposed to have been her date tonight, to help keep her sane. And also to celebrate his own graduation.

Which was clearly not happening now.

"This week sucks," she grumbled. An immature statement, but true.

"Want to order pizza afterward and binge on chick flicks all night?" Lizzie asked, a note of childlike hope in her voice. She'd not be eating much during dinner, not with Lillian Watkins present. The willowy woman strictly controlled Lizzie's diet, claiming it to be her motherly right. *Bitch* didn't even begin to describe her or the way she'd tormented her daughter's self-esteem throughout the last two decades.

Which, of course, meant Stas had no choice but to attend dinner. Someone had to protect Lizzie. Still, that didn't mean she couldn't negotiate a little something here. Peeking up at her best friend, Stas arched a brow. "Can we order one with pineapples and ham?"

"Sure, one of the pizzas can be Hawaiian. I'll pick the other two." Lizzie possessed a love for Italian food that never managed to go to her hips. Amazing, really. She could eat five pints of ice cream a day for a month and still resemble a supermodel.

"Pizza for a week?" Stas mused. "All right, deal."

CHAPTER FOUR

Dinner Crashers

"ARE YOU ALL RIGHT, SWEETHEART?" SUSAN Davenport asked for the fifth time today.

Stas loved her adoptive parents to death, truly, but this line of questioning had to stop. She was close enough to breaking down without the constant check-in on her feelings.

"I'm okay, Mom," she lied. Graduating without Owen this morning had created a bruise on her heart, which left her aching all afternoon.

He's really gone.

She knew that. But the reality of it... She swallowed, refusing to do this here. If she cried, her mother would demand she return to Montana—a threat that had been looming since she told her adoptive parents about Owen's death.

"It's all right to mourn, hon," her father murmured, his hand on her shoulder. "I know it's a big day and all, but you can feel sad, too."

And I do. Trust me, I do.

But tears solved nothing.

She wanted to know who killed him and why. Something the billionaire demon might be able to tell her.

No. Not a good idea.

Except she hadn't been able to stop thinking about him all day. Now that she knew his name, he was suddenly accessible.

One phone call.

One agreement.

He might be able to tell her.

"Stas?" her father asked, his brow furrowing.

"I'm okay," she repeated. "Really."

Their expressions said they didn't believe her.

Good thing she had a distraction plan in place. "The Watkinses and the Fitzgeralds are already here." She gestured to the table in the corner of the dining room where they always sat.

"Are we late?" her mother asked, glancing at her watch.

"No, they're always early." Much to Stas's chagrin. They constantly made her *feel* late. "Come on, I'll introduce you."

Everyone stood to greet them. Doctor Fitzgerald first, his suit immaculate as always and his fatherly grin in place. Tom second, his charming features clearly marking him as his father's son. Then the Watkinses and Lizzie.

Everyone shook hands, Susan blushing fiercely when Doctor Fitzgerald complimented her by saying she didn't appear old enough to have a daughter Stas's age.

It was true.

The Davenports had been in their early twenties when they adopted Stas. But not many knew the truth, so no one clarified the relationship. It wasn't so much a secret as it was a sensitive subject. Stas always referred to them as *Mom* and *Dad* out loud.

"Congratulations on your graduation, ladies," Doctor Fitzgerald said as everyone settled into their respective seats.

"Thank you," Lizzie said softly from beside Stas. Lillian sat on the other side, her expression as constipated as ever. The woman seriously needed to stop investing in face-lifts; it was only making her appearance worse. And her husband, well, he could stand to lay off the sweets. Not that he seemed bothered as he snagged a roll from the center basket.

"How'd your interview go the other week, Stas?" Doctor Fitzgerald asked, his dark eyes crinkling at the sides. The man didn't look a day over forty, despite having a twenty-seven-year-old son.

"It went well," she said, relieved to discuss something normal and non-Owen related. "Human Resources said the job is mine once I finish the security process." Which included passing a polygraph this week. Hopefully, they didn't ask about anything crime-related because she was pretty sure lying to the cops during a murder investigation qualified.

"That's right. You're the one who got our Stas a job at the CRF," her father chimed in.

"Oh, your daughter did that all on her own." Dr. Fitzgerald smoothed a hand over his suit jacket. "I just helped open a few doors, is all." Because he was the CEO and creator of the CRF, she was willing to bet he did a hell of a lot more than that, but she accepted the compliment with a smile.

"The marketing director adores her," Mister Watkins put in with a self-satisfied nod toward Dr. Fitzgerald. "Very pleased with the recommendation."

"But she has to take a polygraph?" her father asked as a tingle itched at the base of her spine. Subtle, but pressing, and prickling the hairs along her arms.

She glanced at the entrance as Issac Wakefield sauntered

into the restaurant dressed in yet another suit. Black jacket, pants, and shoes, and a maroon shirt open at the collar.

With a gorgeous female ornament on his arm.

Her matching dark red dress boasted a V-neck created for a woman with her body type, her breasts proudly on display and barely contained. The back was equally as sinful, dipping to her ass, which swayed as she walked.

Well. So much for Stas's theories about what Issac wanted from her. He clearly already had what he needed in the sexual department.

She barely noticed the shorter male who walked in behind him with his arm wrapped around a similarly dressed model.

"Stas?" her father's voice brought her back to the table.

"Yes?"

"I was asking for your thoughts on the polygraph." He arched a brow.

"I've already given you my thoughts on it," she replied, unsure of why he was bringing this up again. "It's part of the job requirements." The CRF was a privately owned humanitarian organization with ties to various government agencies. It seemed standard practice to require a polygraph, as many of the positions dealt with classified information.

"Yes, but isn't it a bit intrusive for a civil employee?" her father pressed.

Says the high school principal who advocated for athletic drug testing, she thought, recalling the citywide argument regarding invasion of privacy.

"I mean, I can understand employees who handle government documents undergoing the security clearance process, but not everyone else," he added.

"Trust me, if we could avoid it, we would in a heartbeat. Do you have any idea how expensive it is to run a top-secret security clearance on every potential employee?" Dr. Fitzgerald rubbed the back of his neck. "It's not cheap."

That seemed to appease her dad a little, but he still pursed his lips.

"We really appreciate everything you've done for our Stas," her mom interjected, changing the subject before her father could say anything more on the topic. He'd made his feelings on the security process known from the beginning, but Stas didn't understand why he was making such a big deal of it. She didn't have anything to hide.

Well, except for her persuasive problem.

And lying to the cops at Owen's crime scene.

Okay, so she harbored a few secrets, but surely she could pass a polygraph. Right? Maybe?

She glanced at the demon who knew her darkest confidences yet remained a complete stranger to her. He raised a brow in greeting, then tilted his head toward his gorgeous date. Her lips were at his ear. Whatever she said seemed to amuse him, because his lips twitched. The familiar intimacy between them left a sour taste in Stas's mouth, causing her stomach to churn.

This was the Issac she read about in the article—the desired bachelor. He clearly had a different woman on his arm every night.

So what does he want from me?

She forced herself to refocus on the conversation at the table. Something about Tom's recent mission overseas where he helped deliver food and water to a group of orphaned children. She could feel her mother melting into a puddle of goo beside her, while Lizzie focused on her salad plate. The menu was always set before they arrived, a nine-course meal organized daily by the chef.

"Well, it's good to know Stas is working for such an amazing organization," her mother said, her cheeks flushed. "It's hard having her so far away, I mean, but some of my worrying is eased by knowing she has a family here."

"It's been our pleasure, I assure you." Dr. Fitzgerald winked at Stas.

"Of course, the whole thing with Owen has me a bit on edge."

Stas groaned. "Oh, Mom, please don't."

"What? I'm concerned for your safety, Stas. Your friend was *murdered*."

As if she didn't know that. "It's not…"

Sapphire eyes met her own over her father's shoulder. *Oh, shit.*

"Well, isn't this a small world?" Issac said by way of greeting, his lips quirked up into a devious smile as he moved around the table to stand directly behind her, his hands settling on the back of her chair.

Lizzie started hitting Stas's thigh. She assumed the repetitive tapping was Lizzie-code for *Oh. My. God.* But Stas couldn't move. She couldn't even breathe.

"Wakefield." Tom's shoulders were rigid. "Can we help you with something?"

"Oh, I've been helping myself just fine lately, but thank you, Thomas." His palm slid to her shoulder, branding her bare skin and sending a jolt of electricity through her heart. "I apologize for interrupting. I only wanted to congratulate Astasiya on her graduation this morning."

Dr. Fitzgerald raised a dark blond brow. "You two are acquainted?"

Stas wondered the same thing, but about Tom and Issac. Maybe they both attended a "Hottest Bachelors of New York" club. Her lips twitched at the thought.

"We met through a mutual acquaintance," Issac replied. "Owen Angelton. You've no doubt heard of him, yes?" He brushed her pulse with his thumb in a proprietary move that heated her neck.

What are you doing? she wanted to ask.

Dr. Fitzgerald steepled his long fingers on the table, his posture relaxed. "Yes, we were just discussing that. He was supposed to be your date tonight, right, Stas?"

Thanks for the reminder. She cleared her throat. "Uh, yeah, he wanted to meet everyone." She shook the cobwebs from her brain and tilted her head back to meet Issac's gaze. "Thank you for the congratulations, Issac." She used his first name on purpose and found she rather enjoyed saying it out loud.

His responding grin stole the breath from her lungs. Holy crap, a man should not possess such a smile. It could be dangerous for women with certain heart conditions.

"Of course, darling." He squeezed her shoulder before refocusing on her parents. "I don't believe we've had the pleasure of meeting. I'm Issac Wakefield."

"Uh, right. These are my parents. Susan and Henry." Her mother looked ready to faint under the directness of Issac's gaze. Her father, however, seemed to be missing the guns he kept at home. *Great.* They were making assumptions about their relationship.

"A pleasure," Issac murmured. "Do you mind if I steal your gorgeous daughter for a moment?"

Her eyes narrowed up at him. *What game are you playing?*

"Not at all," her mom replied, her excitement palpable.

Stas fought the urge to groan.

Her mother wasn't vain, just excited by the prospect of her daughter seeing someone. Stas's dating history could be counted on one hand. Not for a lack of trying by the male population, but because she just didn't date. School always took precedence.

"Astasiya?" The hand on her shoulder lifted, palm up, a gesture for her to stand.

Well, it wasn't as if she had a choice in the matter. "Excuse me," she said, standing without taking his hand.

"Gentlemen"—Issac's attention shifted to the Fitzgeralds and Lizzie's dad—"always a pleasure."

He pressed his palm into the small of her back, burning a hole through her satin dress as he guided her through the restaurant. Stas would have a lot of explaining to do when she returned. Her leg had taken a steady beating from her best friend's fist the entire time Issac stood behind her. The *"Oh. My. God"* code had changed to *"What the hell is going on?"* after he announced their acquaintance.

The demon escorted her into a dark corner near the elevators of the reception area. She turned right before the wall and put her hands on his sturdy chest when he would have advanced another step closer. "Thanks for that, Issac. They're going to think we're dating now." Which they definitely were not ever going to do.

Warm fingers wrapped around her wrists. "I decided what I want as payment."

Her eyebrows met her hairline. "And you had to tell me now?"

His heated gaze slid slowly over her, taking in every inch of her dress along the way. She fought a resulting shudder, not wanting to react to his nearness or the intimacy of his touch.

Why did he have to be so damn good-looking? Like a supermodel standing inches from her with his perfectly sculpted, aristocratic features.

And those damn eyes…

"You look beautiful in this dress, darling." The accented endearment had her hackles rising.

"Yeah? Your date looks beautiful in her dress too, Issac."

She took a step back into the wall as he advanced on her. The hands on her wrists kept her from pushing him back as he crowded her personal space. Sandalwood mingled with bourbon, a tantalizing combination.

"This is not—"

"Clara is not my date," he interjected, his broad shoulders and substantial height cutting off her view of the restaurant's lobby and forcing her to focus solely on him. "When did you figure out my identity?"

"This morning."

"How?"

"Apparently, you're one of New York's hottest bachelors." Her face warmed at the admission of how she discovered his name. "Lizzie likes society magazines."

His chuckle caressed her in a way it shouldn't, causing her to squeeze her legs together in protest. *This man is fucking potent.*

"Not at all how I expected, but I'll accept it." He stroked his thumb against her wrist. "Were you surprised?"

"Yes."

"Good, I adore that about you. Which brings me to what I want, assuming you still wish to strike a deal with me." More circles against her skin. Each one hot and branding and distracting.

Why did he have to be so close to her?

Every inhale drew his scent closer and every exhale felt too hot.

He came here with another woman.

Who he claims isn't his date.

That's irrelevant.

But he knows what you are…

She swallowed. Not only that, but he had offered to tell her. For a price.

Just this morning she chastised herself for even considering a deal, but now, well, now she wanted answers. Again.

"Will you help me find out who killed Owen?" she asked. Because she knew in her heart the authorities wouldn't be able to solve this case, not after the way they reacted at the crime scene. They just kept muttering the word *impossible* and scribbling nonsense in their books.

Issac tilted his head. "You care more about Owen than your own heritage?"

"I care about both," she clarified. "And I want answers to both."

He released her wrists and rested his arm against the wall over her head while gazing down at her. "Demanding more from me before knowing what I require?"

She didn't back down. "I'm giving you my terms."

"What about mine?"

Her heart hammered in her chest at his nearness, his lips only a few inches from hers. "Name them."

He smiled, indicating those were the words he desired to hear. "I want you, Astasiya."

The image of him stripping off her clothes and taking her up against the wall flashed behind her eyes, making her knees go weak. *That can't be what he means.* The man obviously didn't need to trade answers for sex. "I'm not following."

"Hmm, how to phrase it." The hand lying at his side moved to her hip, his opposite arm still over her head, while her limbs remained limp at her sides. All her focus was on inhaling enough oxygen to keep her brain working. "I need certain individuals to believe we're dating, and for that to work, I require your voluntary participation."

Okay, not at all what she expected him to say. "Why the hell would you want to do that?"

"Maybe I like you."

She narrowed her gaze. "Or maybe you have an ulterior motive."

"Maybe it's both." He shifted closer, the heat from his body seeping into her skin and influencing her in dangerous ways—like encouraging her to tilt her head back as he lowered his mouth to hover over hers.

"Dating for information," he whispered. "A simple quid pro quo situation. You help me and I'll help you."

"How is our pretending to date going to help you?"

The devil grinned in his gaze. "Does the why really matter when I have the answers you seek?"

Did it? She wasn't sure. "If I agree, will you tell me what I am?"

"Hmm." His attention drifted to her mouth, his pupils flaring. "I will after our first date."

"Not now."

He shook his head. "Payment first, then answers." His palm slid up her side to wrap around the back of her neck. "Now, do we have a deal?"

For years, she'd sought an explanation for her unnatural talent. And this man—demon—was the closest she'd come to understanding her condition. He might be able to tell her how her parents died. And Owen.

All she had to do was play along.

A few dates.

Gather some intelligence about the supernatural world.

Find out what happened to her friend and her family.

All by pretending to be Issac Wakefield's girlfriend. Not exactly a hardship. She just had to keep her emotions in check, which wouldn't be a problem. Stas didn't do love or relationships.

"Okay," she agreed softly. "Dating for information. I accept."

"Brilliant." His fingers knotted in her hair, his thighs aligning with hers. "Just one more thing."

She swallowed, her breathing shortening. "Which is?"

He smiled. "This."

"Th—"

His mouth silenced hers, his tongue sliding between her parted lips with the expert ease of a man used to possessing a woman.

And fuck, he tasted divine. Like the finest bourbon, smooth and hot, and edged in age.

Her thighs clenched, her stomach tightening, his kiss dominating her in a way she'd never experienced. One swipe of his tongue and he owned her. Which shouldn't be possible. Not when she knew the truth about him.

Not human. Not real. All a charade.

But the heat pressing into her lower belly certainly felt *real*. As did the way his palm tightened against her neck, holding her for his sensual assault.

He took her slow at first, thoroughly introducing her to his preferences and skill before emboldening the kiss. Each stroke embodied a mixture of warning and promise, telling her just what to expect from him between the sheets. Issac would take what he wanted, when he wanted it, however he wanted it. She had no choice but to accept him, her body succumbing to his every will.

How is it possible to feel so entirely owned from just a kiss?

He branded her.

Controlled her.

Caressed her.

And released her just as her arms encircled his neck.

His hand was still in her hair, his mouth only a breath away from hers. "Thomas." The growled name vibrated her chest.

She blinked. *Thomas?*

"I'm only going to say this once." Issac's broad shoulders blocked her view of what sounded like a furious Tom. "Release her."

Arousal swam in the depths of Issac's gaze. He brushed his lips against her temple and her ear. "Consider our deal sealed." A breath of words meant for her alone. "Is there a problem, Thomas?" he asked, louder now, as he moved to her side, his arm sliding around her lower back.

Tom, Stas thought, frowning. No one ever called him Thomas. Then again, no one called her Astasiya, either. It seemed her demon harbored a dislike of nicknames.

"Go back to the table, Stas." The command in Tom's tone startled her. In the six years she'd known him, he'd never spoken to her like that.

"Excuse me?" she asked, daring him to say that to her again.

"Now, Stas."

Her eyebrows shot up. He'd gone full military officer on her, using a tone he usually reserved for work. Why the sudden protectiveness? Yes, he treated her like a sister, just like Lizzie, but whom she dated wasn't his business.

Not really dating.

Also not the point.

As if hearing her thoughts, Issac nibbled her neck. The look Tom gave him in response screamed murderous intent. What the fuck was wrong with him?

"It's all right, darling," Issac murmured against her throat. "We'll catch up properly later."

"Like hell you will," Tom replied.

Stas gaped at her friend, mortified and at a complete loss for what to say.

"You can stand down now, Sentinel," Issac said, the heat of his body leaving her side. "I'll see you soon, Astasiya." The insinuation in his tone had her stomach clenching. His lips had seared her being, leaving her with a promise of so much more.

It's a charade, she reminded herself. *He's just playing with you.*

But that kiss had certainly felt real…

Tom glowered after her demon, his body tense, his expression darkly serious.

Stas hit his arm to grab his attention and to refocus her own. "What the hell is wrong with you?" Her fingers tingled from the punch, his biceps far too solid. She knew he worked out, but damn. He resembled a rock beneath the suit.

Tom's dark brown gaze reminded her of molten lava as he stared down at her from his over-six-foot height. "He's not who you think he is, Stas."

Yeah, she already knew that. "I can take care of myself, Tom."

"He's bad news," he continued. "You can't date him."

Stas had never been the type to take orders well. "I'm not having this conversation with you." His intentions might be in the right place, but he had no right to dictate her personal life.

"Yes, you are. Tell me you won't date him."

"I'm not going to do that."

"Yes, you will."

"Do you even hear yourself right now?" she asked. He sounded insane.

"I'm just looking out for you."

She sighed, understanding. Issac showed up with a woman on his arm, only to end up kissing Stas outside of the restaurant. Not exactly Boyfriend of the Year material, especially in her friend's eyes. Still, it wasn't any of Tom's business what she did in her personal life.

"How do you know him?" she asked, changing the

subject.

His expression darkened. "Through work."

"Wakefield Pharmaceuticals donates drugs to the CRF?"

He snorted. "Hell no. Look, he's not a good person, Stas. Which is why you need to stay away from him."

And back to the original topic. "I make my own decisions, Tom."

He folded his arms, his expression dubious. "Well, you're making a bad one."

She shook her head, done. "I love you, but I'm not talking to you about this anymore." She brushed past him before he could reply, refusing to say another word. The deal was done. She'd play Issac's game in exchange for answers. Nothing more, nothing less.

The demon in question raised a glass to her as she walked by, as if to say, *Cheers, darling.*

Yeah. Cheers, she thought back at him. *I need a drink.*

~*~

"You're toying with an innocent girl's life," Aidan remarked as he sipped his brandy with an elegance only acquired by time.

"Perhaps," Issac replied as Astasiya reclaimed her seat at the table in the corner of the dining room. That blue dress of hers clung to every curve and revealed a pair of legs that were designed to be wrapped around a man's waist. Preferably, his. "He does appear surprised by our acquaintance, yes?" he asked, switching topics.

"It's genuine," Clara murmured, her perceptive blue eyes on their former ally. Her knack for sensing emotions was why he'd invited her to dinner tonight. "The whole table is shocked." Which meant Jonathan hadn't sent Astasiya to meet him that fateful morning at Owen's apartment. He suspected that to be the case, but he still desired confirmation. Now that he had it, his plan could move forward.

"She's your type," Anya noted, her perfect lips taunting him with a smile. The woman adored flirting, hence the revealing dress she wore displaying all her ample assets. The dark beauty held nothing back. Aidan was a lucky man. "We all know how you feel about natural blondes," she added.

"Except this one seems conflicted." Clara frowned. "I don't think I've ever seen a woman react to you like this, Issac. It's quite phenomenal, really."

He started. "I thought you couldn't sense her?" From what he'd surmised, Astasiya was impervious to supernatural gifts.

"Well, no, I can't, but this one doesn't stare at you in adoration like all the others do."

He followed her gaze to the blonde in question and grinned when he found Astasiya glowering at him. Yes, this woman had spirit. One of her many positive traits. The elder Fitzgerald caught him looking and lifted his brow, his curiosity clear. Brilliant. That marked Issac's secondary goal for the evening as accomplished.

Aidan cocked his head to the side. "She might be useful, Issac."

"Yes." In more ways than one. He could enjoy her company while also using her to exact revenge, and if she lived, he'd give her to Lucian. The Hydraians would be thrilled with the addition of her persuasive power.

"Perhaps you should try not to get her killed?" Aidan suggested over his glass of brandy.

Issac studied the man he considered to be his father, the one who always seemed to know his thoughts and plans before they were fully contrived. "Casualties are a consequence of war, Aidan. You know that better than anyone."

"Ah, but is it her war to fight?"

Issac didn't hesitate. "It is now."

CHAPTER FIVE

Security Clearances Are Bullshit

"LIZZIE?" STAS CALLED AS SHE DROPPED HER purse by the door. "Why does it look like Valentine's Day threw up in your condo?"

There were flowers everywhere.

All shades, sizes, and scents.

"Liz?"

No reply.

Stas ventured into the formal dining area, then the kitchen, and down the corridor to the master suite. Lizzie sat inside with her bare feet kicked up on the desk, her computer keyboard in her lap. She didn't glance up from the screen as she asked, "Did your parents make it to the airport okay?"

"Yeah." It took some reassuring, but they eventually got on the plane. She understood their concerns. However, Stas had never been the type to hide from her fears.

Which was exactly why she'd agreed to date a demon.

He came from a world that fueled her nightmares, but he also possessed all the answers. If he wanted to harm her, he would, with or without her permission. She might as well use him in the same manner he intended to use her.

"So, uh, why does the condo look like a flower shop?" Stas asked, her nose crinkling from the floral aroma.

Lizzie shrugged. "I don't know. Maybe ask your *boyfriend.*"

"What?" *The flowers are for me? From Issac?* "Why?" Was he trying to give her Valentine's Day–themed nightmares?

Her roommate moved the keyboard to her desk. "There's a card by the vase of exotic lilies in the kitchen. Why don't you go read it?"

Right, still mad about the Issac thing.

"By the way, he's not my boyfriend," Stas grumbled as she left for the kitchen with Lizzie right behind her.

"Uh-huh."

"I didn't lie to you, Liz."

"No, you omitted it. I've been trying to get you to go on a date for six years. What happened to *I'm not interested in my MRS degree?*" Lizzie's tone went high as she parroted Stas's favorite excuse for not dating. She went out sometimes and didn't mind sex.

Well, occasionally.

Okay, hardly ever.

To be fair, her experiences weren't something to brag about. With the exception, maybe of last night, and that'd only been a kiss.

Stas found the card on the counter and read it.

I'll pick you up at six o'clock tomorrow. -Issac

Cocky much? Tomorrow was her security interview. What if it ran over?

"For the record, *this*"—she handed the card to Lizzie—

"will be our first date." Assuming she agreed to the high-handed proposal. *Of course you will, idiot.* "And I didn't tell you I met him because I didn't realize who he was until yesterday." Something she already explained after dinner last night.

Lizzie chewed her lip, considering. "What are you going to wear?"

"I don't know. Jeans and a tank top?"

Manicured nails clicked on the counter. "Try again."

"A skirt?"

"And?"

"A tank top."

Lizzie sighed dramatically. "What am I going to do with you?"

"Help me get ready for my date?" she offered, knowing her best friend lived to play beauty consultant. Stas enjoyed fashion as much as the next woman, but no one knew clothes better than her roommate. The woman lived and breathed high society, and if anyone could prepare Stas for a night with Issac Wakefield, it was Lizzie Watkins.

"You need me," her best friend said.

"I do," Stas admitted.

Lizzie tapped her jaw, pensive. "All right, you're forgiven pending an afternoon of chick flicks, wine, and leftover pizza."

That sounded like a horrible way to spend her Monday off. *Not.* "Deal."

Lizzie held up a finger. "*And* you wear the outfit of my choosing on your date tomorrow. I'll put it on your bed before I go to work." She managed an after-school program for underprivileged kids, meaning she wouldn't be home when Stas left tomorrow. And the wicked gleam in her best friend's eyes said whatever outfit she had in mind would double as a punishment.

"You drive a hard bargain, Liz."

Her roommate held out her hand and wiggled her fingers. "Deal?"

I'm so going to regret this, but what choice do I have? She shook Lizzie's hand. "Okay, deal."

* * *

"Have you ever committed a serious crime?"

Stas swallowed. *Don't think, just answer.* "No." *Breathe in, one, two. Breathe out, one, two.* Her reflection in the one-way mirror gave nothing away. She remained poised, confident, and aloof.

The polygrapher—Agent Stark—wrote something down beside her while the machine ticked loudly in her ears.

Don't think, she repeated to herself. If she allowed herself to consider—

No. Stop thinking.

"Have you ever met an Ichorian?"

Oh, this again. The first time he'd given her this question, she'd asked him to define *Ichorian.* He'd stopped the test and reminded her that some of the questions were meant to throw her off, hence the made-up phrases and words.

Now she knew how to answer. "No."

Again with the ticking.

And the scribbling.

They'd been doing this for hours, round and round, question after question.

Does he know about Ow—

Stop thinking!

She focused on her reflection again, studying her blouse. So much more conservative than the outfit Lizzie had picked out for her date later.

Oh, much safer.

Stas pictured the dress as she answered all the same queries.

Have you ever traveled to Greece?

No.

Have you ever manufactured, purchased, or sold drugs?

No.

Have you ever met a Hydraian?
No.

"This now concludes round six of the security interview for Astasiya Davenport. Recording to end in three, two, one…"

A click resounded through the room, causing her shoulders to sag. The contraption around her abdomen dug into her bra, but she didn't care. This whole ordeal was far more exhausting than she anticipated.

"We're done," Stark said, his tone emotionless. He pushed away from his desk and helped extract her from the polygraph instruments without a word. "Follow me" was all he said.

Man of many words.

His muscular stature reminded her more of a military man than a business professional. He possessed a commanding air, one that sent a chill down her spine. This was not a person to defy or piss off.

If he suspects I lied… She swallowed. No. She couldn't think about it. Or Owen. Or the fact that lying to the authorities was most definitely a serious crime. *It's over. It's fine. Everything's going to be okay.*

And what would he do anyway? Drill her about a crime she may or may not have committed?

Except, lying could cost her this job.

Better than ending up in prison for omitting information.

Stark stopped abruptly to knock on an all-white door that matched the pristine corridor. It felt so clinical in the lower levels of the CRF, reminding her of a vacant hospital. No one wandered down here. No paintings or door signs. Just vapid walls revealing a maze of rooms with the occasional security camera dotted above.

The marketing department upstairs was an entirely different world, filled with windows overlooking Manhattan, colorful cubicles, and smiling faces. Perhaps Stark should pay the floor a visit. His stern features could use a little brightening.

A petite woman with darker features and caramel skin opened the door, her gaze lifting to Stark without faltering. "Sentinel."

"Doctor," he returned flatly. "Astasiya Davenport is here for her medical examination."

She gingerly lifted the sleeve of her lab coat and blinked down at her watch. "You're early."

"Her polygraph finished sooner than expected."

Does that mean I passed? Or failed? Stas wondered.

The doctor studied him for a long moment, his expression as stoic as ever. "I see," she said slowly, joining them in the hallway and closing the door behind her. "Then I'll proceed with the exam, if you wouldn't mind…?"

He nodded.

Something passed between them. Something unpleasant.

Clearly a history here. Maybe they used to date?

Stas suppressed a shiver at the wrongness, chalking it up to their clinical surroundings. It just felt so cold down here.

"Astasiya, I'm Doctor Patel." The doctor held out her hand. Despite the smaller size, she delivered one hell of a shake. "If you'll follow me, please."

Stark didn't say anything, but Stas could feel his light eyes on them as they walked down the hall. A glance back at him confirmed her suspicions, the knowing glint in his gaze causing her stomach to churn.

It's just nerves.

Or I failed spectacularly.

But he couldn't know about Owen. No one did except for her demon.

"This way," Doctor Patel said, opening a door to the left.

Stas followed her inside, swallowing the bile rising in her throat. Everything about this felt wrong. *It's the guilt.* There was no other explanation. Yet, what was she supposed to do? Admit everything during the polygraph? She'd come off as a lunatic and would definitely not obtain her clearance for the job afterward.

"All right, have a seat." Doctor Patel gestured to the exam table. Such a simple request, yet Stas's feet resembled lead as she moved across the room. Goose bumps pebbled her skin, her insides twisting at some subtle threat she couldn't diagnose.

What the hell is wrong with me? It's just a physical exam.

"Let's start with your medical history," Doctor Patel said from her computer in the corner. She asked a few standard questions, none of which were all that intrusive, yet Stas still felt that prickle of unease at the back of her neck. Something that told her she was being watched. Carefully.

Paranoia.

It had to be.

This was the CRF, the company she'd interned with for almost a year. The renowned humanitarian agency owned by Doctor Fitzgerald, who had been nothing but a mentor to her for the last six years.

She clearly needed more sleep.

"Vitals," Doctor Patel continued, taking Stas's blood pressure, checking her lungs and heart, and drawing blood for a panel.

All standard.

All completely acceptable.

Until she revealed a tray of syringes.

"What are those for?" she wondered out loud.

"A few common vaccines." Dr. Patel explained as she retrieved a clipboard from the desk. "It's mandatory for CRF employees. You never know when you might have to travel for a work assignment."

"I wasn't aware my position required travel."

"It's standard procedure here." Dr. Patel handed Stas the clipboard with a few documents attached. "These are the consent forms. They explain the three different types of shots that will be administered today and their potential side effects. Review and sign, please."

Stas's brow furrowed. It seemed more prudent for an

employer to inoculate employees after they were cleared for hire. Or maybe even wait until the first business trip. Vaccinations weren't exactly cheap.

"You can always deny them," Dr. Patel added, her near-black eyes eerily observant. "But I'll have to note that in your medical exam records."

Meaning Stas might not be given a security clearance if she didn't agree. Add that to a potentially failed polygraph, and, well, she could kiss her job offer goodbye. Not even Doctor Fitzgerald could fix that problem for her—all of this was mandated by the government, not his company. And those contracts were what kept the CRF alive.

Might as well at least see what vaccinations they were requiring.

Hepatitis. Pretty standard.

Typhoid fever. Not as familiar, but she'd heard of it.

She frowned at the last one. "Nizari fever?"

"It's a recent development." Excitement lit up Doctor Patel's features. "We're seeing a lot of cases in Asia right now, actually. Hence the requirement."

"Oh." It all seemed a bit extreme, but this was the CRF. Globally renowned and respected, and also the company Doctor Fitzgerald had founded. He wouldn't inject his future employees with anything life-threatening. Besides, Stas had never been sick in her life. Not even a common cold. A few shots wouldn't kill her.

She signed the documents and removed her blouse, leaving her clad in a thin tank top that did nothing to protect her from the cool, sterile air.

"Perfect." Doctor Patel readied Stas's arm for the first injection. "Hepatitis is given in three doses, so you'll need to come back for the next two. The details will be with your new-hire paperwork." She administered the shot while speaking and finished with a Band-Aid.

"Okay," Stas replied, noting the requirement to follow up later.

"This might sting a bit," the doctor warned as she

inserted a needle with a peculiar-looking green liquid. "This is for typhoid."

Why is it gre—

Ow!

Sting was an understatement. It felt like the woman had just inserted ice directly into Stas's vein. She bit her lip to keep from crying out. Nerves frayed as the medicine worked its way through her body. It took significant effort not to shiver when the coolness settled around her chest.

"What did you say that was for?" she asked, her voice higher than intended.

"Typhoid. And this last one is for the Nizari."

Another syringe filled with green.

Odd.

She opened her mouth to ask for more time, when Dr. Patel injected her with a shot of liquid fire.

Fuck!

Stas shook from the impact. Cold met heat, causing her mind to fracture beneath the conflicting directives from her nerves.

What in the ever-loving…?

Wow, she was dizzy.

The room swam around her, the lights blinking in and out of sequence. She blinked, her lips parting on a question that her numb tongue refused to help her deliver.

This can't be a normal reaction.

"All done." Dr. Patel's voice sounded far away.

Stas squinted at the tiny woman. *What?* Had she just given her a fourth inoculation? *No, only three on the table. Right?*

"How are you feeling?"

Horrible. Somehow, Stas forced the word "fine" through her dry lips.

"Good. I just need to chart a few things and then Agent Stark can escort you back upstairs."

Stas mouthed, "Okay," welcoming the distraction. Because walking right now was a no-go.

A numbing sensation slithered over her, centering in her chest and expanding outward. She stole a deep breath, hoping to dispel the feeling.

It only worsened.

This can't be a good sign.

But the doctor remained blissfully unaware as her fingers flew across the keyboard in the corner.

Stas closed her eyes and focused, willing her body to accept whatever had been injected into her veins. She could lie down when she returned home. Not here.

It was probably just her nerves catching up to her.

Yes, that had to be it. The guilt brought up by the polygraph coupled with her general unease in the underground of the CRF. She'd feel better as soon as she stepped outside the building. Hell, even off the elevator onto the first floor.

Stas rolled her shoulders, her limbs tingling. But she could feel her arms again—a good sign. Clearly, all just in her head.

She slid from the table to test her ability to stand, and her hands locked onto the exam table to keep her from swaying. Dots danced before her eyes, but she remained upright. A few blinks later and her wits returned, just in time for the doctor to face her.

"You're a little pale. Are you feeling okay?" Frown lines marred Doctor Patel's forehead, but her gaze held a touch of eagerness that sent a chill down Stas's spine.

There is something not right with this woman. How Stas knew that, she couldn't say, but she'd never denied her instincts. Ever.

"Just a little light-headed," she said, forcing a small smile. "It's been a long day." *Can she hear the slight slur in my voice? Or is that just my imagination?*

Dr. Patel studied her for a little longer than was comfortable. "Let me go get Agent Stark, okay?"

Stas nodded once, making the world spin.

Standard vaccinations, my ass.

She'd be researching that Nizari whatever later. After some sleep.

At least the numbness had worn off, leaving her more nauseated than weak. But still dizzy. She focused on re-dressing and forced another friendly exchange when Doctor Patel returned with Agent Stark.

They said some things.

Hopefully nothing important, because she barely heard them. Hardly even paid attention to Stark escorting her back upstairs. Fortunately, he didn't speak much, just instructed her on when and where to scan her badge. He led her to the familiar four-story glass lobby of the CRF and handed over her purse.

Where did you find this?

"Welcome to the CRF, Stas," he said, his light green eyes capturing hers. A hint of familiarity hit her, causing her heart to flutter.

I know you…

Because he just did her polygraph.

Right. Yeah. "Thanks," she said. Or she thought she did, anyway.

With another forced smile, or maybe a grimace, she turned toward the flags decorating her exit. The creepy one in the middle grabbed her attention first, as it always did.

Memento Mori, it said in a fancy scrawl. *Remember that you must die.*

Why, thank you, creepy flag, she thought as she pushed through the doors.

She moved on autopilot, relying on her ten months of experience traveling between the CRF headquarters and Lizzie's condo. Two trains. Walking. Central Park. Oh, Seventy-Ninth Street. Home.

I can sleep now, she thought numbly, half walking, half slouching. *Or maybe I should go to a hospital.*

"Astasiya?"

Her gaze came up from the sidewalk to find Issac leaning against a sleek black car parked outside of Lizzie's building.

Another suit. Of course. At least she had on a blouse and skirt this time. Or did she leave her blouse behind?

She lifted her arm.

Nope.

It was on.

When did I do that?

"Are you all right?" the cultured voice asked, causing her to squint in his direction.

Is he real? She tilted her head. *Looks pretty real. Sexy, too. No, we don't like demons. But this one is nice. Oh, he asked something…*

She blanked on what he wanted to know, not that her mouth felt all that capable of replying. Her tongue felt too big, and wow, the world was really moving, wasn't it? She couldn't distinguish up from down from sideways. Everything started to tilt upside—

Hands gripped her shoulders, causing her to stumble back a few steps. *Issac.* Damn, he moved fast. She could have sworn he stood over ten feet away from her just a few seconds ago.

"Your security interview was today. Did that include a medical exam?" His voice pierced the fog, his handsome face far too close to hers.

"Uh." She had to focus. *What did he ask? About my medical exam?* "Yup. Lotsa shotsss."

"Were any of them green?"

"Creepy green." She shivered. "Cold green. Then sooo hot." *Like you.* Ah, she had to stop that. Maybe not looking at him would help. *Oh, yes, closing the eyes…* A slap against her cheek had her flinching and glaring upward at the too-handsome offender. "Ow."

"I need you to stay awake."

Whoa, they were flying.

No, she was flying.

As in, no longer standing but still moving. In his arms, surrounding her with sandalwood and peppermint and lulling her into comfort. She rested her head against a muscular shoulder, only to be jolted awake and set on something leathery. *I'm in his car.*

"Talk to me," he said from beside her. *Is he already driving?*

"I don't feel right."

"I can see that, darling. Tell me about the vaccinations."

She yawned. "Cold. Fire."

He replied with something, but the pounding in her ears overshadowed his sexy accent. Black painted her vision as her head hit something soft. A pillow? She didn't know. Didn't care. Exhaustion consumed her entirely.

No more pain.

No more dreams.

Just... sleep.

~*~

Issac studied the injection sites on Astasiya's arms, noting the discoloration of her veins. She felt cold—too cold—and her breathing was far too shallow.

She's dying.

"Fuck." This couldn't be happening. But here she was, lying in his bed... dying.

Because of me.

Those three words reverberated in his mind, leaving him helpless at her side. He never meant for this to happen, never expected Jonathan to go to such lengths. Yes, sometimes innocents were a casualty of war. He'd said that just the other night, and still believed it.

But this was a casualty he intended to fix.

No matter the cost.

Hence the incoming presence beside him.

"This better be important, Wakefield," Lucian said as he appeared with his teleporter, Jacque.

Issac didn't bother with pleasantries, jumping right to the point. "Look." He lifted Astasiya's hand to show them the inky green lines crawling up her arm. "Is that what I think it is?"

Lucian eyed Astasiya's skin with interest and knelt beside her for a closer examination. His big hand enveloped her wrist, twisting it one way and then the other. "Nizari poison."

Jacque's dark eyebrows shot up into his moppy hairline. "A fledgling? In New York City?"

Issac ignored the teleporter and focused on the issue at hand. They could discuss her heritage later. "I think it's a variant of the venom." The Nizari assassins didn't know she existed because Issac never reported her existence to the Conclave. And as fledglings were rare these days—a result of the lethal Ichorians killing most of them before their immortal rebirth—most of the assassins were retired.

"It's not the Conclave," Lucian said, his lips flattening. "The mark is too obvious."

Yes, the Nizari were known for making fledgling deaths look like accidents. "I think it's Jonathan." No one else would have any reason to test her ancestry. Of course, this implied that he *knew* about her ability to compel. "The CRF gave Astasiya immunizations as part of her medical exam today. She said they were green," he added while listening for her vitals. *So slow. Too slow.*

"Who is this woman, Issac?" The command in Lucian's tone, coupled with his muscular stature and hard stare, would bring most men to their knees in submission. Women, too.

But Issac didn't heel to anyone, least of all Lucian. They were family, after all, despite living on opposite sides of the immortal coin.

"She's a long story that we don't have time for right now." His phone buzzed, security calling from the lobby. *Finally.* Issac answered and told them to let his physicians up. "I have two of my best infectious disease clinicians coming in to evaluate her. I need you to give them everything you know." Both doctors were on his payroll at Wakefield Pharmaceuticals, and they specialized in orphan drugs. Between their skill sets and Lucian's familiarity with the Nizari venom, they might be able to save Astasiya's life.

"Why didn't you report her presence?" Lucian pressed. "She's a fledgling, and therefore mine. You know the rules, Wakefield."

Sometimes Issac really hated the man he called a brother. "I'm not debating this right now, Lucian. I need you to help my physicians save her life. Then we'll discuss her history and how I know her." He dialed Mateo before Lucian could reply.

His progeny picked up on the first ring. "Sire?"

"I need you to break into the CRF's database and retrieve whatever information you can on Astasiya's medical exam."

A second of hesitation passed before Mateo replied, "When I do this, they may detect my virtual presence." A subtle warning.

Mateo was the only being in existence with the technical wherewithal to hack *anything*. And Issac had kept the extent of his abilities a secret for years, hoping to use him as a trump card at the right moment.

It seemed today was now that moment. Because while the young Ichorian possessed the talent to attack a corporation from inside the system, the woman dying in Issac's penthouse flat could hurt his opponent from a much more vulnerable place.

The perfect revenge.

"I'm aware of the risk," Issac replied, his mind already made up. *She must live.*

"Of course, Sire. I'll send the records to your personal file."

"Thank you, Mateo."

He hung up just as his health care professionals arrived. Jacque went to retrieve them, leaving Issac alone with his old friend. Those hard emerald eyes told Issac exactly how Lucian felt about the situation. As the Hydraian King, he wasn't used to being kept in the dark, let alone ordered around.

"You and I are going to have a very long conversation once this is over." Lucian's tone brooked no argument.

"Save her first."

"Fine."

A violent shiver wracked Astasiya, drawing attention to her rising fever. The damp washcloth Issac had placed on her forehead before everyone else arrived wasn't doing a damn thing. His doctors rushed over to assess her, forgoing the usual greetings. *Thank fuck.*

"I'm going to need a few things." Lucian listed them for Jacque. "And bring Alik. Every moment I spend in this city is a risk to my life." He leveled another sharp glance at Issac, his sacrifice clear. New York City wasn't safe for Hydraians, let alone their King. "I need B and Jay, too," he added.

"On it." The teleporter disappeared, something the researchers failed to notice, as they were too engrossed in tending to Astasiya.

In his bedroom.

Not a guest room.

The decision had been made without thought. An oversight for him to evaluate later.

"You owe me," Lucian said, scribbling something down on a notebook one of the researchers had handed him.

On the contrary, Lucian, Issac thought. *Once you realize how powerful she is,* you *will owe* me. *Assuming she survives.*

CHAPTER SIX

Helpful Hydraians

"START TALKING, WAKEFIELD." LUCIAN STOOD beside Astasiya's comatose form, his thick arms folded over his chest, legs spread. Balthazar sat in the corner chair, while Jayson and Alik stood by the windows, their stances guarded. Every moment they stayed here put all their lives in jeopardy, but it had taken nearly two hours to stabilize Astasiya's vitals.

Now her life was in the hands of the researchers who had left only moments ago to prepare a makeshift remedy at the lab.

Either it would work or it wouldn't.

What if it doesn't?

She appeared so helpless and alone in Issac's bed, her

hair fanned out around her in a halo of gold. A foreign part of him longed to lie with her, to provide her with any semblance of comfort he could, if even for a moment. Odd considering he never wanted to hold anyone, not even sexual partners. He preferred his space, hence his requirements to keep women out of his quarters.

Yet, he hadn't hesitated to place her in his bed.

He still didn't know why, didn't truly wish to consider the cause. It had just felt right to carry her here rather than to one of the guest suites. As if he felt compelled to watch over her, to protect her.

"Fascinating," Balthazar murmured from the corner chair, his lips curled at the edges. The mind reader could hear every thought in the room—no, within the entire building and well beyond it—and was clearly listening to Issac now.

Fuck you, Issac thought at him, edging the words with sarcasm.

Anytime, he mouthed back at him. Somber moments be damned, the man oozed sex in everything he said and did, and he certainly didn't discriminate when it came to bed partners.

Never going to happen. A phrase Issac had thought at the male many, many times. Not that it would deter Balthazar in the slightest. One flash of his sinful gaze sent most women to their knees—men, too. Pair that with his athletic physique and the thousands of years of experience under his belt, and, well, most didn't stand a chance against his charm. Yet, he never tempted Issac. Females, specifically natural blonde ones, were Issac's preference. Like the woman in his bed.

Lucian cocked an eyebrow. "I've done everything I can to ensure her survival, Wakefield. I want an explanation. Now."

Right. Procrastinating the discussion served little purpose. Might as well start from the beginning. "Her name is Astasiya Davenport. We met the morning of Angelton's murder."

Issac relayed the story of their fateful introduction, including details about her immunity to his gift for visual manipulation, and the evidence suggesting her long friendship with Owen.

"Mateo pulled the police records," he continued. "Then additional files on her history. She was adopted at age seven by a couple who lives in Havre, Montana, and it seems someone went to great lengths to cover up her life before that moment. She moved to New York to attend the university, which is where she befriended Owen, as I already mentioned. That's also where she met the young Elizabeth Watkins, who later introduced her to the Fitzgeralds."

Jayson and Alik turned from their perches by the floor-to-ceiling windows at the mention of the infamous names. As Elders, they were considered to be the most powerful of their race, which was why they were here. Allowing their King to visit the most dangerous city in the world for Hydraians went against the grain, but their lifelong friendship with Issac circumvented the rules. These men were family, and no treaty or war would ever put them on opposite sides of the playing field.

"She knows Jonathan," Lucian said, scratching the blond stubble dotting his chin. "Which can only mean one thing. You're using the girl to get vengeance for Amelia."

"I am." The words tasted bitter in his mouth, mainly because he felt responsible for her current situation. He only meant to pique Jonathan's interest. Which he clearly succeeded in doing since the lunatic tried to poison the poor woman.

"But she's a fledgling," Lucian added.

"Yes," he confirmed, aware of what the Hydraian King really wanted to know. Fledglings were rare, and one as powerful as Astasiya was even rarer. "In addition to being resistant to psychic gifts, she has a persuasive talent."

Jayson frowned. "Meaning what? She can coax people into doing things?"

"Not coax. Command. Like Osiris." Stunned silence met his words. Osiris was the most powerful Ichorian in existence. Suggesting her gift rivaled the notorious immortal's spoke volumes about her potential. She would be unstoppable after her rebirth.

"You're telling me, that as a fledgling, she has the power to *command*?" Doubt colored Lucian's tone.

"I observed her use of persuasion twice in casual conversation. It was natural and effective." *And sexy as hell.*

Issac's focus shifted to her prone form. Her heartbeat comforted him only a little. The machines were doing their jobs of keeping her alive, but he had no way of knowing how long it would last.

The urge to lie beside her overcame him again, but he swallowed it. Now wasn't the time to show weakness. Not when he needed to negotiate.

"You're soft on her," Balthazar noted in an unhelpful manner. "I mean, I can see why. Even half-dead she's gorgeous, but it's not like you to delve deeper than the surface, Wakefield. She must be phenomenal in bed." Issac tried not to think about it, but the smile that slipped over those too-perfect lips told him his thoughts came over loud and clear. The bastard let out a low whistle. "Wow. He hasn't fucked her yet. No wonder he wants her to live so badly." At Lucian's cocked eyebrow, the mind reader waved a hand. "Yeah, sorry, carry on."

"Tell me more about her relationship with the Fitzgeralds and why you think she can be used against Jonathan," Lucian said, the rock band logo on his shirt peeking through his folded forearms. Even dressed casually, the man exuded authority. Not that Issac would ever bend to him, but on this, he'd compromise.

He relayed what he knew, which wasn't much, yet enough to explain how the girl could be useful. "We all want revenge, and I think Astasiya could be the key," he concluded.

Jayson twirled a knife between his long fingers. His

shoulders and muscular stature rivaled the others, but beneath it all was a calm lethality underlined in charm. A dangerous combination, one that aided him well when on a mission to assassinate someone. "Can't we just kill the son of a bitch and get it over with?" he asked, his tone far too pleasant for the words.

"Don't look at me," Alik replied. He was the shortest of the group, at just six feet tall, and also the deadliest. "I voted to slaughter him six years ago when he left Eli's head on that godforsaken table beside his headless body holding Amelia's ashes. Talk to the *King*. He's the one who said it was better to wait."

Lucian rolled his eyes at the jibe. The Elders and Issac were among the few who could harass the man about his *regal title*. No one else would dare.

"From what you've told me, she's not going to be easily swayed to our cause," Lucian said, his expression thoughtful, assessing. "Which also means she's not going to be quick to join us in Hydria, either."

An intelligent deduction, and accurate.

"Astasiya requires a slow introduction to our world. It's the only way to build trust, especially after this." Issac considered the woman in his bed, wondering if she dreamt in her deep sleep. Her immunity to his gift made it impossible for him to know, something that intrigued him more than it should. "I'm up for the challenge of teaching her."

"I'm sure you are." Another unhelpful comment from the mind reader in the corner.

Lucian flashed him a speculative glance. "You realize trusting an Ichorian to mentor and groom what could be the most powerful Hydraian in existence goes against the grain, yes?"

Issac snorted. "Don't be an ass." He might not be a Hydraian by blood, but he was a respected member of their society. They trusted him, and for good reason. "Do you remember that time you asked me to trust Eli not to accidentally kill my only sister?" Technically, Amelia was Issac's half sister since they had different fathers. Semantics.

Lucian's blond brows rose. "You mean the one who also happened to be my sister?" Because they shared a birth father—Aidan. The same man who raised Issac as a youth and eventually turned him into an Ichorian.

"Not the point," Issac replied.

"Entirely the point."

"Whatever. Don't be a dick. You know I'm more than capable of mentoring her, Lucian."

"Because you did such a fantastic job mentoring Tristan."

He had to go there. "Tristan has no place in this conversation." Issac's progeny needed some work, but he wasn't *that* bad. "My gift for controlling vision might not work on her, but it works on everyone else. I'll keep her hidden, introduce her to our world at the right pace, and convince her to help our cause."

"That's a hefty task for the CEO of a billion-dollar enterprise." This from the corner again. Balthazar clearly had a death wish tonight. "I would be better suited for the job. My slate is clean, and you know she won't be able to resist this face."

Not after I disassemble it. "No." Flat. To the point. And nonnegotiable. The mind reader could not—*would not*—go anywhere near Astasiya. Ever. He'd try to fuck her, not teach her. "No," Issac repeated. "End of."

"Worried about your competition, Wakefield?" Balthazar's taunt made Issac's hands curl into fists.

"I'm worried you'll be too busy seducing her to teach her anything." *There, that was a fair argument.*

"On the contrary, I could teach her all sorts of things." The deep tenor of his voice implied *what* he intended to show Astasiya. If anyone would be giving her a tutorial around the bedroom, it would be Issac. Not Balthazar. "This territorial thing you've got going on is cute," the mind reader added, smirking.

Careful, Issac warned. One psychic punch would black out the bastard's sight and leave him curled in the fetal position on the floor—a visual tactic Issac had used on the mind reader many times in their long history.

Balthazar blew him a kiss and waggled his dark eyebrows before looking at the man in charge. "I vote we leave her with Wakefield, Luc. There's more going on in that head of his than he's admitting out loud, or even to himself."

"I'll bear that in mind, B." Lucian's biceps bulged as he combed his fingers through his blond hair and then down his face. "Before I agree to anything, I want some clarification."

"Regarding?" Issac prompted.

"You met Astasiya at Owen's apartment, which means two things. First, you kept her existence from me on purpose until now. And second, she knew Owen. Who else knows about her?"

Ah, this is going to start an argument. "Aidan, Clara, and Anya know, but only because I needed backup for…" He trailed off as Astasiya's heartbeat changed.

It was a reassuring rhythm in the back of his mind, until it wasn't.

Issac knelt by the bed and wrapped his fingers around her wrist. *Weak. Too weak.* Alarms sounded from the machines, making his stomach lurch. *Don't do this to me, Astasiya.*

Balthazar joined him, hand on his shoulder. "I need you to move," he said, his teasing nature subsiding to the powerful man beneath the jovial veneer. He'd attended medical school several times, providing him with the knowledge and abilities to treat Astasiya's condition.

It had been Lucian's primary argument for Balthazar being here.

And despite the man's irritating habits, Issac trusted the mind reader when it came to matters of life and death.

Keep her alive, Issac thought at him, moving out of his way. It grated to defer to someone else, to place his faith in another to do what was needed.

But I can't help her. The words bounced around his skull, making him wince. The Nizari poison killed fledglings. No rebirth. No future as a Hydraian. Nothing. Her death would be permanent.

The ache in his chest reminded him of the day he found Amelia's ashes. An inane reaction to a woman he met less than two weeks ago.

Humans died every day.

His relationship with Astasiya was young at best. He knew little about her aside from the research. Her resilience intrigued him, and their brief kiss foreshadowed a passion well worth the seductive effort, but beyond that, what did he know about her?

She's intelligent.

Brave.

Gorgeous.

Dying…

"That's not good enough." Lucian was on the phone. "No. She's not going to make it. Bring what you have and we'll improvise." He hung up and joined Balthazar's efforts to resuscitate Astasiya.

She'd stopped breathing.

Issac collapsed in the corner chair in the sitting area of his room, his head in his palms as he listened to her waning pulse.

This is your *fault*, his subconscious reminded him.

He made decisions every day that impacted the lives of others, but this one grated on him. Left him feeling… *guilty*.

Innocents died in war every day.

Why did this one bother him?

The loss of whom she could have become?

A hard thud brought his head up. Electricity flowed through the room as everyone waited to see how her heart responded to the paddles against her chest.

It was too silent.

His Ichorian senses picked up on the tiniest thump,

followed by another. *Her heartbeat.* The rhythm sounded off, wrong, unhealthy.

"It's only temporary," Balthazar said in his doctor voice, the one void of teasing and seduction. Medicine was one of the few things he took seriously. "I'm honestly surprised she's still alive. Most fledglings die within an hour or two, and she was injected almost eight hours ago."

"She's resilient," Lucian said, frowning. "Do you think Owen knew about her?"

"Yes," Issac replied softly, his body frozen as he focused all his energy on her pulse. *Such a sweet sound.* "Their phone records suggest they've been friends for almost seven years. No way he was around her that long and didn't notice what she could do." Not when Issac figured it out during their second meeting.

"So he knew her for as long as he lived in the city?" Jayson whistled low and shook his head. "That's incriminating."

"It is indeed." Lucian checked something on the machine and gave Issac a nod. "You already know my answer, Wakefield. I'm trusting you to protect what's mine, assuming she lives."

Issac didn't care for the verbal claim. She wasn't an object to be owned or a weapon to be used.

Except isn't that what you're planning to do with her?

Fuck off.

"You know I will," he said, addressing Lucian's comment.

"I do. And you'll call me the second anything changes."

"Of course."

Lucian started to fiddle with one of the cords, then dropped it and pinned Issac with a stare.

And here comes the comment about me talking to Aidan before him, in three, two . . .

"Oh, and the next time you discover a powerful fledgling roaming the streets of New York City? You better tell me before you talk to Dad."

"Duly noted, but let's focus on helping this one survive first." That was all he could think about right now. He needed her alive. He would consider the why of it later.

Lucian nodded. "Fair enough."

CHAPTER SEVEN

A Slow Introduction

STAS'S NOSE TWITCHED AND HER STOMACH growled.

Bacon.

Oh, yes, please.

Lizzie loved to make brunch on the weekends, and Stas adored her for it. Especially when bacon was involved.

Stas stretched her arms and legs, feeling a dull ache inside that left her frowning. She felt exhausted despite the nightmare-free sleep. Odd.

She reached over to grab her phone from the nightstand and hit a fluffy pillow instead. Groaning, she rolled closer and tried again. More pillows.

What the hell? Her bed wasn't this big. She blindly patted around. It wasn't this soft, either.

And what the fuck am I wearing? Yoga pants and a tank top. Stas never wore those clothes to bed.

Yawning, she forced her eyes open for a look around.

Floor-to-ceiling windows with a magnificent view of the Hudson River greeted her.

She flew upward, causing her head to spin. "Ow," she managed through her dry throat. Shit, she felt awful. Like a hangover, but worse. Lying down again helped marginally, her vision no longer blurring.

A high ceiling—not common in Manhattan apartments—met her gaze. Mahogany tones decorated the oversized bedroom suite, and glass doors led to a terrace outside.

Okay, so she was in a building with views of the Hudson River to one side and Manhattan to the other.

Definitely *not* Lizzie's condo.

Stas inched upright and rested against the dark wood headboard, admiring the mahogany tones of the room. Very masculine. A familiar suitcase rested on the floor in the corner beside her purse.

How did I get here?

And when?

She took several deep breaths, calming the spinning in her head. Despite the strange surroundings, she felt safe. An odd sensation, considering, but her instincts rarely failed her.

The familiar scent of sandalwood reminded her of a certain demon, too.

Stas frowned, trying to recall her last memory. Something about the polygraph, being concerned with the serious-crimes question. Everything after that was fuzzy.

Had she drunk too much afterward on her date with Issac?

That would explain her memory loss and presence here, except she rarely overindulged in alcohol. Although, Issac could likely easily drive her to that point. And that would explain the hangover-like throbbing in her skull.

I hope we didn't... yeah.

No, definitely not.

Stas would be naked if they did, not dressed for yoga. And his side of the bed—or what she assumed to be his side—was perfectly made.

Assuming I'm in Issac's room.

She swallowed, her throat reminiscent of sandpaper.

God, she needed water before she figured all this out.

Bathroom.

There, near the glass doors.

Of course, it was across the room.

With a sigh, she slowly slid from the silky bedding. Black spots flashed in her eyes at the undesired movement. Definitely dehydrated and hungover. Great. What had Issac done to push her to drink this much?

Unless he drugged her.

No. No, he wouldn't do that.

Not that she knew him well enough to know for sure.

Her brow crumpled as she gingerly stepped toward the all-marble bathroom. A stack of towels sat on the expensive countertop, the oversized shower behind her a standing invitation. But the giant tub beside it appealed to her more.

Water first.

She grabbed a glass tumbler—there were three—from beside the left sink and filled it to the brim before downing all the contents. The *W* etched into the crystal of her glass further confirmed her whereabouts.

W for Wakefield.

Three cups later, she felt slightly better, but not great.

Although, the brown stone tiles of the shower looked even more inviting now, as did the multitude of showerheads. A glance in the mirror confirmed her need for a wash even more—tangled hair, sunken eyes, pale skin.

"I look like shit," she said to herself, her voice raspy despite the water.

With a shake of her head, she locked the bathroom door,

undressed, and took advantage of the gorgeous bathroom.

It was as she ran a bar of soap over her arms that she noticed an array of colors smattered along her skin. They resembled week-old bruises.

"What the fuck?" she breathed, eyeing her inner elbow and bicep in horror. "*What the fuck?*"

A face flickered in her mind, a short woman with dark hair. Something about injections. And an all-white room.

Stas's legs began to shake, her heart hammering in her chest.

She swallowed and grasped the stone wall for support, the hot water doing little to dispel the chill overwhelming her skin.

Her stomach roiled with a memory she couldn't quite grasp, her mind refusing to release the details.

But something bad had happened.

That's how she ended up here.

What did Issac do to me? She frowned, the thought not quite right. Somehow she knew he didn't harm her. Someone else had.

Stas quickly finished her shower, needing answers. She combed her hair with a brush from one of the drawers, then wrapped a towel around herself before venturing back into the room for the suitcase she'd spotted in the corner. Inside was everything she needed—jeans, tank top, toiletries.

Who packed this?

They'd even included her matching lace undergarments—a penchant she considered to be a secret.

Did Lizzie do this?

Stas quickly dressed before searching her purse for her phone.

Several text messages appeared featuring a conversation between her and Lizzie that she didn't remember ever having.

I guess that date went well, then. You can thank me for the dress advice later.

Stas frowned. She didn't remember wearing the dress.

Thank you, Lizzie, was the reply. In Stas's name. From her phone. But she couldn't for the life of her remember this conversation.

So where is he taking you for the week? Lizzie had asked next.

It's a surprise, she'd apparently replied.

Stas snorted. Definitely a surprise, as she had no flipping idea how she arrived or when or where she even was right now. Aside from in Manhattan.

Well, check in every now and then so I know he hasn't kidnapped you permanently, Lizzie had messaged.

You know that wouldn't entirely be a bad thing, Liz...

Who are you and what have you done with my Stas?!

It's Issac... He's just... The words that followed had Stas's jaw dropping. There was no way in hell she would ever say *that* about a man. "Oh, hell no." She started toward the door, when she noticed the date on her screen.

And froze.

Friday.

Wasn't yesterday Tuesday?

"What the fuck?"

Her legs were moving again with purpose, out the door, down the hallway lined with windows, and into a great room the size of Lizzie's condo.

This place is huge.

And it faced the Hudson River, with towering ceilings above, indicating her location at the top of the building.

An oversized couch with two matching recliners faced a mounted television that would make the entire male population drool. A wall of bookcases graced the opposite wall with an oversized U-shaped couch.

The refined elegance and masculine textures were very Issac.

So where is he?

She hung a left between the two seating areas, toward what appeared to be the foyer, and found another hallway just before it that led to the kitchen—a kitchen Lizzie would obsess over. Marble counters and tiles, hardwood cabinets, an island large enough to host a dinner party, and a half-naked Issac beside the stove.

Flipping a pancake.

In a towel.

Her lips parted, her brain fracturing.

Defined shoulders and a wide, muscular back tapered into a lean waist that disappeared into a blue cloth wrapped loosely around his hips. Fresh water droplets hung from his messy dark strands and dripped over skin that was tanner than she expected. The note of chlorine in the air suggested he'd just come from a swimming pool.

How? Why? Where?

Her tongue felt thick in her mouth as he moved from the stove to the island to pick up a plate.

The front was even better than the back—all rippled, lean muscle. And a dusting of hair leading her eyes on a happy trail to the impressive bulge beneath the towel.

"You look refreshed." Amusement underlined his tone and darkened his eyes to an alluring sapphire she could easily lose herself in. "I'm almost done making breakfast. Would you care for a cup of coffee?"

Gorgeous. Half-naked. And offering her coffee.

I must be dreaming.

"Yes," she whispered, unable to think or focus beyond the offering before her. And she wasn't even sure *what* she was accepting, either. Him? The towel? Coffee?

He handed her a cup with a knowing smirk.

She managed a quiet "Thanks" before diving into the life-reviving fuel. The dark blend with fruity notes warmed her raw throat and chest, eliciting a deep sigh of contentment.

This is exactly what I needed.

What about answers?

Her eyebrows lifted. Shit. The demon had completely distracted her practical senses.

She joined him at the island, her back to the counter as he chopped up what appeared to be a fruit salad. A fucking fruit salad. Like they were in some sort of alternate dimension where they played house together.

"What the fuck is going on?" She meant to ask that the second she saw him, but his lack of clothing derailed her focus. *Maybe this is all just one very fucked-up dream?*

"You have no idea how thankful I am to hear that tone, Astasiya." He sounded so casual and at home, like they did this together every day and his walking around in nothing but a towel was completely normal. He flipped a pancake and turned off the burner before crowding her against the island. With one hand on either side of her hips, he stared down at her. "I'm not sure how to word this without sending you into a fainting fit."

"I don't know what that means, so start talking." *God, my throat hurts.* She took another sip of her coffee, abundantly aware of his nearness and the heat flaring off his bare chest.

His forearms flexed beside her, drawing attention to the muscular masterpiece on display before her. She needed to find him a shirt or something before she lost her mind, because *wow*. And did he have to stand so close?

"The short of it is, you nearly died, but my team of clinicians saved your life."

Okay, forget the damn towel.

"I *what?*" *Did he just say I almost died?* This had to be a dream. Or a different reality. *Something.* Because her almost dying seemed way too far-fetched.

Except I did lose several days of memory.

And the healing bruises…

"The important thing is, you survived. As for the how of it, well, it appears the CRF has manufactured their own version of Nizari poison." The coffee cup fell from her hand and landed in one of his. She didn't have time to contemplate his insane reflexes. Her mind was too busy dissecting his words. "How about you sit down, I'll serve breakfast, and we'll discuss this over food. The physicians said you need to eat, and I'm starved after my swim."

It sounded rational enough, but she needed more

information. *Now.* "Why would the CRF try to poison me?"

He used a hand on her lower back to guide her toward the dining area and pulled out a chair at the oversized table. "That is one question I can't answer."

"Why not?"

"Because it would be speculation on my part." He returned to the kitchen to continue preparing food while she chugged one of the glasses of water sitting on the table. Using the pitcher in the middle of the two place settings, she refilled her cup and hastily gulped down the refreshing liquid before pouring herself a third glass.

Meanwhile, Issac set a few items on the table.

Her brow furrowed. "Baked beans?" That's *what you want to ask about?* Clearly, her mind had up and died.

And apparently so had she.

Fuck.

"It's an English thing," he replied, already heading back to the stove.

"Right." She picked up the coffee mug that had miraculously followed her to the table—compliments of Issac—and noted the slight hint of sugar. *He knows how I take my coffee.* Only her roommate knew that detail. "Who sent all those texts to Lizzie?"

"Hmm, I believe Balthazar did," he replied, his focus on food preparations.

"And who the hell is Balthazar?" she demanded.

"He was one of the physicians looking after you this week."

"You let a stranger talk to my best friend?" *And you thought that would be okay?*

"He's not a stranger." He brought over a frying pan. "He's an old friend whom I occasionally want to punch in the face. Pancake?"

"Sure." *Why not?* She chewed her lip as he added one to her plate and put two on his own. "Okay, I can accept the texts because they kept Lizzie from worrying. But what's a Nizi-whatever?"

"Nizari," he corrected as he brought over a skillet of eggs and bacon, adding two spoonfuls to the space beside her pancake. Then he placed several scoops on his own breakfast array.

Domestic Issac.

I'm totally dreaming.

But why the hell would I dream this?

Issac brought over the fruit bowl and took the seat across from her at the very long, oversized table for twelve.

Okay, seriously, the man really needed to put on some clothes. Those abs were lethally distracting and only half-hidden by the table, and she needed to focus.

"A Nizi-ari-thing almost killed me," she said slowly. "I don't even know what that means."

"Nizari," he corrected again with a chuckle. "Eat something first, and I'll tell you what you want to know."

"I'd rather you tell me now." The scent of bacon taunted her senses while her stomach churned from all the water she'd imbibed. Or maybe it was just the realization that she'd almost *died. What the ever-living hell?*

"Eat," he told her, demonstrating with a few bites of his own.

"Explain," she countered.

His lips twitched. "Nice try, darling. Your health matters more to me at the moment. I spent a great deal of money in resources to ensure your survival, and we will follow the doctors' instructions. Now *eat.*"

Her gaze narrowed at the command in his tone. "I deserve an explanation."

"And I intend to provide one once you're sufficiently fed."

Fucking games. "You told me I almost *died,* and you're going to make me wait for an explanation? Fuck you."

He sighed, setting down his fork. "Astasiya, this is not a two-second discussion." His midnight gaze traveled over her. "The physicians said you're healing remarkably well, which I suspect is a result of your genetics. Those bruises on your arm were fresh a few hours ago, but look days old now. And it would appear the Nizari poison is out of your system. But to maintain your healing, I need you to eat."

She glowered at him. Fine. She'd eat. Using her fork, she cut off a piece of the pancake on her plate—blueberry—and took a bite.

Stas had every intention of swallowing it immediately in a show of defiance and demand, but the flavors on her tongue forced her to savor it. Because wow, whatever he did to that pancake surely fit the definition of *decadence*.

Even the eggs were delicious.

Okay, so she was hungry.

Very hungry.

But she also wanted answers.

"What's a Nizari, Issac?" she asked after washing down some of the food with a glass of water. He had resumed eating while she gave in to the temptations on her plate. It hadn't been her intent, but the flavors, paired with her growling stomach, forced her hand. Literally.

Issac regarded her while chewing, his chiseled jaw flexing with the movements. He picked up his coffee, taking a long sip, eyeing her the whole time. "How about we make a deal?"

Her eyebrows lifted. "What kind of deal?"

"I'll tell you what you need to know, but not everything. Not yet, anyway."

That sounded like a horrible idea. "Why the hell would I agree to that?"

"For several reasons, the foremost being you're not ready to know everything yet, and the second being you still owe me a few dates. Dating for information, remember?"

"I think my almost dying voids our deal."

"It voids nothing, but I'll give you the details you need, and I'll continue to give you information as we date."

Her fists clenched. She wanted to throttle him. "Tell me what the hell a Nizari is, Issac." Stas wove a hint of compulsion into her tone, causing his nostrils to flare.

"It's a poison that was developed by an elite group of Conclave assassins who used it centuries ago to slaughter fledgling immortals after realizing their threat to the Ichorian race. The assassins were referred to as the Nizari. Hence, the elixir they created was named after them. However, the one used on you was a variant, not the pure substance." His gaze narrowed. "Now, compel me again, darling. I dare you." The threat lingering in his tone was lost to her chaotic thoughts.

Conclave.

Assassins.

Ichorian. Hadn't her polygrapher mentioned that term?

"Fledgling immortals?" she managed to ask out loud, her brow crumpled.

"Yes. It's what we call your kind. Fledgling for short." He waited for her to comment, but she had nothing, her mind running all the words in a loop, searching for some aspect of familiarity.

Nothing.

Issac ate another bite, leaving her to her thoughtful silence.

Maybe he'd been right about the need for slow information because none of what he'd said made a lick of sense. All she'd gathered so far was that someone had tried to poison her. And apparently her *kind* was referred to as *fledgling immortals.*

Is he implying I'm immortal?

But he also said she'd almost died.

"How are you feeling, Astasiya?" he asked softly after nearly finishing his plate. "I know this is a lot to take in, but I mean physically."

That seemed like a safer topic, one she could actually understand and focus on.

How was she feeling?

"Dehydrated," she decided. "My throat is sore, my head hurts like I'm hungover, and I think this might be the first time I've ever been sick." She frowned at that last part. *It's also the first time I've ever almost died, apparently.*

How is this my life?

"You've never been sick?" he asked. "Not even a cold?"

"No." Something she chalked up to always keeping herself in decent health, but was likely related to her... *immortality. I'm a fledgling? And assassins want me dead?* "Can we go back to why the CRF would want to hurt me?" Because she couldn't wrap her head around that. All she remembered was her polygraph. Had something happened after that?

"I suspect the CRF used the Nizari poison on you to test your bloodline. But as I said earlier, that's speculation on my part."

"When?" she asked, completely lost.

"When they administered your vaccines during the physical exam." He frowned at her. "Do you not recall telling me about the green shots?"

That woman's face flickered through Stas's thoughts again. A tray. Needles. A pristine room. Something about papers and weak explanations. "It's fuzzy," she admitted, worrying her lower lip and shaking her head. "I don't remember much after the polygraph."

"Well, it seems the CRF gave you a series of inoculations, one or several of which were a manufactured compound of the Nizari poison."

"But why?"

He sighed. "To test your fledgling bloodline, or that's my theory, anyway."

Right. Speculation. And he'd already said that.

But it didn't make sense. Why would a renowned humanitarian agency dabble with poison that killed fledglings? They didn't even know about immortals, right?

"Have you ever met an Ichorian?"

Wasn't that the term Issac had used just moments ago?

"What's an Ichorian?" she asked.

"What I am," he replied smoothly.

"And..." She paused, thinking back over his

explanation. "They kill fledglings?" *Like me?*

"Yes." No hesitation. No hint of remorse. Just a straight response paired with an unreadable expression.

Well, shit. She licked her lips, considering. She could ask him why he didn't just let her die, but she suspected he would answer evasively. He wasn't ready to admit her purpose here, or he would have told her already. He didn't strike her as the kind of man who waited when he wanted something.

"During my polygraph, the agent asked me if I knew any Ichorians," she said slowly, pairing what Issac had accused the CRF of doing to her with her experience during the security process. There had to be a logical association, one that didn't equate to them trying to kill her. This was Doctor Fitzgerald's organization. The man she considered her mentor. The father of one of her friends. He would never hurt her.

"I'm not surprised. Did the polygrapher ask about Hydraians as well?"

She blinked. "Yes." That had been the other term Agent Stark mentioned. "What's a Hydraian?"

"Your future," he answered vaguely.

"Meaning?"

He smiled. "Astasiya, I'm thankful you're alive, more than you know, but that doesn't mean I'm going to answer every question."

"That makes you an ass."

He folded his arms over his bare chest, drawing her attention to all those defined ridges of muscle decorating his abdomen. "Sure. An ass who saved your life and made you breakfast."

"That's not fair."

Issac leaned toward her, his blue eyes narrowing. "Who said anything about fair?"

He stood to casually stretch his arms over his dark head. Every sinewy inch of him not covered by the towel was on display, something she suspected he'd done for her benefit.

Amusement flirted with his lips, confirming her suspicions, as he lowered his hands.

Devious man.

Demon.

"Hmm, I'm feeling generous," he murmured. "So I'll answer something you haven't actually asked yet. Not with your mouth, anyway."

"Yeah? And what's that?" She couldn't help the sardonic note in her tone, irritated with his evasiveness. He'd barely told her a damn thing. The damn—

His towel dropped.

"A swimsuit, darling," he said with a wink before turning to leave.

Stas tried to scowl. She really did. But the swim trunks showcased strong legs and an exquisite ass. The man was walking perfection.

"Oh, and don't go anywhere," he called back to her over his shoulder—a muscularly lean shoulder that melted into a sexy-as-fuck backside. "We're not done yet."

He disappeared, taking the gorgeous sight with him.

Stas groaned, her forehead hitting the table as she attempted to beat some sense into her brain. She *never* swooned, but Issac, well, he'd certainly awakened some feminine-nonsense gene inside of her.

Lizzie would be so proud. After years of only having passing interests in men, Stas finally found one undeniably attractive. And it was one she most certainly should not be fawning over.

Damn demon Ichorian.

Whatever the fuck that all meant.

Ugh, she was in trouble. She needed to follow him and demand more answers, but pissing him off, especially after he saved her life—assuming that was true—didn't seem like the smart play. While her command earlier had worked, he'd clearly been irritated. And his explanation hadn't made an ounce of sense, really.

Still, she had one answer.

I'm a fledgling immortal.

This man, being, Ichorian, whatever, clearly had the answers she'd been searching for the last seventeen years. Too bad he wouldn't just give her all the details now. There had to be a reason, something she wasn't understanding.

The CRF?

What would have happened during her polygraph if she had admitted to knowing an Ichorian?

She drummed her fingers against the tabletop. Issac's accusations regarding the CRF didn't marry up to the organization she knew and adored. How would a humanitarian organization know anything about the elixir that almost killed her? They were involved in international affairs, not supernatural nonsense. Issac had admitted it was speculation, meaning it may have been someone else who poisoned her, but who?

He saved me. That part radiated true within her heart, igniting another question. *Should I trust him?* Her instincts whispered, *Yes,* but common sense held her back.

She needed more information—information Issac didn't want to give her yet.

Fine.

They'd play this little game.

And if that didn't work, she'd tie him to a chair and compel him to give her answers.

CHAPTER EIGHT

Gifts from Hydria

ISSAC PAUSED ON THE THRESHOLD OF HIS living area to admire the view of Astasiya lounging on his favorite couch. All that glorious blonde hair was pulled over one shoulder, leaving her neck exposed.

The innocent gesture taunted the predator within him, exciting his hunting instincts.

He hadn't fed in nearly two weeks, a long time for an Ichorian. But he'd been slightly preoccupied by the female on the couch. Maybe he should snack on her, provide her with the true definition of his kind.

Vampire—a word he loathed.

Monster.

Fallen angel.

She shifted, pulling her jean-clad legs beneath her, not yet sensing his presence. Something had consumed her attention. It appeared to be a book of sorts.

What did you choose, darling?

Issac finished fastening his cuff links while approaching the beauty on the couch. He moved silently behind her to peer over her shoulder, Astasiya too engrossed in her book to sense him.

What he saw in her lap made his blood run cold.

It wasn't a book at all, but a photo album. One that held cherished memories he preferred not to revisit.

"Where did you find that?" he demanded. Because it didn't belong here.

Stas's fingers trembled as she touched the page. "You knew Owen." Her softly spoken words alleviated the pressure in his chest, but only slightly.

"We were acquainted, yes. Did you find that on the bookshelf?" He would bet good money Jacque put it there. *Damn teleporter.* He loved leaving little reminders of Hydria all over Issac's condo. A not-so-subtle hint to visit.

"You told me you didn't know him." Accusation underscored her tone.

Issac couldn't recall his precise phrasing. Had he implied he didn't know Owen? "We weren't so much friends as we were acquaintances."

Laying his jacket over the back of his couch, he sat beside her.

She traced the photo, her lower lip trembling. Ah, the date, yes. Not to mention the attire. She'd clearly identified a key element in Owen's existence—his immortality.

"I don't miss the fashion of that decade," Issac murmured, noting the bell-bottom jeans and flowery shirts in the photo.

"He was an Ichorian, too?" she guessed.

"Not quite, no."

Her full lips curled downward. "This photo looks like it's from the seventies. It's decades old." A clear deduction that didn't require his confirmation. She looked at him. "If he wasn't an Ichorian, then what was he? Because he obviously wasn't human if he still looked twenty-something today."

"He was a Hydraian."

She continued to stare at him. "Okay, so what's the difference between a Hydraian and an Ichorian?"

"Telling you that would require defining Ichorian." Which he couldn't do yet.

A slow introduction would foster trust and understanding, something they required between them for this partnership to work. If he told her everything now, she'd run screaming.

Or worse, she'd go straight into Jonathan's waiting arms.

And Issac couldn't risk that, not when he was so close to achieving his goals.

Yet, he'd seen the look in her eyes when he mentioned the very likely scenario of the CRF trying to poison her— doubt. Until he broke that barrier, they couldn't move forward. Her faith was too intertwined with the Fitzgeralds and Watkinses to listen to him. He planted the seed of doubt by speculating about the CRF's intentions. It would be up to her to put the puzzle pieces together now.

"Okay." Annoyance flashed in her green eyes, making him want to kiss her. "So are there more types I should know about?"

"It depends on who you ask. Ichorians and Hydraians are the most prominent, but there are those who believe Seraphim still walk the earth. They're rare and supposedly the creators of my race, but I've never met one."

"Seraphim." Her lips twisted. "Like angels?"

"Why are you giving me that look?" It held traces of laughter and surprise, offending him slightly. "Are you surprised I may be a descendant of the divinity?"

"It…well…" She bit her lip, her eyes crinkling with mirth. "I sort of nicknamed you *demon* when you wouldn't give me your name."

Oh. He grinned. "You gave me a pet name."

"No, I gave you a *name* when I didn't have anything else to call you."

"It's cute." The indignant look she gave him was adorable as well. *So feisty.* "Ichorians are descended from a fallen Seraphim, or so the rumor says, so it's still appropriate." He brushed his knuckles down the curve of her neck. Her soft skin blushed a pretty shade of pink in response. "Mmm, I like my pet name."

"It's *not* a pet name." She flipped to the next photo and his smile died.

He didn't know Owen well, but Amelia did. She knew all the Hydraians.

"He looks so happy here," his blonde murmured, not realizing the turmoil building in his chest.

Issac would be sending this particular reminder back to Jacque.

"Do you know why he was killed?" Astasiya asked while turning the page to display another memory. The blue eyes staring up from the page haunted Issac's soul. He didn't need the fresh reminder. Not today. He took the album from her and closed it.

"I have my suspicions, but nothing concrete." He stood and returned the album to the shelf, his touch lingering on the familiar binding. Amelia's creativity was etched into every groove. There were hundreds of these books in Hydria. Jacque knew what he was doing when he dropped this particular one off. It seemed a call to the young teleporter would be required this afternoon.

"Who is she?" Astasiya asked, her arms folded tightly around her stomach from her position on the couch. "The woman in all those pictures, I mean."

Issac longed to change the subject, but the memories troubling her gaze reminded him too much of his own. This woman understood loss. Not just Owen, but her birth parents as well. The information Mateo provided said they died in a house fire. Clear human fabrication. Whatever happened to her parents weighed heavily upon her. It was evident in the way she studied him now.

"My sister, Amelia." He held out a hand to help Astasiya stand. It served as an excuse to touch her, one she accepted with minimal hesitation despite the shocked expression on her face. Questions brewed in her eyes, ones he had no interest in addressing. Ever.

Besides, they had business to discuss.

"I have to attend a gala tonight, and I would like to take you with me," he told her. "As my date." He dropped her hand and feigned fixing his already immaculate tie. The blood-red color suited his current mood. Having a delectable yet unavailable woman in his bed for three nights was enough to drive a sane man mad. He would definitely need to feed soon. Too bad what he wanted wasn't on the menu.

Issac retrieved his jacket from the back of the couch and put it on while she considered his request.

"Okay," she said slowly. "But only if you give me five more answers to whatever I ask and tell me what an Ichorian is."

His lips curled, intrigued. *Playing with fire, are we, darling?* He welcomed the challenge, especially after that unfortunate walk down memory lane. This—negotiating— he could do. "Are you trying to make a deal with me, Miss Davenport?"

Fierce green eyes met his, provoking all manner of inappropriate thoughts. Like what they would look like in the throes of passion. "No, I'm giving you my terms."

He nearly laughed. No woman ever gave him terms for a date. Not that this necessarily qualified since he considered it more of a business arrangement. They needed to be seen in public together for his plan to work, and to put to rest any suspicions the CRF had about her reacting to the Nizari poison. Winning her over in the process would be an added bonus, one that would make her more helpful.

"I will give you two answers." He tucked a soft strand of

her hair behind her ear and let his fingers drift down her neck. "And I will consider defining Ichorian more clearly for you." *By showing, not telling.*

She licked her lips and shook her head. "Three answers and you define Ichorian now."

He moved into her personal space, gripping her hip with one hand to hold her in place when she tried to move away. Their foolish conversation had already gone on longer than he intended. "We leave at seven." He bent so their mouths were a hairsbreadth apart. "And I will only answer your three questions after the gala, not before or during."

Her breath fanned his lips, encouraging him to close the gap between them. But he waited, wanting her consent first.

She gave a tiny nod, her lips grazing his. "Okay." A single word that he took to mean so much more than it really did.

His free hand tangled in her hair as he took her mouth with his. There was nothing tentative about his movements, all power and demand, and she melted into him the way she had the other night at the restaurant. Only this time he didn't hold back. Wrapping his arm around her waist, he pulled her closer and devoured her.

Three days of having her near, but so far away, fucked with his senses. He wanted this woman on a near-lethal level despite hardly knowing her. But when did he ever truly know his conquests?

I want to know her, he thought, deepening their kiss. *Very, very badly.*

She moaned, her tongue engaging his in a sensuous dance that fueled the need growing inside him. Every touch, every stroke, every nip made his intentions clear.

I want you.

And I will have you.

Her body responded in kind, already yielding to his experience and desire.

His hand tightened in her hair, holding her closer. He left nothing to the imagination, showing her exactly who he was and what he would demand, and she didn't back down, meeting him move for move, showing him exactly what kind of lover she would be.

An equal.

Fierce.

Confident.

Her sweet arousal teased his senses, demanding more. Mmm, he longed to take her up on that unspoken offer. Alas, this was only meant as a proper introduction to his needs and intentions. He hardened the kiss, proving his dominance in a single swipe of his tongue against hers. She groaned in response, succumbing to his touch and command.

Oh, yes, they would pair well in the bedroom.

He eased back slowly, showing her with his eyes how she affected him. Promising her more. Vowing to finish this. *Soon.*

"Hmm, I would continue this discussion, but you need to be seen in public." He nipped her lower lip, not hard, just a soft tease for them both.

"Public?" she repeated, her expression dazed.

"Yes." He nuzzled her nose, his palm sliding to the back of her neck. "It will help dispel any uncertainties surrounding your reaction to the Nizari poison."

She blinked, some of the fog lifting from her heated gaze. "You think someone noticed my reaction?"

"It's possible, but seeing you alive and healthy will negate any suspicions. Which is why my driver is waiting downstairs to take you out for an afternoon of pampering." He brushed his lips against hers, enjoying the shiver it evoked from her. "Try to be ready by seven."

"I'll just take the subway home. I have a few cocktail dresses in my closet. I don't need any *pampering*." She made little air quotes with her fingers before gripping the lapels of his jacket. The possessive action warmed him inside, as did her words. A woman denying his gifts provided such a rare experience. He rather liked it, not that he planned to allow it.

"It's nonnegotiable, darling. I've already arranged everything and requested a friend to pull a few dresses for you to choose from."

"Should my closet be insulted?"

He grinned. "No, I rather enjoyed going through your clothes, especially your lingerie. Someone has a lace fetish." He nipped her bottom lip again as she struggled for a response. She'd failed to ask about her suitcase, something he attributed to her general alarm and confusion over the week's events.

"You were in my room?" she finally asked, her voice breathy.

"It was that or dress you in my clothes." An appealing thought, actually. The woman would look fantastic in a pair of boxer briefs and a white T-shirt. No bra or panties, just his clothes against her flesh. Mmm, he would tease her nipples through the thin fabric with his mouth until her taut peaks were visible beneath the shirt.

A beautiful image, one that left his pants a little tight.

He stepped away before he made the image a reality. Astasiya needed time to recover. He also didn't have enough time to indulge in her the way he desired. Perhaps later, after the gala. Something to anticipate.

"Do I want to know how you got into the condo?" she wondered.

"Probably, but I'll have to count it as a question and you owe me a date first." He patted her on the ass because he could, and started toward the foyer. "Enjoy your spa day, darling."

"I don't remember agreeing."

"I don't remember offering a choice." He called over his shoulder. "See you at seven."

CHAPTER NINE

Smile for the Cameras

SHE'S IN THE CONDO.

Issac read the text message from his driver, Benjamin, as he exited Wakefield Pharmaceuticals' headquarters.

He typed a reply saying they would be ready for pickup in twenty minutes. It was only a five-minute walk to his condo building, and he'd changed into his tuxedo at the office. One of the perks of owning the company and the Wakefield Pharmaceuticals' building meant he had another penthouse with a full bedroom and en suite bathroom. Not that he used it often. He much preferred his place off Chambers Street.

He ran a hand over the silk lapel of his buttonless jacket, approving of his Italian designer's creation. The wool kept him a bit warm for this June evening, but the overall fit worked. He'd paired it with a black vest, silk button-down, and trousers. Black on black—his trademark gala attire.

"Evening, sir," Paul greeted as he opened the door to the condo building. It was always "sir" or "Mister Wakefield" no matter how many times Issac suggested otherwise.

"Hello, Paul." He gave the man a nod as he headed toward the elevators.

There were only two condos on his floor, both of which he owned. The larger one he used for himself, while his guests stayed in the smaller residence.

Astasiya, however, waited inside his suite, an intimacy he reserved for only his closest friends and family. She'd stayed in his condo for several days already, nearly died there, so why not give her full rein? It would make her more comfortable.

And yes, perhaps a small part of him enjoyed having her in his space.

Not that he cared to investigate that feeling. There was no future for them. She didn't know that, but he did.

He entered the condo and followed the sweet aroma of lavender and soap to the great room. Astasiya stood by the windows, admiring the view. The evening hours always provided a glorious sight, but he couldn't be bothered to appreciate it now. Not with the gorgeous blonde standing before him.

Sapphire silk hugged her curves, flowing over her long legs to the floor. Two thin straps were all that kept the fabric from falling, leaving her entire back exposed to his touch. The hairstylist had piled Astasiya's blonde hair up high on her head, exposing her neck and making him regret that he'd not had time to feed today.

She'd be taunting him all night.

Perhaps he would return the favor in a slightly different way.

"Hello, darling," he murmured, trailing his fingers down her spine. Her resulting shiver caused his lips to curl.

"You're stunning."

"And you look more expensive than you usually do" was her greeting.

Cheeky minx.

His hand fell to her hip as she turned. The slit up her left leg exposed her upper thigh and provided a glimpse at the silver heels she wore. They added several inches to her height and lengthened her already long legs. *Glorious.*

"How was your afternoon?" he wondered, caressing her hip with his thumb. The designer dress certainly met his approval for the evening, though he'd have preferred a dipping neckline to the sweetheart cut.

"The pampering was all right, I suppose." Delight played over her full lips.

Cheeky indeed. "Just all right?"

"It was an experience."

He grinned. "Are you ready for another?" Issac could think of several entertaining activities for the evening, none of them just *all right*. One such activity? Finding out what color lingerie she'd selected. No bra, clearly, but he could feel the faint hint of lace against her hip. He traced the seductive texture with his thumb to the small of her back.

Her pupils dilated, the unveiled suggestion stirring her interest. "Maybe."

Not exactly consent, but he could work with it.

He placed his palm against her bare back, her skin warm beneath his touch. "Shall we?"

Not waiting for a reply, he applied just enough pressure to encourage her to move with him. She did and grabbed a black clutch from the table as they passed it.

"So where is this gala?" she asked as they entered the elevator.

"The Pierre." The flare in her gaze told him she knew of it. Most New Yorkers did. It was a popular place for events. "Benjamin is driving us."

"The tall, chatty guy who took me all over the city today?"

"That would be him." The old man started working for Issac over a decade ago. A kind soul he paid handsomely to keep quiet about his personal affairs. Talkative he might be, but he understood the value of secrets.

"He doesn't get the night off?" she asked.

"Not tonight." Issac didn't feel too bad about it; the man had been given most of the week off. A result of Issac staying cooped up in his condo waiting for a certain blonde to wake up.

The gray-haired man greeted them as they exited the building, and opened the limo's back door.

"What happened to the car?" Astasiya asked, referring to the four-door vehicle Issac's driver typically used for daily errands.

"I upgraded it," Benjamin replied, grinning.

"Some upgrade," she said as Issac helped her into the limo.

Two flutes of champagne waited for them inside. He handed her one after settling beside her and took the other for himself. "To experiences, darling."

"I have no idea why we're doing this, but sure." She tapped her glass against his and took a healthy sip. "I hope there's food at this event."

"You could say that." These galas were more about the alcohol than the sustenance.

She groaned. "It's going to be one of those hoity-toity affairs, isn't it? With artistic food meant for looking at and not eating?"

"You sound familiar with them. Have you attended one?" He'd never seen her at a charity event, but then again, he usually attended these affairs with a date, so he may not have seen her.

No. Not true. Issac definitely would have noticed her.

"Yeah, no. Not my scene, but Lizzie's been to several. She always complains about the food afterward."

Always piquing his curiosity and surprising him. "Why isn't it your scene?" he wondered out loud. Most women adored lavish affairs.

"I'm more of a movie-date or coffee-date kind of a girl."

"Go on." He made a show of getting more comfortable and widened his legs enough to press his thigh against hers. It was the left one, exposed by the slit in the dress. His hand itched to settle there, slide his fingers beneath the silk, and explore. He busied himself with finishing his champagne and pouring a new glass instead.

"You know, typical stuff. Like spending Friday night at home with a book or watching a movie. I don't like the whole socialite thing. That's Lizzie's scene."

"Yet you appear to be fully ingrained in their world."

"Only by association."

"That's all it takes."

"But it's not *my* scene. I only tag along to keep Lizzie company."

He considered. "Your friendship with Elizabeth is interesting." The Watkinses were social climbers, their daughter a notorious CRF science experiment—not that anyone knew, of course. The stunning redhead wasn't related to her parents at all, something she seemed oblivious to. He wondered when George and Lillian would break the news to her. Allowing her to attend university and work full-time could not be their ultimate plans for the poor girl.

Though, she had met Astasiya in the process.

Was that an accident or something done on purpose?

"How did you meet Elizabeth?" he asked.

"We met during our freshman year at Columbia. She was my assigned roommate. It was awkward at first. She likes pink, I mean *really* likes pink, and hugs, and she can be a bit boy crazy. We had a few ground rules to work out, but she's become my best friend over the years." She smiled. "She's Lizzie."

Ah, so potentially an arrangement then if Elizabeth was her roommate. Interesting. "And that's how you met the Fitzgeralds?"

"Yeah. Sunday brunch. It's a monthly tradition. I think

it started before Lizzie was born."

"I'm certain it did." George helped create the CRF and was one of the few who knew what the organization was designed to do. "How are you feeling, by the way?" He'd meant to ask earlier but had been too caught up in her dress. She appeared perfectly healthy, all her bruises healed. A happy circumstance of her immortal heritage, no doubt.

Astasiya swallowed the last bit of her champagne and set it on a table off to the side. "Physically? I feel fine."

"And emotionally?"

"Well, I'm a mix of pissed off, confused, and overwhelmed."

"All reasonable reactions." He leaned over her to set his glass beside hers. Her pulse leapt, enticing the Ichorian within him. Hmm, she needed to add *aroused* to her emotional list.

Issac extended his arm across the top of the seat behind her head while gently tracing the slit of her dress with his opposite hand, crowding her, testing her boundaries.

"I do like this dress," he murmured, studying her reactions.

"That's good, because you paid for it." The confident words almost hid the breathy quality of her voice. Almost.

"Does that bother you?" he asked softly, referring to him paying for her outfit. He typically sponsored his dates' attire for events because he required a certain level of fashion and expense to maintain his public image. However, the spa treatments and allowing the woman to pick her own dress were not typically included in the routine. That had been for her benefit and her benefit alone.

"Not really, but only because I don't know how much you spent on it all. They wouldn't let me pay for anything." She said that last part with an adorable glare. She didn't like him taking care of her. Too bad because he had no intention of stopping anytime soon.

"You would be the first woman to ever complain about that in my presence," he admitted.

"We've already gone over the part about me not being a socialite. Besides, we're not really dating."

"No?" It certainly felt like they were. At least tonight. His thumb slipped beneath the silk, lightly brushing her inner thigh.

"No, it's a business deal. Although, I really don't know what you're getting out of it."

He leaned in closer, his palm sliding up her leg. Her shuddering breath fanned his lips. "Are you sure about that, Astasiya?"

~*~

Stas forgot how to speak, her tongue useless inside her mouth.

That look, the one in his sapphire eyes, set her blood on fire. She fought the urge to clench her thighs, knowing he'd feel her reaction. But fuck, she needed something, *anything*, to alleviate the ache stirring inside her.

This is so wrong.

Yet, nothing had ever felt more right.

If she tilted her head just an inch, their mouths would touch. The temptation had her licking her lips, yearning for a taste. His all-black ensemble was lethally seductive, the vest hugging his muscular torso and highlighting the physique she knew lurked beneath.

His palm branded her thigh, his thumb drawing delicious circles against her bare flesh.

They should just skip the gala and stay here all night.

Except she'd wanted something from him earlier, a thought or question that had weighed on her mind all day.

Fuck if she remembered it now, not with his alluring scent mingling with her every breath.

The champagne was not helping.

Neither was the hot male cage surrounding her.

His arm dropped to her shoulders. "By my calculation, we have about five minutes before we hit Sixty-First Street," he whispered against her parted lips. "Not nearly enough time."

"We could just not go," she suggested, her voice holding a husky quality she'd never heard before.

This man was unraveling all her layers, exposing a part of her she'd never truly explored.

A very sexual part that failed to heed reason.

Her hands went to his chest, the pads of her fingers reveling in the feel of silk against stone. As much as she adored the tuxedo, she wanted to remove it, to explore his bare skin and the ridges of his abdomen.

"A tempting offer," he breathed. "Consider this a prelude."

She opened her mouth for him, accepting his tongue as he thrust inside, taking command in a way that was all Issac.

Her heart raced.

Everything tingled.

And fire licked across her skin, radiating from his palm on her leg.

Devastating, dominating, determined.

Stas lost herself to his embrace, completely intoxicated by Issac's kiss. He lifted her onto his lap, forcing her to straddle him. He palmed the back of her neck, holding her in a way that allowed him the deepest access to her mouth.

She forgot how to breathe.

Forgot how to think.

Her nails embedded in his silky shirt, holding on for dear life, as he devoured her to completion.

Oh God...

She needed more, her lower body shivering with a craving only Issac could satisfy. He kept his grip on her neck while his other hand returned to her thigh, sliding upward beneath the fabric to the lace beneath.

"Issac," she sighed, willing his fingers to move a few inches south to where she desired him most.

"Fuck," he whispered, reclaiming her mouth.

Yes, she thought, writhing over him, searching for

purpose.

A flash brightened the air, followed by another.

What? She tore her mouth from his to peer out the tinted windows, her jaw dropping at the line of photographers standing outside the limo in front of them.

"They can't see inside," Issac said softly.

She shivered both from the feel of the hot, aroused male beneath her and the realization that she was about to be surrounded by vultures with cameras. "Shit." Her shoulders stiffened, the reality of their impending situation cooling her heated blood. "Can't we just go to the movies like a normal couple?"

Issac's chuckle vibrated through her as he removed his hand from her thigh. "We're a couple now, are we? I thought this was a business deal, Astasiya."

She swatted his chest and climbed off of him. "You know what I mean."

He leaned over to fix her dress with the ease of a man who tousled women in limos often. Not something she wanted to think about.

His focus went to her hair as he said, "I have to make an appearance tonight; otherwise, I would take you home and do *normal couple* things to you." His blue eyes met hers to mock those two words before he continued messing with her hair. "How do you feel about art?"

"Uh." *Art?* "It's not something I know much about."

"Then we'll skip the auction. I'm not much of an art connoisseur anyway."

"There's an art auction?"

"It's a gala, darling. The auction is a fundraiser for tonight's charity." His fingers trailed down her neck to her arms. "There you are, gorgeous as ever."

His English lilt intensified the compliment, making her warm all over. If anyone was *gorgeous*, it was him in that tux.

He smiled. "Three, two…" The door opened beside him.

A middle-aged man wearing a penguin suit greeted Issac

by name, his smile bright.

"Evening, Claude. How are the wife and kids?" Issac asked as he stepped outside.

Stas frowned while the man answered, his tone jovial. *Issac must visit the hotel frequently to be so familiar with The Pierre's staff. How many dates has he entertained here?*

Does it matter?

Not really, no.

"Brilliant. Happy to hear they're doing all right," Issac said, his hand appearing in the doorway.

An invitation to escort her into the frenzy that waited outside.

Cameras.

Vultures.

Most of them were waiting, but a few were already taking photos of the famous Issac Wakefield.

And now he wanted her to join him.

Just one night.

She'd be known as the random blonde on his arm, not nearly as notable as all the models and famous actresses who typically accompanied him to these types of affairs. Which, of course, meant they'd all be comparing her to them. *No pressure.*

He peered down at her with a humored look. "Scared, darling?"

Yes. "No."

His lips curled. "Liar."

She took his hand to prove him wrong and allowed him to assist her out of the limo. Lightning flashed around her before she could level a retort, causing her to shelter her eyes. Issac wrapped his hand around hers, guiding it downward between them and exposing her face to the onslaught of hungry photographers.

"Just breathe." His lips brushed her ear as the hand not holding hers slid around her waist to hold her close. "And maybe smile."

"Why, because you always smile?" she retorted.

"Meaning?"

"You never smile in photos." She must have gone through thousands of event photos while researching him Monday night. Never once did he grin, or even crack a smile. "So why should I smile?"

A hint of amusement flickered through his dark blue eyes. "What else did you learn about me, Astasiya?"

"Nothing useful."

"My net worth didn't intrigue you?"

She snorted. "Assuming it's even true, no. Your biography read like a page out of the playboy handbook."

His resulting laugh sent a shiver down her spine. Such a lovely sound, one that caused her lips to curl in response to his open charisma.

Tightening his arm around her, he kissed her on the temple before returning his mouth to her ear. "Your honesty is refreshing."

"Does that mean you'll repay the favor?"

"Perhaps later." He nibbled her neck before returning his attention to the photographers. They were eating up his display of affection, making her wonder if this was the real him or an act.

With the ease of a professional used to navigating paparazzi, he angled them closer to the entrance, pausing every few seconds for another photo. He made a show of grinning for the cameras. There were going to be a lot of broken hearts tomorrow when the pictures surfaced, because Issac's smile, paired with that tux, was devastatingly beautiful. Stas paled in comparison at his side but did her best to pose along with him while the media shouted questions at Issac.

"Tell us about your date."

"Give us a name!"

"How did you meet?"

She lifted up on her toes to whisper in his ear. "Doesn't this exhaust you?"

He trailed his fingers up her exposed spine to fondle a

strand of her hair as another photographer snapped their picture. "I doubt I will ever tire of having my hands on you, darling."

"I think we're past pickup lines, Issac."

"I don't use *lines*, something I believe I demonstrated in the limo. Or do you require another, more public demonstration?" The hand playing with her hair moved to her neck. He dipped her back, his opposite hand grabbing her hip to hold her steady as he lowered his mouth to hers. "I'm happy to oblige." He spoke each word against her lips, eliciting a shiver from deep within.

Lights flashed around them as he held her just out of view of their audience. The questions continued, sailing over their heads, all unanswered.

"What's her name, Issac?"

"Who is she?"

"How long have you been seeing each other?"

Oh God. If Issac had done all this with the goal of distracting her from almost dying this week, he'd succeeded. She couldn't decide if she wanted to hide forever or kiss him.

"I think I might have to hurt you," she said, meaning it.

"You could try." He pulled her upright, aligning her body with his. "I would very much enjoy punishing you for it."

Desire pooled in her belly. It went against all her ingrained ideals to be turned on by the thought of being *punished*, but her hormones weren't on the same wavelength as her brain. She would be having a serious discussion with her common sense later.

"Smile, darling. Your natural blush is quite lovely." He returned her to the view of their spectators and gave them all another adorable grin. Warmth crept up her neck as she forced her lips to curve upward.

These were not pictures she wanted to see tomorrow.

"Well done," Issac whispered as he escorted her into the palatial lobby of the hotel. Several employees stood by, but

Issac bypassed them all, leading Stas to an opulent room with over fifty dining tables set up before a center stage. Chandeliers hung from vaulted ceilings, and candles decorated the walls between lavish red curtains. The ornate tiled floor gave the room a classical appeal, dating the hotel's wealth and grandeur.

Issac escorted her to a table near the middle of the room with a clear view of the podium, where she left her purse. Several recognizable celebrities mingled around them, suggesting the wealth and influence of the charity. A number of them greeted Issac by name as they sauntered by, acknowledging him as part of the beautiful-people club.

I so do not belong here, she thought as he handed her a flute of champagne from a passing waiter. His lips quirked at whatever expression she wore.

"Cheers, darling," he murmured, tapping his glass against hers.

She took a fortifying sip in response, enjoying the bubbly sensation against her throat. "This is quite the life you lead, Issac."

"The night's only begun." He kept his arm around her, holding her close while he socialized with the guests. She gathered this forced conversation was a pre-dinner requirement since no one had bothered taking a seat in the full room. A few waiters wandered around offering appetizers, but a subtle shake of Issac's head told her not to try one.

"Plastic tastes better," her demon whispered before continuing a conversation with some politician. She knew *demon* was no longer the appropriate term, but it suited him too well to stop using it. *Okay, so maybe it is a pet name.* Not that she would admit it out loud.

He introduced her to each newcomer, but most of them ignored her in favor of the handsome CEO of Wakefield Pharmaceuticals. She didn't mind, preferring to watch him work. This was his world, where he thrived in seducing the crowd while inspiring appreciative grins from all over the room.

"Stas?" The familiar voice gave her pause.

She'd called Lizzie this afternoon to ask for pointers about the gala tonight. It served as a way for her to explain where she'd been all week and to stay on her best friend's good side. But it never occurred to her that Lizzie wasn't her only friend who attended high-society events.

Until now.

"Hey, Tom," she greeted, smiling at his handsome appearance. The man wore a tux very, very well. Lizzie's jaw would be on the floor. Alas, Stas preferred his usual attire of jeans and a leather jacket—his comfort zone.

Silence fell around them, making her realize they'd interrupted Issac's conversation with a couple of politicians. Or were they actors? She couldn't tell anymore.

But Tom knew them all, shaking their hands, addressing them formally, and sharing several smiles.

There really is a hottest-bachelor club, and both of them are clearly members. The appreciative looks from around the room agreed with Stas's thoughts.

When Tom's focus reached her demon, his easy grin fell. They didn't shake hands. "Wakefield."

"Thomas."

Testosterone radiated between them, causing the hairs to dance along Stas's exposed neck. Issac's arm flexed against her lower back, holding her closer while Tom narrowed his gaze.

Yeah, this isn't awkward at all, boys. And everyone around them seemed to feel the same way, their intrigued gazes on the two men. Did Issac and Tom have a history of disliking one another? Because the lethal air emanating from Tom made her skin crawl in warning.

He's livid. Why?

"How kind of your father to give you the weekend off," Issac said, breaking the tense silence.

"Oh, don't let the suit fool you. I'm always working," Tom returned.

The words sent a chill down Stas's spine.

Seeing her friend had felt so natural, so incredibly normal, that she hadn't thought at all about the relation to him and *work*.

The CRF.

The organization that may or may not have tried to kill her.

Shit.

What if it's true? That they really did try to kill me?

Had it only been this morning that she woke up after nearly dying?

The harsh reminder made her shiver. All the pampering and grandeur of today had distracted her from real life.

A life she almost lost.

What am I doing here?

What if they know?

Is it even true?

Did they really try to poison me?

Nothing felt real, almost as if this was all a dream. She didn't know what or whom to believe, and the fact that she seemed fine now didn't help matters.

What really happened?

Issac nipped her neck and brushed his lips against her ear. "Breathe. You're safe."

Yeah? I don't feel very safe. Not with Tom glowering at her demon like that.

Doctor Fitzgerald approached from the left, his expression holding a touch of adoration—a stark contrast to the irritation vibrating from his son.

"Hello, Stas," Doctor Fitzgerald greeted, kissing her cheek. "You look lovely, dear. Issac." He nodded.

"Doctor," Issac returned, smiling. "Good to see you."

They shook hands while Doctor Fitzgerald replied, "Likewise."

Some of the tension dissipated as the crowd refocused on the renowned humanitarian. Everyone wanted a piece of him, just like Issac, leaving Stas again on the sidelines to observe.

She expelled a long breath, her heart beating a chaotic rhythm against her rib cage.

Pull it together, she whispered to herself. *It's all just speculation. Doctor Fitzgerald is a friend, mentor, father figure.*

And he proved it by charming the crowd around them, his smile genuine and reaching his dark eyes. Tom remained at his side, ever the dutiful son, mimicking his father in kind. They really could have passed as brothers, Doctor Fitzgerald not looking older than forty. It only added to his appeal, as several of the women around them seemed to notice. His wife had died over a decade ago, leaving him very, very single.

This world is—

"The good doctor is receiving an award tonight," Issac murmured against her ear. "They're also sitting at our table."

She glanced at him sideways. "Thanks for the warning." Sarcasm underlined each word. He could have given her a heads-up in the limo.

Amusement brightened his gaze. "You're welcome, darling."

"This is the second time I've seen you two together this week," Dr. Fitzgerald mused, breaking from the crowd. Genuine curiosity lit his handsome features, his lips twitching at the sides. Unlike the man beside him, who appeared to be contemplating the best way to disfigure her demon.

"Worried I might steal her?" Issac asked, his lips brushing her cheek, earning him a harder glare from Tom.

What is his problem? she wondered. Issac might not be Boyfriend of the Year material, but he wasn't *that* bad.

Jealousy popped into her head as a potential cause, but she quickly tossed it out. Tom treated her like a younger sister, just as he did Lizzie.

No. Something else was at play here. But what?

Dr. Fitzgerald arched a dark blond brow. "Should I be worried?"

"Absolutely," Issac replied against her neck, his possessive touch causing her to shiver. *Careful, Stas. Just a business deal.* "Are you ready to eat, darling?" he asked softly, ignoring all the eyes on them and focusing on her.

More than a few of their spectators wore surprised expressions, including Dr. Fitzgerald. Stas's stomach fluttered and heat crawled up her neck. She much preferred being the ignored arm candy to being the center of attention.

"Sure," she managed to reply, her throat dry. A light buzz hummed in her head from the two glasses of champagne she'd consumed on her empty stomach. So yes, she should probably eat something, too.

"Brilliant." Issac engaged the others in a few parting words, his smile enigmatic. When the Fitzgeralds joined the conversation, she had to fight the urge to fan herself. The three of them were magnetism on steroids. Further proof that this was not her world. Not by a long shot.

"Shall we?" her demon asked when the crowd dispersed.

Dr. Fitzgerald led the way. Tom lingered for a moment longer before he finally turned to follow his father. Stas took a step, only to be pulled back into Issac's side.

"Don't mention your reaction to the immunizations." The words were a breath against her ear, so low she almost missed them. "If they ask, the inoculations made you queasy, but you were otherwise fine."

Her stomach clenched, the stark reminder drizzling ice through her veins.

Human Resources had left her a voicemail during her hair appointment today. She passed her security exam, and they wanted to schedule her orientation.

That was what she meant to tell Issac. She wanted to know why he suspected the CRF's involvement in her near-death experience because he never actually told her.

This whole day had been a fairy-tale escape from reality.

And now that reality sat several feet away at a table they were all meant to share for dinner.

"Are you implying they know about the poison?" she asked, studying Issac's face for something, anything, that would give her reason to believe him. To suspect the man she considered a role model of having any involvement in her experience this week.

Because if his company truly was poising potential employees, he would know about it.

He'd never authorize such methods. Would he?

"I'm warning you that anyone could be listening," Issac replied softly. "Do you understand?"

She did, but that wasn't what she'd asked. "Does he know or not, Issac?"

"That's not for me to say. Observe and learn." He brushed his lips over hers, holding her gaze with an intent that made her heart race. "Trust me."

CHAPTER TEN

Dangerous Romance

OBSERVE AND LEARN.

Stas could do that.

Issac sat on her left, his palm resting on her upper thigh. His warm fingers caressed her bare skin through the slit of her dress while he engaged Doctor Fitzgerald in a conversation about the stock market. She gathered they shared similar investment strategies. Their easy candor also suggested they were friends, something Issac had failed to mention.

Yet, he'd accused Doctor Fitzgerald's company of trying to kill her.

One would think a friendship with the organization's CEO might be a useful detail, or a point of discussion.

Nope.

It left Stas irritated and confused, and that casual touch against her leg really needed to stop because it only bewildered her more.

So remove his hand.

Such a simple idea, one her mind understood where her body didn't.

I'm going insane.

"So, how is Aidan?" Doctor Fitzgerald asked as he set his napkin down on the table. He'd finished his food, while hers remained mostly untouched. Not because she disliked the taste, but because her appetite appeared to be nonexistent—a complication of her nerves rioting inside. The last thing she wanted to do was eat and be sick all over the table.

"He's well, which, of course, you already know," Issac replied, his thumb still against her skin.

Doctor Fitzgerald grinned. "Yes, true. I was surprised to see him at dinner the other night."

"That's one word for it," Tom remarked. He sat between his father and a young blonde woman. Her name began with a *T.* Tina? Taylor? Tiffany?

Whoever she was, she belonged to the family who filled out the rest of their table. All blondes, though Stas suspected the mother might dye her hair to match. She possessed a fake quality that several others in the room rivaled.

"Yes, he considered stopping by to say hello but didn't want to make the table uncomfortable," Issac said with a pointed look at Tom.

Doctor Fitzgerald chuckled. "Something you had no problem doing, hmm?" He winked at Stas, the indication clear.

They're talking about graduation dinner. Aidan must have been the male at Issac's table.

"Ah, well, I had a reason to stop by." Issac squeezed her thigh as he tilted his head toward her. "My beautiful woman."

She snorted. *Cheesy line.*

He must have sensed her thoughts because his fingers trailed higher, his thumb nearly caressing the edge of her lace thong. The actions were hidden by the table, his expression politely bored.

Stas fought the urge to squirm, not wanting to draw attention to herself, but holy hell, her skin was on fire.

"I'll extend your regards to Aidan," Issac said smoothly. "He's in town for another week or so."

Goose bumps scattered down her legs as he began to sketch a foreign pattern against her flesh. Every upward swipe caused her muscles to tighten, the taunting motion so incredibly inappropriate. Yet, her hands refused to react, her fingers curling into her palms instead as she fought the sensations he stirred inside.

This is wrong.

I shouldn't be enjoying this.

There's clearly something wrong with me.

She glanced at him, catching the wicked twinkle in his gaze. And it hit her—the purpose. Not necessarily to seduce, but to distract. She'd been unnaturally quiet through dinner, hardly touching her food, something that wasn't like her at all. Something others who knew her might notice.

He wanted her to relax.

Or maybe he wanted to take her mind off her situation.

Devious man.

She almost grabbed his wrist, but his thumb finally found the fabric between her legs. A subtle brush, one that caused her nipples to stiffen and her breath to catch.

So decadent and wanton, and not her at all.

What is this man doing to me?

She squeezed her legs together, realizing too late that the move trapped his hand.

Shit. This—

The clearing of a throat had her glancing at Doctor Fitzgerald. He gazed at her expectantly. She must have missed a question.

"Uh, I'm sorry, can you repeat that?" The breathless note in her voice seemed to amuse her demon. His lips twitched as his gaze dropped to her breasts—slowly, purposefully.

If she could move her legs, she would kick him. But she'd trapped his fingers between her thighs. Who knew what he'd do if she released him.

"I asked if you heard from Human Resources yet on your start date," Doctor Fitzgerald said.

Her heart dropped to her stomach, her limbs loosening. Issac slid his palm down to her knee and gave it a gentle squeeze, playtime over. His touch, however, meant everything to her. *I'm here*, he was saying. And she believed him. An indication of trust that surprised her enough to clear the cobwebs from her throat and allow her to reply.

"Yeah, they called today to schedule my orientation, but I received the voicemail too late to phone them back." Mostly true. She hadn't wanted to call them back, unsure of what to say.

"Fantastic. The clearance process can take so long that I was worried it might be a few weeks before you heard anything. Are you excited?"

She tried for a smile and hoped it translated. "Of course."

A round of applause saved her from commenting further as a short, white-haired woman took the podium to introduce the evening's keynote speaker. Stas recognized the name, but not the man who approached. He had a nice voice, one that carried and captivated as he highlighted various humanitarian efforts throughout the world and commended the committee who organized this event. Stas gathered by the end that the gala's purpose revolved around raising money for various relief organizations.

The elderly woman took the podium again to thank a few key sponsors, including Wakefield Pharmaceuticals and the CRF, who were both noted as top-level supporters.

There were a few other items mentioned to draw out the program before she finally moved on to announce this year's recipient of the Humanitarian of the Year Award.

Everyone clapped as Doctor Fitzgerald made his way to the stage, his popularity amongst the gala attendees evident. He grinned before holding up a hand to quiet the warm welcome. Charismatic and commanding, he calmed the audience with that gesture alone.

"Good evening. I can't even begin to say how honored I am to be here tonight, receiving the Humanitarian of the Year Award. I honestly don't feel I deserve it, as I'm only doing what my heart tells me to, and really all the hard work is done by a team of ten-thousand-plus employees. I just show up every day and try to direct them." He gave a self-deprecating laugh that earned him several grins throughout the ballroom.

He continued speaking, the adoration and respect palpable throughout the room.

With each word, he reminded Stas why she idolized him. Why she wanted to work for him. Why she *trusted* him. He was magnanimous and humble, and not the kind of man who would authorize poisoning his employees.

There had to be another explanation.

Maybe someone else poisoned her on her way home Tuesday. The whole afternoon was fuzzy, making it entirely plausible that someone slipped her something without her knowing. That made more sense than her employer trying to kill her. The CRF wasn't even related to the supernatural world. They had no reason to give her the Nizari serum because they didn't know fledglings existed.

Except…

"I suspect the CRF used the Nizari poison on you to test your bloodline." Was it only this morning Issac spoke those words? They implied the CRF might know about the supernatural, but he never explained his suspicion.

He's wrong. He has to be wrong.

Six years of knowing the enigmatic man onstage

trumped a fake two-week *relationship* with a demon. Stas didn't even know how to define *Ichorian*, for crying out loud.

Maybe Issac saved her life... or maybe he was toying with her.

This whole arrangement made no sense. *Dating for information.* She saw the way other women looked at him. Issac Wakefield didn't need to bribe a woman for a date. There was more to this that she didn't know.

Because he won't tell me anything.

Annoyance bubbled inside her, every passing moment making her want to turn and demand answers right now. He'd distracted her earlier with his seductive touch and smile and general sex appeal. Ridiculous. She'd never allowed a male to corrupt her in this way, and she'd be—

The crowd erupted into a standing ovation, pulling her back to the stage, where Doctor Fitzgerald stood with a slight flush painting his cheeks. He never could take praise very well, always deferring to others he felt deserved it more.

Not a killer.

Or a psychopath.

Unlike the demon beside her, whom she found outside a murder scene.

Owen...

Why was Issac there that day? He never explained, just kept her in suspense while forcing her into this charade for answers. Answers he didn't seem all that keen on giving.

But he did save my life.

Maybe.

"Aidan and Osiris would approve," Issac murmured as Doctor Fitzgerald rejoined them.

"Yeah? Maybe you'll try for it next year," her mentor replied, smirking.

"Not bloody likely."

History radiated between them, underlined in a palpable fondness that left her even more flabbergasted. How could Issac possibly suspect the CRF of trying to kill her? Unless he knew something about the organization that she didn't.

Ugh, she was thinking in circles and giving herself a headache.

The older woman stood at the podium again, making parting comments about the art auction and recommending everyone keep drinking champagne and wine. While Stas agreed wholeheartedly in the alcohol plan, she needed to take a breath. Alone.

"I'll be right back," she said quietly, excusing herself for the restroom.

She found it just outside the doors and quickly grabbed an embroidered cloth towel from the stack. *Definitely a fancy hotel.* Running it beneath cool water first, she used it to dab at her face, frustrated by the two splotches of pink decorating her cheeks.

Alcohol mingled with confusion created a decidedly unattractive look.

Just breathe, she told herself. *This is almost done. Then you can demand some answers.*

Or maybe just march back to the table, grab Issac by the arm, and growl a few demands in his ear.

No. That'd just create a scene, and she preferred to stay hidden.

She tossed the cloth into the basket by the door and walked out to find Tom waiting for her. He leaned against the wall, one foot crossed over the other and his hands tucked into his pockets. Lizzie would have swooned at the sight, his blond hair messy as if he'd just run his fingers through it several times.

But there was nothing attractive about the fury radiating in his gaze as she approached him.

"The Arcadia, ten o'clock tomorrow night. Go there, then tell me if Wakefield's still worth it." Tom pushed away from the wall and started down the hall. She caught his arm.

"Tom, what—"

"No, Stas." He shook her off and leveled her with one of the harshest looks she'd ever received from him. She took a step back. This was the man who led rescue missions all over the world, the domineering leader, not the big brother she knew and adored.

"Don't give me that wounded look. I've tried to warn you, but you won't listen. So go tomorrow and see for yourself. I suggest you wear something black. Call me when you're ready to talk about it."

His long strides ate up the hallway too fast for her to keep up.

"Tom, hold—" She cut off the command, knowing it would have forced him to halt in place. A dark part of her yearned to take over and demand he listen, and she almost did. But she knew better. People died when she used her abilities.

Like my parents.

Tom didn't pause or glance backward, just followed the stairs down to the lobby instead, bypassing the ballroom.

Her heart stuttered, her heels rooted to the floor. *What am I supposed to do with that?*

Doctor Fitzgerald walked out of the ballroom, frowning after the direction his son had headed. "Did Tom just leave?" he asked when he realized she stood only a few feet away from him.

"I think so," she said, swallowing.

He sighed and gave her an apologetic shake of his head. "I hope he wasn't too hard on you. Issac isn't his favorite person."

"I've gathered that."

"Don't worry. He'll come around." He put a hand on her shoulder and rubbed it in a fatherly way. "I meant to check in on you this week to ask how you're feeling."

Her brow furrowed. "Feeling?" she repeated, warning bells sounding in her head.

He nodded. "Yeah, I saw you leaving the building Tuesday and you didn't look like yourself. Was everything all right?"

Every muscle in her body threatened to lock in place, but the hand on her shoulder forced her to remain calm. If she reacted outwardly in any way, he'd sense it. "Yeah, it was the shots. They upset my stomach."

Shock lit his features. "Shots?"

"From the medical exam."

"You were given injections during your exam?" Did he look uneasy, or was that her imagination?

"Uh, yeah. Doctor Patel said my job might require travel."

His blond eyebrows met his hairline. "Really?"

Not a comforting reaction. "So, uh, that's not normal, then?"

"No, it most certainly is not. Inoculations are meant for our paramilitary unit only." He let go of her shoulder to pull out his phone. He typed while he spoke. "I'll be meeting with the medical director first thing Monday. This is news to me."

Her muscles went weak as all the tension left her body. If the CRF really did try to poison her, Doctor Fitzgerald hadn't known about it.

"Anita should have asked you basic questions, taken vitals, and let you go," he continued. "The vaccinations didn't negatively impact you at all, did they?"

Her lower back tingled, right around her birthmark. She fought the urge to scratch it while considering how to reply. Part of her yearned to tell him the truth, but instinct pulled her back from that leap of faith. There were too many missing pieces in this puzzle to trust anyone. He'd never believe her anyway, and she really didn't want to have to prove it by using her persuasive gift.

She cleared her throat. "Honestly, I felt a little woozy after the exam, but I slept it off."

"You felt sick afterward?"

More tingling. So annoying.

"Yeah," she admitted. "I felt pretty nauseated when I got home, but I think it was the stress of it all." Her stomach twisted with the lie, the wrongness of omitting the truth physically paining her. She really needed to change the subject, or maybe just alter it slightly. "So, uh, you think she followed the wrong protocol on purpose?" *Does that mean Doctor Patel knows I'm a fledgling?*

Ice drizzled down her spine at the thought.

What if Issac hadn't been the only one who saw her compel that reporter after Owen's memorial? He'd told her to be careful, that there might be others watching. What if he'd issued the warning too late?

"I'm not sure, but I promise to personally look into it," Doctor Fitzgerald said.

"Thank you."

"No need to thank me, Stas. I'm truly sorry this happened."

"It's not your fault."

"Well, not directly, anyway, but I still take ownership for it." He studied her closely, his brown eyes edged in concern. "I really hope we won't lose you over this. You're going to be very successful at the CRF."

"No. No, of course not." She shook her head as if to dispel the foolish notion. Although, a part of her thought perhaps she should walk away and never look back. But she'd never been one to run away, even when she should. "I'm very thankful for the opportunity," she added, forcing a smile.

At least she knew the CRF hadn't tried to kill her.

Just, maybe, Doctor Patel.

Which meant *someone* suspected Stas of being a fledgling.

"You earned it," Doctor Fitzgerald said, his smile crinkling his warm eyes. He gestured toward the ballroom. "I'll let you get back to your date, even if I think you can do better." *What a dad-like thing to say.*

"Thanks, and congratulations on your award. It's well deserved."

His cheeks flushed. "Thank you, Stas."

He went off in the direction of his son, while she ventured into the ballroom.

Their table was empty.

Where did you go, demon man?

She searched the room, spotting him near the dance floor in the company of three supermodels.

The tightness in her stomach grew, knotting uncomfortably as she started toward them.

This was the man she'd read about—the perpetual playboy, already picking out his next date despite still being on this one with her. Of course, this wasn't real, just a business arrangement.

One where he fondled and kissed her a lot.

Maybe he did that with all his business partners.

"Ah, darling, there you are," he said, holding his hand out for her as she approached. "Ladies, if you'll excuse me, I promised to give Astasiya a tour of the hotel."

Stas fought the urge to roll her eyes as all three women pouted. What did they think he was going to do, invite them along?

He linked his fingers through Stas's and led her away from the trio of simpering debutantes.

"Are you sure you don't want to finish your interview?" Stas asked, batting her eyelashes. "I don't mind waiting." She could peruse some art. Not that she would understand any of it or could afford it, but it would serve as a distraction while he flirted.

"My interview?"

"You know, for your next conquest, or date, or whatever you call them."

He paused to study her, his luscious mouth curling upward. "Hmm, yes, green is not your color, though it does match your beautiful eyes."

"What?" That line didn't even make sense.

"Jealousy, darling. It's not very becoming."

Her eyebrows shot upward. "Did you just accuse me of being jealous?"

He pulled her along beside him, his amusement evident. "No accusation necessary."

"I'm *not* jealous."

"Whatever you say."

"I'm not." What was there to be jealous of? This was his life. She knew that.

"Don't fret, darling. I'm here with you, not them."

"Right, as part of a business arrangement," she reminded him, ignoring the *fretting* part. "And where are we going?" They were heading toward the lobby exit.

"To complete our *business arrangement* in the limo."

"We're leaving? I thought we were going on a tour." Not that she particularly cared, but the hotel was gorgeous and a historical site.

He stopped again, this time raising a perfectly sculpted brow. "I only said that to maintain my image, but if you want to grab a hotel room, I would be happy to oblige."

She gaped at him. "Are you propositioning me?"

"You were the one expressing regrets over our missed tour. Who propositioned whom in that scenario?"

"You're impossible. You know that, right?"

His grin was too damn alluring. "We can conclude our agreement in bed or in the limo. Which do you prefer, Astasiya?"

With a growl and a muttered curse, she pulled him toward the doors. *Tempting demon.* Her common sense wouldn't stand a chance in bed with him, and she needed to focus. There were too many unanswered questions between them.

Benjamin stood waiting by the limo outside with the door open. She murmured a hello and climbed inside. Issac sat right beside her—despite the spacious backseat—and draped his arm over her shoulders. At least he'd left her thigh alone this time. His burning touch made it difficult to think.

"So, it's okay to leave this early?" she asked as the limo inched forward. It seemed early.

"The sizable donation I left excused us from the art auction, which means we can search for something more edible to eat. I'm craving Italian, but I'm open to other

136

suggestions." That explained his eagerness to leave. He was hungry. *Typical male.*

"Does that mean I have to wait until after dinner for answers?"

He considered while toying with one of her blonde strands. "I suppose you've upheld your side of our bargain for the night. What would you like to know, Miss Davenport?"

"Everything."

"I believe our arrangement was for three questions."

"Fine."

~*~

Astasiya was adorable when frustrated.

That little growl she gave Issac in The Pierre lobby almost had him hoisting her over his shoulder and carrying her upstairs to a room. It wouldn't be the first time he booked a suite after a gala, but tonight he craved something different.

He wanted her in *his* bed—a foreign concept, one he'd never indulged in before.

But Astasiya was special, different, a new challenge he would thoroughly enjoy conquering.

He *liked* her. Perhaps more than he should. However, wasn't that half the fun?

She remained thoughtful beside him, her fight subsiding as she contemplated what questions to throw his way. He waited patiently, using the time to pull the pins from her hair. Although he enjoyed her updo, he wanted to see those natural blonde waves of hers on full display.

When he plucked the last pin free, he combed through the thick strands and luxuriated in the soft, alluring texture. All men had a trait they adored; for Issac, it was natural blondes. A night of passion would cure this intoxicating desire for her, but for now, he chose to revel in it, allowing the attraction to consume him.

He should wait, should ensure her trust first, but he wanted her. And he would have her.

Then they could return to business.

His phone vibrated, causing him to sigh. He used his free hand to remove it from his jacket and read the incoming message.

A summons. Of course. Issac nearly rolled his eyes at the timing of it all.

He could ignore Osiris, but it would be prudent to accept and play along. For now. He slipped the mobile back into his jacket pocket and pressed a button to talk to Benjamin.

"Change in plans, mate. We need to take Miss Davenport home. I believe you have the address."

His driver confirmed and Issac closed the connection.

"Sorry, darling, where were we?" He moved his hand to her neck to massage the tense muscles there. "Right, you were about to ask me a question, yes?"

"What do you want from me, Issac?" she asked, the words spilling from her mouth. "What are you really using me for?"

Her questions struck a deep chord, tugging at his chest. That wasn't what he expected her to ask at all, especially not while he'd been in the process of seducing her. "You think I'm using you?"

"I know you are, but I don't know why. Is it because I'm a fledgling?"

It would be so easy to refuse her, but this she deserved an answer to. Even if it wasn't an answer he wanted to give. He continued rubbing her neck, moving upward into her scalp, in an attempt to ease some of her tension where his words could not.

"This isn't about you," he started softly. "Not necessarily, anyway. I'm righting a wrong, and fate placed you in the center of my plans. You see, you're quite literally the perfect pawn."

The pink flush in her cheeks died as her body stiffened

beside him, her muscles tense again. His words might not be what she wanted to hear, but they were at least true. He could have lied, but for what purpose?

"Are you going to elaborate on your plans?" she asked.

"I will when you're ready."

"Any idea when that will be?"

Considering how well the evening went... "I suspect it will be very soon."

She studied him for a long moment, a war of emotions dancing behind her gorgeous gaze. Whatever she wanted to ask, she wasn't sure she desired the answer. But he caught when her curiosity won in the end. "Are you going to get me killed, Issac?" Such a quiet query, spoken in a way that said she already knew his response.

This had definitely not gone according to plan.

He expected her to demand a definition for *Ichorian*—something he'd intended to give her. Not questions about his plans or how they may impact her life.

Are you going to get me killed?

He swallowed. "It's a distinct possibility, yes." Of course, she would wake up immortal. A loss for him, but a gain for her. She had the potential to become a powerful Hydraian, if Lucian allowed it.

"Then why bother saving me?"

His lips flattened. What a ridiculous waste of a question. "Because I need you alive."

"But only until you're finished with your plans."

"Well, yes." Then she would be free to accept fate whenever she liked.

Her hands balled into tiny fists, her frustration evident. That, he could have accepted. What he didn't like were the tears that flickered in her eyes—eyes that were too beautiful and fierce to showcase such pain.

Hurting her had never been his intention but seemed to be an inevitability. Just because his plan might kill her didn't mean he wished death upon her. He found her company rather enjoyable, a rarity these days. She made him laugh.

The last person to do that was Amelia.

He waited for the pain that usually arose with thoughts of his sister.

Nothing.

Odd.

Perhaps the movement of his plans had granted him a reprieve. Tonight had been a spectacular success, something to be celebrated.

But the tear rolling down Astasiya's cheek dampened his celebratory mood. She flicked it away and turned to look out the window.

"I didn't mean to hurt you," he said softly.

"I'm fine."

Issac gripped her chin and forced her to look at him. Her vivid gaze startled him.

Astasiya wasn't hurt.

She was furious.

The tension in her shoulders and the mutinous line of her jaw both indicated she wanted to throttle him.

"You're angry," he said, sounding like a complete fool for uttering the obvious.

"And you're perceptive," she retorted.

The limo came to a stop just outside her building. Seeing it, she opened the door beside her and jumped out without waiting for Benjamin or saying another word.

Issac climbed out on his side and cut her off on the sidewalk.

"I'm sorry; did you want a thank-you?" Hostility poured off her in waves.

He frowned. "This bout of childishness is not attractive."

Her expression told him that was the wrong thing to say, despite it being the truth. "Childish? You think I'm being *childish*? You know what? Fuck you." She moved around him and marched off in a manner he considered to be the definition of immature.

Eyes rolling heavenward for patience, he started after

her. She made it through the lobby before he caught her by the elbow. He maneuvered her into the elevator and hit the button for her floor. "Right, I can see you're furious with me and no amount of groveling is going to fix that quickly." So he did the only thing he could do.

He kissed her.

Hard.

When her lips parted in protest, he took full advantage and showed her with his tongue what he couldn't say with words.

He wanted her.

The thought of her dying burned him despite it being her fate. They had little time to share together, and wasting it being angry over words wasn't acceptable. Most women preferred honesty, and he'd given her just that.

Because he cared.

Because he needed her to know the truth.

Because he longed to enjoy these short moments with her.

Issac cradled her face between his hands, kissing her soundly, begging her to reply in kind. *Needing* her to respond.

Don't block me out. Not over this. Not yet.

Astasiya sighed, a low moan of approval escaping her throat as her nails dug into his suit jacket. Not to push him away, but to pull him closer. An emotional battle raged inside her. He could feel it in the way she poured her frustration and anger into the kiss, the sharpness of her grip on his tux.

She was angry.

But she still wanted him.

If only they could take this back to her bedroom, he could make this right. The summons was in thirty minutes. Not nearly enough time.

The elevator doors opened.

He backed her out and up against the wall, not giving a damn who might see them. He ground his hips into hers, letting her feel the evidence of his desire, needing her to know that while he considered her the key to his success, that wasn't all she meant to him. It might just be lust, but that had to be better than nothing. It had to be enough.

Astasiya's tension lessened with each stroke of his tongue against hers until she melted into his embrace, succumbing completely to his will.

He knew how to work with this, his hand sliding to her breast to tweak her hard nipple through the dress. She arched into him on a groan, all inhibition thrown to the wind. He did it again because he could, reveling in her response and taking full advantage of the thin silk. Her breast fit perfectly in his hand.

The thin straps of her gown taunted him.

One tug and the fabric would pool around her waist.

Alas, that was a temptation to be fulfilled another night.

He broke the kiss despite wanting to do the opposite and palmed her cheeks.

"You seem to mistake truth for what I want to happen," he whispered. "Fate has a path for you that doesn't involve me. I'm only borrowing you while I can. Please don't waste it by staying angry over a few honest answers."

Arousal illuminated her gaze while fiery embers ignited in her pupils. She was turned on and angry. A heady combination that had him reconsidering his evening plans.

"You only saved me to use me," she accused.

"I saved you because I need you."

"To fulfill your plans that might get me killed."

"All mortals die eventually, Astasiya."

Some of her ardor died. "*That's* how you justify it?"

He closed his eyes and tried to find his old friend, forbearance. This was why he only *fucked* women. Emotions were complications he avoided. Yet he felt compelled to placate her. When did he start caring so bloody much about hurt feelings?

"You're a fledgling, Astasiya. When you die, you'll be reborn a Hydraian. *That* is how I justify it." He pushed away from her and led the way to her door. She trailed a step behind him, then leaned against the wall beside her residence.

"You're saying when I die, I'll become immortal?" she asked as he pulled her clutch from his jacket pocket. She'd left it on the table earlier in the evening, and he worried she might forget it. Her eyes widened as he handed it to her, confirming his thoughts on the matter.

"Yes, a Hydraian," he replied.

"Then why bother saving me this week if I would just wake up?"

"Because the Nizari poison was specifically designed to make sure you wouldn't." He tucked a strand of her hair behind her ear. "I believe you are over your quota for the evening, darling. I'll be out of touch for the remainder of the weekend." He didn't allow her a chance to reply, just pulled her in for a kiss before starting down the hallway. "Sleep well, Astasiya."

Her muttered curse followed him all the way to his meeting. He was going to have some serious groveling to do when he saw her again.

CHAPTER ELEVEN

The Soultaker

TOM SUGGESTED STAS WEAR SOMETHING black. What he'd failed to mention was the lingerie part.

She stood off to the side of the dance floor in a clingy black dress she thought would work for a nightclub. Almost all the other women here were in bras and skirts, or less. Translucent black seemed to be the better wardrobe requirement.

Stas sipped her drink while the deep bass of the Arcadia vibrated through her limbs, her nerves frayed.

What did Tom want her to see here?

Something about Issac, clearly. But he'd claimed to be busy the rest of the weekend. Had he meant he would be busy *here*? Because it was pretty obvious what this club catered to—sex. She'd caught several couples on the leather couches lining the walls already engaged in passionate affairs, hence her presence at the edge of the dance floor, where it was safe.

Except most of the people before her seemed to be taking pointers from the seductive beats playing overhead.

She searched the entire lower level for her demon, all the suit-clad males blending together with the pass of her gaze. A roped-off staircase near the middle led up to a VIP area, somewhere she couldn't access.

Are you up there, Issac?

Is this where you come when you need a break from toying with me?

She suspected Tom wanted her to catch Issac here, hooking up with another woman. Stas didn't exactly want to see that, but she could use the reminder of their business arrangement. Last night's date had felt a little too real, at least until he'd ruined it with the truth.

"You're quite literally the perfect pawn." His words reverberated through her heart, making her even more furious. Not necessarily at him, but at herself. Because at some point in the last week, she'd developed *feelings*. And those *feelings* were not acceptable.

She knew better.

This wasn't a real relationship. He needed something from her, plain and simple. They just happened to also be attracted to one another, a complication that could be solved by one night in his bed.

Or maybe a weekend.

Unless her emotions latched on, which they seemed to be doing.

She scanned the lower level once more, focusing on the dimly lit bar, and then the couches again. If she found Issac with another woman—

Awareness prickled her spine, her senses picking up something.

No, not something, *someone.*

There.

At the top of the stairs, dressed in an all-black suit like every other male in this club. Yet he owned it in a way the others never could.

And damn if he didn't look good.

She stepped to the side, admiring him as he descended with two other men. No women. Her shoulders relaxed, her stomach loosening at the sight of him without a date.

Not the right reaction.

Fuck off.

The three men garnered attention around them as they hit the bottom floor, several women already turning their way, but the trio moved through all of them with ease, their disinterest clear.

Stas stepped to the side, trying to keep them in her sights, when a finger boldly traced her spine, setting off her pulse.

Danger, her instincts whispered, her skin tingling with alarm. An unspoken threat had lingered in that brazen touch, stirring unease inside her.

"Hello, lovely." A low murmur against her ear, barely audible over the music. "Care to dance?"

She didn't even need to turn around to know the answer to that. *No.* But another caress of her back said this one wouldn't be swayed easily.

"I'm actually looking for someone," she replied while stepping out of his reach and to the side, where she nearly tripped over her own heels.

Oh, fuck.

It was the guy from Owen's apartment.

The one she'd nicknamed *Hank.*

"I'm looking for someone too," he replied, his muddy gaze sliding over her neckline and lower to her exposed legs.

She swallowed. Twice. Working on a reply that wouldn't come out in a screech. Because holy shit, he'd somehow been involved in Owen's death. Or at least the world that killed him.

"Sorry," she said, clearing her throat. "I meant I'm meeting someone." Those words usually worked, but Hank remained unfazed, his lips twitching at the side. The words seemed to go right through him as he moved into her personal space. She took a step back into a wall of male and spun to the side. The glass fell from her hand, shattering on the floor.

Brutus. His lecherous gaze stroked over her while Hank crowded her from the other side, both men trapping her with an ease that made her stomach churn.

Do they recognize me? She'd been in several of Owen's photos and had been friends with him for years. *What do they want?*

"What did you find, Mike?" Brutus asked, lifting his stubby finger to fondle a strand of her hair.

"Something delicious," Hank—or rather *Mike*—replied from behind her.

Her pulse raced, the need to duck out of their masculine cage clawing at her insides. But as she stepped to the side, they followed, edging her closer to the couches, and farther from the exit.

"It's cute. She thought my asking her to dance was a request." Mike sounded genuinely amused.

"I guess she's not into the gentlemanly thing, so should we get right to the point?" Brutus's lips were far too close to her neck, his words damp against her skin.

"That's certainly how I'm interpreting it," Mike replied, grabbing her hip, pulling her ass up against his groin.

"You really don't want to do this," she said, meaning it.

Command them to release you, the devil on her shoulder whispered.

Consider the consequences, her common sense replied.

One demand and they would have to leave her alone, but it wouldn't be subtle enough for them not to notice. And the last thing she needed was these two becoming aware of her persuasive abilities. They were probably about as human as Issac.

"Upstairs?" Mike asked.

"Yeah, she seems like a screamer. Do your thing, buddy."

How about we not...

"Gladly." Mike whirled her to face him, his grin menacing.

She pressed against his chest, not at all impressed by the stench of smoke surrounding him. "Really, I don't want—"

"Gentlemen," a new voice greeted, the owner standing just behind Mike. "I do hope you're planning to share."

Forest-green irises met hers, his face immediately familiar. *One of the men walking down the stairs with Issac.* Momentary relief flooded her, followed swiftly by dread. Cruelty lurked in this man's features, providing him with a lethal edge that matched his sharp, athletic form.

"She is a tempting morsel, indeed," he added with a smirk that sent a chill down her spine.

What kind of needs does this club cater to? Because she was starting to think this place might be a dungeon of sorts, for unwilling participants.

"Back off, Tristan," Mike growled, his grip tightening. "We found her first." Challenge lurked in his voice, his muscles flexing. Brutus joined him, his stance and presence menacing.

Tristan smirked, arrogance dripping off him as he ran his gaze lazily over the other men. He stood a few inches shorter, but violence radiated off him. The other two were more bodyguard types, all intensity and bulk. Tristan's lack of concern told her just what kind of man lurked beneath the suit.

"Did you, though?" he asked, cocking his dark head to the side. "I fear you might be wrong about that." The two brawny males visibly stiffened as a familiar warmth caressed her back. Tristan lifted his gaze to the one behind her. "You need a better leash for your pet, Issac."

A palm grabbed her hip, yanking her backward and away from Mike.

"Indeed," Issac murmured, his opposite hand circling her neck to hold her captive against him. "Thank you, Tristan."

"Sire." Tristan bowed his head and took his leave.

Mike and his friend stuck around, their eyes locked on the demon behind her with a mixture of uncertainty and resigned reverence.

"Gentlemen, my apologies for the misunderstanding." Issac's lips skimmed her thundering pulse, the heat from his body burning her back. "This one belongs to me."

What? I belong to no one.

But yeah, she wasn't going to argue right now. Not with him saving her from the two goons in front of her. Whatever they'd planned for her upstairs was definitely worse than being manhandled by her demon.

"S-sorry, Wakefield," Mike stuttered. "We didn't know she was yours." He put his hands in front of him, his expression contrite.

"Yeah, we didn't mean anything by it," his buddy added. "We're really sorry."

The two groveling idiots took a step backward, their gazes downcast.

They were terrified.

Stas frowned. What had them scrambling to get away from her demon? Sure, he maintained a daunting presence, but this was more than mere intimidation. They were *submitting* to him.

"An oversight on my part, I assure you. You're forgiven." Tension radiated at her back. Issac was livid. At her?

Mike and Brutus excused themselves in a similar fashion to Tristan, inclining their heads in a gesture of respect, before prowling about for another victim.

The fingers curled around her throat tightened. "What are you doing here, Astasiya?"

She tried to turn to face him, but he held her in place. A jolt of simmering electricity flashed through her veins, leaving her breathless and mute in his arms. The display of dominance should have pissed her off, yet it left her feeling… conflicted.

"Answer me," he demanded.

Right. Her presence at the Arcadia. She couldn't exactly tell him she'd come here searching for him at Tom's advisement. "Don't most people go to clubs to dance?" she asked, feigning innocence. A ridiculous excuse, one he had to see right through.

"I don't see you dancing," he growled, the sound rumbling through her ears, heightening that sizzling energy flowing through her.

"That's because I'm being manhandled," she replied, ignoring the sensations his nearness provoked and focusing on her sarcastic tendencies.

"This is not a game." The low pitch of his voice caused her to squirm, visions of his bedroom materializing behind her eyes. That was the kind of tone a man used in bed. An experienced one. A male who knew how to properly fuck a woman until dawn.

God, I need this to end. I can't focus around him, this attraction—

Issac bit her ear, interrupting her thoughts and sparking new ideas.

What would that mouth feel like on other parts of her body? He seemed to enjoy nibbling. Her nipples tightened at the prospect of him focusing his attentions there.

Think of last night. How he called you a pawn.

Her blood cooled.

Yes, that's what she needed to remember. His intentions with her.

"Who told you to come here, Astasiya?"

"Why do you care?" she countered, her voice higher than she intended. He evoked a response from her unlike any other. Not that her limited experience was much of a comparison.

"Because whoever sent you here is trying to get you killed."

She frowned. Tom wouldn't put her life in danger. He might be angry with her, but he still cared about her.

"Look around you," Issac said, angling her toward the back of the room.

She much preferred the view of the dance floor and the door. "I'm not really into voyeurism, Issac." She tried to look away, but the hand on her neck held her in place.

"Watch."

Not having much choice, she studied the threesome occurring on the couch nearest them. The mostly naked woman seemed to be enjoying herself with one man at her exposed breast and another beneath her skirt. Her dark head was tossed back in bliss while both men worked her over with frantic mouths.

"Is this what you're into, Issac? Kinky shit?" she asked, wondering if this was what Tom meant for her to see.

"Oh, darling, you have no idea what I'm into." The gentle kiss Issac laid on her neck belied his furious tone. "Look closer. What are they really doing?"

Swallowing, she eyed the ménage à trois again.

More ecstasy.

Mouth opened on a cry of… pain?

Her brow furrowed. *Is that blood?*

She sucked in a breath, her eyebrows lifting. The man at the woman's chest was lapping up a trail of dark liquid pooling from an open wound over her nipple.

And the one between her legs wasn't angled right.

They're not pleasuring her.

They're drinking from her.

Oh, what the fuck?

Two couches over, a foursome of three women and one man in a similar position. His mouth parted, eyes closed, one female on her knees bobbing her head while the other two suckled his neck and bare chest.

Vampires.

"Yes, you see it now, don't you?" Issac's harsh whisper heated her cooling skin, his lips at her throat. "Now tell me

151

why you're here. Who sent you to die, Astasiya?"

"No." She tried to shake her head, but his grip forbade the movement. "He wouldn't. He just wanted..." Wanted her to what? Realize Issac wasn't human?

Her pulse leapt.

That would imply Tom *knew*.

How could he know something like that? Her knees shook, her limbs threatening to give out. Because if Tom knew, Doctor Fitzgerald knew, which would imply the CRF...

She couldn't finish that thought, her vision darkening before her eyes.

Issac's speculations...

No. No way.

She couldn't believe any of it. There was no way Tom knew what she would find here.

Then why send me?

Fuck.

"Thomas," Issac snarled against her ear. "That's what he told you in the hallway last night. To come here."

She barely heard him, her focus on the nightclub. The feeding. The vampires. Everywhere. On the couches, against the back walls, on the dance floor, even at the bar.

She'd missed all of it in favor of finding Issac.

Tom had led her to a blood den.

A club meant for demons.

"An Ichorian club," she realized out loud, her voice barely audible. That was the only explanation for this, for Issac's presence, why Tom told her to come here.

Her stomach twisted.

Why not just tell her the truth? Why put her at risk like this?

"Indeed, it is," Issac confirmed softly. "Come, I—"

"Is there a problem, Issac?" The cultured voice came from her right, interrupting Issac.

Stas hardly registered the newcomer, her gaze still on the couches. She spotted a third group—two men fucking a woman between them while openly feeding from her neck. Her face had taken on an unhealthy ashen tint rather than a euphoric one. *She's dying...*

"No problem, Osiris. Just having a conversation about what happens to women who are disobedient." Issac's harsh words drew her attention to the bald man standing before them. Dark brows, olive skin tone, harsh jawline, all wrapped up in a dangerous aura that sent a shiver down her spine.

The slight tightening of Issac's grip told her to stay quiet, a warning she didn't need.

This man was a predator.

A threat.

And ancient.

She shivered, her instincts telling her to run. This male could hurt her. Badly. And the cruelty lurking in his green eyes said he'd enjoy it.

He studied her intently, his gaze seeming to memorize every line and detail as if searching for her very soul. The slight pinch in his mouth suggested he found her lacking as he finally returned his attention to Issac.

"Eager to join us, is she?" he asked, his accent distinctly other. *Old. Very, very old.*

"Something like that," Issac replied.

"Bring her tonight. We could all use a diversion, and your punishments are always so creative."

The way he said it, so cold and calculating, scattered goose bumps down her arms. *This* was the man in charge. No question. And he would kill her without remorse. She could see it in the way he regarded her.

As an object beneath him.

A toy.

Just a passing amusement.

How could Tom send her here knowing the danger this place possessed?

Issac stroked his finger down the column of her throat as he considered the proposal. Her pulse raced as she

153

waited, wondering what he would do, if he even had a choice. "As much as I would enjoy providing some evening entertainment, I fear her punishment will be for my eyes only tonight," he mused softly. "She's made me quite hungry, and I don't feel up to sharing."

"Disappointing." From the look he gave Issac, she could tell this man didn't appreciate being *disappointed*. "Bring her anyway."

She recognized the power in those three words, the familiar note of persuasion one she often heard in her own voice. *He can compel.* Even she felt pressured to obey, despite not knowing where he wanted Issac to take her.

Holy shit.

"Of course, Sire," Issac replied smoothly.

Tristan had used that term earlier. *Sire* must be a term of reverence or superiority, similar to how one would address a king.

"We'll see just how eager she is to join us afterward," Osiris mused.

Ancient eyes met hers, freezing her inside. She couldn't even breathe, let alone speak.

"I suggest you behave, little one. Issac is not known for his mercy—a trait I admire deeply." With that solemn warning, the man sauntered over to the staircase and ascended it. The guards bowed their heads as he passed, adding to his air of authority. *Yes, definitely the one in charge.*

Her chest ached from the lack of air, her throat burning beneath Issac's touch.

"Not a word," he whispered against her ear. "You need to do exactly what I say. Now walk with me."

Cool air met her neck as he dropped his hold, her lungs still not working the way they should.

I need to get out of here.

Except Issac guided her in the opposite direction, one of his hands meeting the small of her back to propel her forward—toward the same staircase Osiris had ascended.

Oh God...

Her legs locked, her heels cementing to the ground, but a subtle push against her spine forced her to move alongside Issac. Up the stairs. Past the nodding guards—no bowing. When one of them eyed her with unveiled interest, she stepped closer to Issac's side, seeking his protection and warmth.

He kept walking, guiding her upward into the VIP lounge filled with more couches and chairs. One of the patrons waved, her striking features familiar.

Clara.

The woman's face broke into a wide grin at Issac's approach, only to fall when she noticed his arm around Stas.

Issac shook his head once, earning him a pouty face from the woman.

This must have been whom he'd been entertaining before venturing downstairs with his two friends. It didn't take a genius to figure out what they'd all been up to, not with Clara wearing a black negligee and nothing else.

I see. This was what Tom wanted her to discover—Issac with Clara at the Arcadia. That made more sense than him sending her into a demon club.

Or maybe that was just her hoping for the best.

Issac led Stas into a rear hallway lined with doors, causing her to frown back at the reception area. A booth, in the open, surrounded by people, seemed like a much better plan.

He stopped at a random door, twisted the knob, and practically pushed her inside. She opened her mouth, but no words slipped past her lips.

Because she didn't know what to say or where to start.

The door slammed with a finality, shrouding them in darkness and silence.

"I-Issac," she whispered, her heart in her throat.

She squeaked as he grabbed her and pushed her up against the wall, his hands in her hair, his mouth a hairsbreadth away from hers.

It happened so fast.

Too fast.

Stealing her breath and her fight all at once.

"There are cameras everywhere," he warned, a dark edge highlighting each word. "And they all have night vision, so put your hands on me and make it look like you're enjoying this."

She swallowed and lifted her arms to wrap around his neck. *This is Issac. He won't hurt me. He needs me.* If she told herself that enough, she'd believe it. Maybe.

"What are you wearing under this dress?" he asked, his mouth brushing hers, the words whisper-soft.

Not what she expected him to say. "E-excuse me?"

His teeth sank into her lower lip, making her yelp. "Focus."

On what? The demon club? The humans dying downstairs? The fact that you're a fucking vampire? Where should I begin?

He sighed, his forehead falling to hers. "Astasiya, we have very little time to sort this before the Conclave. I need you to work with me. Both our lives depend on it. What are you wearing?"

She cleared her throat, her hold on his neck tightening as if needing his support to respond. And maybe she did. This was all a lot to take in. "A, uh, thong," she managed to say. "And a strapless bra." Both black and lacy, but she didn't add that part.

One of his hands drifted from her hair to her waist, then down to her ass. His palm flattened and forced her to arch up into him. A breath hitched in her throat at the feel of his growing arousal.

He's turned on… here… now?

She trembled, the heat of his body seeping into her cool skin, warming her blood. They were standing rather close. And he smelled amazing, as always.

Anywhere else, in the dark, she'd have kissed him.

But here…

"The dress will have to stay, then," he said, the disappointment evident in his voice.

She frowned. "What's wrong with my dress?" It hit her midthigh and clung to her curves. She looked good in it.

He ignored her, his mouth brushing hers in a chaste kiss as his hips pressed firmly into hers.

Definitely aroused.

"You're going to see things tonight that will make you want to scream, but you must remain calm and quiet. Mortals who overreact die, and they die badly."

"Wh—"

Issac lifted her off the ground one-handed, her legs wrapping around him automatically for balance. And, oh God, that placed his thick erection right against the scrap of lace between her thighs.

Any other place and time, her body's instinct to move against him would have won out, but not now. The shiver that traversed her spine was from his words, not his touch.

Mortals who overreact die. Her arms tensed around his neck.

Issac had already admitted that her involvement as his pawn would likely lead to her death. And now…

I'm going to die here.

"It's imperative they believe you're human," he whispered, his groin moving in a sinful circle against her. Such a subtle move, but one that sent tingling sensations through her entire body despite his words.

I should not… This cannot… Oh, he just did it again…

"I need to know you understand me." His peppermint scent seeped through her parted lips as he spoke the words against her mouth, stoking a forbidden fire inside her.

Pull yourself together, Stas.

This isn't the right place.

Just ignore—

His hard length caressed her hot center again, causing her to arch against him in a blissful mix of confusion and need. The heady combination left her light-headed, lost, unable to focus.

Who knew fear could be such a turn-on?

"Astasiya." He punctuated her name by nipping her

lower lip, causing her to cry out. Whether in protest or because she liked the other things he was doing to her, she didn't know.

Reality started to blend with desire, making it difficult to discern right from wrong. It was as if her mind had shut down in favor of her body's needs. So much easier to rely on than to think about what she'd learned, what she'd observed, or the fact that she may very well die here.

"They cannot find out what you are," he growled against her mouth. "Both of our lives depend on it."

His words registered through the haze of passion clouding her mind. "No persuasion," she repeated. That seemed like common sense considering their surroundings. As did not giving in to her baser needs. *Logic.*

"One last thing." Issac licked her bottom lip, eliciting a stinging sensation. His bite had broken the skin, and the way he laved the wound now sent tingles down her spine.

Why does that feel so good?

"You can't enter the Conclave unmarked."

"Conclave?" she repeated.

"A meeting of sorts for Ichorians." His tongue traced a pattern against her mouth before dipping in to dance with hers.

What are we doing? she wanted to ask. *Why are we doing this?*

Instead, she kissed him back, welcoming the reprieve from her mind, needing a break from the danger lurking around them.

Not smart.

I don't care.

Think.

No.

She gave in to the urges, her mouth moving against his without restraint. It felt so natural, so calming, so *real*. Every embrace between them seemed experienced somehow, as if they'd been kissing each other for years. She already knew him, his wants, his needs, his desires, and she unleashed that knowledge with her mouth.

He groaned, his hips grinding against hers, their passion no longer an act, but true. One palm remained against her waist, his other wrapping around her nape. He slid his lips across her cheek to her throat, his exhale warming her skin.

"It's either this or we both die," he whispered. "And I'm particularly fond of living."

"Issac?" she breathed, uncertain of what he meant.

"Forgive me, darling."

CHAPTER TWELVE

Broken Blood Laws

WHAT THE HELL WAS THOMAS FITZGERALD thinking sending Astasiya here? The bloody idiot threw her right into the middle of an Ichorian haven.

Fuck.

Issac wanted to torture and maim the imbecile, but first, he had to focus on protecting Astasiya.

By marking her.

His lips skimmed her pulse, the delectable scent taunting his senses. He meant to feed yesterday, or earlier this evening, but hadn't, his tastes for this woman all that drove his desires. And now he had her pinned against a wall, his mouth against the very artery he craved.

Consent mattered to him.

The rolling of her hips against his, despite the confusion underlying her voice, provided him with the acquiescence he required. Not all consensual cues were spoken; some were given through body language, and Astasiya's lithe form sang of approval, of a yearning just as fierce as his own.

"I need to bite you," he whispered. "To mark you as mine to protect you."

She swallowed, her hesitation palpable. After a beat, she breathed, "Okay."

His incisors ached from that one word alone, her blood so close, so potent, so *perfect*. He sank his teeth into her skin, breaking the surface swiftly and efficiently and eliciting a sharp squeak of protest from her throat. It was quickly replaced by a heady moan as he unleashed the endorphins into her bloodstream—a mechanism used by Ichorian kind to help subdue their prey.

Astasiya's arms tightened around him, her lower body arching and seeking purpose against his cock.

Mmm, what he wouldn't give to be inside her right now, to feel her slick walls tightening around him as he fucked her into oblivion. That was how he preferred to feed, but tonight required a more delicate introduction, one that would leave her well sated while only providing him with the sustenance he needed for survival.

She tasted amazing—sweet with a hint of fiery power that called to his very soul.

Such a unique flavor, unlike any he'd ever sampled.

Addicting.

Powerful.

A few pulls of her blood rejuvenated his spirit, energizing him in a way it shouldn't. Not yet. It usually took a few pints. But her essence, *fuck*, it was amazing. He swallowed more, savoring every drop, loving the way her heartbeat accelerated as if wanting him to devour her.

Astasiya groaned, her lower body pressing into his as the euphoria from his bite lit her on fire from within.

Fucking glorious.

A younger Ichorian would be lost to her responding passion, especially one who had gone so long without feeding, but he held himself in check, ensuring her pleasure while indulging in her blood.

Her head fell back against the wall, eyes glazing over in confused bliss. Balancing her between his torso and the wall, he slid his palm from her luscious ass to her exposed thigh, delighting in the energy traversing between them.

So perfect.

Delicious.

More…

He explored upward, eliciting a gasp from her as he found the lace undergarment adorning her hip. Her penchant for lingerie was fast becoming his favorite trait about her. If only he had time for a preview.

Alas, he'd kept the lights off for a reason.

If she saw the torture instruments surrounding them, she'd fall into a fainting fit.

"Issac." His name on her lips undid something inside of him, his control hanging on by a thread.

He wanted her more than anyone he could remember ever wanting before.

Maybe it was the moment.

This place.

Her.

He didn't know. Didn't care. He just wanted to rip the thong from her body and take her. Hard. Fast. To possess every inch of her and stake his claim. The possessive need overwhelmed him, calling to the predator inside and sending a tremble through his limbs.

This is dangerous.

Issac never felt this way for anyone, never even bedded a woman twice, but Astasiya had him wrapped up in a web of sensation carefully woven with feelings he couldn't even begin to define. As if his very purpose on this planet was to be with her.

I hardly know her.

But she's already mine.

The thought shook him to his core, forcing his teeth from her skin on a shudder so violent it was a wonder he kept her against the wall.

Her whimper confirmed he wasn't alone in the passionate struggle.

A weekend in bed. That's what they required, all he would allow, to kill this unhealthy obsession between them. But first, they had to survive the Conclave.

Issac traced the tempting line of lace beneath her dress, allowing himself one last indulgence. *So alluring. So gorgeous. So ready.*

"If we live through the night, I want to see what these look like without the dress," he whispered, his tongue tracing the marking on her throat. He left her purposely unhealed, needing everyone to know whom she belonged to, even if just for tonight. "If I had it my way, we'd be on our way to my bed right now, Astasiya. I want to devour every inch of you."

"Yes," she hissed, her agreement a welcome sound in his ear.

He took her mouth with his own, binding the agreement between them with his tongue.

She would be his—soon.

He would possess her.

Worship her.

Mark her in a way no other ever could.

And he promised her that with his lips, carving his name into her very being.

She was his, for now. No one else would touch her, taste her, or fuck her. Only him. Astasiya responded in kind, solidifying the vow, the heat pouring off her sinking into his skin, to his blood and soul.

This was never his intention, an infringement on his plans, but he cared fuck all about everything now. Only their survival mattered tonight.

An image of a clock flashed in his mind, courtesy of

Tristan. He followed it up with a vision of the door, a silent way of saying that he and Mateo both stood in the hallway waiting. Issac manipulated the picture to show five minutes on his wristwatch. He wasn't done here yet.

With a final thrust of his tongue, he broke the kiss and pressed his forehead to hers, loving the way her exhales feathered over his lips.

Since when do I enjoy embraces such as this?

He shook off the bizarre, undesired feelings and focused on the task at hand—remaining alive.

"Ground rules," he started softly. "Do not speak to anyone even if they speak to you. Do not comment on anything. Do not react. Do not scream. And most importantly, do *not* use your talent for persuasion. If you break any of these rules, we both die. Do you understand?"

Her pulse kicked up a notch, flaring the mark he left on her neck.

He frowned. His predatory response to mortal fear didn't appear, only a foreign urge to console her. *This woman has clearly broken me.*

Yes, part of the blame fell on him for her presence here. Had he properly warned her of his kind, she'd not have felt the need to explore. And now she might die as a result. Or worse.

However, Thomas deserved substantial credit for her being here.

Yet it was up to Issac to protect her.

And I will. No alternatives. She would not die here tonight.

He grabbed her hips and helped untangle her limbs from his body, encouraging her to stand on her own. Her nails dug into his suit jacket, her heart rate shooting higher. Terror poured off her, the reality of their situation settling between them.

Issac cupped her cheek and brushed his lips over hers softly, tenderly, providing the only semblance of support he could offer. "You're in the heart of my world right now,

Astasiya, and it's not kind to mortals. Especially those with psychic abilities."

Another kiss, this one lingering as her pulse slowly calmed, her grip on his clothing loosening, her body melting once again.

"You have to do what I say and trust me," he whispered against her mouth. "Can you do that?"

She remained quiet, her expression invisible in the dark. Predator he might be, but night vision was not one of his strengths. Unfortunate, considering the situation, as he enjoyed the way her eyes telegraphed her thoughts. Particularly as he couldn't access her mind in the way he could everyone else's.

"I'll protect you, Astasiya. You have my vow, but I need your cooperation for this to work."

"You need me alive," she finally said, her voice careful.

"I do," he agreed, his fingers sliding to the back of her neck, tightening. "But more importantly, I *want* you to live." An admission that cost him more than she'd ever know. Because he'd just confessed something to her he'd not wanted to disclose to himself.

I don't want to lose her.

A dangerous, lethal realization, one he would pay for dearly later.

Alas, that was a concern for another time. Tonight, he already had his hands full.

"Oh." A puff of air against his lips followed by more silence.

His palms began to perspire, his heart in his throat. They could not leave this room until she agreed. But if they were late…

He winced at the line of thought.

Being late was not an option. "Astasiya—"

"Yes," she interrupted. "I'll trust you. Tonight."

His shoulders fell, his forehead finding hers again. "Thank you." He meant it, something that seemed to surprise her, as she stilled against him.

He busied himself with fixing her dress, pulling the fabric over her ass—something she'd yet to do after he set her down—and running his hands over her sides to ensure it was in the right place. Then he adjusted his own clothes, specifically his pants, and ran his fingers through his hair.

The rumpled look would serve them well.

As would the fresh bite on her neck.

No one would question his intention with her, though they would be curious. Issac never brought pets to the Conclave. Ever. That alone would garner quite a few stares.

Issac pulled Astasiya's blonde waves over one shoulder, leaving his mark exposed. *This is the best I can do.* "For what it's worth, I'm sorry."

He opened the door before she could reply and linked his fingers through hers to pull her into the hallway before she could glance around the room they'd just occupied. It would only worsen matters, and he finally had a grasp of control between them, one he desired to keep.

Mateo and Tristan stood just where he expected them, the picture of elegance and superiority against the hallway wall.

"Miss Davenport," Mateo greeted, his charming grin in place as he openly tested Astasiya. "Lovely to finally meet you."

She glanced at Issac, deferring to him. That couldn't have been easy, but it confirmed she'd heard his rules. A good sign if they wanted to survive the night. Oddly, however, he missed her voice already. *Strange.*

"Oh, look at that. You trained your pet," Tristan said.

Issac gave the jackass a hard look. Sometimes he wished one could disown progeny, but turning Tristan into an Ichorian made him responsible for the bastard, even when he chose to be an ass. As he clearly intended to be now.

"Well done, Issac," Tristan added, smirking.

Issac lifted Astasiya's hand and placed a kiss against her wrist, a formal declaration of ownership in his world. "Astasiya, I believe you've already met Tristan. Might I introduce my other progeny, Mateo?"

She gave Mateo a small smile but didn't say anything.

Brilliant.

Unfortunately, this was just the easy part.

"Shall we, Sire?" Mateo asked, gesturing down the hall.

"Yes," Issac replied, squeezing Astasiya's hand once more for reassurance.

Tristan led the way, stopping when they reached the elevator and stepping inside when the opulent gold doors opened. These led to the underground. The only other way downstairs was through Osiris's private quarters. He owned this building. Hell, the Ichorian owned half the city. He was the most powerful being of their existence, and ancient, too.

Tension radiated through Astasiya's arm as they exited, her fledgling instincts no doubt picking up on the danger emanating from their destination.

Many humans died here.

Particularly those with unique abilities or those who had seen too much. Astasiya fell into both categories.

Issac despised the Conclave and its purpose—a standard show of status and authority, meant to establish the Ichorian hierarchy. He attended to protect his progeny from potential challenges. Centuries of lessons had taught his lesser brethren not to test his bloodline, but there were a select few who craved power beyond reason.

They entered through the traditional arch, the auditorium already bustling with darkly dressed Ichorians mingling near their designated seats. Aidan sat waiting in the front row with Anya draped across his lap. Clara and Nadia were behind him, engaged in conversation.

The three-story room fit over two hundred Ichorians comfortably, the marble columns and beige walls lending an opulent feel that belied the gruesome intention of the theater. And overseeing it all was a mural of angels painted into the ceiling in shades of blue.

Such blasphemy.

Aidan lifted his gaze from the gorgeous woman in his

lap to greet Issac as he approached. His shrewd gaze landed on Astasiya, the lack of surprise a result of having seen them waltz through the VIP lounge only thirty minutes prior.

"Osiris was disappointed that you refused his offer to entertain, Issac," Aidan said in lieu of a greeting, the words holding a hidden meaning. "But I reminded him of your proclivity for private affairs."

Hmm, yes, refusing Osiris's wishes earlier was a risky decision. Fortunately, the hunger radiating from Issac's pores explained his ungiving mood. Even the master Ichorian would have sensed and understood that.

Although, apparently, he'd expressed his frustration to Aidan. And if Issac followed Aidan's comments correctly, he'd handled the issue on Issac's behalf.

"Cheers," he said, thanking him for fixing the problem. The last thing Issac wanted was a required punishment ceremony.

"Seeing your new toy up close, I can understand why you want to keep her to yourself," Aidan added, his green eyes— identical to Lucian's eyes—danced appreciatively over the woman frozen at Issac's side.

"Might I introduce Astasiya?" he offered, glancing down at his gorgeous blonde. "Aidan is my Sire. He made me who I am today." He added the last part for her benefit because she wouldn't know what *Sire* meant.

"A pleasure, dear." Aidan gave her a gentle smile before focusing on the two men climbing the stairs. "Tristan, Mateo, how do you feel about the potential new addition?"

Interesting.

Issac never mentioned wanting to turn Astasiya—an impossibility due to her bloodline. Which meant Osiris must have inferred that little lie from Aidan's words during their conversation. It would have helped to explain why Issac didn't want to punish her before the masses. He wouldn't want a future progeny to appear weak in any way.

Clever ruse, Issac thought, his lips twitching.

"Thrilled," Tristan deadpanned. "Issac could use

another blonde in his life. Clearly." He stroked Clara's hair while giving Astasiya a pointed look.

All right. Issac narrowed his gaze. A conversation with his progeny would definitely be needed because that comment was unfounded and unnecessary.

Tristan didn't appear contrite in the slightest as he sat beside Clara. She immediately draped her legs over his and laid her head on his shoulder. Her empathetic ability left her craving physical contact, something Issac's best friend had no problem providing despite the platonic nature of their relationship.

"Well, I think she suits Issac's tastes," Mateo said. He gave Aidan a polite bow and took the chair beside Tristan.

Astasiya remained silent at Issac's side, eyes trained on him, awaiting instruction. He pulled her closer to brush his lips against her temple. His silent way of reassuring her. He followed it up with a squeeze, hoping she understood that he had a part to play next.

"Come," he said, his voice stern as he tugged her with him to the chair beside Aidan. He sat and yanked her down onto his lap, the show of force required for those around them.

Placement in the room indicated power. The rows at the back contained the weakest of their kind. Strength increased with each step toward the bottom, where the oldest and most powerful bloodlines resided. Aidan's ancient blood paired with his progeny's psychic talents put them in the front two rows.

"She's delicious, Issac," Anya murmured, her dark irises raking over Astasiya with abandon. Her full lips curved. "I'm Anya, by the way. I look forward to getting to know you very well."

"Let's not terrify the poor girl, love," Aidan murmured, nipping Anya's ear.

She swung her leather-clad legs around to straddle him, her arms wrapping around his shoulders. "Then entertain me a different way."

"Happily," Aidan replied against her mouth.

Issac chuckled and focused on situating Astasiya in a more comfortable position on his lap. Several interested gazes followed his movements, many accompanied with raised eyebrows. Most lovers shared chairs, making his choice typical. The fact that it was *him* sharing a chair was what garnered so much attention. In his over three hundred years of existence, he never brought a human with him to the Conclave.

Not that he minded.

Actually, he rather liked the way she felt against him, her head against his shoulder and her legs draped over his.

Mine.

At least for tonight.

Issac kissed the mark on her neck for everyone to see and secured her in his arms. He'd done what he could to ensure her survival.

The rest was up to her.

CHAPTER THIRTEEN

Master of Ceremonies

THE AUDITORIUM GAVE STAS THE CREEPS.

It sat deep underground, like some archaic ceremonial ring surrounding a center stage with one lonely chair. Oh, the adornments of gold and the white tile floor gave it an expensive feel, but she sensed the history lurking here.

The hint of death.

The terror.

And she had a front-row seat from Issac's lap.

This situation far outweighed the worst-case scenario she pictured for the evening—catching Issac in the act with another woman.

An underground colosseum filled with demons gathering around a black-and-white marble stage never once crossed her mind.

The throne in the center had seen better days. Blood stains. Charred material. A stone back. *People die there*, her instincts whispered. *They burn.*

She shivered as a vivid image of Owen flashed behind her eyes.

Unrecognizable head on a table.

Skin burnt to a crisp.

The horror he must have experienced...

What if—

A light tug on her hair drew her attention to the hard body beneath her and the arm wrapped around her waist. She met Issac's blue gaze and noted the admonishment there.

Control your reactions, he seemed to be saying. Likely because he could feel her pulse racing, or perhaps even heard it.

She reached up to touch the mark on her neck, only to have her wrist caught between his fingers and brought to his mouth for a nibble.

Don't, his eyes said.

Okay.

He released her hand and palmed her nape to pull her down for a kiss. Not the soul-destroying kind, but the comforting kind. A soft brush of his lips. An attempt to help her relax. Or perhaps he meant it as a show for their audience, because she could feel all their eyes on them. Observing. Studying. She shivered against him.

This whole room freaked her out.

All the attention on them didn't help.

I'm surrounded by demons.

The same demons who may have killed Owen.

The same demons who did *kill my parents.*

Oh God...

Was the culprit here? The man with the gold-flecked black eyes?

Her heart stopped.

What if he recognized her?

What if someone here knew about her friendship with Owen?

She'd end up in that chair, the throne in the center of the room.

"Mortals who overreact die, and they die badly."

Issac's palm squeezed, his lips trailing over her cheek to her ear. "Relax," he whispered. "Your fear is seducing the room."

Because *that* helped.

"You're mine, Astasiya. No one will touch you without my permission." He nipped her earlobe hard enough to bleed, something she assumed was more for show than a reprimand.

Or maybe he did mean to punish her.

She didn't know because she barely knew *him*.

"Trust me," he added on a breath, as if sensing her thoughts. *"Please."*

That last word gave her pause. It came off as a near-silent plea, a word she doubted Issac said often. She moved back to catch his gaze and caught a flicker of emotion before a mask of casual elegance took over his features.

The air chilled behind her.

Issac nodded his chin at the center, telling her to refocus and pay attention.

The show was about to start.

Osiris's ancient green eyes captured hers as she turned, freezing her in place. His lips curled into a cruel smile that had her digging her nails into the skirt of her dress. Issac remained completely relaxed beneath her, one arm wrapped around her to support her lower back, his other falling over her lap to conceal her hands. Her legs dangled off his left knee, leaving her cradled against him like a child. But as that seemed to be the norm of the room—she'd noticed several others in this position upon entering—she didn't question it.

Silence fell over the room, the auditorium lighting

dimming, confirming her theory about Osiris being the one in charge. Because he stood in the center of the marble floor, hands clasped before him, the stage lights flickering to life around him.

Several people—Ichorians, she guessed—scrambled to their seats.

Displeasure radiated from Osiris as he watched the latecomers take their seats, his lips flattened, his chiseled jaw clenched.

"Lucinda," he called into the stillness.

A curvy female seated a few chairs down from Aidan smiled, her painted lips a cruel red color that matched her hair. "My love?"

Osiris flicked a hand in the general direction of the last man to arrive.

Issac's arm tightened, providing her with a subtle warning as a lanky man went up in flames several rows back. His shriek tore through the room, sending her heart into a chaotic rhythm.

Fire.

Momma screaming.

Daddy writhing in agony.

That cruel man's laugh echoing across the yard.

A pinch to Stas's side brought her back to the auditorium, her gaze finding Issac's and holding for a beat. He gave nothing away, but that small touch told her he'd caught her drifting.

Deep red nails twirled in her peripheral vision, the fingers belonging to Lucinda. She circled them once, twice, then paused at Osiris's nod.

The flames died, sending the burnt man—still alive—to his chair on a grunt.

No one spoke or moved. Not even the women on either side of the victim, each of whom had specs of ash dusting their clothing.

They're used to this, Stas realized, swallowing. *This happens often.*

"Blake, is it?" Osiris's tone resembled frost in the already chilly room. "Next time, arrive punctually, or I'll let Lucinda play with you until the next Conclave."

The curvy female's lips curled with feline grace, her eyes screaming *sadistic bitch*. She wore a black teddy—similar to many others in the room—and a pair of metal cuffs linked to a set of chains. Stas followed the metal to the two collared males behind her.

Note to self: stay far away from that one.

"Now, where were we before I was so rudely interrupted?" Osiris continued, his commanding presence overpowering the room. "Right. Some of you may be aware that we recently underwent a breach in our beloved city. A Hydraian masquerading as a graduate student, of all things."

Stas stopped breathing.

Owen...

A Hydraian—something Issac had confirmed—graduate student.

What did Osiris mean by "breach"? Were Hydraians not allowed in the city? Like Fledglings?

"Now, you may be wondering, as I did, how he went undetected." Osiris paused as if waiting for someone to guess. No one replied. "It's quite troubling, really. You see, I've recently learned that one of our own helped him hide. And as you all know, that's a direct violation of our sacred Blood Laws."

Whispers flooded the room, ranging from outraged to shocked. Osiris appeared politely interested, but the slight twist of his mouth suggested he approved. No, not just approved, *expected* this reaction.

A theatrical man, thriving on chaos.

Issac twirled a strand of her hair around his finger, studying it with a bored expression. Not at all concerned or entertained by the proceedings. *An expert at controlling his facial tells.*

"Yes, shocking, I know," Osiris said over the crowd. "And what's more shocking, the culprit's currently sitting in this room."

The murmurs escalated, exciting the master of ceremonies. He grinned—the gesture charismatic yet underlined in evil intent, a contradiction that sent a chill down her spine. This man knew how to seduce a crowd, and he enjoyed it.

"So who would defy one of the oldest orders of our kind and assist a Hydraian?" He scanned the room while slowly rolling up the sleeves of his dark shirt, revealing tanned forearms corded in muscle. "Of course, I could demand the damned step forward, but where would be the satisfaction in that? I'm curious to see if anyone can work it out alone first. Whom here would you accuse?"

The shouts started immediately.

Some in foreign languages.

Some in English.

All including names.

Issac's chuckle vibrated Stas's side, his fingers still combing through her hair. "Well, this ought to be entertaining," he said.

"Indeed," Aidan agreed, his gaze roaming the room in interest. Anya seemed equally piqued.

They think this was fun?

The energy in the room shifted from calm stillness to chaos as pandemonium ensued. Threats littered the air, causing the hairs along Stas's arms to dance.

Magic.

She could taste it, the magnetism calling to her inner gift, itching her to play. Stas swallowed, her throat reminding her of cotton balls.

I need to get out of here.

It wasn't safe.

Issac's lips brushed her pulse, nipping at the bite on her neck. Surely, he could feel her heart racing. He probably wanted her to calm down. But how? Violence tinted the auras of every single person—demon—in this room. They wanted to argue, to brawl, to *harm.*

Osiris raised his hand, silencing the room instantly.

Sweat dotted Stas's spine despite the cold temperature of the auditorium, the lethal atmosphere humming over her skin. *Someone is going to die tonight.*

"It's fun to learn how we really feel about each other, isn't it? I imagine some of you may be leveling challenges later this evening, hmm?" He chuckled, that charismatic grin in place. "Alas, I failed to hear the guilty party's name among the accused. Not surprising, really. I never would have guessed it myself." His eyes danced tauntingly over the audience. "Well, before we get to that, another matter of business first. Mike?"

Stas's heart dropped to her stomach. *Mike.* She didn't want to see him again.

But the burly man sauntered into the room holding a metal leash. He gave it a harsh tug, eliciting a yelp from the other end.

Oh my God. Issac caught Stas's hand before she could lift it to her mouth, his arms tight around her, reminding her to remain calm.

But on the other end of that leash was a frail woman.

Her dark head bowed.

Dressed in chains.

Crawling across the floor like a fucking dog.

Stas's stomach heaved, the alcohol she'd imbibed earlier threatening to expunge itself onto the floor.

Issac squeezed her hand, not in a gentle or reassuring way, but in warning. Things were about to get worse. *Fucking fantastic.* She wasn't sure how much more she could take.

"What's your name, sweetheart?" Osiris asked, his voice deceptively gentle as he stroked the woman's sunken cheek. Her dark features and caramel skin hinted at the foundations of a beautiful woman. But whatever these assholes had done to her had turned her into a shell of skin and bones with no substance.

"*Fuck you.*" Despite the woman's frail condition, her voice carried through the dark room.

"Intriguing name," Osiris replied, inspiring several laughs from the audience. "A result of conditioning, I'm sure." His smile died as he looked to the man holding the metal leash. "Now, who was it that brought her to your attention?"

"Jarod."

"Ah yes, Jarod." All part of the show, he searched the crowd and flashed a jovial grin at a tall male lurking near the back of the room. "Good man, please come join us."

Jarod meandered down to the stage with long, sure strides. He bowed low, kissing the olive skin of Osiris's hand before standing upright.

"You found this one in a brothel, yes?" Osiris asked.

"Yes, S-sire," Jarod stuttered, his meek voice not at all matching his impressive build.

"Only adds to her name." Osiris smirked at the laughs his crude statement garnered. "In any case, you noticed she had a peculiar ability, did you not?"

Stas's lungs stopped working.

A gifted mortal surrounded by Ichorians.

"It's customary for one in my position to kill you on sight," Issac had said what felt like years ago.

Was Stas about to learn what he meant by that? To witness exactly what his kind did to fledglings such as herself?

"I-I did, Sire. Her t-touch was hypnotic," Jarod stammered.

Stas frowned. A prostitute with a hypnotic touch? How was that considered evidence?

"Ah, how very intriguing. Have you or the others been able to re-create it, Mike?" Osiris asked.

Mike flashed a lascivious glance at the woman. "I don't know about hypnotic, but her touch sure is inspiring."

Ugh, gross.

"Not exactly proof, then." Osiris tapped his chin. "If only we had someone here who could sense immortal bloodlines." He smiled, his focus shifting over the crowd with a knowing gleam. "Oh, but we do, don't we? Sierra, love, why don't you join us?"

Chapter Fourteen

A Gift for Words

ICE HELD STAS CAPTIVE, REFUSING HER THE ability to move or breathe.

An Ichorian with the ability to sense immortal bloodlines.

Fledglings.

Me.

Issac had listed all the ground rules, never once mentioning that someone might be able to sense her. An oversight? Or because he didn't consider the approaching woman a threat?

He didn't seem at all bothered, his body just as relaxed as before. He was even drawing patterns against her thigh with his thumb.

She forced herself to inhale. If he wasn't concerned, then

she would be fine. Right? She exhaled through her nose. Okay, yes, this would be fine. Everything would be fine.

If she told herself that enough, she might just believe it.

"What do you think, dear?" Osiris asked as a woman with black slacks and a tank top joined him on the stage. She had to be the most conservatively dressed woman in the room.

Something about her struck Stas as familiar. Short blonde spikes, metal bar through her nose, short, plump, hmm… *Where do I know you from?*

Sierra's hand wavered a little, belying her confident stance, as she touched the brunette. Anticipation stirred in the air, everyone awaiting her verdict.

"I sense nothing, Sire," Sierra finally said, releasing the woman.

"Really?" Osiris's expression indicated surprise to the crowd, but it appeared too contrived. The slight flattening of the mouth, imperceptible to the back of the room but noticeable to those in the front, suggested he held something back.

Or maybe Stas was just starting to understand his tells. Something about him struck her as familiar, too. Like she *knew* him from a different life. *I'm clearly losing my mind.*

"She's not a fledgling, Sire." Sierra bowed her head and turned to leave, a flush creeping into her cheeks.

Oh, shit.

In two seconds, she would spot Stas.

Would she recognize—

"*Stop.*" Power buzzed through the room, singeing Stas's senses. It felt so familiar, calling to her own ability to compel. "Don't move until I tell you to."

Stas's lips parted, understanding finally dawning. She'd felt the urge to obey once before tonight. To feel it again contradicted coincidence.

Osiris can definitely *compel.*

Just like me.

Only his gift appeared to be far more powerful.

"Carl, join us." Another demand, tightening her stomach into knots.

No restraints. The man just wielded his gift like a whip, controlling the room with mere words.

This was one of Stas's darkest concerns—that she could someday give in to the sinful instincts brewing inside her. Compelling others could easily become addictive, and a very wicked part of her enjoyed it.

A lanky male dressed in the trademark black strode down the stairs across the room, his expression blank. He didn't acknowledge Sierra as he stepped onto the stage, merely arched a thick, bushy brow at Osiris after bowing his head in respect.

"Are you aware of your progeny's evening activities?" Osiris asked.

"Sierra bartends at Louie's."

Stas's lips parted at Carl's mention of Owen's favorite bar. She went there regularly with him. *Is that how I know Sierra?*

"Yes, indeed she does," Osiris agreed. "And do you know who was a frequent visitor of the establishment?"

Oh God… Stas had been right before. *This is all about Owen.*

Issac's thumb drew a circle against her lower abdomen, his touch burning through her dress. *Remain calm*, it said. *Don't react.*

She swallowed, trying to heed his advice, recalling all his warnings.

Breathe, she told herself. *Breathe.*

"Owen Angelton," Osiris said, confirming what she already knew. "You see, I've been trying to piece it all together, and I recently discovered that he frequented your progeny's club on a weekly basis. Yet, she never mentioned a word to me. Interesting considering her ability, is it not?"

Carl's stony mask didn't falter, his beady black eyes refusing to acknowledge the trembling woman frozen a few steps away from him. Fear radiated from Sierra, suggesting she would run if she could.

But Osiris's persuasion kept her feet glued to the floor, forcing her to face the open ridicule growing in the crowd. They were all piecing together the accusation, realizing that Sierra had been the Ichorian who aided Owen. And they were not happy.

"Jarod, you're a telekinetic, right?" Osiris asked.

The lanky man's nod was unsteady. "B-but only with objects of a certain weight and within d-direct line of s-sight."

"Right. Useless. Go back to your seat." A cold assessment that had Jarod cringing, his shoulders hunching over in defeat.

Stas almost pitied him. Almost.

At least until she remembered the woman on the floor covered in chains.

The bastard deserved a lot worse than being called out for his lacking ability.

"Oh, and, Jarod?" Osiris called as the cowering male started up the stairs. "Good prostitutes are all hypnotic. That's how they make their money. Try not to waste our time at the next Conclave."

Stas half expected him to use the fiery redhead to underline his statement, but he flicked his wrist in dismissal instead, his focus returning to the "hypnotic prostitute" on the floor.

"Now, what do I do with you?" he mused, tapping his chin. "It's possible you're gifted, but how will I know for sure? Can't trust anyone these days. Decisions, decisions." Movement from Stas's right startled her. Aidan's hand waved just once, low over the armrest, but enough to draw notice. "You have a suggestion, Aidan?"

All eyes turned in their direction, causing her skin to crawl. The lack of response in Issac's posture indicated he wasn't surprised by Aidan's boldness. Osiris seemed to share the sentiment, his expression showing mild interest.

"An auction," Aidan said.

He couldn't mean to auction off a human? Like an object?

Except the gleam in Osiris's gaze told her that was exactly what Aidan had just suggested. He seemed quite pleased—too pleased—by the idea. "When?" he asked.

"After the trial. To lighten the mood and perhaps inspire the famished?" Aidan spoke the words so calmly, as if they were debating the weather, not a mortal life. Anya demonstrated her approval by nipping Aidan's lip when he finished speaking, and he flashed her an indulgent smile before redirecting his focus to the stage.

Demons.

No, vampires.

They were talking about auctioning off an innocent woman as if she were property, not a living, breathing human being. *Who does that?*

"Excellent." Osiris snapped his fingers in Mike's direction. "Give the girl to Aidan. He'll watch her until the auction."

"Happily," his minion said, tugging harshly on the leash.

The woman gagged, her knees scraping over the ground as she crawled along behind him. "Assss," she hissed under her breath, causing Stas's eyebrows to lift.

This female was a fighter. Being beaten, starved, and dragged around by a metal leash hadn't dampened her fire in the slightest, as was evidenced as she continued to curse and mutter obscenities at Mike.

"Charming," Issac remarked, his tone cold and chilling her to the bone.

No remorse.

No concern.

Just a flat comment followed by a snort of disgust as the prisoner growled crudely at Anya—who had taken control of the leash.

"Indeed," Aidan replied, sounding just as frigid as Issac.

"Hmm, I don't know," Anya murmured, running her gloved fingers through the woman's dark mass of tangled hair. "I rather like the feisty ones."

Stas's stomach churned at the display, her blood freezing in her veins.

"Do try to contain your gifts, yes?" Osiris said, his affectionate gaze on Anya.

She waved her leather-clad hand at him, mischievousness dancing across her striking features. "I'm wearing protection."

Several chuckles vibrated around the room, including one from Issac. His hold around her abdomen loosened just enough for him to draw his fingers up and down her side.

The touch warmed her through the fabric, confusing her instincts. Part of her longed to cuddle closer, to seek his comfort and lean her head against his shoulder. Yet logic held her in place.

I should hate him, not trust him.

Except he'd warned her tonight would not be easy. And it wasn't his fault she sat here.

No, the blame lay at Tom's feet and her own. She never should have come here. If only—

Osiris's hand clamped around Sierra's throat, freezing Stas midbreath. He dragged the woman backward and tossed her unceremoniously into the chair while Carl observed emotionlessly.

Oh God...

The worst had yet to come, the truth of that lurking in Osiris's smile as he addressed the crowd. "Let the trial begin."

~*~

Sierra's screams echoed through the room as Osiris slid the razor across her mutilated skin.

This was one of the ancient immortal's favorite methods of torture, something he reserved for those he planned to kill. It didn't matter what the woman said, she would die tonight.

Astasiya remained rigid on Issac's lap, her nails biting

into her palms. She'd clearly ascertained that Osiris could compel, something the Ichorian had made obvious when he commanded Sierra to sit in the throne without restraints while he skinned her alive.

A violent shudder had rocked Astasiya as a result, her understanding and horror palpable.

Issac had done everything he could to distract her from the stage before them. Fondling a lover during a ceremony such as this was expected and allowed, as many of his kind preferred the darker pleasures in life. Not Issac, but his brethren didn't need to know that.

He nipped Astasiya's shoulder, shifting her focus from the gruesome scene back to him. Her dilated pupils showcased her terror while her heartbeat remained normal. He hoped that was because of the diversions he continued to offer her—little kisses, bites, and touches.

"Why was Owen in New York City?" Osiris demanded for the fifteenth or sixteenth time. The bastard could just compel the information from Sierra, but he adored entertaining. And Issac's brethren thirsted for blood, furious at one of their own for breaking the precious Blood Laws.

Fucking archaic laws.

They were established after the Treaty of 1747 as a defensive measure. The Hydraians had grown too powerful, hence the reason the Ichorians lost. So the new plan was to prevent the Hydraians from amassing more power by cutting them off at the source.

Forbidding the creation of fledglings meant no new Hydraians could exist.

The rules against consorting with Hydraians was just an additional measure to ensure Ichorians and Hydraians didn't develop any *new* partnerships. Those of certain birthrights were grandfathered in, their relationships allowed to remain so long as they didn't break the treaty. Ergo Issac and Aidan were permitted to contact Lucian and the others.

Of course, that didn't mean Issac could invite the

Hydraian Elders to New York City.

And that definitely didn't grant him the right to a relationship with Astasiya—a known fledgling.

Complicated laws.

Bullshit rules.

With very serious consequences.

"I don't know!" Sierra screamed, referring to Owen's purpose in the city.

"Truth," three women said in unison. They stood just behind Osiris, having been called down for their aptitudes for mind reading. Whenever one of them expressed even the slightest hint of doubt in Sierra's answer, Osiris repeated the question while removing another layer of skin.

Poor Sierra would have very little skin left to remove soon. Osiris had already divested her of her clothing and scalped her. The areas he focused on now were ones that would drive a sane person mad. And the hysteria in Sierra's gaze said she was well on that road to insanity.

"A pity he didn't tell you why he was in New York," the ancient murmured as he wiped the razor against a towel Carl held beside him.

Sierra had divulged very little information, only noting that Owen had paid her handsomely to keep his presence a secret and to provide him with notice of any upcoming Conclaves. Everything else she mentioned was inconsequential.

Osiris clearly knew she was out of details, the last several rounds meant to be a statement more than anything else. A lesson to those considering disobedience.

Like me.

Alas, Issac chose his path centuries ago, choosing to ally with the Hydraians while remaining in New York as an informant. Because while a treaty may exist between the races, everyone knew it was temporary.

One day, the agreement would fall. And Issac wanted to be able to provide his family and friends ample notice of that day.

So he played this game, attended the Conclaves, and worked his own angles.

A leathery bit of skin fell to the floor—the remainder of Sierra's thigh.

Astasiya swallowed, her attention having drifted back to the throne. Another question hung in the air, this one about whether or not Sierra knew of anyone else in the city aiding Hydraians. She responded in the negative between shrieks while the hive of mind readers confirmed her truthfulness.

Issac and Aidan were very good at keeping their personal affairs private.

No one suspected a thing about them, and they would keep it that way.

Osiris sighed theatrically and stood, trading his weapon for a clean towel from Carl. Having Sierra's maker involved in the ceremony only added to the punishment because, technically, the man could speak up on her behalf, attempt to negotiate a lesser sentence. That he said nothing spoke volumes about the kind of immortal he'd become and what little care he had for those he'd turned.

Issac would never allow his progeny to suffer in this manner.

Aidan wouldn't either.

"Tristan, would you mind?" Osiris asked while cleaning his hands with the bottle of water Carl had brought him.

"Of course, Sire," Tristan replied, instantly silencing the room.

This was why no one challenged Aidan's bloodline. Between Issac's aptitude for manipulating vision and Tristan's ability to control sound, they were a formidable team. Couple that with Anya's gift for killing by touch and Aidan's gift for intelligence and strategy, and they were unstoppable.

Astasiya shifted, her wide eyes lifting to Tristan in wonder and awe, clearly grasping what he'd just done.

Tristan sat lounging in his chair, petting Clara's arm. He gave Astasiya an indulgent look. "Impressed, pet?" he taunted, mouthing the words at her.

Her responding expression said, *Yes.*

Issac drew his finger down her spine and pressed his lips to her throat again, claiming his mark. It should have stirred unease inside him, yet all he felt was immense satisfaction. He was enjoying this charade far too much, but fuck if he cared enough to stop. After the evening they'd endured together, he'd earned a little pleasure in their situation.

"I'm assuming no one else has any final questions or last words for the accused?" Osiris's voice carried an ominous chill.

Sierra's seconds are numbered.

Issac wrapped his palm around Astasiya's neck, forcing her to study him, not the stage. She didn't need to see this next part.

Sierra's mouth parted on a silent scream, her eyes wild. She couldn't move, Osiris's command having paralyzed her from the neck down. He'd only allowed her head to move, requiring her voice, which Tristan now silenced.

A horrible, excruciating way to die.

Issac couldn't even imagine how much it had to hurt to remain seated from a command while in such pain. Osiris certainly knew how to put on a show.

"Well, hearing none, I think it's time to deliver punishment," Osiris said.

Because skinning the woman alive had clearly not been enough for him or the audience. Howls of approval followed, eliciting a grin from the mastermind on the stage.

Meanwhile, Astasiya began to tremble, something Issac attempted to dispel by tightening his grip on her neck. She remained cradled against him, her ass on his groin, her legs over the armrest. There was only so much he could do to hide her reactions, such as the goose bumps pebbling up her bare legs.

He nuzzled her throat again, attempting to mask her reaction as one of arousal, not fear—the two were closely related, after all.

"Sierra, Ichorian daughter of Carl, I find you guilty of breaking one of our most sacred laws," Osiris announced, his authoritative voice adding to the theatrics. "Consorting with Hydraians is a crime punishable by death. Carl, as is custom, I leave you with the honors. You know what to do."

Ah, a way to punish them both. Forcing an Ichorian to kill his progeny was a punishment in itself, one Issac could never accept.

But Carl left the room without a word, returning several minutes later with a ceremonial sword and a bottle of alcohol.

There were only two ways to kill an Ichorian—destroy the blood flowing through their veins or poison one by forcing them to ingest Hydraian blood.

Sierra had already started to heal enough for her mind to grasp Carl's intentions, her eyes pleading with her soundless mouth. He ignored her and instead showed the overproof hard liquor label on the bottle to the audience. Upon a few murmurs of approval, he upended the contents over her head.

Issac's palm slickened against Astasiya's skin, but his grasp remained firm. She would not handle this next part well.

Hell, she'd not handle *this* part well.

Sierra's agony was palpable, the alcohol sliding over her exposed flesh.

Despite anticipating the scene, Issac's stomach still churned. He'd witnessed this dozens of times over his life span, but it never grew easier. Osiris, however, seemed quite pleased. Eager, even.

Carl picked up Sierra's discarded shirt and pulled a lighter from his pocket, flicking it to life and lighting the fabric on fire.

This was the part Issac sought to protect Astasiya from, having noticed her reactions to Lucinda's little trick earlier.

Astasiya is afraid of fire.

Given the history of her parents, he couldn't blame her.

Carl tossed the flaming shirt onto Sierra's lap, the alcohol spreading the blaze rapidly over her form, destroying her. And still, she didn't move because of Osiris's command.

Astasiya stopped breathing, sensing the massacre behind her. Issac pressed his lips to hers, again attempting to hide her reactions from the room. He refused to let her end up on that stage, no matter the cost. Everyone would assume him infatuated, an oddity in his life, but one he accepted.

Consider me mad with lust. It's not exactly a lie.

He held Astasiya to him when she tried to pull back, her fear heightening.

Not yet, darling, he wanted to tell her. *Give it another minute.*

The sword glinted in the light, Carl slicing it through the air, putting Sierra out of her misery while her body still burned.

Astasiya's nails bit into the jacket covering Issac's forearm, which lay across her lap. He released her mouth and neck, having kept his lips there to keep her from screaming. She immediately turned, her spine rigid as she found Sierra's mutilated corpse.

Fortunately, the majority of the fire had died off, leaving her burnt and headless in the chair. Similar to Owen.

Which meant someone with Conclave knowledge had killed him. The mystery nagged at Issac, not feeling right. This whole evening had been about the Hydraian lurking in New York City, Osiris's displeasure over not knowing clear.

So who killed the Hydraian if not an Ichorian?

Osiris kicked Sierra's head across the floor, giving it an offending glance for having soiled his shoes. "Let this be a lesson to you, Carl. I allowed you to clean up your mess this time. I won't be so lenient on your next offense."

"Thank you, Sire." Carl bowed, then left the room, sword and bottle in hand. The body continued to smolder in his wake.

Astasiya's breathing evened, but she continued to clutch Issac's suit jacket. He flattened his palm against her thigh, giving it a gentle squeeze to remind her of his presence. If it helped, she didn't show it, her focus on the stage.

If only he could tap into her mind, he could alter the scene before her, help to lessen the impact. Although, he suspected she wouldn't appreciate that. His blonde was a fighter, the type of woman who chose to face her fears rather than run from them. That much he ascertained last night at the gala. She could have demanded he take her home and answer her questions, but she stayed beside him instead.

Osiris clapped his hands twice, his smile wide. "Now, let's have some real fun."

Astasiya tilted her head, her attention returning to Issac. The purpose of tonight's lesson lurked in her gaze, as did a hint of dismay. He'd told her during their second meeting that it was customary for one in his position to kill her kind. She now understood just what he risked in breaking that rule.

Why? she seemed to be asking.

Of course, she already knew the answer—he needed her alive. But it did indeed go deeper than that. Deeper than he cared to admit, even to himself.

"You all know how this works," Osiris continued, gesturing to the prostitute and giving Anya a knowing smile. "Bring her forward."

"Happily." Anya stood, her stilettos clacking over the marble as she dragged the human along behind her. Mike gingerly accepted the handle, careful not to touch Anya despite her wearing gloves. Rather than return to her seat, she remained on the stage.

Osiris arched a brow at Aidan, who shrugged. "She decided she wants a new toy. You know I can't say no to her."

"It's going to make this a very short auction," Osiris replied, glancing around the auditorium. "Is there anyone here who wishes to duel Anya for property rights?"

Astasiya had gone stiff again, but it wasn't so much fear

Issac sensed from her as it was rage. While he preferred that emotion to terror, he needed her to calm down and conveyed that with a nip against her ear. She startled and glanced back at him again.

Calm down, he told her with his eyes.

"Anyone?" Osiris called again, sounding disappointed.

Anya had slipped off a single glove to study her ruby nails. "Cowards, the lot of them."

Osiris chuckled. "I think everyone is tired of dying by your hand, dear."

She pouted. "But it's been so long since my last challenge. I'm starting to get bored."

"Perhaps you can find entertainment in your new pet," Osiris offered, his tone and manner indulgent. She could literally poison the blood through a single touch, a rare gift that he adored and used on occasion.

"Does that mean I win?" Such a brilliant actress, she even sounded hopeful.

"Yes, dear. I don't think anyone is willing to take the risk." He sounded disappointed, but he grinned as Anya skipped over to the woman on the floor. She crouched down to trace her bare finger over the woman's mouth.

"Ow!" She yanked her hand back and waved it in the air. "She bites!" Her dark head swiveled in their direction. "Oh, Aidan, she's perfect."

The fond smile he gave her belied his shaking head. "I don't know what I'm going to do with you, sweetheart."

Issac smirked, feigning amusement for the charade at play. "I think we all have a pretty good idea of exactly what you'll do with her."

Astasiya flinched, clearly not appreciating the humor in his tone. It was all for show, but she'd have no way of knowing that since he never explained any of this to her.

"Anya's touch is lethal," he murmured against her ear as the woman in question dragged the human across the stage again. "That's why no one will challenge her."

"Sit," Anya commanded before sliding back into Aidan's

lap.

The human on the floor didn't exactly obey so much as collapse into a heap, her fight depleting.

Just hang on, Issac thought at her. *You'll be all right.*

"Well, this wasn't nearly the diversion I hoped for," Osiris mused. "Does anyone have any grievances they wish to air? Punishment to deliver, perhaps?" He blinked long lashes in their direction on the latter inquiry, his question pointed.

No way in hell was Issac dragging Astasiya up on that stage.

Knowing how Osiris preferred to play, Issac maintained a bored expression, neither shaking his head nor nodding. If he showed no outward reaction, the older Ichorian would grow bored.

Several shouts graced the air, a disagreement being voiced from across the room. Osiris shifted focus with interest, his curiosity piqued.

Ah, a power struggle.

Issac nearly rolled his eyes at the blatant stupidity of his brethren.

Energy flickered across the auditorium, Ichorians using psychic powers to dismantle their challengers. A few ended up on the stage, fighting to prove their worth and status.

No one attempted to test their luck with Aidan's line.

Astasiya calmed with each passing minute, seemingly more comfortable with Ichorians harming one another. She almost appeared bored by the end, or perhaps just so emotionally exhausted that she could no longer feel.

It'd been hours since she last spoke. Issac found he missed her voice. He missed *her*.

Brushing his lips against her temple, he guided her closer to his chest, encouraging her to lay her head against his shoulder. She didn't fight him, didn't even flinch, her body melting into his as if it always belonged there.

Definitely fatigued.

It took significant energy to suppress natural instincts,

something he knew all too well from centuries of experience.

Fights continued throughout the room, spoiling the pristine marble floors.

Blood.

Smoke.

Unmentionables.

Astasiya seemed oblivious to it all, having lost herself to her own thoughts. It concerned him to see her so broken, the mental abuse of the evening taking its toll.

Don't leave me, darling. We're not through yet.

The challenges withered, the bloodshed done.

Osiris seemed pleased with the outcome, enough that he excused the room, ending what had turned into a very long Conclave.

Finally.

Issac roused Astasiya on his lap, her eyes having fallen closed some time ago. She blinked, her green irises holding a dark note that disturbed him. He would fix that soon.

"She did well," Osiris said, approaching them.

"Mmm, yes, she did." Issac nuzzled her neck, expecting her pulse to spike, but it remained steady. *Too steady.* As if she no longer cared, the night having deadened all her instinctive reactions.

Not good…

Osiris assessed her slowly, thoroughly. Aside from a shallow swallow, she didn't outwardly react, both pleasing and concerning Issac.

Had she figured out how to mask her reactions already? Or had tonight left her so fractured she could no longer feel?

"Any idea what her talent will be?" Osiris asked.

Issac nodded, having already thought of a clever truth should this question arise. "She has an affinity for language, so likely something vocal."

"Fascinating. Do let me know when it's done." Osiris's statement implied he approved of Astasiya joining the

Ichorian ranks.

Too bad that was an impossibility. "Of course," Issac said out loud, knowing those were the words his leader desired.

Osiris refocused on Astasiya and gave her a doting smile. "It was nice to make your acquaintance, young one. I look forward to knowing you better in the centuries to come." He didn't wait for a response, meandering toward the other side of the room to begin chatting with another group.

CHAPTER FIFTEEN

The World Has Gone Silent

"WE'RE DISMISSED." The words were a breath against Stas's ear. They should have elicited relief, but she felt nothing.

For years, she knew this world existed and what it could do, had witnessed the darkest heart of it when her parents were burned alive. But tonight's live horror show took her expectations to a whole new level of hell.

Pure evil existed here.

Demons.

Blood.

Torture.

Strong hands went to her hips, helping her to stand on numb legs. An arm wrapped around her waist, holding her

197

close to a hard, masculine body.

Lips brushed her neck, words whispered in her ear.

She heard nothing.

Understood nothing.

They started walking, Issac's palm against her lower back, his body between her and the macabre scene. Not that it helped. Sierra's remains were forever burned into Stas's mind.

So similar to Owen.

To her parents.

She shivered, thinking about how much this world had taken from her. And she didn't understand why. Not entirely, anyway. Something about laws and an ancient history she knew nothing about.

Issac possessed all the answers.

Do I still want those details?

Not right now. Maybe not ever.

The night air ruffled her hair. *We're outside.* Another fact that should have calmed her, yet nothing happened. Her heartbeat remained a dull thud in her ears, her hands cool, her body moving without her direction.

Issac opened a door, guiding her inside and onto a leather seat. *His car.* He could take her anywhere he wanted. That should have provoked some semblance of fear, a question, *anything*, but she didn't have the energy to try. What did it matter? This world was destined to kill her anyway.

On a throne.

Surrounded by hungry demons.

Having her skin stripped from her bones.

Burnt to a crisp.

She gagged, the acrid scent still very much alive in her nose. God, would she ever rid it from her clothes? Her hair? Her *skin*?

Issac's palm squeezed her thigh, his other hand on the steering wheel, already driving. How did she keep losing time? Or was he moving faster than her mind could comprehend?

She closed her eyes, too exhausted to debate the semantics.

"Astasiya, what did I tell you about using your persuasive talent?" Daddy's brow lifted in that way that meant she was in big trouble.

She bunched her mouth to the side, thinking. "Not to use it on strangers," she admitted slowly. "But I wanted that ice cream and he wouldn't give it to me."

"That's not a reason to demand it."

She folded her arms. It seemed like a good reason to her. The ice cream man had chocolate and she looooved chocolate. "But you demand Mom do things alllll the time that she doesn't want to do because you want something."

Momma didn't say anything, but her eyes sparkled as she waited for Daddy to reply.

"What I do with your mom is very different and private. Do I persuade strangers?"

Astasiya pinched her lips again and slowly shook her head. No. "We don't show strangers."

"And why don't we persuade strangers?" he asked, his voice soft and soothing.

"'Cause they don't understand and can make bad things happen."

And bad things did happen.

They died.

A warm palm cupped her cheek, stirring her from her memories. A blink outside showed they were parked near Lizzie's building.

Stillness surrounded them, the late hour leaving Seventy-Ninth Street quiet.

"Do you want to talk about it?" Issac asked softly, his thumb tracing her skin.

She frowned. *Do I?* "I…" She cleared her dry throat, the sandpaper texture a result of hours of disuse. "No." She didn't want to talk at all.

Issac studied her for a long moment before opening the door. He appeared beside her too quickly, pulling her from her seat and guiding her to the building's entrance without a word.

"Key?" he asked.

He didn't remark on the placement as she pulled the item from her bra. She hadn't wanted to carry a bag tonight. Good thing, too, because she probably would have left it behind and then that psychopath would have her address. If he didn't already.

She trembled at the thought, Issac's palm against her skin doing nothing to dispel the chill overwhelming her body.

Osiris knows my name.

What if he came for her? Did he sense her fledgling status?

"Do let me know when it's done?"

What did that even mean?

"Is Elizabeth home?" Issac asked. They were already outside her door.

She frowned. When did they even go into the elevator?

"Astasiya," he murmured, his hand on her face again. "Is Elizabeth home?"

Lizzie? Stas shook her head. Her roommate volunteered one Saturday night a month at a children's shelter in Harlem. She wouldn't be back until late tomorrow morning.

Which meant Stas would alone tonight.

Her stomach churned at the realization, the nightmares already playing behind her eyes. *Oh God…*

The door opened.

She disabled the alarm on instinct, moving on autopilot to the kitchen. *Water.* She needed a big glass of it. Followed by some alcohol.

Issac followed her, his jacket having disappeared with his tie.

Did he leave them in the car? Her closet? She couldn't even remember if he wore them inside.

Whatever. She chugged her cup, not caring at all what he thought of her inelegance, and poured herself another. It cooled her throat, easing the burn with each gulp. She closed her eyes, her shoulders falling, her back resting against the refrigerator.

Her stomach rumbled, the tightening in her gut reminding her how many hours had passed since her last meal. As if she could eat something now, or ever again. The mere thought of it made her nauseous.

No. No food.

"Talk to me, Astasiya," Issac murmured, the heat of his body seeping into her pores as he stood beside her.

She didn't look at him.

Didn't reply.

Because she had no idea what to say. Or perhaps she had too much to say.

"Please, love." He tucked her hair behind her ear, his touch lingering against her neck.

His bite.

God, she had a fucking vampire in her kitchen.

No, a demon.

An Ichorian.

Whatever the fuck any of that even meant. They burned people alive after skinning them. Certainly *not* angels despite what Issac had told her about descending from one. *Seraphim.*

She nearly laughed, the hysterical summarization taunting her sanity.

"Talk to me," he urged, his thumb tracing the column of her throat. "I miss your voice."

He misses my voice? He was the one who told her she couldn't speak all night.

Fucking rules.

Laws.

Trials.

A tear slipped from her eye that he caught with his thumb, brushing it to the side. His lips pressed against her forehead, his arms wrapping around her as he pulled her into a hug.

She couldn't return the embrace, her arms too stiff, the

glass still in her hand.

"I never meant for you to witness any of that," he whispered, his hand rubbing her back. "It's a harsh world, but there are moments of light. If you allow me, I'll introduce you to some of them."

Stas snorted. *Light? Yeah, right.*

He sighed, pulling back to cup her cheeks between his hands, his dark eyes capturing hers as they opened. "Please tell me what you're thinking."

Her eyebrows rose. "You want to know what I'm thinking?" The words sounded normal now, unlike in the car, her throat properly working again. But they were also edged in an incredulity she couldn't hide.

Relief flourished in his features. "Yes, I very much would."

"Okay." She could do that. "I'm thinking about this." She pointed to the bite mark on her neck. "And about how Ichorians are apparently vampires, not angels. I have no idea what the fuck a Hydraian is, but obviously, they're not welcome here. And helping one, or a fledgling like me, earns the culprit a death sentence. But not just any standard sentence. No, you're burned alive. Like my parents. And Owen."

Images of charred flesh flashed behind her eyes. Fuck, she felt queasy. Like, really, really queasy.

She spun to set the glass in the sink and gripped the counter beside it, lowering her forehead to the cool marble. Issac gathered her hair away from her neck, the air cooling her skin.

Stas swallowed once. Twice. Calming her insides and willing the contents of her stomach to stay there.

"Your parents were murdered in the same style as Owen and Sierra?" he asked softly.

Of course he chose that topic. "Yes."

"You witnessed it?"

"I was hiding in the fucking trees while that monster tortured and maimed my mother, then set my father on fire for her to watch." Her knees wobbled, her mother's screams haunting her thoughts. Stas had wanted to go to her, to help her, but a hand had held her back. *Whose?* she wondered for the millionth time. Her mind refused her, only providing her with a partial memory that felt altered on some level she couldn't understand. Psychologically she understood it was a defense mechanism, her seven-year-old self's way of protecting her, but one day, she'd break down that wall and remember everything.

She rolled her forehead against the marble, aware that she must look deranged, and not caring. The cool texture felt good against her clammy skin.

"It's believed that Ichorians descend from a cursed line of fallen angels, and the curse requires my kind to drink human blood to survive. Not daily, or even weekly, but enough to remain breathing. Some indulge in it more than others." Issac's thumb brushed her pulse. "This mark declares you as mine."

Startled by his admission, she stopped moving her head. "Why?"

"To protect you."

She straightened slowly, his words slowly registering.

He gripped the counter on either side of her hips as she turned to face him. "Do you want to know how a fledgling is created?" he asked.

She nearly rolled her eyes but refrained due to the headache brewing behind them. "You know I do."

"By a male Ichorian parent, which means your father was an Ichorian. The fact that you *knew* him as a child tells me he broke several Blood Laws. He not only created a fledgling, meaning you, but he also allowed you to live. I'm guessing that is what brought about his death sentence. Your mother was just a casualty of being with the wrong man."

She stiffened, her hands tightening into fists at her sides. "Are you saying it's their fault for being brutally murdered? That they brought about their own fate by creating me?"

"Of course not. Their fate was the fault of antiquated Ichorian laws."

Not what she expected him to say. She relaxed marginally, her limbs beginning to tingle from fatigue. She really should have removed her shoes at the door. Because *ow*.

"So, you don't agree with the rules," she said, noting his tone.

"You being alive makes that obvious."

True. Except… "You're only keeping me alive because I'm the *perfect pawn*." The words tasted bitter in her mouth, as did the memory of him saying them. Was that only last night? Because it felt like a year had passed since the gala.

"Hmm, I see that bothered you." He tilted his head, gaze thoughtful. "You are indeed the perfect pawn, Astasiya. But that's not why I risked my life for you tonight." He brushed a strand of her hair away from her face, his thumb tracing her cheek. "I meant to introduce you slowly to my world, to not overwhelm you. Alas, that's no longer possible."

She swallowed. "Yes, I think tonight was the equivalent of being thrown into the deep end of the pool." And Issac had been her life raft.

"I'd liken it more to the darkest depths of the ocean, but yes." He pulled her to him, wrapping his arms around her. "There is still so much you don't yet understand."

An understatement. Her head fell to his chest as she returned his embrace. It felt so natural, so right, to melt into him, to borrow his strength, to bathe in the heat of his body.

This is so wrong.

He's a demon.

His friends took home a human slave, for fuck's sake.

She stiffened at that last thought. "What will happen with the girl?" she asked, his button-down shirt muffling her words.

"The prostitute?"

She nodded, not sure she wanted the answer, but needing it all the same.

"She'll be saved," he murmured, his fingers combing her hair. "Another aspect you don't yet understand that I intend to rectify. But trust me, she's safe."

Trust me. Two words that requested so much of her. This man had evaded her questions at every turn while also providing her with more information on the supernatural than anyone else in her existence ever had.

A conundrum that left her dizzy.

And in her current state, she couldn't ponder it much more. Stas needed a few hours of sleep, to recharge and face another day.

Her legs shook, her limbs threatening to give out on her. Holding back her emotions all evening had taken a toll not just on her mind but also on her body.

She was fucking exhausted.

Her eyes closed, her breathing steadying. The bedroom was so, so far away. She didn't have the energy, didn't want to even try, just wanted to lie here for a few moments and rest.

"I can't," she whispered, her fingers curling into his shirt. "Issac, I… I can't."

He must have understood her because he lifted her into his arms, carrying her with ease to her room. That he knew which one was hers confirmed he'd been here before, which she already knew—he'd packed her a suitcase earlier this week.

Only a few days ago?

Time was moving abnormally slow for how fast everything seemed to be happening.

Her mattress reminded her of heaven as he set her down. Pajama pants and a tank top seemed to appear beside her seconds later, his concerned expression flickering in and out of focus.

"Can you dress yourself?" he asked softly. "Or would you like assistance?"

So formal.

As if he hadn't just asked if he could remove her clothes.

Of course, he hadn't meant it that way. Maybe he should. No. No, that wasn't a good idea at all. Except it sounded like an amazing plan to forget everything.

Okay, yeah, that's not happening.

Stas forced herself to sit up and twirled her finger, signaling him to turn around. He smirked but did as she requested.

Wait, he should probably just leave…

She'd handle that in a minute.

Shoes first—on the floor. Good.

Dress next. She reached around to fiddle with the zipper, tugging on it unsuccessfully. Damn. This was one of those dresses where she had to zip it up in the front, then twist it because the damn hook sat right between her shoulder blades.

She huffed a breath.

All right. Either she slept in the dress or she asked him to help. And as he'd already offered, she might as well take advantage.

"Can you help me unzip my dress?" It came out rougher than she intended. She blamed the exertion of trying to grasp the zipper for her shortness of breath.

He rotated and eyed the fabric glued to her body. "I'll need you to stand."

Right. Yeah. This really wasn't an ideal position at all.

He held out a hand to assist her, which she only accepted because she didn't trust herself not to face-plant on the carpet. Who knew emotional burnout carried similar side effects to drinking too much alcohol? Because she felt drunk as fuck.

Issac gathered all her hair over one shoulder and traced the material along her upper back to the zipper, then drew it down far too slowly. Almost hypnotically so. Or maybe time was messing with her head again. She really couldn't tell the difference anymore, her reality fracturing into a sea of absolute madness.

The dress loosened around her top, causing her hands

to lift automatically to keep it against her chest as he exposed more of her spine.

Almost there.

Any second now.

His lips caressed the back of her neck, eliciting a shiver from deep within. She nearly dropped the dress, her instincts to melt into him overriding logic, but his touch disappeared in the next breath.

She glanced over her shoulder to find him facing the wall again, hands in his pockets.

Stas swallowed, a hint of disappointment pricking her chest. A reaction that made absolutely no sense whatsoever. This was neither the time nor the place. Not to mention, she'd hardly enjoy it in this state. And neither would he.

Dropping her dress, she pulled on the pajama pants and tank top, and collapsed on the bed from the exertion. She couldn't remember a time when she'd been this tired.

"I'm decent," she managed to say with a yawn.

"Not the adjective I'd use to describe you," he replied as he sat near the headboard of the bed. "Come here, love."

Love. She puzzled over the word, not sure she heard it right. Though it was a very English thing to say, and his accent clearly thickened with the term.

He raised an eyebrow when she didn't move, and patted the pillow.

Demands in the bedroom never bothered her. Actually, she preferred them.

And this one was not an exception to the rule.

She crawled up to the pillows ungracefully and curled into a ball beside him as he pulled the blankets over her. *Mmm, so nice. Comfortable. Warm.*

His fingers ran through her hair, his lips against her forehead. "I'm sorry about your parents, Astasiya. I'm sorry about tonight, too. And Owen. If I could change fate's cruelty, I would."

She lifted her eyes to his, lost in the cloudiness of the moment. "Is it always that way? Your Conclaves?"

He sighed, lying down beside her on top of the blankets, one arm hooking beneath his head as he stared at the ceiling. "The Conclave is our governing board, so to speak. A show of power to keep everyone in line and they only occur when someone breaks a Blood Law."

"How many Blood Laws are there?"

"Three primary rules, all involving fledglings and Hydraians." He glanced sideways at her. "As you may have guessed, my kind is not fond of the other immortals."

"And you?" she asked softly. "How do you feel about Hydraians?"

"I think that should be obvious to you by now given what I've already stated about the archaic laws." His dark lashes fell, fanning his defined cheekbones. "Good night, Astasiya."

She blinked at him. "You're staying?" *Wait, why is he even here?*

"Apparently."

"Why?"

"It feels right." He looked at ease, like he stayed in her room all the time.

"And you typically sleep in a dress shirt and pants?" It wouldn't surprise her. She rarely saw him in anything else.

One eye peeled open to look at her. "Are you giving me permission to undress?"

"Depends. What do you have on under that?"

He grinned, lowering his lashes again. "Go to sleep."

With you in my room? "Easier said than done." Except, his presence here did feel right. Like a comfort she'd never known. As if destiny had placed him here with a purpose—a good one.

She frowned, uncertain if her instincts were fried from the insanity of the day or if a moment of clarity had surfaced.

Regardless, she needed to sleep.

If Issac had wanted to hurt her, he could have done so several times over. Instead, he seemed to keep saving her.

Because he needs me alive.

Or maybe… maybe he wants me alive, too.

Banishing the inane thoughts, she reached over and turned off the lamp, shadowing the room in darkness.

After a few hours of rest, she'd be able to think more clearly and figure out why she thought Issac staying over was a sound idea.

Yes. Good plan.

Too drained to think anymore, she closed her eyes.

And fell into the dark abyss.

Chapter Sixteen

Water Nightmares

STAS COULDN'T BREATHE.

Thick black bands held her legs hostage as she tried to kick to the surface. Water clogged her airways, trapping her screams inside.

Yet, she lived.

Her body begged for oxygen.

Her skin decaying from years—decades—of living beneath the surface.

Her blonde strands resembling ash.

Everything hurt. Her heart, most of all. She missed *him*, her other half, her—

Oh, not again. Please, not again!

Slipping. Dripping into the world of nothing. Dying.

Again.

Except she didn't; she remained waiting, her consciousness nagging at the obvious.

This isn't really happening.

The water swirled around her, a whirlpool of sensation whirling her into an inky hell and throwing her into a spotlight glistening off marble tiles.

Osiris.

He sat on the throne, his cruel lips twisted in delight. A bloody razor sat beside him and a scalp of blonde hair. Stas touched her head, feeling the blood and gore, her lips parting on a silent scream no one could hear.

Oh, fuck, he found her! He knew!

And now she sat bound to the chair, leather ropes holding her down as he chuckled maliciously before her. She sobbed, begging him to stop, not wanting to die like this, here and now. She didn't mean to fall into this world, didn't know why she existed.

Please don't! Please, not again!

Astasiya! Find—

Stas flew upward on a gasp, her lungs screaming for air. Her throat felt sore, used, horribly raw. She couldn't swallow, couldn't breathe fast enough, her heartbeat in her ears.

"Astasiya." The voice penetrated the drumming only barely. Masculine. Deep. Familiar.

Heat enveloped her, hands on her face, lips in her hair.

She struggled, alarmed by the presence of another, only to inhale the soothing scent of sandalwood. *Issac.* She collapsed against him, her face meeting his bare skin, his arms forming a protective shield around her back.

He's here.

I'm safe.

Stas shuddered, bits and pieces of the too-real nightmare flashing behind her eyes. A deep ache stirred in her chest, her mother's broken features so clear and vivid in her mind. It'd been her mother tied to that chair, begging for help before drowning all over again.

"He wouldn't let her move," she whispered on a sob, the vision flickering between her mother and Sierra. "The razor..." She buried her face against his shoulder, needing his familiarity and warmth.

"I know," he murmured, stroking her hair down to her back. "But you're safe here. I won't let that happen to you, Astasiya."

The vow in his voice circled her heart, soothing some of the pain radiating through her body. Still, Osiris's eyes haunted her, his malicious smile as he wielded that blade forever ingrained in her memory.

Just like the man who burned her parents alive.

She didn't see him tonight, had searched for him, wondering if he'd appear. Some part of her knew he wasn't there, the part that swore she'd recognize him without even seeing him. He had a lethal presence about him—a memorable one.

Issac's lips brushed her temple, his hands sliding over her, providing the comfort she craved. It went against reason to trust him, to give in to the lure of his protection, yet she did it with ease, as if they'd been doing this all their lives.

I trust him, she realized. Perhaps not logically, but she did nonetheless. Her breathing slowly returned to normal, her gaze clearing as Issac continued to caress her, his touch working magic against her back and neck.

She swallowed, her palms and legs informing her of his current state. He'd undressed while she slept, leaving him clad in only a pair of boxers. One of her thighs had lodged between his, the top of which absorbed the heat of his groin. And her hands had ended up on his bare shoulders, clutching his strength.

I'm cuddling a nearly naked Issac. In my bed.

"I can't remember the last time I had to wake someone the old-fashioned way," he said softly, completely unaware of the shift in her mind and the fresh wave of warmth flooding her veins. "Your immunity to my gift is quite tiresome."

She cleared her throat, her brow furrowing, not following his comment. "Your invisibility?"

"My invisibility?" he repeated.

"Yeah, your gift, right?" How would that help wake her up?

He chuckled, the sound warm and affectionate and not at all helping to dispel the heat flooding her body. "That's cute. Invisibility isn't my gift." He started massaging a tense spot on her neck, sending tingles down her spine.

Oh, so not helping with the attraction problem, but definitely not going to ask him to stop. Because wow, that feels… mmm.

"I control vision," he continued, his fingers working her muscles with expert precision. "The day we met, I was hiding my presence from everyone in the building by controlling their sight. Except it didn't work on you. I tried to access your visual receptors tonight, and I mean, I *really* tried, but your nightmare eluded me. Your mind is dark to me."

"You control vision in real time, like what I see right now, and in dreams?"

"My gift extends to the dream realm, yes. Vision is about what your eyes allow you to see, and those sensors are connected to the brain. I manipulate the part of the mind that tells a person *what* he's seeing or how to interpret an image. That extends to the imagination as well, such as how someone might picture something. I can make a person think he's sleeping when he's not, based on the dream playing out inside his head. Which is why I tried to access your nightmare—to stop it—but as I said, I can't touch your mind."

She blinked. Okay, visual manipulation was far more impressive than invisibility.

And he had hidden his presence in Owen's building by manipulating everyone's sight? Several hundred people lived in that apartment building. How many of them did he control that morning?

This is why others fear him, why they respected him at the Conclave.

What a terrifyingly powerful ability.

"I'm immune?" she asked, part alarmed, part relieved.

"Yes, to all power, it seems."

She lifted her head to look at him, but the darkness of the room hid his features. "Is that normal for a fledgling?"

"No, not at all. You're the first I've ever met. However, Aidan told me about someone he knew long ago with a similar ability."

"He knows about me?"

"Of course."

His quick, nonchalant answer made her shiver. Aidan reminded her too much of Osiris. They both possessed an air of age about them that lent to a disregard for humanity. His callous suggestion to auction off a mortal woman marked him as one of the last people she ever wanted to see again, but apparently, he knew about her. That didn't bode well for her future.

She rolled onto her back, away from Issac's magical hands, needing a moment. The way she accepted his comfort unnerved her. Trusting him defied rational thought. Their acquaintance nearly killed her, something he admitted might happen again, and he was using her.

He also saved my life at least twice now.

She almost growled, frustrated and exhausted by the confusion rioting inside her.

A glance at the clock showed she slept two hours at most. Not nearly enough, not after everything she'd been through.

Issac shifted beside her, his palm cupping her cheek as he hovered over her, removing the space between them. "Hmm, you and I are going to have a very long talk tomorrow, love."

Love. What happened to *darling?*

"However," he continued softly, his mouth lowering to

hers. "We require more rest first, and fortunately, I know exactly how to help us achieve that."

She parted her lips with a reply that he interrupted with his tongue. Her heart stopped beating, her breath frozen.

He started slow, his tongue gliding against hers in a way that coaxed her into returning the kiss. Each slide and dip caressed her senses, causing her pulse to kick-start into a rhythm that bowed to his control. It decelerated when he went soft and accelerated when he deepened their embrace, his palms sliding down her neck and arms.

God, this man knew exactly how to destroy her, to plow through every wall, to bring her to her knees with a simple stroke of his mouth over hers. Each nibble and lick fractured another brain cell, leaving her mindless beneath him, and captivated.

He was fast becoming her darkest addiction, his touch something she craved more than air itself. Right and wrong fled her system, leaving a puddle of desire in their wake that only he could satisfy. She no longer cared about anything or anyone—except him.

And to release all those emotions, all that pain, was a gift in itself, one she couldn't refuse.

"More," she moaned. "More, Issac." Because if he stopped at just kissing her, she'd kill him. They'd danced around this attraction for too long. Fuck everything else, all that had happened, she wanted relief. "Please."

"Don't worry, love. I'm going to give you what you need," he whispered, his lips hot against hers. "What we both need."

His thigh slid between hers, pressing into the most sensitive part of her.

Yes…

She moved closer, her hips undulating beneath his, seeking the friction she so badly craved.

Dangerous. Wrong. Wanton.

But she gave in to the allure anyway, seeking the comfort he offered.

"Yes, love." His palms slid up her sides, beneath her top. "That's it." He peeled off her strapless bra, tossing it to the floor and revealing her breasts to the night air. "You're gorgeous," he whispered, his lips on her neck. "Utter perfection."

She threaded her fingers through his thick hair, her other palm against his shoulder.

So strong.

So soft.

So... *mine.*

The thought came unbidden, nearly derailing her from the moment, but the pinch against her nipple captured her attention, eliciting a groan from deep in her chest. *Fuck.* His hands really were enchanted. He knew exactly how to touch her and where, both rough and gentle, his strong thigh flexing between hers.

"Issac..." His name a prayer and a promise, wrapped up in a sultry voice she hardly recognized. Already she felt a sensuous storm brewing inside her, culminating in her lower abdomen. No one had ever done this to her, brought her this close, without *really* touching her.

But then again, none of her previous lovers rivaled Issac in any way.

His lips traced a wet path down her chest, his tongue teasing her stiff peaks. It made her want to explore him in kind, causing her palm to drift down his muscled back to his firm ass. The silky texture of his boxer shorts teased her fingertips, sliding across her skin as she ventured around to the front to palm his impressive erection.

He hissed her name, his teeth scraping her skin.

She stroked him through the fabric, only to find her wrist captured and pulled over her head. Her lips parted on a complaint that he swallowed with his mouth. His lower body settled between hers, the head of his cock right against her clit. And when he pressed into her, she saw stars.

Oh, fuck...

So close...

The minimal clothing between them didn't matter, not with him moving like *that*.

Her nails bit into his biceps, her back arching as she thrust upward, chasing the sensation tingling throughout her body.

Just.

One.

More.

"Now, Astasiya," he growled, his teeth sinking into her lower lip.

God, that voice, coupled with the things he was doing to her, pushed her over the precipice into oblivion. Sensual energy unlike anything she'd ever experienced flooded through her, his tongue absorbing each of her moans as he drove her to madness.

She quivered.

Quaked.

Exploded.

Her vision going dark and then light, every part of her melting beneath his assault. And then she was floating, lost in a cloud of bliss she never wanted to come down from.

"Glorious," he murmured, his lips tracing her jaw to her throat. "You're amazing."

His praise warmed her in a way she didn't expect. She should be the one commending him, not the other way around.

Because wow.

He sent her to heaven and back without really touching her. It was a testament to his skill and her lack of recent experience. Or maybe the culmination of all the foreplay between them.

His tongue laved her bottom lip before his mouth took hers in a kiss underlined in unspoken words. *Feelings*. They were walking a dangerous rope, this connection between them bordering on something decidedly deeper than mere lust.

It wrecked her.

Floored her.

Excited her.

"Sleep well," he whispered, pulling her against him, his hot arousal against her thigh.

"But—"

"Shh." He nuzzled her hair, tightening his hold. "Another time, Aya. We will have many more nights together. Trust me."

Aya? She wanted to ask him what he meant, but her yawn dispelled her ability to speak. Mmm, in the morning. She'd ask him then.

If she remembered.

CHAPTER SEVENTEEN

Afternoon Ride

ASTASIYA'S HEARTBEAT CHANGED, SIGNALING her awareness. Her abrupt intake of air had Issac's lips twitching, but he remained otherwise still, his arm draped loosely across her waist.

He never held women like this, nor did he ever sleep beside one, but he rather enjoyed waking up with Astasiya snuggled up against him. His cock enjoyed it, too, especially as she stretched.

She froze as her ass brushed his groin.

Yes, darling, that would be for you.

Except they couldn't do anything about it right now. Elizabeth had returned home an hour ago, hence the reason Issac was wide awake now.

Astasiya shifted slowly, as if to not disturb him. He allowed it, deciding to give her the moment to herself she seemed to need. She crept quietly away from the bed and closed the door to the bathroom behind her.

He chuckled, sitting up with a shake of his head. Most women fawned over him, desiring to please him with their mouths and bodies just for a few minutes more of attention. Astasiya, however, couldn't get away from him fast enough.

The challenge she provided thrilled him. As did many other aspects of her body and mind.

Rolling out of bed, he pulled on his trousers and picked up his phone from the nightstand. Lucian had replied to the text he sent last night, agreeing to a meet.

Brilliant.

This whole slow-introduction idea with Astasiya had clearly not worked out as planned, so they needed a new course.

Checking the current hour, Issac sent back a message with a reasonable arrival time and pocketed the device.

The water flipped on in the bathroom, giving Issac pause as he began buttoning his shirt. Joining Astasiya in the shower would be most pleasing. He pictured the water trickling over her naked skin and his tongue following a droplet to the delicious juncture between her thighs. Mmm, an activity for later today if all went as planned. Because if they started now, they'd never make the meeting he'd just arranged.

Needing a distraction, he made her bed and left the room in search of Elizabeth Watkins. His curiosity over the woman had piqued when she appeared seemingly from nowhere at the age of eighteen.

From all that he'd observed, she appeared to know nothing about the supernatural. An impossibility, it seemed, with her birthright and those who surrounded her. She even had a Sentinel detail assigned to her security, something she definitely knew, as Issac had seen her speaking to them more than once.

He found her in the kitchen, humming over the counter as she whipped something in a bowl. Her summer dress seemed better suited for a day out with friends, not an afternoon at home, but Elizabeth seemed to fancy high fashion. She even wore stockings.

"Hello," he said with a slight knock, hoping not to startle her too much.

She squeaked, jumping backward and flinging what appeared to be egg all over the cherry wood cabinet.

So much for not surprising her.

"Sorry, Elizabeth, I didn't mean to cause alarm. Here, let me help." He reached for the paper towels by the sink, but she grabbed the roll before he could reach it.

"I-I have it," she stuttered, her brown eyes round, her cheeks pink. "You just caught me off guard." She was already wiping up the mess and bending to retrieve what appeared to be specialized wood cleaner.

Issac frowned. He knew she was an experiment of sorts, but she acted so incredibly human. Well, a clone of a housewife, anyway. *What did Jonathan do to you?*

"I, uh, was making an egg casserole," she explained, gesturing to the mixture and then the flaky pie crust beside it. "Stas loves bacon and eggs. Hopefully, you do, too, because I doubled the recipe."

He leaned against the counter, arms folded. "You knew I was here."

She tossed out the paper towels and began fiddling with her mixture again. "The expensive jacket and tie in the hall closet gave you away." She smiled at him over her shoulder. "Stas isn't dating anyone else who can afford that brand."

Oh, now that was an interesting statement. "Who all is she dating?" he wondered aloud, his eyebrow arching.

Elizabeth giggled, the sound one he heard far too often from simpering beauty queens, but hers came off as more genuine. "No one. Stas doesn't date."

"She doesn't?"

"Well, it seems she does *now*." She poured the mixture

into her dish, adding a layer of cheese to the top. "But no, she didn't date much throughout college, too consumed with her studies."

Excellent segue. Thank you, darling. "Because she was focused on her future with the CRF."

Elizabeth snorted. "I guess, yeah." She put the casserole in the oven and started the timer. "Definitely not my first choice."

The muttered words surprised him. "What, working at the CRF, you mean?"

A faint red crept up her neck. "Sorry, I didn't mean for you to hear that."

And now he was very intrigued. "Your distaste for the CRF?" Which he heard clearly in her voice. "Or the comment about it not being your first choice?"

Her cheeks matched her auburn hair, her eyes widening. "I really need to learn to just not speak, like, at all."

"That would be a shame, as you have a lovely voice." He meant it as a compliment, not in a flirtatious manner but in a friendly one. "Why do you dislike the CRF?" he pressed, changing the subject back to what he really wanted to know. *Is this all a charade? Do you know what I am? Is your friendship with Astasiya by coincidence or on purpose?*

Elizabeth chewed her lip. "I don't not like it."

"But you're clearly not their biggest fan either," he pointed out, reading her body language and tone. If this was an act, then the woman deserved an award for her performance because the female radiated innocence. Especially in the way she continued to blush and lower her gaze.

"They just… I know how consuming they can be. I grew up with a father who was never home, and I don't want that for Stas. I hope she can find a balance. That's all."

Her words floored him, particularly the way she spoke about her father—George. Almost as if she truly believed she grew up with him working all the time.

Oh, there were birth records and other official

documents that indicated she grew up with the Watkinses. But that family had been under surveillance for over two decades, and Elizabeth didn't appear in those videos or notes until six years ago.

Except it seemed she was completely unaware.

She appeared quite human.

Were his instincts wrong? Could she be the result of something else? Why go through the hassle of creating a history for someone who has no otherworldly powers or purpose?

One thing he knew for certain—she was not related to her parents.

But the experiment piece he now had to question. They all just assumed the CRF created her because where else would she have come from? Yet her mannerisms and emotions didn't suit that theory at all.

Are you a failed project at the CRF? A sleeper agent of some kind? Or something else entirely?

"So, uh, yeah. I'm happy for her, and it's nice to see her dating, too." Elizabeth's eyes sparkled over that last part, her lips pulling upward into an eager smile. "I saw the photos from the gala. How did you talk her into wearing that dress?"

"My stylist picked it out for her."

Elizabeth gave him a look. "Yeah, I figured that much. But how did you get Stas to wear it?"

He wasn't following. "Why wouldn't she wear it?"

"Uh, because it would have cost a fortune."

What kind of man did Elizabeth think him to be? "She didn't pay for it." He'd never force a date to buy their own gown.

Elizabeth made a noise in the back of her throat. "No, that's not— Okay. Let me start over. How did you convince Stas to let you buy her a dress? And not just any dress, but *that* dress? I can hardly get her to borrow my shoes, and they have nothing on that designer label. So how? How did you do it?"

Such a trivial topic and so very human. *She really has no idea who or what I am, does she?* Because anyone else in this situation would never think to question such a frivolous detail. "I didn't give her a choice."

She considered that, her lips scrunched to the side. "I see." She tapped her chin with a manicured nail. "You didn't tell her how much it cost."

"The topic didn't arise, no."

"And she didn't recognize the label, because it's Stas, and she wouldn't." She laughed and shook her head. "I'm very impressed. I hope she keeps you around."

"Thank you, I think."

"It's a compliment." She busied herself with the coffee maker, grabbing three mugs from the cupboard. "Can I offer a suggestion?"

"Yes." That didn't mean he'd take it, but this woman did appear to be Astasiya's true best friend. Not because of outlying circumstances, but because of pure fate. *Fascinating.*

"Never give her a price tag. Ever. Especially if you plan to dress her up again."

"You're recommending I not mention the cost?" he asked, sensing Astasiya's nearing presence. Her delectable blood sang to his senses, reminding him of how she tasted. He desired more. He desired *her.*

"I'm just saying she might not be as appreciative as your other more, uh, *money-savvy* dates. She's not ignorant or anything, just not..."

"Shallow?" he offered, aware that Astasiya lurked in the hallway now, listening.

"Right. That's a good word, or *materialistic.* She's not a fashion person, if that makes sense."

"Duly noted." He paused, waiting for his blonde to enter. Hmm, it seemed she wanted to hear more. All right. Then he'd continue pressing Elizabeth about her life and purpose in this world. "Astasiya hasn't told me what you're doing post-graduation?" He phrased it as a question, hoping she would elaborate from there.

Are you going to work for your father?

For Jonathan?

Or is your purpose darker? What are they planning to do with you?

And more importantly, what exactly are you? Because she wasn't an Ichorian or a Hydraian, from what he could tell. For all intents and purposes, she came off as completely human. Which couldn't be the case at all with her family history and ties to the CRF.

"Oh. I'm working with a kids' shelter in Lower Manhattan, and I volunteer with one in Harlem, too. That's where I was last night, but I work for the other full-time."

"Teaching the underprivileged?" That wasn't at all what he expected.

"Yeah, I lead their reading and writing programs."

"Very commendable." He meant it. "How do George and Lillian feel about it?"

Astasiya's pulse escalated, his question clearly striking a nerve. She appeared in the doorway, her expression concerned.

"Yeah, they don't like it much," Elizabeth replied, nose scrunching. "Oh, hey, Stas."

Issac smiled. *Eavesdropper*, he accused with his eyes.

The look she gave him screamed defiance. *What are you going to do about it?*

He shrugged, not at all bothered. Given the direction of their relationship, he had nothing left to hide.

"Casserole is in the oven," Elizabeth added.

"Yes, you live with quite the master chef, Astasiya," he murmured. "I'm impressed."

Astasiya grinned, approval radiating in her expression. He'd clearly said the right thing, and that pleased him far more than it should.

"Yeah, I sort of love her," she admitted, giving her roommate a side hug.

"Sort of?" Elizabeth gave her a reproachful look. "You adore me."

"It's true," she agreed.

"My sister would have liked you a great deal," Issac said, surprising himself with the words, yet meaning them. "She loved cooking and baking." Amelia spent most days in the kitchen, always entertaining and feeding everyone. His lips actually curled with the thought, astounding him. Usually, thoughts of his sister resulted in pain.

"You have a sister?" Elizabeth asked, brow furrowing.

"I had a sister, yes. It's not well known." Because he didn't contrive his new public image until after her death, and at that point, it wasn't worth the trouble of painting her backstory.

Elizabeth openly cringed. "Oh. I'm sorry."

"No need to apologize. She passed some time ago." And he certainly didn't want to elaborate on that right now. He smiled at Astasiya, needing a new topic. "I want to take you somewhere today. Interested?" He wouldn't exactly accept a negative response, but he'd negotiate as needed.

She cocked her hip against the kitchen table, expression curious. "That depends on where we're going."

He could withhold the truth or dance around it, but after last night, he felt compelled to be honest with her. Always. "The Hamptons."

Her eyebrows rose as Elizabeth nearly dropped the cream she'd just pulled from the refrigerator.

"The Hamptons," Astasiya repeated. "Why?"

"I'm expecting some friends, and I would like for you to join us." At her incredulous look, he added, "Might be an informative experience."

Understanding darkened her gaze. "Friends like the ones I met last night?"

"Similar, but much more hospitable."

"I assume that means you'll miss dinner tonight?" Elizabeth directed the question to her roommate.

"Fitzgerald and Watkins dinner," she translated on a groan. "Don't we get a reprieve? We just ate with them last weekend."

"That's what I said, but my mom said it's mandatory. For me, anyway, not you."

Astasiya looked positively pained, her expression falling. "I… I don't know if I'm ready for another dinner with them. But if you need me to go, Liz, I can."

"Oh, no." Elizabeth straightened, her gaze filling with purpose. "You totally go to the Hamptons when Issac Wakefield asks you to go to the Hamptons." She winced, seeming to remember the man she addressed by full name stood in the room. "Uh, I mean, you should go."

So much more nonchalant and natural, causing him to smile.

"I agree with Elizabeth," he said. "When I ask you to go somewhere, you say yes. Beautifully accurate advice."

Astasiya gave him a look. "Not biased at all."

"Naturally not, no," he murmured.

Elizabeth cleared her throat. "So, uh, do I just tell them you're together?"

"I've not agreed to go yet," Astasiya pointed out.

"She means yes," Issac translated.

"Like in a relationship or just a date?" Elizabeth asked, her focus completely on him.

"Both," he replied, wishing he could be there to see the look on all their faces at dinner. Maybe he'd ask Mateo to hack into the dining room security feeds, just for a laugh.

"You don't do *relationships*," Astasiya said, her cheeks bright with color.

"I also don't see a woman more than once, yet here we are," he pointed out.

"You can't be serious."

His lips curled into a taunting grin. "I'm very serious, love." *Especially when it comes to you.*

Elizabeth smiled. "So, I can refer to you as her boyfriend, right?"

Astasiya looked positively affronted by the notion. "Seriously—"

"Absolutely," Issac replied, cutting her off.

She sputtered. "I don't get a say in this?"

"No."

Elizabeth squealed and clapped her hands. Her yellow sundress flickered beneath the kitchen lights as she skipped around, her happiness making him smile. *Definitely a genuine friendship.* And it seemed she approved of him, too.

"Chick flicks and whatever pizza I want for a year," she announced, pointing a finger at Astasiya and waggling it. "And *you* have to pay for it all." Another squeal followed by an impressive ballet move that had Issac really wondering about her history and upbringing.

Where did she learn to dance like that?

"Oh God." Astasiya's head fell to the wall behind her as she shook it back and forth. "I can't believe you remember that."

"Of course I do. I've waited six very long years for this moment. Freakin' finally!"

"What am I missing?" Issac asked, completely enamored by the display between them.

"Oh, please don't," Astasiya groaned.

"Stas swore up and down that she would *never* have a boyfriend. It wasn't *her thing,* and she has no interest in her *MRS degree.*" She used her fingers to quote Stas. "We made a bet that whenever she got a boyfriend, she would let me choose movies and pizza for a year, at her expense. That was how sure she was that she would never date."

"Hey, I dated."

"Oh, that Jake guy so did not count. You went home with him after that wedding. That's not a date. That's called a hookup."

Bright splotches of pink painted Astasiya's features. "Lizzie!"

"Okay, fine, Pete kind of counted. You went out with him twice, but he wasn't a *boyfriend,* and you didn't even sleep with him. And then there was that one guy, uh, Brian? Brandon? Whatever. He lasted for, like, two seconds before you got bored, and then—"

"Oh my God, just stop!"

"Oh, like he cares. He's a walking tabloid." Her cheeks reddened. "No offense."

"No offense taken, darling," Issac said, his mouth hurting from smiling so much. "However, please, do continue. This is all very enlightening."

"No," Astasiya snapped.

"The only other one was that Paul guy who wouldn't leave you alone, and none of it counted, but you're finally dating. Like, *really* dating." Elizabeth started dancing again.

"I daresay dear Elizabeth is more excited than you are," he noted.

Astasiya glowered at him. "Oh, I'm just thrilled." She moved to grab some plates as the timer on the oven sounded, and paused at something resting on the counter.

Issac glanced over her shoulder to read the headline.

Mystery Woman Coaxes Smile from Billionaire Playboy.

He was already laughing before she grumbled, "You've got to be fucking kidding me."

"Oops," Elizabeth said, grimacing.

Issac plucked the magazine from her hands and tossed it in the bin, where it belonged. "Ignore it, love."

She gave him a look. "The headline is wrong. You only smiled for show."

"If that's what you want to believe, then so be it." He knew the truth and that was all that mattered. Cupping her face, he pulled her closer, needing an answer. "Now, will you go with me today? Please?"

"To the Hamptons."

"Yes."

"To meet more friends."

He nodded. "You'll like them. They remind me of you and Owen."

Her eyebrows lifted at the subtle context underlying his words, and he nodded again at the silent question in her eyes. *Yes, they are Hydraians.*

"Please, Astasiya?" he asked softly. "Come with me

today. You won't regret it."

She swallowed, a hint of emotion flickering in her gaze. "Okay," she whispered.

"Brilliant." He smiled, pleased. "We'll go after we finish eating."

"Okay," she repeated.

"Go pack a few things," he added, aware of their audience. "We might stay a few days."

"What?"

"Trust me." He couldn't elaborate in front of Elizabeth. She clearly knew nothing about his world, despite her surroundings, and he wouldn't change that for her.

Astasiya held his gaze for a beat, more of that emotion spilling through her expression. She finally nodded, agreeing. "I'll grab a bag."

Elizabeth stood behind them, the casserole already on a cooling rack. She grinned widely as Astasiya turned.

"Stop gloating, Liz," she muttered.

"*Pretty Woman* and a pizza with extra pepperoni. That's my first order," she replied.

"I hate you."

"You love me."

"Uh-huh." Astasiya grabbed her and hugged her tight, her words low as she added, "Call me if you need me tonight. You know I'll be there."

Something akin to relief graced Elizabeth's features, her expression turning somber. "I know. Thanks, Stas. But go have fun. You deserve it."

"Thank you," Astasiya replied, leaving the room. "I'll be back in a few minutes." She glanced at him. "With a suitcase."

He smiled. "Brilliant."

Chapter Eighteen

Will You Dance with Me?

Issac hadn't visited Wakefield Manor in several years, his memories of the grounds tainted by that day in the ballroom.

The day he found Eli's headless body holding an urn of Amelia's ashes.

With each approaching mile, the ache in his gut grew stronger. He didn't want to do this, but the woman beside him required it.

Astasiya remained quiet and unaware in the passenger seat, taking in the summer scenery. The Hamptons were truly gorgeous, with all the manor-style homes and white picket fences. His estate rested on the water, a few streets over. Amelia had loved the beach, spending hours lounging in the sun with Eli at her side.

He swallowed, taking the turns and driving on autopilot.

The familiar gates loomed ahead, a *W* etched in the middle. He pulled a device from the glove box and clicked the button. The iron moved slowly, opening up the driveway. Usually, he went left at the split to park in one of the garages, but as he had a guest today, he bypassed it for the loop around the fountain in front of the mansion.

Fifteen bedrooms.

Just as many bathrooms.

Several living areas.

A pool house equipped with two pools.

And a guest home.

The abundance of space had been required to accommodate the parties Amelia enjoyed throwing here during the summers, many of the Hydraians choosing to stay overnight. They were just far enough outside of New York City to feel safe, especially with the security system at Issac's estate—built by Mateo.

He parked in the cobblestone drive outside the front and smiled as Robert opened the French doors. Issac could have phoned ahead with a warning, but he opted to surprise his estate manager instead. The ruddy color on the rotund man's cheeks said Issac had achieved that goal in spades.

"Welcome to Wakefield Manor," he murmured, setting his sunglasses on the dash and unbuckling his seat belt.

"It's gorgeous," she breathed, her eyes on the oversized windows and brick siding.

While he agreed, he didn't comment and instead unbuckled his seat belt as his door opened.

"I couldn't believe it when I heard the gate open," Robert said, bouncing on his heels just outside the car. "My Cherie is going to be thrilled."

Issac chuckled and stepped out to shake hands with the much shorter man. "How are the children, Robert?"

"Oh, Rebecca is married and just had a baby, making me a proud granddaddy to an adorable new granddaughter. She inherited all the fairer genes from Cherie's side of the family, too."

Issac had listened while walking around the car to open the door for Astasiya. "That's fantastic, Robert." He held out a hand for her, which she accepted as she joined him and stood by his side. "Why didn't you tell me?"

"Well." The man clasped his hands over his rotund belly. "Whenever we talk, it's usually about business. Didn't want to waste your time with family news and all that."

"You becoming a grandfather is hardly a waste of my time, Robert," Issac replied, disappointed that he would feel that way.

"Maybe, maybe." He rocked back and forth with the words. "So, who do we have here?" he asked, his hazel eyes crinkling as he studied the blonde at Issac's side.

"This is Astasiya Davenport. Astasiya, this is Robert Allmond. He lives here."

Robert blew a raspberry. "He means I live over there." He pointed in the direction of the guesthouse near the garages. "Cherie and I just keep up the grounds for Master Wakefield. Speaking of which, I better go tell her you're here. You know she's going to expect you to stay for dinner."

"Yes, I'm expecting company as well. Lucian and likely a few others."

"Oh!" Robert hopped with excitement. "I'll ask Shelly to help me ready some of the guest rooms. She's back from college for the summer."

Ah yes, the youngest of the Allmond family. "Is she enjoying Duke?" Issac asked, curious.

"Loving it, of course. I'll make sure she stops by to thank you."

Issac waved him off. Paying her tuition had been a natural favor. The Allmond family took amazing care of his estate, and he returned the favor in kind. "There's no need for that, but I would enjoy an update. I haven't seen her since she was thirteen or so?"

That seemed to calm the man a bit, his hand coming up to scratch his jaw. "Yeah, about that long, huh? I was starting to think the next time I'd see you would be at my funeral."

"Foolish thoughts."

"Not for an old man, they're not." There was a hint of chastisement in that statement that twisted Issac's heart. *Fair point.* "Okay, so four or five rooms will do? Yours as well?"

"I'll handle mine, but if you wouldn't mind the others?"

Robert puffed out his chest. "Master Wakefield, I've had six years of nothing to do other than keep the dust from settling around here. I do not mind one bit, and you can bet Cherie will feel the same."

Has it only been that long? It felt like a century had passed since Issac last set foot on these grounds.

"Thank you, Robert," he murmured.

"My pleasure, sir." He bowed and scampered off down the driveway.

Issac chuckled after him, shaking his head. He'd missed the jovial man, perhaps more than he realized.

"You have a manservant," Astasiya said, eyebrows raised. "And apparently a house in the Hamptons you don't use often. At least I know the tabloids were right about your net worth."

He snorted. "Hardly, on all accounts." He tugged her toward the still-open doors of the house. The Hydraians wouldn't arrive for another hour or so, which gave him plenty of time to change and give her a proper tour.

A twinge of excitement dispelled his unease, the idea of showing off a bit appealing to him far more than it should.

"Uh-huh. So why are we here, again?" she asked, her eyes dancing over the three-story foyer as they entered.

"To meet friends, but first, I need a shower." If Lucian or Balthazar found him like this, there would be comments galore. Issac never wore the same suit two days in a row, and the stubble across his jaw would certainly indicate his lack of a proper shave. That, he might keep, but the rumpled appearance required replacement.

"Not liking the whole walk-of-shame look?" she teased, a devious twinkle in her gaze. So much better than the dead eyes from last night.

He pulled her close, his lips brushing her ear. "Or liking it too much."

Her breath hitched, a slight pink creeping into her fair skin. She cleared her throat. "I mean, I guess I can keep myself entertained. Anything off-limits I should know about so I can start there?" Her voice held a sultry edge to it that lit his blood on fire.

He would have her beneath him.

Tonight.

Issac let her see that in his expression as he slowly perused her legs—exposed by her jean shorts—and her clingy tank top. She swallowed as he met her gaze, recalling her question about anything being off-limits.

"Only the master bedroom," he lied, knotting his fingers in her hair to guide her into a kiss. Fuck, he wanted her now. The last few days had been torture, his need for her escalating by the second. But he had to change first. He traced her lower lip with his tongue, allowing himself one final taste of her before stepping back. "I'll find you."

~*~

Issac disappeared down the hall rather than up the stairs.

Stas gazed left and right, surrounded by opulence and wealth. Above her hung a chandelier that glistened from the sunlight streaming in through the windows.

"Wow," she breathed. This place was unreal. Everything held a note of extravagance, even the furniture. She was almost afraid to touch anything.

Closing the front doors, she followed Issac's path, curious, and found herself in a vast dining area with doors that overlooked a huge porch. And beyond it, a pool. Not just a dipping pool, but a full-length water arena equipped with waterfalls and various plant life that she felt sure were not native to New York.

She should have brought her swimsuit.

The row of trees lining the back of the property hid the beach and ocean from her view, but she knew Issac's estate was situated on the water. She could smell it outside.

A kitchen Lizzie would have fainted at the sight of joined the dining area, expanding outward to showcase several ovens and stoves, two refrigerators, and an island that doubled as a dining table.

She snapped a picture with her phone, sending it to her roommate. Because wow.

Continuing her journey, she found another seating area near the back of the house with more doors that led outside to the patio, and ended her journey at a set of oversized doors. Finding them unlocked, she twisted the knob and froze.

Two stories of windows stared back at her from three angles. Thick velvet curtains were tied into the corners, granting her a magnificent view of the property and the ocean beyond.

"Holy fuck," she breathed, twirling in the oversized ballroom. No furniture or decorations in here, just a polished hardwood floor with a grand piano in one corner.

She left her sandals and purse by the door and padded barefoot into the room. Another one of those chandeliers hung above her from the vaulted ceiling. Definitely a room designed for entertaining and dancing.

Stas twirled in the center, picturing masquerade balls and parties in this room. It wasn't her usual scene, but she'd enjoy watching one. Especially if Issac were a star performer.

Having no training and not caring whatsoever, she danced around the room, letting go of the last twenty-four hours and just *being*. She felt light and carefree, as if she hadn't almost died last week. The Conclave disappeared, along with her troubles, and when she opened her eyes to find Issac leaning against the doorjamb, all she could do was smile. He brought her here. He did this. And it'd been so worth it for even the few moments of freedom she'd found in this room.

He'd traded his suit for a pair of jeans and a fitted gray shirt. No shoes. Hair damp. It was the most casual she'd ever seen him, aside from this morning when she woke up to his mostly naked body.

"This was Amelia's favorite room," he said, his voice soft. "She used to dance in the center where you're standing now while Eli played the piano."

"Eli?"

"I guess you could say he was my brother-in-law. He and Amelia never married, but they were romantically involved for centuries." Meaning his sister had been an immortal as well. Stas supposed she could have guessed that from the photo books in his condo. All those photos were decades old, yet Owen remained the same in all of them. Because he was a Hydraian. Did that mean Amelia had been one as well?

Fledglings were created from an Ichorian father and a mortal mother. Then fledglings became Hydraians—the enemies of Ichorians.

Stas frowned. She understood the creation bit but couldn't fathom a reason for why Ichorians would loathe their children. That part made no sense.

And what's more, Issac didn't seem to have an issue with fledglings or Hydraians. So why did he break all the rules? There were clear consequences, as she observed last night. Yet, here she stood in a ballroom while he fussed with an electrical board on the wall beside the door.

She was about to ask him when music began playing overhead, drawing her attention to the speakers. The lights flickered overhead next, setting a romantic mood in the room.

"Amelia taught me how to dance when we were young," he said over the music, sliding a wooden panel to cover the electrical switches he'd just altered. "She claimed it was the best way to win a woman's heart. I always said I had no interest in a woman's heart."

He sauntered onto the floor, extending his hand as he approached.

"Care for a demonstration, my lady?" he offered.

"You're asking me to dance?"

"Amelia would scold me if I didn't."

"Would she scold me for refusing?" she asked, even as she accepted his hand.

He chuckled. "She definitely would, yes." He caught her hip with his free hand and pulled her closer. "And I should warn you, my sister was known to make many grown men cry. I don't recommend upsetting her. Now put your other hand on my shoulder."

She did as instructed. "Okay, but I'm warning you, I'm not a great dancer."

He walked her two steps backward, then one to the side, as if testing that theory. "Not an issue. It's all about the leading, love."

"Uh-huh." He wouldn't be saying that when she kept stepping on his feet.

Issac seemed to take her words as a challenge, as he proved his point by moving her across the floor with a few subtle nudges of his hand against her hip. His hand in hers helped as well, as did the slow beat of the song. He'd clearly chosen this one on purpose.

"Good," he praised as they returned to their starting place. "Now, let's make it interesting."

His palm slid from her hip to the small of her back, the gentle pressure encouraging her to shift with him as he introduced her to a slightly faster rhythm. She mimicked his motions, keeping pace with him and smiling when she realized this wasn't nearly as hard as she expected.

"I don't know how you're doing this, but I'm dancing." And she wasn't terrible, either.

His lips twitched as he lifted the hand holding hers and

led her into a twirl. She gasped as he caught her around the waist with his opposite arm, her pulse racing at the fluidity of his movements.

Okay. Issac could dance. Like, really, legitimately dance.

"Mmm, yes, I daresay, Astasiya, you move quite well." He spun her around him again, this time dipping her close to the floor before righting her against him. "Amelia would approve."

Her breathing escalated as he picked up the pace to match the new song. Each touch and brush of his hand caused her hips to sway with his, her body syncing in time with his and following his lead entirely.

Issac twirled her, bringing her back to his front, his hands on her hips holding her to him.

"I bought this estate for Amelia," he murmured against Stas's ear. He slowed their swaying as the music melted into a sensual tune. "She wanted to be closer to me but couldn't stay in the city. So this was the best alternative. I thought it would keep her safe." He rotated Stas back around to face him and gazed down at her. "I was wrong."

Despite the emotion thickening his voice, he continued their movements, whirling her about the floor with an ease that spoke of years of training. Stas's pulse quickened with every twirl, her body trusting him to catch her. He never missed a beat, his tempo in line with the rhythm regardless of the song. She wondered if this was his outlet, his way of moving through the pain.

"What happened?" she finally asked, her voice breathy from all the activity.

"Jonathan happened." Lifting her hand, Issac propelled her into a twirl that was faster and harder than the others. She spun twice before he caught her against him, her heart fluttering at the intense contact. "He made it look like the Conclave did it."

She swallowed, her feet missing a step as ice drizzled down her spine. "Like Owen?"

Issac masked her stumble with another spin, helping her

to rebalance and continue. "Yes, the same methods."

They danced in silence for a long moment, her mind processing his admission. "So you think Jonathan killed Owen?"

"I've considered it," he murmured, slowing their momentum to a sway that seemed to fuse their bodies together. "But everything with Jonathan requires a motive, and I cannot think of a reason for him to have killed Owen."

Well, Stas couldn't think of a reason for *anyone* to kill Owen. But it seemed this mysterious Jonathan had a penchant for arranging murder scenes into a Conclave-like setting.

So, who is Jonathan? Another Ichorian? Whoever he was, she doubted she knew him. Although, she must have some tie to him if Issac felt she could help him in seeking revenge. "What was his motive for Amelia and Eli?" she wondered out loud.

"I believe he wished to incite a war. The Hydraians are very protective of their Elders, of which Eli was one."

"An Elder?" she repeated.

"Yes, the oldest of the Hydraian race. There were five. Now there are four."

"So by killing him…?" It turned into a question because she couldn't puzzle it all out.

"Hydraians and Ichorians have long been at odds with one another, something you may have gathered last night during the Conclave. However, there's a truce of sorts in place. Assassinating an Elder, someone the Hydraians held very dear to their hearts, was a surefire way to invoke an emotional need for retaliation. Add Amelia, and, well, it's a wonder Lucian could control his Hydraians."

"I'm not sure I completely follow," she admitted. "But I understand the gist of what you're saying: Jonathan had a motive."

"Yes."

"And how did you figure out it was him?"

"Ah, that is a much longer story." He twirled her with

the words before pulling her flush against him again. "The short version is, a bottle of red wine tipped me off. I found it in the fridge, not fully chilled, and it came from a vineyard only one person I know fancies."

"Jonathan." A reasonable guess considering what he said before about Jonathan having killed his sister.

"Indeed," he replied. "There were other factors at play, but I'm positive he had a hand in my sister's murder."

"What happened when you accused him?" she wondered, curious as to why or how the man still lived. Given what she'd observed of Issac's world, his kind wasn't afraid to kill. And Issac certainly had the motive to seek revenge.

"Nothing, as I've not informed him." He dipped her backward, his lips at her neck. "I've let him think that I believe the Ichorians killed my sister."

Her eyes flew to his as he righted her again, her breasts against his chest. "Why?" she asked, breathless.

"Because the best revenge takes time and careful planning. It requires the perfect pawn." Another pivot ending in a dip that brought her dangerously close to the floor. Her chest heaved against his as he held her there, his body bent over hers as her hair brushed the polished wood. "Me."

"Yes." He slowly guided her upward, her body flush with his. "But last night changed everything. You meeting Osiris was a consequence I never could have predicted."

"Meaning what? I'm no longer the perfect pawn?"

"Oh, you're still perfect for my plans." The hand on her back drifted lower, sliding over her curves. His lips were a hairsbreadth from hers. "But I'm rather fond of you being alive." She shivered at the heat in his voice. They were no longer moving, just locked in an intimate embrace that left her craving more.

Clapping shattered the moment, a low whistle added for effect. "Not bad, Wakefield," a deep voice praised. "Not bad at all."

Chapter Nineteen

Blood Ties

BALTHAZAR, Issac mentally growled, not at all amused.

"I give it a seven point eight out of ten on the seduction scale," the mind reader informed Issac as he lowered the music to a soft background murmur. "Points deducted for a lack of disrobing and missed opportunities for light petting."

"You're an ass," Issac said, stepping in front of Astasiya.

"I'm only trying to be helpful. Shall I demonstrate the disrobing part while you take notes?" The suggestion underlying his voice had Issac narrowing his gaze.

Fuck. Off.

Balthazar grinned wickedly instead, intent and sin

dancing across his features. "Oh, I wouldn't go that far, sweetheart. I'm always up for a good challenge."

Issac frowned. "What?" That didn't even remotely make sense. And since when did Balthazar refer to Issac as *sweetheart*?

Amusement played through Balthazar's dark eyes. "I'm replying to your little blonde vixen's lascivious thoughts. You've unleashed quite the fancy in that one."

Astasiya's gasp had Issac glancing over his shoulder. She peered around him at Balthazar, her expression boasting shock and dismay.

Hmm, most women reacted like this when first meeting the sensual Elder. The man practically oozed sexual intent, and his outward confidence confirmed his ability to follow through. Issac shook his head, giving the mind reader a knowing look. "Nice try, Balthazar. She's immune to immortal gifts."

"Sounds like a performance issue, Wakefield. Might want to get that checked out because I hear her loud and clear. She's a fan of your ass, in case you were wondering."

Issac studied Astasiya, who now wore several shades of red.

"You're practically screaming it, sweetheart," Balthazar added, causing her lips to part.

Somewhat telling, but not. "You're going to have to do better than that." Sensing a woman's interest in another man didn't require mind-reading abilities, especially for someone as old and as experienced as Balthazar.

Balthazar's chuckle echoed across the room. "Now she thinks you're arrogant. Which, by the way, sweetheart, I've seen his ass, and I can firmly say he's well within his rights to be arrogant about it."

Astasiya blanched, her face giving everything away. Even Issac could tell what she was thinking.

All right, Balthazar. You want to prove you can really read her thoughts? Let's go for something harder.

The mind reader gave him a look that said, *Challenge*

243

accepted.

"What are the names of your birth parents, Astasiya? Their real names?"

"Why?" The word came out on a breath, as if shocked he would ask. "What do they have to do with anything?"

"Caroline and Seth," Balthazar said, disapproval radiating from the downward angle of his lips. "That wasn't very nice, Wakefield."

Astasiya took a step to the side, her focus on the mind reader leaning against the wall. He'd chosen a casual outfit, as always, of jeans and a maroon shirt. This was why Issac had chosen to dress down—he knew the Hydraians would arrive in similar attire.

"How did you know that?" she asked, her hands shaking at her sides.

Okay, that had been the wrong question to ask, clearly. Because she appeared ready to fall apart.

Balthazar tapped his head. "Mind reader, sweetheart."

"Impossible," she breathed, accusation lurking in her gaze as she faced Issac. "You said I was immune to Ichorians and their psychic gifts."

"You are." Of that he was certain.

"Then explain him?" She pointed at the smirking male across the room.

"He's not an Ichorian, but a Hydraian like Owen." A thought occurred to him, shifting his attention back to Balthazar. "Who else is here?" Maybe someone else could test a gift on Astasiya to see if this was just a fluke or if her supernatural resistance only applied to Ichorians.

"Ash and Jay. Jacque went back to get Luc a few minutes ago. And yeah, I think you should run that theory by your leggy blonde before you test it."

Issac's jaw clenched. "Get the fuck out of my head." *Or I'll play in yours.*

"It's just been my experience—of which I have a few millennia more than your three centuries—that most women don't like men thinking for them." He winked at

Astasiya, which only pissed Issac off more.

Stop flirting with her.

Balthazar seemed amused, his eyes saying, *I've only just started.*

"What theory, Issac?" Astasiya demanded.

I fucking hate you, Balthazar, he thought while pinching the bridge of his nose. The damn mind reader adored throwing Issac off his game, like a perpetual competition with no true winner. Because truthfully, they rivaled each other in many, many ways.

"You're immune to Ichorian gifts, but Balthazar's ability to read your thoughts suggests you might not be immune to Hydraian gifts. The only way to test that theory would be to have other Hydraians use their respective talents on you." There. That sounded scientific and sound.

Except the raising of her brows said she didn't agree with that logical idea at all. "You want to make me a guinea pig?"

"You could really use some work on your bedside manner, Wakefield."

"Oh, do shut up." Issac envisioned punching Balthazar in the face and forced the image into the mind reader's visual preceptors. The bastard staggered sideways on a gasp, only to shift the opposite way as Issac cast another visual spell—this one showcasing a hit to the stomach.

"As for you," he added, turning to Astasiya. "I thought you might want to test your immunity against psychic abilities in a safe environment. But what do I know?" He stalked out of the room in search of Lucian.

Astasiya needed someone reasonable to introduce her to Hydraian life. Not the seductive Elder with only one goal in mind.

Touch her and I'll kill you, Issac thought at him, knowing Balthazar could hear him. He didn't really mean it.

Or maybe he did.

Fuck, this woman had him tied up in knots over absolutely nothing and everything. He just felt so out of sorts around her, as if he were trying to fix something elusive.

No, that wasn't it.

He felt threatened.

Not by her, but by Balthazar.

Issac paused in the hall, startled. He *never* felt this competitive with anyone, least of all the Elder. So why now? Why her?

Because she'll never truly be mine...

His lips flattened. Since when did he care about the long term? Was it the element of the forbidden that taunted him into these thoughts and feelings? The fact that their relationship was a true impossibility, therefore making it safe to yearn for more? But why bother? Issac preferred one-night stands, easy relationships with no strings or expectations. Why would Astasiya be any different?

He shook his head. *This isn't me.* He needed to rein in these wayward inclinations and refocus on the task—to introduce Astasiya to the future.

And for that, he needed Lucian. Her destiny.

~*~

Okay, someone's angry, Stas thought, gaping after Issac. He'd just stormed out of the room, his shoulders tense, hands fisted at his sides.

And whatever he'd just done to Balthazar... wow. The man was still recovering, hands on his knees, his breathing harsh.

"Why is he so pissed?" she asked, confused as hell. She didn't want to be the object of an experiment. Was that really so infuriating?

"No, it's my fault," Balthazar said, coughing. "I underestimated his fondness for you and pushed too far." He shook his head and finger-combed his dark hair, righting himself. "Not that I regret a minute of it."

His licentious gaze made her snort. Sure, he was

attractive—almost lethally so—but she only had room for one too-gorgeous man in her life right now.

"I'm more than mere looks, sweetheart," he murmured, his tone one that alluded to silky sheets and long nights spent naked between them. "Why else would your Issac feel so threatened?"

She swallowed. *First, not my anything. Second, I'm not even going to consider the first comment.* Because if she did, she might believe him, and the last thing she wanted to do was fantasize about a *mind reader.*

"Ah, but fantasy makes it all so much more interesting." Sensuality seemed to ooze from his pores, his handsome face and deep voice a combination that no doubt brought most women to their knees. "Men, too," he added for her.

Her gaze narrowed. "You must get the biggest headache reading minds all the time."

"He loves it," a deep voice drawled from the doorway. "B?"

"She's not a threat, but I would be happy to search her more thoroughly." The wicked twinkle in his gaze only added to the smile he flashed her.

A charmer—not in a creepy way but in an experienced way.

This man knew how to seduce women, and if she weren't so wrapped up in Issac, she might be more intrigued.

"That won't be necessary," the newcomer replied, stepping into view.

Her lips parted. *Are all of Issac's friends gorgeous?* Because fuck, she couldn't handle more of these guys. She had enough between Balthazar and Issac. Now she had a third.

Lizzie would be losing her shit.

Stas just, well, stared.

"Can you give us the room?" the new male asked, his authority clear in both tone and stature. Tall, broad shoulders, sturdy jaw dusted in blond stubble, and emerald eyes that seemed to pierce her to her very soul.

Why does he look so familiar? She tried to place the features, but the connection refused her. It wasn't *him* she recognized, but something about him.

"Be careful with this one, Luc," Balthazar warned as he walked by him. "Issac has her all riled up." He glanced back at her, devious energy smoldering in the depths of his chocolate irises. "I look forward to getting acquainted, Stas. Let me know when you're ready for a real immortal."

The new male demigod—because what else could she call these guys? (They certainly weren't human)—shook his head with a chuckle while shutting the door.

"B will never learn," he said, more to himself than to her.

B is a nickname for Balthazar. Got it.

And what was this guy's name? She'd been too consumed by his size and striking features to hear it. Those features only grew more powerful and gorgeous as he approached her.

"I'm Lucian, but call me Luc." He held out a palm that was twice the size of hers.

Yep, definitely some sort of god. "Stas," she managed on a squeak as she shook his hand.

He released her from his hold, his shake firm and quick. "Yes, I know." He flashed her a devastating smile that had her taking a sharp breath.

Okay, so not only did Issac belong to the hot-bachelor club, but he also seemed to be part of some sort of secret society for lethally attractive men. This... was distracting.

"You can't read minds, right?" she asked, realizing that her thoughts were going south fast.

"No, my gift is more strategic. Some call me omniscient, but it's not the correct term. I also possess a sensual talent, but it's not relevant to our discussion."

"Oh." A sensual talent? Like a supernatural-style gift or just an overconfident statement about his bedroom skills? Given Balthazar's introduction, it seemed appropriate to assume the latter.

What is with these men? No, not men. Gods.

"I hear you're gifted with persuasion," he said, his words dumping a figurative bucket of ice water over her head. "That's a very unique talent, even more so since you can apparently already access it."

She swallowed, unsure of how to reply to that. *Where's Issac?* He mentioned telling Aidan about... Her eyes widened. *That* was how she knew this man. "You look so much like Aidan." The words left her mouth without thought.

"Yes, he's my father." His eyes crinkled with his smile. "You met him last night, right? During the Conclave?"

Her palms were clammy. "I... yes." Wait, did those rules still apply here? She took a step back. *Is this man an Ichorian? One who knows about my gifts? Oh, fuck, is he here for me?* She searched the room, expecting more of them to appear, but hoping Issac would be among them. *Where did he go?*

"Relax," Luc murmured, holding up his hands in a placating gesture. "I'm not your enemy, Stas. I'm actually very much your ally."

Yeah, she doubted that. Not after the introduction she received last night, courtesy of Osiris.

"Issac has explained that you're a fledgling who will one day become a Hydraian, right?"

She didn't trust him enough to answer that, so she said nothing instead.

"I'm a Hydraian, Stas," he said softly. "The oldest, actually. Aidan is my Ichorian father, who created me with a mortal mother several millennia ago."

Her lips parted. "Several..." She couldn't finish that phrase. *How old is this guy?*

"Balthazar, whom you just met, is nearly as old. I met him during a time you can't even begin to fathom, and we've existed together for thousands of years. It may seem impossible right now, but you can trust us, and you will. Because we're your future."

Issac chose that moment to open the door, his expression far less irritated than before. "When I mentioned bringing some of the others, I didn't realize you intended to invite an army to my house."

Luc grinned. "You're just sour that B tagged along."

"One of these days, I'm going to shoot him."

Luc shrugged. "He'll wake up."

"I know. That's precisely why I've not bothered." Issac stopped beside the blond male, their contrasting appearances giving her whiplash. Women everywhere would weep at the sight.

This sort of thing should be illegal.

"I was just introducing myself to your Stas, as she's apparently unfamiliar with my name." A hint of accusation lurked in those words.

"Yes, we've not yet touched on Hydraian hierarchy." His sapphire gaze captured hers. "Lucian is the eldest of his kind. Thus many refer to him as their King."

Luc rolled his eyes. "Great introduction."

"It's true."

"It's ridiculous and you know it," Luc replied, not at all amused. "They consider me a leader because of my vast experience."

"He remembers everything," Issac added helpfully. "He's omniscient."

"See, this is what I referred to earlier, Stas. Everyone makes this assumption about my gift, but it's really just that I store every detail from every experience, of which I've had many due to my age."

"Otherwise known as omniscience."

Luc shook his head. "Not by definition, which sta—"

"Okay," Stas interrupted, grimacing when both men focused on her. "Sorry, I need some clarifications."

"Then you're definitely in the appropriate company," Luc replied, smiling. "What can I clarify?"

Uh, everything. But she chose to start with the basics. "What are the rules for today?" It was something Issac should have covered with her prior to this introduction.

"There are none," Issac replied. "This meeting defies

them all."

Because Hydraians and Ichorians weren't supposed to consort with one another. Right. "Isn't that dangerous?"

"Absolutely." This from Luc. "But you're well protected here."

"Hence the Guardians taking over my kitchen," Issac muttered.

Luc chuckled. "I'm fairly certain the majority of them came to see you, not to protect me. You're missed on the island."

They shared a moment, some hidden conversation flowing between them that left Issac nodding. "I should visit more."

"Yes. You should." The command in Luc's tone startled Stas. This man truly was a leader, and it showed in the way he gripped and squeezed Issac's shoulder. But something else lurked between them, something brotherly.

Aidan is Luc's biological father.

Aidan also turned Issac.

Did that make them family?

"Where does Amelia fit in all this?" she wondered out loud, earning her an arched brow from Issac.

"My sister is dead."

"Right, I know. I'm just…" She winced, uncertain of how to word it. "This is all, well, confusing."

"Aidan is my father," Luc said, repeating what she already knew. "He was also Amelia's birth father. Making her a Hydraian, just like me."

That was the connection she needed. "So you're all friends because Aidan created you."

"Yes, but not quite." Issac scratched his stubbled jaw, his expression thoughtful. "My father died when I was two. Then my mother—a widow—met Aidan a year after, and he became her consort of sorts because my mother didn't wish to give up her title and fortune. Amelia was born shortly after."

Meaning Amelia and Issac shared a mother. "And then

Aidan turned you into an Ichorian later."

He nodded. "Precisely. I grew up with him as my father figure, even referred to him as such for many years. Which is why I consider Lucian a brother."

Luc grinned. "In a world of black and white, there is also gray."

"Yes. So perhaps now you see why I'm not a fan of our archaic laws, hmm?" His lips quirked at the sides.

"Why have the laws to begin with?" she asked, still uncertain of that part. "I mean, why would fathers want to hurt their children?" Because clearly they did. Case in point—Owen.

"Ah, families have fought over much less throughout existence. But in this case, it's the oldest reason known to man: fear." Luc's gaze took on a faraway gleam, seeming to lose himself in the past. It was then that she saw it—his age.

Like Osiris.

Luc resembled a normal man. Well, a ridiculously handsome man captured in the body of a god. But not exactly *old.*

Yet those eyes held thousands of lifetimes of knowledge.

"What are they afraid of?" she asked softly, both curious and confused.

"Power," Luc murmured, still seemingly lost in his own mind. "And blood."

She frowned. "I don't understand."

He blinked, refocusing on her. "Hydraians are dually gifted, while Ichorians are singularly powerful. That's how the jealousy began, long, long ago. Our kind inherits the talents from their fathers and their mothers, both of which manifest during rebirth. Many thought to use us, even isolated us on an island. But then they realized the darkest secret of all, something we kept hidden for nearly two thousand years."

Issac's face was artfully blank, his gaze almost bored. Very unlike Stas, who felt as if Luc had left her on the edge of her seat. "What was the secret?" she asked, hoping he would tell her.

"Our blood is toxic to Ichorians," Luc replied. "Which means, Stas, that once you're reborn as a Hydraian, you will be hunted by every Ichorian in existence. Because not only can a single drop of your blood kill one, but you'll also be able to persuade them to drink it."

CHAPTER TWENTY

A Crumpled Charade

ISSAC CAUGHT ASTASIYA'S HIP AS SHE SWAYED, his gaze locking on Lucian. He could have eased her into that truth rather than flaying her alive with it.

"But... But..." She touched her neck, gingerly stroking the healed mark against her skin. It had disappeared overnight, something that disappointed him more than it should.

"You're a fledgling," he reminded softly, his lips at her ear. "Your blood isn't venomous to me yet."

She clutched his shirt, burying her face against his chest as he wrapped his arms around her. Lucian raised his brows, the display of affection evidently surprising him.

"Let's prepare for dinner," Issac suggested, knowing

254

Cherie and Robert would be over soon with a feast. "We can discuss more later." Because they were nowhere near done yet. They hadn't even skimmed the surface.

"Can I have a moment?" Astasiya whispered. "Please?"

"Of course, love." He kissed her temple and signaled for Lucian to leave with a nod of his head. *I'll handle it.*

The much older man nodded. "I look forward to getting to know you better, Stas."

She didn't return the sentiment, her body shaking against Issac.

Lucian didn't press, merely left the two of them alone, the door closing quietly behind him.

"We're alone," he murmured, stroking his fingers through her hair. "I know this is a lot to take in and understand. It's why I wanted to introduce you to it slowly." Because he knew it would overwhelm her, specifically when she realized her future—not just that she would become a Hydraian, but also a powerful one. Perhaps the most powerful in existence.

She would have many enemies.

Fortunately, she would be equipped to handle herself. There was a reason the Elders survived as long as they did, and they would teach her as they had many others throughout their millennia of existence.

Rendering me useless to her.

He pushed that thought away, focusing on the trembling woman in his arms. "Ask me anything," he whispered. "I'll answer it."

She shook her head, her arms twisting around his waist. "I don't even know where to start."

"You could ask me when or how immortality will occur." That's what he wanted to know when Aidan first told him about this world. "And I would tell you it's your decision. You won't become a Hydraian until you die, even if it's a decade from now. As long as your bloodline remains, you'll be reborn."

"My bloodline?"

"Hmm, yes, it's speculated the immortality lives in our blood. Destroying it, such as by fire or severing the flow to the mind, are two ways to kill an immortal, including a fledgling."

She shuddered. "The Conclave."

"Yes, the ceremony is driven by the final death—the only way to guarantee an immortal will not awake."

"Owen…"

He nodded. "Exactly, yes. Whoever killed him knew how to ensure he would be unidentifiable to the authorities, and never rise again. I suspect the same was applied to your parents."

"Yes." She fell silent, her body no longer quivering. He continued combing her hair and lightly rubbing her back, offering what minimal support he could.

"Lucian and the others are nothing like the immortals you witnessed last night," Issac promised. "Have dinner with them and give them a chance to prove it to you. I'm certain you won't regret it."

She cleared her throat and finally looked at him, her eyes clear. "I have so many questions, Issac."

"I know, and the others and I can answer them. We won't lie to you. *I* have never lied to you." He added the last part to prove a point, to remind her that he'd done everything in his power to earn her trust, even when trying the slow approach.

Astasiya studied him for a long moment, her wariness evident in the way her nostrils flared. But eventually she nodded, the motion tentative. "All right."

He wrapped his palm around the back of her neck and pulled her into a kiss, needing to taste her. Tonight would change everything. She'd learn more about her destiny, which didn't involve him.

She's not for me.

His gut ached with the thought, his grip tightening as if to hold on to her for just another moment. He'd never felt this way about anyone, had never desired to be this close to another. But Astasiya had changed him on an irrevocable level.

He wasn't fond of it.

Preferred to avoid it.

A night in bed could cure them both, or worsen it.

Maybe I should end it now, before this feeling deepens.

Her tongue slipped into his mouth, distracting him from his thoughts, her talented mouth returning his kiss.

Oh, fuck the idea of pushing her away.

No, he wanted her closer.

He wrapped an arm around her waist, holding her in the position he preferred, and devoured her. Her nails bit into the back of his neck as she clung to him, hanging on as he kissed her beyond reason. This was how he would take her body—hard and thorough. All night. Until they both couldn't walk, and then he'd do it again. Because he needed her out of his system, and their time together was limited.

"Aya," he breathed, the nickname falling from his tongue unbidden. It came to him last night, and hell if he cared to analyze it now. If there wasn't a room full of Hydraians waiting for them, he'd take her now. "Fuck, I want you."

Her shuddering exhale tasted of mint, necessitating another kiss, this one longer and harsher.

He unloaded his conflicting emotions into it.

Frustration.

Confusion.

Apologizing for last night and the Conclave.

Expressing gratitude for her survival.

Sealing it all with a hint of anger for causing him to feel this way, for making him second-guess his plans and reprioritize his needs… for *her.*

And ending it with a whisper of a pledge for more. Later. As soon as they finished dinner.

Her pulse beat in time with his as he pressed his forehead to hers. Their breaths mingled, both coming in pants.

"That…" She swallowed. "I… Yes."

He chuckled. "What are you agreeing to, love?"

"You. This. Whatever this is."

He cupped her cheek, brushing his lips over hers. *It can't last*, he wanted to say but couldn't, his lips refusing to utter the words he normally had no problem saying. *One night. No strings.* He said that to every woman he ever fucked. But the phrases clung to his tongue, refusing to be released.

Issac cleared his throat. "We need to go to dinner first." A coward's excuse, but he required the distance. This *connection* between them was confusing his senses. Being around his family and friends would help. She needed to meet them all as well.

"Okay." Disappointment lurked in her tone, but she nodded. "Dinner."

~*~

Stas sat beside Issac, her heartbeat thrumming in her ears. She'd expected a horror show, or fighting, or some sort of power challenge. Not laughter. Or love. Or light teasing.

These immortals acted... normal.

Like friends.

No, closer than friends.

Like family.

A very good-looking family. Even the females were flawless. Stas was starting to understand Issac's theory regarding descending from angels. Because yeah, they possessed a heavenly appearance, as if marked by the gods themselves.

Their names were all beginning to run together, but Luc had taken the chair beside her while Balthazar sat at the head of the table. Everyone else filled in the spaces between, and few lounged outside, enjoying the evening breeze on the illuminated patio.

"Syrup shots," one of them was saying, her big eyes on Issac. Her name began with a G. Gretchen? Greta? Georgia?

"You're joking," he replied, glancing over her head at

Luc. "Tell me she's joking."

"There is nothing wrong with maple shots."

"There is everything wrong with maple shots," Issac fired back. "Syrup belongs on pancakes, not in a bloody glass."

"It belongs on waffles, actually, and you shouldn't knock my invention until you try it."

Issac shook his head, his disgust clear. "I'll pass, thank you."

"But it works!" the woman said, her excitement clear. "He demonstrated them last month in…" She trailed off, frowning at Balthazar. "Where did we go?"

"Aruba," he murmured. "You'd have enjoyed the body-shot display, Wakefield."

"Not with maple shots, no," Issac replied, his arm around Stas's chair, his thumb brushing her shoulder. They'd already eaten, the immortals proving to have hearty appetites. And now it seemed they were playing a game of catch-up, going through stories she knew nothing about.

Such as this one about maple syrup that she gathered Luc had turned into some sort of liquor.

The banter continued, providing such a different atmosphere than what she expected. An almost average night, minus the abnormal beauty and hints of immortality floating around the room.

Issac sipped his wine, chuckling and shaking his head at his friends. He was much more relaxed than last night. This felt real, as if he'd given her a glimpse into the true Issac Wakefield. Surrounded by Hydraians.

And breaking all the rules.

Now that she understood why Ichorians disliked Hydraians, the Blood Laws Osiris had mentioned made sense. Learning about Issac's familial ties helped her comprehend why he risked so much as well, why he'd kept her alive.

But he never told her about his plans for revenge or how he planned to use her.

"So, Stas, tell me about your job at the CRF," Luc said before taking a swig of his beer. The table fell silent at the request. She hadn't said much since introductions, and even then only a polite hello. They probably wondered if she could speak.

"Uh, I work with the marketing team. I started as an intern last year, but they just offered me a full-time position a few weeks ago." Not all that interesting yet everyone gaped at her. "I, uh, just passed my security exam. So I start next week." Assuming she remembered to call Human Resources back tomorrow.

"Hmm." Luc nursed his beer, his gaze pensive. "Issac mentioned you're close with the CEO and his son. How did you meet?"

"Through my roommate, Lizzie. Her father works at the CRF too."

"Ah yes. Elizabeth Watkins. I've not yet had the pleasure, but I know of her. What did you say she's doing?" The question went over her head to Issac.

"She's teaching," he replied.

"Teaching?" Luc repeated. "That's… unprecedented."

"Indeed."

Stas frowned between them. "What's unprecedented about teaching?" Lizzie adored kids. It seemed a natural path for her to pursue education.

"It's just not what I would have expected," Luc said. "With her upbringing and all, I mean."

"If you mean because she grew up with Lillian, then I understand." But something told her that's not what he meant at all. "How do you know of Lizzie?"

"Not the right question. How about a new route?" he suggested. "What is Doctor Fitzgerald's first name?"

What? "John. Why?"

He nodded. "Commonly short for Jonathan, yes?" The innocence underlying Luc's tone didn't match the intelligence radiating from those sharp green eyes.

She nearly snorted at the inane commentary when she

realized *what* his words implied. Her gaze shot to Issac, who sat beside her, swirling his red wine, awaiting her reaction.

"*No.*"

"Afraid so" was all he said. So casual. So nonchalant. So uncaring.

She pushed back from the table, knocking his arm from her chair. "No."

"He tried to ignite a war between our worlds. I assume you've informed her?" Luc's voice still held that note of innocence to it.

"I have." Issac. Still nonchalant.

Stas's hands fisted at her sides, her breath coming in erratic puffs. "No. I don't believe you."

"He tried to make it look like the Conclave, thinking it would incite my kind to finally seek revenge against our makers, the Ichorians. With Eli being an Elder and Amelia being my half sister, it almost worked. Issac was the one who realized what really happened. He saved a lot of lives in the process." Luc's rendition of the story matched Issac's from earlier, but she refused to accept them.

"You're wrong." Doctor Fitzgerald would never do that. He was her mentor. Her friend. Tom's father. "It's not true."

"Unfortunately, it is," Issac said, standing.

She took several steps back until she came up against a wall, her head swaying back and forth, rejecting his claim. Not Doctor Fitzgerald. He was world renowned for his humanitarian efforts. How could they accuse him of being a murderer? "You're wrong," she whispered. "He wouldn't—"

"I'm not wrong, Astasiya. The Sentinel program that Thomas belongs to, the very one *Jonathan* manages, is a military unit whose primary task is to hunt and kill rogue supernaturals. And—"

"They perform humanitarian missions," she interjected, her blood running hot. "I've done the press releases for them, Issac. I've seen the photos."

"You've seen what Jonathan allows you to see, Astasiya. And while, yes, they may perform some missions for media purposes, they're designed to take out immortals. Why do you think they gave you a full medical checkup?"

"Doctor Fitzgerald said that was an error."

"And you believe him?" he pressed. "Did he ask you if you had any adverse reactions?"

"Well, yes, because he *cares* about me."

He shook his head sadly. "No, Astasiya. He doesn't. He cares about my perceived interest in you, and he tested that theory with the Nizari poison."

"He's telling the truth, Stas," Luc added softly. "Think about it for a minute. Why would Jonathan try to provoke a war?"

"He wouldn't," she whispered, tears prickling her eyes. "*He wouldn't.*"

"He would." Issac sounded so emotionless, so certain of his accusation. "If a conflict between Ichorians and Hydraians was to ever spill over into the mortal realm, who would be there waiting with a solution?"

"The CRF's Sentinel program," Luc replied.

"Which has been researching immortal-killing weaponry for the last three decades," Issac added. "It's ingenious, really. War is good for business, and Jonathan knows that better than anyone."

"You're lying." The words came out on a choked sound, her voice failing her. "You're friends." She saw him with Dr. Fitzgerald. They shared jokes and stories like old colleagues. How could he accuse his *friend* of doing this?

Because he's right, her subconscious whispered.

She shoved the voice to the back of her mind, refusing to hear it. Doctor Fitzgerald would never do this. He didn't know anything about the supernatural.

Yet, Tom sent me to an Ichorian club.

Because he knew what she'd see.

Not Issac with another woman, but drinking blood.

Which implied—

"Remember what I told you just hours ago?" Issac asked, breaking into her thoughts. "The best revenge takes careful planning. Jonathan thinks I blame the Conclave and therefore trusts that our relationship is intact. He's comfortable. Exactly where I want him to be."

She shook her head, trying to clear it, but he kept talking.

"Think, Astasiya. What humanitarian organization subjects its civilian staff to full-blown security clearances? How about the Nizari poison that almost killed you? Do you think that's standard for all employees, because I'm guessing it's not. I'm betting that Jonathan requested his medical staff administer it after he saw us last weekend. Our little kiss did not go unnoticed, and neither did my unabashed pursuit of you. Jonathan and I have known each other for centuries. I don't date women. I fuck them. My interest in you only piqued his curiosity."

An arrow through the heart would have hurt less.

This explained all the attention, the black-tie event, the kiss in the hallway at the restaurant. He meant it all for show, something she knew already, but his abrupt confirmation still burned a hole through her chest. His blatant lack of remorse turned her inside out. He just stared at her with an expectant look, waiting for her to understand the validity of his words.

The security clearance she understood. Several government agencies required it.

But the questions about Hydraians and Ichorians during her polygraph provided damning evidence. One could be a coincidence, but two demonstrated a knowledge of this world most mortals didn't possess.

She trusted Doctor Fitzgerald, knew he would never hurt her, yet he had been interested in her reaction to the vaccinations. Because he cared, or had something else driven his interest? What would he have done if she'd admitted to becoming sick? Kill her?

She shivered. For six years, she looked up to him. He wasn't a cruel man. He couldn't be building an army. How would he even be getting away with it? Wouldn't Osiris know and do something to stop him? The master Ichorian didn't seem to handle rebellion well, and this would be the epitome of defiance.

Her head spun, a battle waging in her mind.

Loyalty fighting logic.

Desire brawling with truth.

The facts are damning.

Everything she'd learned over the last week painted Doctor Fitzgerald in a guilty light. Did he really authorize the Nizari poison? Did he suspect her of being a fledgling? Or was that standard protocol? Only he could tell her. Would he admit it?

Wait, did Issac say he's known Jonathan for centuries?

Is Doctor Fitzgerald immortal?

He didn't look a day over forty, yet Tom, his son, was twenty-seven. And Tom clearly knew about the supernatural world. Because his father told him? Because Tom himself was also immortal?

Fuck. She squinted her eyes closed, her vision spinning.

If all this was true, then Tom had sent her to the Arcadia not to find Issac cheating on her but to show her demons existed.

He sent me to a fucking slaughter.

Stas stumbled to the side, her equilibrium tilting.

She couldn't do this anymore. She needed a break. A fucking drink. To run. To… To… *Something.*

Issac lifted a hand, causing her to flinch.

"Don't fucking touch me," she growled. He lost that privilege when he admitted to her purpose in his life. A *perceived interest* to *pique Jonathan's curiosity.* Well, he'd fucking succeeded.

Issac scowled, her command clearly registering. Because yes, she'd threaded those words with power. And now he couldn't touch her. Too bad she had no idea how long it would last.

The narrowing of his eyes scattered goose bumps down

her arms. That look told her to run. Fast.

And she did, taking off down the hall toward the ballroom. She skidded to a stop by the closed doors, her purse and shoes nowhere to be found.

Issac sauntered down the hall toward her as she turned, his expression one of unveiled annoyance.

"Where's my purse?" she demanded.

"Why? Are you going somewhere?" he asked, his voice the epitome of calm. And that just pissed her off more.

"Not yet." She walked around him, aware that he still couldn't touch her.

"And where will you go? To Jonathan? To tell him you're a fledgling and hope he uses you for research instead of killing you outright?"

She stopped at the back staircase, refused to turn around. "That would just suck for you, wouldn't it? All that work you put into your pawn, just to lose it to the man who supposedly murdered your sister?" Water welled in her eyes, blurring her vision. "Well, I'm sorry you wasted your precious fucking time. Now, where's my purse?"

"In the pool house with your suitcase," he said, somehow driving the knife further into her gut. He couldn't even offer her a room in his home? She nearly laughed. No, those were for family and real friends. She was just the pawn in his game, a woman he wanted to fuck, but nothing more.

Why does that hurt? I never wanted a relationship. Neither did he.

But the truth slapped her across the face, leaving her weak in the harshest of ways.

Swallowing her pride, she went through the patio doors near the rear of the house and ignored all the Hydraians seated on the patio. Walked down the long path by the pool to the house beyond it. A kitchen with a breakfast nook was situated just inside the doors, a bowl of fruit on the table.

How fucking welcoming, she thought, hating it immediately.

A set of double doors were open beyond it, displaying a huge room with a four-poster bed.

Ah yes, the bed Issac had likely planned to fuck her on before heading back to his room in the house. Well, she despised that too.

She pulled her phone from her purse as Issac came to stand beside her, arms folded over his chest.

Why was he even here? Hadn't he said enough? She knew her purpose now. Not exactly how he'd intended to execute his plan, but it wasn't like she planned to stick around to hear about it.

There was only so much damage her heart could take in one day. Stupid mercurial organ, falling for a man she had no business falling for.

He's a demon, for crying out loud.

The waterworks threatened again.

Ugh, I'm losing my fucking mind.

Refocusing on her phone, she noticed several missed calls from Tom and a text from Lizzie telling her dinner went okay. She hadn't realized how late it was until she read the time. It would be well after midnight by the time she returned to the city. Then what would she do? Confront Doctor Fitzgerald? Talk to Tom?

A hysterical laugh threatened to bubble out of her.

The phone trembled in her hand. She didn't know who to call.

She couldn't bring Lizzie into this mess.

Owen was dead.

She no longer trusted Tom.

Her parents were too far away, not that she would allow them anywhere near this world.

A cab would do, but she wasn't sure where to go. What little money she had wouldn't last long.

Fuck.

She texted her roommate back with a quick, *I definitely won't be home tonight. Don't worry about me.* She didn't give a location because she didn't know where to go.

Her throat tightened. Dropping her phone into her purse, she let the bag fall to the floor.

I have no one.

Even if Issac was wrong about the CRF, she couldn't risk going back to the city. Not after everything she now knew. It'd been a miracle she'd survived this long as a fledgling in the middle of Ichorian territory.

"Talk to me," Issac said, standing a few inches behind her.

She swallowed, refusing to turn, not wanting him to see the tears glistening in her eyes. "Why?"

"Because I need to know you're okay."

Are you fucking kidding me? Of course I'm not okay. She took a deep, fortifying breath instead and muttered, "I'm fine."

"Your little show of persuasion out there says otherwise." His warmth cocooned her back, his step forward silent on the plush carpet.

Don't touch me, she begged. Because if he did, she'd break. Stas couldn't handle her body caving to him, not after everything he revealed. He toyed with her emotions just to pique the interest of Doctor Fitzgerald.

"I don't date women. I fuck them."

The words prickled her heart, straightening her backbone. She took a step away from him but faced him. *Let him see the emotion in my eyes. It's not like it matters.*

"I know you don't really care." The defeated note in her voice couldn't be helped. All she wanted was to be left alone, and he wouldn't even grant her that. "So why even bother? Just go back to your dinner party. It's not like I'm going anywhere. You can even take my phone if it makes you feel better. I'll be fine."

The latter was a lie. She would never be fine, at least not inside. Outside she could pretend. She mastered the art of concealing emotions at a young age. That would come in handy now.

"I know you're not going to run, Astasiya. That's not why I'm standing here."

Wrapping her arms around herself, she sighed. "Then what do you want from me?" What would it take to get him to leave her alone?

He started to lift his hand but dropped it. Those beautiful eyes almost looked troubled. An act, no doubt. She didn't understand it, couldn't determine the purpose.

"You never handle anything the way I expect you to," he murmured. "It's amazing."

Wow. Okay. "Happy to amuse you. Can you kindly fuck off now?" It came out as a question rather than a demand.

His eyes widened. "You're furious with me."

How good of him to notice, she thought, arching a brow.

"Because I told you the truth about Jonathan?"

She just stared at him. He couldn't be serious. "Why are you still pretending to care? Do you get some sort of sick pleasure from it? Trying to see how long you can toy with your little pawn before it finally breaks?"

"Astasiya—"

"No. This charade thing is done. You made yourself very clear. Your feigned interest piqued Doctor Fitzgerald's curiosity. Given that he nearly killed me with that Nizari crap, I'd say you did a fine job. What I don't understand is why you're still standing in front of me, acting like you give a shit when we both know you don't."

Silence.

A fire lit his blue irises, making her stomach flip. She wasn't sure if he wanted to kiss her or kill her. The intensity pushed her back a step, the back of her knees hitting the nightstand.

"While true that my interest in you also intrigued Jonathan, there is nothing *feigned* about it. If I could touch you right now, I would demonstrate thoroughly." He uttered each word slowly and precisely, his gaze smoldering.

I... I don't know how to reply to that.

"Do you understand why Lucian is here?" he continued, not giving her a chance to speak. "The danger you were in last night, well, let's just say I haven't felt that way in a very long time. That's why I called Lucian. He's here to help you become a Hydraian and to help keep you alive."

She bit the inside of her cheek. That's what he meant about her packing a few things, but he phrased it as a choice. Like she *might* decide to leave. "But what about your revenge?" That was the whole point of their association.

He palmed the back of his neck. "It seems my desire for you to live trumps my need to avenge my sister's murder."

He opened the drawer of the dresser beside them and pulled out a pair of swim trunks. She frowned at it. Storing swimwear in the pool house made sense, but there were other clothes beside it.

Issac took several steps toward the door before pausing, not meeting her gaze. "I'm going for a swim. Let me know if I need to find somewhere else to sleep tonight. I'll understand if you need space."

He closed the door behind him, disappearing from view.

His parting words had her studying the room around her. Dark, masculine tones, an oversized bathroom with a Jacuzzi tub, and beyond it a walk-in closet filled with suits.

Her lips parted, the obvious clues having been missed due to her emotional state.

This is Issac's room.

Chapter Twenty-One

Making Waves

OKAY, I MAY HAVE OVERREACTED.

Stas stared at the vaulted ceiling from Issac's bed, her lips twisted to the side. The shock had slowly melted into mortification at how she'd behaved. Because yeah, she'd definitely taken out her frustration on Issac. Which he sort of deserved, but not really.

It may have started as a charade, but the attraction between them wasn't a lie. He'd proven that several times. And he'd again confirmed he cared about her by following her to his room, where she found her suitcase and purse.

Still, he should have told her about Jonathan from the beginning. That would have saved them a lot of confusion and heartache.

Would you have believed him?

Ugh, she hated that voice. Such doubt. Such irritation. And so right.

Because she wouldn't have believed him at all. She wasn't even sure she did now. All the evidence backed up his claims, but her heart longed to reject the truth. Once she gave in, she'd have to admit that Doctor Fitzgerald was a monster, and she wasn't ready for that.

She dug her palms into her eyes, the temptation to scream hitting her hard.

Why did this have to be so difficult? Why her? Why was all this happening?

Because I'm a fledgling.

My blood will be toxic to Ichorians, like Issac.

The same man who had seemingly chosen her over his need to avenge his sister, a woman he clearly loved.

"I'm an idiot," she muttered to herself. She'd accused him of not caring when he clearly did. And now he'd left her in his room.

She needed to find him. To talk to him. To apologize.

Right.

No time like the present.

She rolled off the oversized mattress, the tile cool beneath her feet. The window above the kitchen sink showcased the beach, and the moon shining brightly over the water, causing her to pause and admire the view. She wondered if the curtains along the back of his room revealed the same view or if those covered windows overlooked the trees.

Hmm. Stas would investigate later.

Her musings shifted as she found Issac in the pool, swimming laps. He seemed to cut through the water, his strokes measured and sure, surprising her. She knew he enjoyed the sport after the towel incident from the other day but had no idea he excelled at it.

But of course he did.

The man exemplified perfection in every way.

She tested the water with her toes and found the temperature to be pleasant enough. Sitting on the edge, she allowed her legs to dangle over the side, her focus on the sexy swimmer gliding across the pool.

He completed another lap before stopping in front of her. The water hit him mid-torso as he stood, making the depth around five feet or so. He pulled off his goggles and tossed them onto the deck beside her, his expression wary.

"I may have overreacted," she admitted. "I'm sorry."

His shoulders visibly relaxed. "You don't need to apologize, love. It's a lot to take in."

"Which is why you preferred the slow approach," she said, understanding that now. "I just wish you'd have told me your suspicions about Jonathan sooner."

"Would you have believed me?"

A question she'd asked herself more than once in the last hour. "Probably not," she admitted, drawing a circle in the water with her finger. "A part of me still doesn't, even now."

"Do you require more proof?"

She shook her head. "No, I think what I need is more time." She twisted her lips to the side, unsure if that would really help or not. "There's something I don't get." Well, there were a lot of things she didn't comprehend yet. But on this topic, something really stuck out to her. "Osiris is all about rules, right? Why would he let Doctor Fitzgerald create an elite immortal-killing unit in the heart of Ichorian territory?"

"Ah, a question we've been contemplating for nearly three decades. He's clearly worked out some sort of arrangement with Jonathan, though we're not sure what." He pushed onto his back, his hands sculling beneath the water to keep himself afloat as his legs came up.

She tried not to admire the rippled abdomen on display.

And she failed miserably.

The man's body was a moving distraction.

"Aidan believes Osiris has hired Jonathan's team to target specific immortals, and in return, he allows the

Sentinel unit to exist."

"So Jonathan is an immortal," she said, having already guessed as much.

"An Ichorian, yes."

"And Tom?" He looked too much like his father to be adopted.

"A fledgling, just like you," Issac confirmed. "Which is why we're certain Jonathan has an arrangement with Osiris—because he's allowed Thomas to exist."

"So…" She paused, swallowing. "Tom knew what he was doing when he…?"

"Sent you to the Arcadia?" Issac finished for her. "Yes. Although, I don't think he knew about the Conclave. But he definitely knew the activities and behavior common in the club."

She expected as much given everything she now knew. "So he wanted me to find you with another woman." Not necessarily in the throes of passion, but to catch him *feeding*.

Issac lifted a shoulder, still treading water. "That, or more likely, he wanted you to see the world I belong to. I rarely feed at the Arcadia, if ever. And I certainly didn't last night. Not until you arrived."

Her heart skipped a beat at the memory of his bite. She hadn't understood it at first. Then, by the time she realized what he was doing, she could hardly think.

It'd been so intense.

Addictive.

Crippling her mind and thoughts, stealing her from reality, and sending her to a place she'd never been.

A place she would happily visit again.

"Does…?" Heat crept up her neck. "Does it always, uh, feel like that?"

"It can, yes." Sin danced across his features, curling his lips. "Care for another bite, love?"

Such a loaded proposition, one that warmed her in a way it probably shouldn't. "Maybe," she managed, her throat dry.

He stood again, a dark emotion flaring in his midnight irises, one that sent off a flurry of butterflies in her lower abdomen. That was the kind of look a man gave a woman before he devoured her.

She started to scramble backward, but he caught her by the ankle and yanked her into the water.

Shit!

Completely submerged.

Hair and all.

She pushed up from the bottom of the pool. *Fucking demon.*

Spitting out a mouthful of water, she glowered at the laughing male beside her. "What the hell was that for?"

"Payback for earlier."

She snorted and splashed him, the move automatic and far more playful than she intended.

He slowly wiped the droplets from beneath his eyes, then narrowed his gaze in her direction. "All right, Aya."

He lunged for her.

With a shriek, she kicked onto her back to escape him, unsure of what he intended to do. But he was much faster, grabbing her hip with one hand and fisting her wet hair with the other. He tugged her to him, his body hot and hard in all the right places.

"Issac..." She put her hands on his shoulders, winded from her poor attempt at outswimming him. "Let's talk about this."

"Talk?" He arched a brow. "All right, then. For the record, I do not appreciate edicts of any kind, especially ones that forbid me from touching you."

Okay, not what she expected him to say. "I, uh, I'm—"

His mouth took hers in a punishing kiss that seemed to vibrate through her, stroking her very soul. *Holy wow.*

He'd kissed her several times over the last few days, but this one threatened to blow her mind. So much frustration and heat and pent-up *need.* His grip tightened, holding her exactly where he wanted her, ravaging her mouth, destroying her, claiming her.

She trembled against him, lost to his will, silently begging him for more.

But he pulled away, his forehead touching hers, their exhales mingling. "Not being allowed to touch you was physically painful. Please don't do that to me again, Astasiya."

If this was the expected result? "No promises," she breathed. She'd take a dunk in the water any day if it meant ending up in his arms.

"Mmm, then I better take advantage of touching you while I can." He led her backward beneath the waterfall, effectively hiding them from view of anyone outside. Her back met the wall, his body caging hers. "You're decidedly overdressed, Astasiya. How about we fix that?"

His hands fell to her tank top, giving it a tug.

"Yes," she managed, her voice husky.

Devious intent darkened his features as he guided the fabric over her head, casually tossing it aside without a glance. His thumb stroked the button of her jean shorts next, flicking it open and pulling down the zipper without faltering.

Her heart was in her throat, a thundering cacophony of beats in her ears.

He tugged the material from her hips, sliding it downward with the ease of a man used to undressing a woman, the water providing minimal resistance as he went.

Flames erupted inside her, igniting her veins and sending a tremor down her spine. By the time he finished his task, she could hardly stand, her knees threatening to buckle.

"I truly adore your penchant for lace, Astasiya," he murmured, his focus on her blue bra, his palm on her ass. He lifted her one-handed, forcing her to wrap her legs around his waist. "You questioned my desire earlier. Are you questioning it now?" He punctuated the words by grinding his hips into hers, his erection hot and hard against her.

Fuck.

She arched into him, wanting to feel more, to put this intense passion between them to the ultimate test. Her lips parted, but all that escaped her was a moan that sounded a lot like his name. Issac captured her mouth once more, his lips bruising against hers, his tongue fucking her mouth the way she wanted him to take her body.

Oh, he'd held back before.

Now? He gave her everything.

She felt branded.

Owned.

Possessed.

Every touch stoked the need inside her, enflaming her with a passion no one had ever come close to sparking.

"Issac," she breathed, needing more.

They still wore too many layers.

Her nipples chafed against the bra, causing her to whimper. Not enough friction. Not enough *Issac.*

Desire controlled her every move. One hand went to his hair, the other to his back, enjoying the feel of him. All hard, hot male pressed up against her, just begging her palms to explore every muscular inch.

His hands returned the favor in kind, sliding up to palm her breasts. She arched into him on a groan, meeting the delicious hardness settled at the apex of her thighs. He rotated his hips, hitting her most sensitive spot and shooting sparks through her system.

"Do you feel how badly I want you?" he asked, his lips whispering over hers.

"Yes," she hissed. If he'd just remove the rest of their clothes, he'd feel how much she wanted him, too. Damn, she needed to free him, to *feel* him. Her fingers traced the ridges of his abdomen to the happy trail leading to the edge of his swimsuit.

"No." He grabbed both wrists and held them over her head in one hand, the devil smoldering in his gaze.

Her complaint came out as a gasp as he pressed into her,

his arousal nudging the place she desired him most. *Too many fucking clothes.*

"How does it feel to not be able to touch something you want, Aya? Does it burn you the way it burned me?"

She shivered at the possessive hold and nipped his bottom lip in protest. "I could command you to let me go," she said, her voice drowsy with lust.

"But that requires you to have a voice." His mouth covered hers, taking her slowly, making his point clear. His free hand returned to her breast before drifting down toward the sweet spot between her thighs. He found her clit through the fabric, pressing it with his thumb.

She cried out against his lips, evoking a grin from him.

"Try commanding me now, little fledgling." His teasing tone made her want to do just that, but he distracted her by rolling the pad of his thumb in a sensuous circle, her hips bucking in response.

A growl caught in her throat as he pressed harder, energy humming up and down her spine, her abdomen overheating. "*Fuck.*"

"Another demand, love?" He removed his thumb, eliciting a curse from her very soul. "Is this what you want?" he asked, sliding his fingers beneath her panties to part her slick folds.

"Oh…" Her hands fisted, her head falling back against the wall on a groan.

He was killing her in the most delicious way, his fingers teasing her into oblivion while only barely brushing where she desired him most.

She bit her tongue to keep from screaming, her need overwhelming all of her senses.

So close.

Just right.

Not enough.

"Issac." It came out as a plea as she writhed against him, her body on fire. "Please."

He bent to nibble one of her aching nipples through the

lace, intensifying the sensations and worsening them. It almost hurt, but it felt so, so good.

His thumb found her clit again, pressing down hard and bringing her to the precipice, only to disappear just before she could fall over the cliff into oblivion. His teeth sank into her nipple, evoking a scream from her throat.

"Issac!" she cried out, trembling with need, tears glistening in her eyes. "Fuck! What do you want?" she asked, begging now. "An apology? For me to promise never to compel you again?" It fucking hurt to be brought to the point of no return only to be denied.

"No, darling." He kissed her hard and ripped the lace from her body, leaving her naked and gasping against him. "Keep your hands there." He pressed her wrists into the wall beside her hips.

God, this man was going to wreck her. Inside and out. Heart, body, and mind. It terrified her, floored her, excited her.

He slowly removed his swimsuit, inch by inch, revealing his gorgeous form to her gaze.

And damn, every part of him was perfect. Long. Lean. Strong.

She shuddered, desperate to explore him but fearing he would stop if she did. Stas couldn't bear if this ended now. She'd surely explode. Ruined. Destroyed. Expired.

Her limbs shook from the onslaught, electricity humming like a live wire through her very being. One stroke and she'd combust.

She wanted him inside her. Now. If only—

"I admire your persuasive talent, love," he whispered, his lips against her jaw. "Even when used on me." He knotted his fingers in her hair, his mouth brushing hers. "Never apologize for what you can do." His fierce words only added to the sensations building inside of her.

"Okay," she managed, her throat dry, her legs quivering around his waist.

"Touch me," he mouthed, his cock hot and heavy

against her lower abdomen.

Finally.

She grabbed his shoulders, sliding her hands down his back to his ass and back up again. Silk. Muscle. Man. Her own personal heaven.

His palms went to her thighs, his arousal prodding her entrance.

She arched into him in invitation. "Yes…"

Her nails bit into his back as he pushed forward, his gaze holding hers.

The intimacy of it nearly undid her, his intensity almost unbearable. There were so many unspoken emotions lurking in his blue eyes, emotions she knew were rivaled in her own.

But she couldn't look away.

Not even as he slid deeper, all the way to the hilt, filling her almost to the point of pain.

He took her mouth in a thorough kiss, his body still against hers, giving her a moment to adjust. Her minimal experience hadn't prepared her for him—for this.

"Aya," he whispered, the nickname tasting sweet on her tongue. "What are you doing to me?" he asked, wonder in his voice.

She parted her lips, only to find them occupied again, his mouth memorizing and training hers for his use alone. Every kiss, every caress translated to a claim, her body slowly submitting to him.

I'll never want another.

Only Issac.

She'd never experienced such passion with another, never knew it existed. But as his hips began to shift, she learned a whole new dance of life. One underlined in adoration and overwhelming sensation.

God, he can move.

She threaded her fingers through his hair, holding on as he took her without remorse, fucking her the way only Issac could. There would be bruises tomorrow. She didn't care.

Not when it felt so incredibly raw and true and amazing.

"Fuck," he groaned, his lips falling to her neck, his teeth scraping her pulse without breaking the surface.

Her thighs clenched around him, the heat inside climbing to insurmountable heights.

So hot.

Burning.

Need.

His hand drifted between them, his thumb finding her clit and pressing down. "I want to feel you fall apart." His voice was rough and growly and so fucking arousing. "Come for me, love." He intensified his thrusts while circling her bundle of nerves, the heady combination too much for her senses.

I'm falling.

Too much.

Oh, fuck.

"Issac." Her nails bit into his back, needing to hold on as a tumultuous wave of energy shook her very being. It heightened, grew, all centered in her lower abdomen and spreading. It hurt, tightening all her muscles.

"Now, Aya." The command in his tone shattered her, spiraling her into a tornado of heated oblivion that blinded her vision.

She couldn't move.

Couldn't breathe.

Couldn't think.

Only feel. Her heart hammering in her chest. Her lungs burning. Her lips parted on a soundless scream.

She squeezed her legs, capturing him, her mouth against his shoulder, her arms around his back. He drove himself into her, his penetrating movements only prolonging her ecstasy as he slammed her hips against the wall. Each stroke set off a new quake, her limbs shaking and burning around him.

He groaned her name, his muscles stiffening beneath her touch, his orgasm exploding inside her. The heat of it sent another shock wave crashing through her, shaking her to her very core.

Stas panted, her exertion overwhelming and exhausting, and yet so very exhilarating.

Issac kissed her, his mouth worshiping and adoring, her name murmured between nips and licks. He remained hard inside her, the water still rippling around them from his exertion.

We just fucked in the pool, she realized dizzily. And water resistance hadn't impacted him in the slightest. *What can he do on a bed?*

"I need more," he whispered, as if reading her mind. "Much, much more."

She undulated her hips, silently urging him to proceed. She'd be sore tomorrow. But who the hell cared? She'd enjoy every minute of the sensual ache, thinking of Issac the entire time.

He grinned against her mouth. "In the bedroom, love. I want to taste every inch of you."

Chapter Twenty-Two

A Lesson in Exclusivity

ISSAC COULDN'T STOP TOUCHING ASTASIYA.

She slept soundly beside him, exhausted from their night in bed. The woman was fucking flawless, meeting him move for move and kiss for kiss.

He'd entertained numerous women over the centuries, but none of them aroused him like the woman sleeping in his arms. Even now, his cock desired more, pressing against her ass, urging him to wake her with an orgasm.

But they had company, something he suspected she wouldn't be pleased about when she woke up.

Issac kissed her neck, her bare shoulder, and along her arm as he slid his palm down her stomach to the apex between her thighs. She squirmed, her heartbeat escalating in his ears.

"We missed breakfast," he murmured, guiding her onto her back, his lips against her hip. "A shame, really, as I'm starved. Someone kept me up all night."

Perhaps he could coax her into a good mood so his news of who had dropped by for a visit wouldn't be so upsetting. He nipped her skin, tracing a path along her lower abdomen with his tongue.

Bedroom eyes gazed down at him, her pupils dilated from sleep and flickering with wonder. "Oh God…"

"Mmm, no. Issac," he corrected, smiling against her skin.

"Fuck." She clutched the silk bedsheets on either side of her waist, her gorgeous breasts on display from the sunlight streaming in through the translucent curtains.

He licked the sensitive space between her legs, teasing her, adoring her, memorizing her. "Good morning," he murmured, his lips grazing her mound. "Or should I say 'afternoon'?"

"I'm… You're…" She shuddered, her thighs tensing as he settled between them.

"I'm what?" he asked against her damp flesh, her arousal taunting him in the most sensual of ways. "Hungry? Yes."

"That's—" She bowed off the bed, whatever she'd been about to say wrapped up in a moan as he tasted her. He'd wanted to do this last night, had meant to lick every inch of her, but the sight of her in his bed had derailed his focus. Being inside her had become his obsession, his primary goal of the evening.

Now, he wanted to worship her the way she deserved.

His guests could wait.

One night hadn't been enough. Hell, a month wouldn't suffice at this point. This woman was under his skin, his new addiction in life.

He devoured her, loving the way she writhed and moaned. Her hands moved to his hair, holding him to her, encouraging him to explore more, to take her over the edge.

Rather than oblige, he shifted out of her reach, eliciting a guttural growl in response.

"Tease," she accused, her breath harsh.

He grinned against her inner thigh before moving upward to her breasts. They were flushed and aroused, just the way he liked them. He took a tender bud deep into his mouth and rolled it with his tongue.

"I want you to shatter so hard that you think of me all day, Aya." He bit the sensitive peak, evoking a whimper of need from her. Oh, he loved that sound. He inspired another by nibbling her breast, her pleasure addictive.

"Tell me what you need," he whispered sliding down again, his tongue dipping into her belly button. "My hands? My cock? My tongue?" The last word was spoken right against her swollen clit.

"Yes," she hissed. "Yes."

He slipped a finger through her wetness, teasing her. "Yes?" he repeated. "Yes what?"

"Just touch me, Issac," she begged, her words healing a wound deep inside him. Being told he couldn't have what he desired had physically hurt. Her plea now counteracted the command from last night, lifting a bruise from his heart he hadn't realized was there. He *needed* to caress her, to adore her, to please her.

His lips closed over her sensitive bud, and she cried out his name.

Yes.

He swirled his tongue over it before sucking her hard into his mouth, causing her to buck against him.

So beautiful.

So gorgeous.

So *mine.*

He'd never felt this possessive over anyone, but Aya awoke the predator inside him, the one who desired her more than any other. And she was his. Writhing. Wet. Willing. In his bed. Where she belonged.

Issac's palms skimmed her legs, her abdomen, and

breasts, urging her to come, needing to feel her pleasure beneath his touch and tongue. He sensed her teetering, her muscles clenching around him, her body frozen on the precipice.

And falling.

His name a scream in the air.

Her fingers gripping his hair, her body trembling, coming undone in the most gorgeous sight he'd ever witnessed. Fucking beautiful. Glorious. And he wanted to see it again. He wrung every drop from her, waiting until her quakes shifted to quivers, and climbed up to cage her between his arms.

"I absolutely adore hearing you say my name like that." He kissed her thoroughly, allowing her to taste herself on his tongue. "And I'm going to enjoy hearing you say it again just like that later." He would do so now, but she wasn't ready for him again yet. Just pressing his cock against her center had her wincing. "Mmm, we need to get ready. Shower with me?"

Her brow furrowed. "But... don't you... I mean, shouldn't we, uh, finish?" She cleared her throat, her cheeks flushed with color.

"You're quite charming when flustered." He brushed his lips over hers before rolling off of her and standing, hand palm up, waiting for her. "That was for you, love. The shower is for me."

"Oh..." She pushed up onto her elbows, her eyes roaming over him with interest.

He chuckled and scooped her up off the bed, tired of waiting, and headed toward the bathroom. "We have people waiting for us."

"What? Who?"

"I mean, I realize I fucked the sense right out of you, but did you miss Lucian and all the others at dinner last night?" He set her on the counter, his hands gripping the marble on either side of her thighs.

She narrowed her gaze. "That's a bit cocky, isn't it?"

"Confident," he corrected, smirking. "And also, true." He went to the walk-in shower to turn on the water and found the items they needed under the sink. "Can you stand yet, darling?"

"So arrogant," she muttered, sliding to her feet. "We'll see if I return the favor now."

"Who said that's what I have in mind?" He pulled two oversized towels from the cabinet to set aside on the heat rack before stepping onto the stone floor of the shower. "Join me, Aya. If you dare." She brought out a playful side to him that he barely recognized after centuries of disuse.

Astasiya made him feel young.

Alive.

Buoyant.

Her arms slipped around his waist as she entered the shower, her breasts against his back. "I'm not afraid of you."

His lips curled. "That sounds like a challenge."

"Take it however you want."

He angled the showerheads over both of them and turned in her arms. She tilted her head back beneath the spray, her eyes closed, her expression angelic. He slid his mouth over hers, needing to kiss her, his dick throbbing against her lower belly. Fuck, he wanted her again. And again. Alas, he meant what he said. This wasn't about reciprocation but about a different type of seduction.

Threading his fingers through her hair, he combed through the long, damp strands while gently teasing her lips with his tongue. She sighed against him, her hands exploring his back.

"Mmm, I could kiss you forever, it seems," he whispered, picking up the shampoo. "But we need to talk about today." He lathered a healthy amount into his hands and ran his palms over her head, taking care of her in a way he rather enjoyed.

"What about today?" she asked, gazing up at him through thick lashes.

"Well, first, a few others have arrived." He rinsed the

suds from her hair and repeated the actions for himself before picking up the soap.

"Who?" she asked as he guided the bar over her arm, painting suds over her skin.

"Aidan and his harem, as well as Tristan and Mateo."

"Harem?" she repeated.

"Anya, Nadia, and Clara." Technically, the latter wasn't involved with Aidan sexually, but Issac didn't want to go into that topic now.

"He has a harem?"

"He created them all, yes." Issac slipped the soap between her breasts, taking tender care of her core and loving the way her nipples beaded in response to his teasing touch.

"So they're like your siblings?"

He nearly laughed. "Hardly. He may have turned them, but our relations are somewhat estranged. I grew up with Amelia and knew Lucian at a young age, while Aidan's newest additions came from different occurrences throughout the last few decades. We're all friends, of course, but I don't consider them family." Especially Clara. That would be wrong on a variety of levels.

Issac soaped the tops of her thighs and knelt to reach the rest of her legs before telling her to spin so he could approach her from behind.

"How is an Ichorian created?" she asked, curiosity evident in her tone.

"It's a blood exchange process that ends in death and subsequent resurrection," he said, his focus catching the mark at the base of her spine as he massaged her ass with both hands.

"So not through procreation," she continued, causing his gaze to snap up.

"What?"

"Well, you said an Ichorian mating with a human creates a fledgling. Fledglings become Hydraians after their rebirth—which I interpret to mean they wake up immortal after dying?"

"Yes," he confirmed, his attention shifting back to the mark on her skin. He traced it with his finger. Small, heart-shaped, almost like a tattoo, but not quite.

"What happens when an Ichorian has sex with another Ichorian?"

"Aside from sharing pleasure?" *Assuming both parties are into that kind of thing.* "Nothing. Ichorian females are infertile, and my kind are immune to disease."

"What about a Hydraian and a mortal?"

"Hydraians are also infertile." He stood and finished soaping off her back, the blemish imprinted in his mind. "And before you ask, so are fledglings." He rotated her to face him. "Which is why we didn't use protection." With humans, he always wore a condom. Astasiya didn't require it, something he very much enjoyed and would be taking advantage of again soon.

She bit her lip, nodding. "Probably should have discussed that pre-sex."

He smiled and helped her rinse the suds from her skin. "There wasn't anything to discuss, love. I can't impregnate you, nor would diseases impact us."

Another nod. "Well, that's good, then."

He handed her the soap. "Your turn."

Delight radiated from her expression. "Yes, please."

She started with his abs, causing him to smile. He hadn't given her much opportunity to touch him last night, his hands too busy controlling hers as he took her in various ways. All of which she enjoyed, as did he. So much so that he'd completely missed the symbol on her lower back.

Astasiya lathered his chest, his arms, and continued lower, her fingers wrapping around his base to give him a firm stroke.

"Careful, darling, or I'll accept that as an invitation."

"Just being thorough," she replied, all innocence, aside from the sinful intent dancing in her gaze. She fisted him again, squeezing harder this time, her palm slick and confident against his shaft.

"You're playing a dangerous game, love."

"Me?" She batted her eyes at him. "Never."

Another stroke that had his balls tightening, his abdominal muscles clenching. Part of him wanted her to continue. The sadist in him preferred to wait, to delay his gratification until they had more time to prolong the experience.

He caught her wrist, stilling her movements. "Keep pushing and you'll end up on your knees with my cock down your throat." Not an idle threat, which she must have seen in his features because she shivered.

"I… I might enjoy that." Soft words.

He smiled. "If we didn't have everyone waiting on us, I'd test that statement." And enjoy every fucking minute of it.

Her grip loosened. "Why are they waiting on us?"

Hmm, time to kill the fire brewing between them. He'd reignite it later. "Because they want to talk about your future, and I believe Aidan has news on Owen."

She froze. "Owen?"

Issac took over soaping his body. "Indeed. He sent me a series of visions when he arrived, Owen being one of them."

Her brow furrowed. "Visions?"

"My gift, Aya." At her continued frown, he added, "I'm constantly tapped into everyone's vision, within a certain mile radius, of course. As my Sire, I'm very attuned to Aidan."

"Miles?" she asked, her lips parted in awe.

"Roughly one or two, depending." He swapped the soap for some conditioner, applying it to her hair first.

"That must be overwhelming," she said after a minute.

He chuckled, recalling his early days. It'd been an absolute nightmare learning control, but residing in London for a few months had done the trick. "I liken it to having the tele on in the background without sound. Switching them all to the same channel is an easy skill. It's making them see different things that can be more cumbersome."

"And what you did to Balthazar?" she asked as he rinsed her hair.

He smirked, recalling the way he'd handed Balthazar his ass yesterday. An overreaction, sure, but the bastard deserved it. "Child's play."

Issac rinsed his hair and brushed his lips against hers once more before shutting off the water. Her eyes glimmered with questions, causing him to arch a brow. "Is there something you want to know, love?"

She nodded slowly, her cheeks reddening.

"And?" he prompted, intrigued.

"You didn't... We didn't..." She pinched her lips to the side. "You didn't bite me again. Last night, I mean."

He wrapped a freshly warmed towel around her shoulders, grinning. "I typically only feed every two weeks or so. But if you're craving a bite, I'll be happy to oblige." He nipped her chin playfully.

"And you usually feed during sex?" she asked as he grabbed his own towel.

"Yes." He met her gaze. "Is this where you ask about my experience?" Because he really didn't want to have that conversation.

She shook her head. "No, I'm well aware of your playboy reputation. As you said, you don't date women, you fuck them, right?"

"Hmm." He caught her around the waist and yanked her to him. "I'm not sure I like that tone, Aya."

"Just stating facts." The bitter quality in her voice had him narrowing his eyes further. "And what does *Aya* mean?"

"It's my nickname for you," he murmured, his palm wrapping around the back of her neck. "Just yesterday you protested Elizabeth referring to me as your boyfriend. And now, your mood has soured over a few experience-related questions. Why?"

"Those are two very unrelated topics."

"Oh?" He tightened his hold around her when she made to step backward. "Allow me to relate them, then. You don't want me to be your boyfriend, yet you ridicule my relationship behavior. So which is it?"

"I don't…" She shook her head. "What are you asking me?"

This was why he avoided dating. Too much confusion and emotions. But with Astasiya, he found he wanted that.

While he hadn't realized it yesterday, her outright rejection had hurt a bit. Never in his life had he ever considered a romantic relationship with anyone. Then the first one he desired to truly court—Astasiya—had seemed quite affronted by the proposition of a label.

"Would you like me to be yours exclusively, or not?" he asked, tired of dancing around this topic. Either she admitted her feelings ran as deep as his own or she laughed him off.

Her eyebrows rose. "Like seriously date? Not just a charade?"

"If this were a charade, love, we wouldn't have just spent a night fucking in my bed." She was the first woman he'd ever entertained here. Typically, he reserved his Hamptons estate for family and friends only, since Amelia and Eli were the primary inhabitants. Until recently, anyway.

"Oh." Her cheeks pinkened. "You want this to continue."

"That is the general idea, yes." And he'd really appreciate a more telling response on the prospect sooner rather than later. He couldn't be the only one who felt this intensity between them.

"Exclusively," she added.

"Now you're just repeating my phrases." He released her to run a comb through his hair before handing it to her. "That mark on your lower back—how long have you had it?"

She looked taken aback by the abrupt subject change,

but as she didn't seem ready to discuss their future, he switched to a more practical topic.

"I... The what?"

He pressed his palm to her lower back over the towel, rubbing the spot to the left of her spine with his fingertips. "There's a heart-shaped blemish here, and I'm wondering how long you've had it."

Her brow crumpled. "Uh, my birthmark? Forever. Why?"

"I don't think it's a birthmark." He kept replaying the image in his head, the details too exquisite and contrived to be of natural occurrence. "I think it might be a rune."

"A *what*?"

He didn't bother repeating the term. She'd heard him. "With your permission, I'd like to show Aidan and Lucian. They'll be able to confirm for sure."

She blinked. "You want me to let them examine my lower back?"

"No." He tapped his head. "I can provide the detail they need."

"Ah, right." She started combing her hair, her lips curled down. "I mean, if you think it's useful, then okay. But only my lower back, Issac."

He chuckled and kissed her temple on his way to his closet. "As if I would ever share the rest of you with anyone." He meant that in a multitude of ways. The idea of another seeing her naked, or worse, *touching* her, had his fists curling around the jeans he'd just picked up.

No. Definitely not sharing her. Ever.

Except, one day he'd have to. Because a Hydraian and Ichorian relationship was too risky to consider.

So we'll date until we tire of each other.

That would work.

Astasiya didn't have to join the Hydraians tomorrow. She could wait a year, or five.

He selected a gray shirt, his movements stiffer than intended. Clearing his throat, he reentered the bathroom to find Astasiya pulling up a lacy blue thong from her suitcase. She added a matching bra that had him regretting having to join the others in the main house.

"You're killing me," he said, his voice hoarse.

Her gaze ran over his bare torso to the towel wrapped around his hips. "Likewise." She sauntered toward him, a smile in her eyes. "Yes, Issac."

"Yes what?" He hadn't asked her a question.

"I want you exclusively." She went onto her toes to kiss him softly. "Feel free to bite me anytime." She nibbled his lip and took a step back, her hooded gaze nearly undoing him.

He dropped his clothes and pulled her into him again, his mouth on hers. She couldn't just say that and wander off. No. He needed to feel her promise against his lips, to taste it with his tongue, to memorize the words with his heart.

She grabbed his shoulders, her nails claiming him as she dug them into his skin.

He had no idea what they were doing.

But fuck if he cared.

For the first time in his life, he allowed emotion, rather than logic, to drive him, and he followed the sensations to his very soul.

A handful of images flashed in his head from the others, as well as a timer that Tristan seemed to be imagining.

Countdown, Issac translated, slightly irritated by the clear intention to interrupt.

With a sigh, he slowly released Astasiya, his forehead falling to hers. "The others are getting impatient."

"You can hear them? Like, telepathically?"

"God, no. That'd be awful." He shuddered at the thought. "I just *see* them. Tristan, specifically. He's planning his interruption."

"The Ichorian who can control sound."

"That'd be the one," he murmured, stepping away to retrieve his clothes as a buzzing sounded through the room.

"What the hell is that?" Astasiya asked, her gaze darting back and forth.

"Tristan being an impatient ass," he growled, pulling on his jeans. He sent his progeny an image of his middle finger, and the noise stopped.

"That's... Is he outside?"

"No, he's in the main house."

"Is he able to manipulate sound for miles the way you can influence vision?" she asked while rummaging through her suitcase.

"Yes. Our powers rival one another." He ran his fingers through his hair, not caring at all to style it. "I suspected what he would be able to do based on his affinity for music. He was actually quite famous in the late eighteenth century, renowned for his skill with a harp. I met him in New York, during one of his visits. He fancied the States, you see, and, well, the rest is history between us."

"Eighteenth century," she repeated, a few articles of clothing in her hands. "Do I even want to know how old you are?"

He chuckled, amused. "Nearly four hundred, which is quite young compared to Aidan and all the Elders. They've experienced several millennia, Aidan being the oldest of us all."

"I... This... Yep. Completely surreal." She shook her head and focused on choosing an outfit.

She donned a blue sundress that hit her midthigh, and left her hair damp over one shoulder. No makeup. No styling. Just all-natural woman, which he appreciated considering his usual female company.

Pulling his shirt over his head, he walked over to nibble her pulse.

"You're gorgeous, love," Issac whispered.

"Even with my supposed rune?" she asked, her tone teasing. "Which, by the way, they're going to tell you is a birthmark."

"Are they?" He gazed down at her. "Care to wager on

that?"

She laughed. "Yeah, I have about ten dollars in my purse, but why not?"

"You know I'm not interested in money," he reminded her, pressing his hips into hers. "But I'll wager other, more pleasurable activities."

She licked her lips, intrigue flashing in her features. "Such as?"

"Hmm." He pressed his lips to her ear. "If I'm right—which I am—then I get to fuck you however and wherever I want."

"And when I'm right?" It came out breathy.

"You can tie me up tonight and do whatever you want." Which he wouldn't enjoy nearly as much as being in charge, but he could concede to her for an evening. Not that he would need to. The mark was most definitely a rune.

"Yeah, I'll take that bet," she agreed.

"Brilliant." He nipped her lower lip. "Ready to face the others?"

She scrunched her nose, clearly not ready at all. "There are no rules, right?"

"Oh, I can come up with some, if you like." He wrapped his hand around her throat, giving it a gentle squeeze. "Maybe later in the bedroom."

She swallowed, her pupils dilating. The interest flaring in her gaze intrigued him. They would definitely be exploring that later. "I meant with the Ichorians," she said, her voice husky.

I know. His palm slid upward to cup her cheek. "You're free to do whatever you want, love. We're surrounded by friends here."

"Your friends."

"They'll become yours as well, over time." He kissed her gently, lingering. "Can you do something for me?"

"Depends on what it is," she whispered, her lips moving against his.

"Hear them out," he replied, just as soft. "Let them show

you who they are before you judge them. And remember, your decisions will always be your own. No one can make them for you. All right?"

She was quiet for a long moment, a million emotions flashing through her features. But eventually she nodded. "I can try, yes."

CHAPTER TWENTY-THREE

Once upon a Time

STAS'S RESOLVE TO TRY FOR PATIENCE AND understanding went out the window when she entered the house. Her grasp on Issac's hand tightened, her legs threatening to give out beneath her.

The female auctioned during the Conclave sat at the dining table with her arms wrapped around her middle. Incredulity radiated from her dark irises. At least she appeared to be in better health—minus her frail state. But someone had clearly offered her a shower and clothing.

"Ah, Stas," Luc said from the head of the table. "I was just telling Eliza about Hydria."

Eliza? That must be the woman's name.

"Hydria?" Stas repeated.

"It's where they all live," Eliza replied, her voice far stronger than Stas expected. "An island near Athens."

Luc nodded. "Yes. It's technically owned by Greece. However, we're self-sufficient and report the bare minimum to the Greek authorities to maintain citizenship status. Everyone on the island has a job, whether it be in Athens proper, part of the security system, or other, more lucrative means."

"Investments," Issac added as he took the chair catty-corner to Luc. He held out the one beside him for Stas, his indication clear. *Join me.*

The only reason she didn't protest the request was because of the food on the table—cheese, fruit, and a relish tray. Her stomach growled at the sight, her fingers snagging a raw pepper as she sat down.

He smiled as she ate, the gleam in his gaze suggesting he knew what had inspired her appetite. Their midnight snack and early-morning post-sexathon meal hadn't been enough.

Issac poured her a glass of water from the pitcher on the table while saying, "When you live forever, you invest and watch the money grow. That's the lucrative side Lucian is referring to, which is a skill set I've cultivated over the last few centuries."

"Yes, Issac is one of our advisors on the subject, having amassed billions over the centuries." Luc shrugged. "No one wants for anything, but we do support each other."

"So you can live forever and you all choose to work," Eliza said, sounding very unimpressed. "How boring."

The Hydraian King's lips thinned. "Survival requires even the most menial of tasks. It's a strategy that works."

She snorted. "Okay, so my work history involves sex. What will my job be on your island?" Sarcasm colored her tone and radiated from her eyes. A clear defense mechanism, one Stas understood all too well.

"My suggestion? College, to acquire a more marketable skill that will benefit everyone." Luc leaned back in his chair, his muscles flexing with the movements.

"You don't find sex to be an adequate skill?" Feisty energy poured off Eliza. This woman had spirit, even after the Ichorians tried to break her.

Speaking of which... "Where are Anya and Aidan?" Stas asked softly, her focus shifting to Issac while Luc and Eliza continued their conversation beside them.

"In the living area with the others." He wrapped his arm around the back of her chair, leaning in close, his voice equally hushed. "It's been a while since we were all together."

She started to nod, then frowned. "So this isn't a unique occurrence?"

"No, we used to gather more frequently before Amelia and Eli passed."

"In the Hamptons?"

"Sometimes. The location shifts. Aidan and his harem currently live in Vancouver, while I've resided along the East Coast for the last century or so. The Hydraians are just off the coast of Athens, as Lucian said. Jacque's ability to teleport facilitates matters, at least now. He's actually quite young for an immortal, only a hundred or so."

Teleporter.

Right.

She shook her head to clear it. "Okay, help me understand this. You all gather like this, frequently, despite the Blood Laws urging you not to? Does Osiris know?"

"If he did, we wouldn't be here having this conversation right now."

Fair enough. "But you just risk it anyway?"

"We're family, Aya. You have to realize that up until the eighteenth century, Hydraians and Ichorians lived in peace. The war between our kinds started when Ichorians realized the threat lurking in Hydraian blood."

"War?" she repeated, her eyebrows lifting.

"It didn't last long," Luc cut in. "Also, I'll add, the only reason we lived in peace, as Issac calls it, is because the Ichorians put us all on an island—Hydria—and withheld

299

resources. They wanted us weak, to cripple our dual gifts, but what they created was a brotherhood founded by the desire to live. We knew for over three thousand years that our blood could kill an Ichorian. However, we kept it quiet and safeguarded the secret, knowing they would round us up and kill us. And instead, we worked as a cohesive unit to become stronger so when the inevitable happened, we could protect ourselves."

"The Ichorians tried to eradicate the Hydraians," Issac murmured, his thumb brushing her bare shoulder. "They failed miserably. Not only were they outmatched in power, but several Ichorians refused to fight. Including myself and many others with personal ties to Hydraians."

"In the end, Aidan, Osiris, and I drew up the Treaty of 1747—a tentative agreement evoking peace." Luc leaned forward, hands clasped on the table. "The Blood Laws were created as a result, to deter fraternization between the immortals."

"Yes, Osiris is a clever leader," Issac added. "He's biding his time, breaking down the relationships built over the centuries through fearmongering, and, we believe, will one day lead another attempt against the Hydraians. Hence the reason Aidan and I and the others play nice and attend the Conclave meetings."

"You're playing the role of double agent," she translated, completely awed by the history and purpose he just detailed. "I don't know whether to call you brave or suicidal."

He chuckled and tugged on a strand of her hair. "I'll accept 'brave.' As I told you the other night, I have no intention of dying."

A collection of giggles coming from the hallway interrupted them as Balthazar entered with his arms around Anya and Clara. All three of them were dressed for the pool, or maybe a magazine spread. For a sexy magazine. Because the girls were in thongs and tops that barely covered their breasts, and the man between them… *wow*.

"Oh, you're here!" Clara bounced over to Issac's chair

and wrapped her arms around him from behind, her lips against his cheek.

He grabbed her wrist to press a kiss to her hand. "Yes, just rehashing history with Lucian."

Clara didn't move, her breasts firmly pressed into Issac from behind, her lips still near his face. The ease with which she touched him indicated a history, one that soured Stas's stomach.

Yes, they'd just discussed exclusivity.

But this, well, she didn't like it. Not one bit. Especially the part where Issac kept holding Clara's hand.

"You should invite Aidan," Clara said, a smile in her too-blue eyes. "You know how he adores a jaunt through the past."

"I do," Issac agreed, releasing her. Finally. "Are you off to have a swim?"

"Balthazar challenged us to a round of water volleyball." She flipped her long blonde hair over her shoulder as she stood, cocking a model-worthy hip at the man in question.

"I merely suggested a friendly game," he murmured, his arm still around Anya. "The girls took it as a challenge. Luc, you in?"

"I'll have to pass for this round," Luc replied, disappointment evident in his tone. "Are Jay and Alik playing?"

A snort from the doorway had him looking over his shoulder at a man in a leather jacket and jeans—the attire far from appropriate for the hot summer day. "Why the fuck would I play volleyball?"

"Because it's fun?" Clara suggested.

The athletically lean male folded his arms and gave her the kind of smolder that could silence the room. "Fun would be driving to the city and slaughtering some Ichorians."

Clara shivered. "Always so dark."

Yes, that was an apt description. Lethal energy radiated from the man, one Stas didn't recognize as having joined them for dinner last night. Another Ichorian? Or a Hydraian?

"Alik," Balthazar said. "Meet Stas. Stas, this is Alik. He likes to brood more than socialize."

"And you all wonder why?" the male—Alik—replied, pushing off the doorway. "I'll be out patrolling with Jeremy. At least he understands the value of silence."

Nice to meet you, too, Stas thought at his back.

"Don't take it personally, sweetheart." Balthazar gave her a soft smile. "Alik isn't a fan of being this close to Ichorian territory, and he's feeling protective."

"He's an Elder," Issac added. "One of the four I mentioned as the oldest of Hydraians. Balthazar, Lucian, Alik, and Jayson."

"Present," a new voice said as another godlike male joined the room clad in a swimsuit. "I thought we were playing a game in the pool?"

"We are, but we stopped to chat while waiting on you." Balthazar gave him a grin. "Ready to strip some women?"

"Always."

"I thought you said this was a friendly game." Anya batted her eyes demurely.

"Of strip water volleyball, yes." Balthazar smiled, his dimples making his face even more breathtaking.

Yep. Totally giving in to the angel myth because how else is this much beauty in a room possible?

"Then why the hell are we still standing here? I can't wait to make you parade around the deck naked." Anya gave him a little push that earned her a laugh.

"If all you want is a show, just ask," he said, heading toward the door.

The newcomer smirked. "Like B needs a reason to lose his clothes."

"Right back at you, Jay. Now, let's teach the girls a lesson." Balthazar opened the back door, leading Anya and the one called Jay—which Stas assumed was short for Jayson—outside.

"It's like Hydria just exploded in my dining room," Issac remarked.

"You miss it," Clara accused, winking at him. "Admit it."

"Never."

"Liar." She blew him a kiss and flounced over to the exit. "Oh, and this new emotion? You wear it well. I like it." Her gaze rose to Stas. "Thank you for brightening his aura. I hope to know you better soon."

She disappeared before Stas could fathom a reply. Which probably would have been... *Huh?*

"Clara's an empath," Issac explained.

"And bubbly," Eliza muttered. "Like, overly bubbly." She visibly shuddered.

Stas grinned. Now, this woman? Yeah, this woman Stas could see herself befriending in a heartbeat.

"Right, shall we move this discussion to the living area?" Issac suggested. "I believe Aidan has a few matters to discuss, and there's something I want to show you both." He squeezed her shoulder with the words, his intention clear.

My birthmark.

Which he thought was a rune.

Why the hell would I have a rune on my back?

Luc's eyebrows rose. "I'm intrigued."

"I thought you might be," Issac murmured, his lips tilting.

Had he just shown Luc a glimpse of it with his mind? The way the Elder's green eyes focused on her, she suspected he did.

Both men stood, Issac holding his hand out for Stas. "Aya?"

"Can I have a minute with Eliza first?" she asked, hoping he would allow it.

He didn't hesitate. "Of course, love. We'll be in the other room." He gave her shoulder another squeeze before leaving with Luc at his side. "It's a rune, isn't it?"

"Show me a more detailed view," the Hydraian King

replied.

"When we're all together, I will." Issac's words drifted down the hall. "I want Aya to hear the results."

She smiled, pleased that he wanted her involved.

Then she remembered their bet.

Right. He wanted to win, and to gloat if he did. *Devious demon.*

"Stas or Aya?" Eliza asked, tilting her head to the side.

"Stas," she confirmed. "Eliza, right?"

The woman nodded. "You were there, weren't you?"

"At the Conclave?"

Another nod.

"Unfortunately." Stas almost felt ashamed, not that she could have changed fate. "I'm sorry about what was done to you."

Her nostrils flared, anger flashing through her features. "Don't fucking pity me."

"No, I know. I mean, I'm not..." She trailed off because, yeah, she had felt bad for her. And yes, that was tied to pity. *I need to start this over.* "Okay, you're right. It's just..." *No, not a good route.* "Have they been, uh, nice to you? The Ichorians, I mean."

A note of understanding cooled her expression, but the irritation still lurked in her dark gaze. "You want to know if you can trust them."

"Sort of. I don't know. It's all been a bit overwhelming." An understatement. She looked at the ceiling and then back at Eliza. "Did they tell you I'm a fledgling?"

"Yeah, they mentioned it. Apparently, we're pretty rare."

Stas blinked. "We?"

The other woman stared at her. "Uh, yes. *We.* I'm a fledgling, too. Didn't you know that?"

"I thought Sierra said you weren't one? That the idiot who accused you was just an inexperienced asshat?"

Eliza's lips curled. "'Inexperienced asshat,' not a bad description." Then her smile faltered, a memory haunting her eyes as she dropped them to the table.

Stas saw it then, the broken woman hiding behind a charade of bravery—a coping mechanism for whatever had happened to her. Which was why pity infuriated her, because she had to be perceived as strong.

Stas understood that, had experienced something similar when her parents died.

This world had been cruel to them both.

"So you're a fledgling," Stas mused, trying to bring Eliza back to their conversation. "Are you able to do anything special now?"

"What do you mean?"

"Like, do you have any gifts?"

Eliza lifted her focus from the table, her mouth curling down at the edges. "No. Luc said they won't present themselves until I become a Hydraian."

Oh. Stas had hoped she might know what it's like to hide a gift in the mortal world for years. Alas, it seemed Stas was still alone on that front. "So how do they know you're a fledgling?" she wondered out loud.

"Aidan had someone—one of Luc's Hydraians—test my bloodline somehow. I guess she has a similar gift to the woman from the, uh, Conclave. The one who could sense immortal genetics or whatever." Eliza twisted her lips to the side. "You don't think they'd lie about it, do you?" Her eyebrows rose. "Oh, sorry, I didn't mean—"

"I don't think they'd lie," Stas interjected. "But I understand why you might not believe them." Because she felt the same way.

A moment passed between them, a mutual respect.

They were one and the same.

Yet completely different.

"They've treated me very kindly," Eliza said after a long moment. "As soon as we left that night, Aidan gave me his jacket. They allowed me to shower. Gave me clothes." Her gaze fell again. "They held me while…"

While I cried, Stas inferred, her heart breaking for the woman.

She swallowed the reaction, hiding it, not wanting Eliza to sense her pity again.

"You're very strong," Stas whispered, emphasizing the other emotion flourishing inside her. Admiration. "Stronger than most women I know." She reached across the table to squeeze her hands, but Eliza quickly pulled back, her aversion to touch evident.

Of course. Stas should have expected that.

"Maybe we should go see what they're discussing," Eliza said, standing, her limbs quivering. "Make sure they're not talking about us."

"Sure," Stas agreed, recognizing a wall when she saw one.

Eliza wanted space.

Stas comprehended that need better than most.

She pushed away from the table and joined her in the hallway, careful to keep physical distance between them.

"Stas?" Eliza whispered, pausing on the threshold. Her midnight irises lifted, a glimmer of respect shining in their depths. "Thank you."

Chapter Twenty-Four

A Financial Trail

Issac held his arm out for his Aya as she entered. He sat on the love seat across from Aidan, Lucian, and Mateo.

"Such a good pet," Tristan mused from the recliner in the corner as Astasiya joined Issac. "Coming when the master calls her."

Astasiya stiffened, her sharp gaze going to Issac's asshole of a best friend. "Excuse me?"

"Ah, but she speaks." Tristan tsked. "Such a pity, Issac. I prefer them silent."

"Then it's a good thing she's not yours," Issac returned, a hint of censure in his voice. One his progeny ignored.

"Not my type, I'm afraid." He eyed Eliza, who had

chosen a chair against the wall, her legs tucked beneath her.

Hmm, yes, Tristan preferred submissive females, the kind who fancied pain over pleasure. He wasn't gentle by any measure of the imagination, and while Issac might enjoy dominance in the bedroom, hurting a lover didn't appeal to him.

"The feeling is mutual," Astasiya replied, distaste clear in her tone.

"Such disrespect." Tristan pressed a palm to his chest, feigning an affronted look. "This one is certainly a downgrade, Issac. Especially considering your usual fare."

"Careful," Issac warned, his arm tightening around Astasiya.

"When have you ever known me to mince words?" Tristan tossed back. "Just stating a clear observation."

"You're just sour over losing your wingman," Nadia said from the stairs. Ash and Jacque were behind her, all three of them dressed in swimwear. Balthazar must have requested more players for his shenanigans outside.

"No, I'm trying to understand how he could find this option more attractive than Clara, who was literally made for him." So callous. So nonchalant. But the devious twinkle in Tristan's gaze demonstrated his intention to hurt, and the gasp at his side said the verbal barb was translated and received.

"That's enough," Issac stated, done with this ridiculous banter. "Either fuck off or shut your goddamn mouth." He would deal with his disgruntled progeny later, the fuckwit. "Aidan, Mateo, what did you find on Owen?"

The energy in the room shifted, Tristan's shock at having been dismissed evident in the way he didn't retort or move. Nadia, Ash, and Jacque quietly slipped down the hallway toward the pool.

"As you know, Eliza is in fact a fledgling," Aidan started, reiterating the topic they'd been discussing before Astasiya and Eliza joined them. "Which I found curious since Sierra claimed her not to be one during the Conclave."

"Making it a good thing Osiris never asked for clarification during the trial," Issac added. Because the mind readers would have caught on to the lie.

"Indeed," Aidan agreed. "But it was strange, right? Why would she lie? So I tasked Mateo with finding out more about Sierra and her ties to Owen. What he found was, well, fascinating."

Mateo slid a tablet across the coffee table, the screen displaying some sort of legal document—a deed. Issac lifted the item, reading through the details as Mateo said, "The bar Sierra worked at was owned by Owen. He purchased it over twenty years ago."

"What?" Astasiya asked, joining Issac in reviewing the documents. "Why?"

"While a fascinating question in and of itself, there's something even more pressing. *How*?" Aidan asked. "Owen was too young to have amassed the wealth required to purchase a property in Manhattan, so how did he acquire it?"

Issac flipped the tab, seeing the answer as Mateo voiced it. "A shell corporation," his progeny said. "Called Gabriel."

As someone well versed in setting up such organizations, Issac had never heard of this one. "Who owns it?"

"I don't know." Those three words were rare, particularly in regard to Mateo's ability to find every detail known to man in cyberspace.

"As in you've never heard of him, or you can't find him?" Issac asked.

"The latter. Whoever set it up is one of the best I've ever seen. The work reminds me of a previous mystery."

"Jonathan," Issac translated. "We've always wondered how he acquired the funds to create the CRF," he added for Astasiya's benefit. "Whoever granted him the funds is a ghost. Mateo can't find any trace of the benefactor."

"Yes, only mentions of him in certain CRF project files," Mateo muttered, his frustration over this particular puzzle evident. "And this new corporation, Gabriel, has the same feel. No bank accounts, no names, not even a place. Almost as if it exists in space."

"How is that possible?" Astasiya asked.

"Great fucking question," Mateo replied, running his fingers through his short blond hair. "There's always a trail. *Always.*"

"Mateo harbors a gift for technology that goes beyond the standard hacker and into the supernatural," Issac explained softly as he passed the tablet back to Mateo. "He manages most of my accounts as a result. He's well versed in moving properties and money around, creating identities, and so forth. But for him to not be able to trace a lead speaks of divine intervention."

"Another immortal," she replied.

"Yes, exactly." He shifted his attention to Aidan. "This suggests a link between Owen and Jonathan."

"It does," he agreed. "Which provides a potential motive if a working arrangement between them went sour."

"What I have trouble grasping is a purpose for their partnership," Lucian said, his expression artfully blank. Hearing that one of his Hydraians may have been working with the infamous CRF CEO had to hurt.

"I can't find anything in the CRF files that addresses that point," Mateo said, his eyebrows drawing downward. "But there's a part of his servers I can't seem to reach."

That was news to Issac. "Since when?"

"I imagine it's always been the case," he replied. "I discovered the wall when searching for information on the Nizari poison last week. The medical research side was easy, most of the researchers leaving a multitude of back doors for me to pass through. But there's a vault deep inside that I can't access with my psychic abilities."

"Similar to the ghost trail," Issac replied, drumming his fingers against his knee. "Is there any way around it?"

"Not without going inside the CRF, which we can't do for obvious reasons."

Issac nodded. "The runes."

Jonathan had somehow crafted a layer of magic to secure the perimeter. Ichorians and Hydraians would be defenseless inside, stripped of their powers, and essentially mortal. Issac had seen the markings outside, etched into the stone pillars adorning the iron gates. They circled the property. And bore similar notations to the design against Astasiya's lower back.

"That reminds me," he murmured, pressing his lips to her ear. "May I show them now, love?"

She blinked at him, her eyes holding a myriad of questions. "My birthmark?"

He nodded.

"I… If you think it's relevant." A touch of incredulity lined her words. "I mean, I doubt it's related."

"I beg to differ." It all seemed very much connected. Owen befriending Astasiya. Her roommate-pairing with Elizabeth during their freshman year. Obtaining employment at the CRF. "There are a lot of links, Aya."

She studied him for a long moment, her uncertainty melting to concern. "You think Owen befriended me on purpose."

"It's starting to sound that way, yes."

"Okay, but that implies the CRF knows about me, that Jonathan knows I'm a fledgling."

"Yes, it does."

"Then why wait until the security exam to test the theory?" she asked. "Why go through all the hassle of a six-year friendship?" She shook her head. "No, it doesn't feel right. Owen… He was one of my best friends. I *knew* him."

"Except you didn't know he was a Hydraian," Issac pointed out softly, rubbing her upper arm as he secured his hold around her. "It's possibly a coincidence—Owen having a similar financial supporter capable of hiding his tracks, like the CRF does—but it all feels too close, too purposeful. Even Elizabeth being your roommate is a bit contrived considering her ties to the CRF."

"Lizzie?" Astasiya pulled back, angling her body toward

311

him. "Now you think Lizzie befriended me on purpose, too?" The squeak at the end of her voice pierced his heart. He hadn't meant to upset her. Again.

"Your friendship with Elizabeth is too heartfelt to be fake," he said quickly. "I'm suggesting that someone may have coordinated your living arrangements, that your pairing as roommates may not have been fate so much as designed."

"When did you meet Owen?" Lucian asked before she could reply. "Was it after you met Lizzie Watkins?"

"Yes, but there's no way she's in on it. And Owen..." She shook her head. "No. We're... we *were* close friends. He cared about me. I'm sure of it. He'd never hurt me."

"Perhaps Jonathan became aware of you through the random housing assignment and tasked Owen to get to know you better," Aidan suggested. "I wonder if Jonathan requested Owen to do something in regard to you that he refused."

"Such as administer the Nizari poison?" Lucian said, scratching his jaw. "Actually, that provides ample motive. If Owen suspected Stas of being a fledgling, which I imagine he would have had to after six years of knowing her, then he'd know the cost of administering the poison."

Aidan nodded. "And because he cared about her, he declined the task."

"Thereby earning his death," Lucian finished. "It's exactly the kind of retaliation Jonathan prefers, especially when a minion doesn't do his bidding."

"Indeed." Aidan focused on Issac. "Show me the rune."

Astasiya shook beside him, her fingers trembling as she twisted the cloth of her dress against her thighs. "He...he died because of me?" she whispered, her big green eyes looking to Issac as if she needed him to deny it. "You think D-Doctor Fitzgerald...?"

"We don't know for certain, but it does seem plausible, yes."

"H-how? W-why?" She swallowed. "H-how do we...? I

mean, there isn't proof. We c-can't know for—"

An alarm sounded on Mateo's tablet, silencing the room.

Issac's progeny lost himself to the technology, his fingers dancing over the screen with a dexterity few possessed. He managed the security of Issac's estate, his strategically placed devices monitoring the grounds and nearby surroundings for any potential threats. The system activated whenever Issac or Amelia entertained Hydraians on the property, a fail-safe to ensure everyone remained alive and protected.

"Tom Fitzgerald is a mile away," Mateo said, his focus on the screen. "He seems to be alone."

"What?" Astasiya gaped at him. "How could you possibly know that?"

"Facial recognition," Mateo murmured without looking up. "I have all potential threats cataloged and categorized to notify me when in proximity."

"Like..." She cleared her throat. "Does it include all Ichorians?"

He nodded. "Of course."

"Their faces?" she pressed, causing Issac to frown, curious as to what she truly wanted to know.

"Yes, well, no." Mateo typed something and bent over the screen. "He's definitely headed our way." He finally straightened, meeting Astasiya's gaze. "The program has no pigment, just bone structure and dental records. Think skeletons, but alive. Would you like to see it?"

She grimaced. "No, not really."

"What did you want to know, love?" Issac asked, holding her close.

"I, uh, I was just thinking." She paused, her fingers clenching the fabric of her dress. "I thought, maybe, if he has all the Ichorians, I might be able to find the man who killed my parents."

Ah yes. He imagined she would want to know his identity.

"You saw the man who murdered your parents?" Aidan

asked, head tilted. "What did he look like? Perhaps Lucian or I have met him."

With their penchants for remembering every detail of their lives, it would seem quite probable they could help Astasiya identify the killer. If only Issac could see the vision in her mind.

"That'll need to wait," Mateo said, standing. "Tom just turned onto the street outside the gate. He's definitely on his way here, and he's not trying to hide it."

"Who's Tom?" Eliza asked, having been quiet and studious by the wall throughout the conversation.

"A friend of Astasiya's," Issac replied. "Who also happens to be a Sentinel with the CRF."

"Like the humanitarian organization?" She frowned. "Is that the company you keep talking about?"

"Yes, they have a paramilitary unit that specializes in assassinating immortals," Lucian summarized as he stood. "I'll brief you more on it later." He held out a hand for her. "We need to join the others, just in case Tom has brought a surprise with him."

Balthazar and Jayson entered at that moment, towels wrapped around their damp waists. The mind reader must have heard the thoughts inside and set everyone in action.

"Is Eli's armory unlocked, Wakefield?" Jayson asked.

Issac nodded, sending them upstairs with Ash and Anya right behind them.

It seemed the pool party had moved inside.

Amelia would be positively appalled by the wet footprints across her marble foyer.

Sorry, he said, glancing upward on instinct.

"Can you at least tell me why we're going upstairs?" Eliza asked, her arms wrapped around her middle, shaking. "Please?"

"For protection," he replied, his voice coaxing and tender and very unlike the authoritative one he typically favored. "The Hydraian who used to live here maintained a fully stocked weaponry, which my people are going to use if

Tom has brought anyone with him."

She didn't look very convinced. "And what are we going to be doing?"

"Talking." He held out his hand again. "There's still so much for you to learn, but you can trust me."

"They're not going to hurt Tom, right?" Astasiya asked, her voice tight and distracting Issac from the couple across the room. "They can't hurt him, Issac. They… He's…" She swallowed. "He's still my friend."

"He sent you to the Arcadia."

"I know, b-but… Please, Issac. Don't let them hurt him. Maybe he just wants to talk." The plea in her gaze had him sighing.

"All right. No one will touch him unless he enters aggressively," he vowed. He made his voice loud enough for everyone to hear him on the ground level.

Balthazar, don't hurt the nitwit. Aya wants to talk to him first. Despite their differences, Issac trusted the mind reader to spread the word to his cohort. On this, they would share a side.

"I'm too racked to be bothered, really. What with the edict not to kill and all." Tristan's Irish lilt always became more pronounced when agitated. "How very unlike you," he added, the words pointed.

"Maybe you should have stayed in the city," Issac replied flatly, done with his childish behavior.

His best friend narrowed his gaze, then chose to say nothing as he joined the others upstairs.

Smart man.

"Tom's at the gate," Mateo informed just as the buzz sounded from the security panel against the wall. "And he's alone."

"Well, it seems Thomas is braver than I anticipated," Issac murmured, standing. "Let him through."

Chapter Twenty-Five

Queen on the Board

FUCK, WHY IS HE HERE?

Stas stood beside Issac in the foyer, Aidan and Mateo just behind them with guns in hand. A few other Hydraians lurked about, all with names she couldn't remember.

Tension radiated through the room, not at all helping the ache in her stomach.

Owen working with Doctor Fitzgerald.

Lizzie potentially being set up as her roommate.

How long has the CRF known about me?

Was any of it even true? She felt in her gut that they were missing something vital, some key piece of information that would exonerate both her best friends.

And Tom.

Yes, he sent her to the Arcadia.

However, she knew he cared about her. She couldn't be that blind to emotions and instincts; otherwise, she'd been living in a lie for the last six years. Stas refused to accept that, refused to believe it.

"Let me talk to him first," Issac said softly.

She eyed him warily. "Why?"

"To determine his intentions." He pulled her close, his lips at her ear. "And to give you an opportunity to prepare for whatever you need to say to him."

She studied his expression, soft and knowing and filled with understanding.

How was it possible for someone to comprehend her on this level? To know what she needed before she realized it herself?

She started to shake her head to clear it, then realized it came off as a denial. "Okay," she said and swallowed. "But I want to listen."

"Of course." He gestured to a stop behind the door, and she moved just as Tom knocked, his fist loud against the wood panel. "Ready?" Issac asked.

Not really. She nodded anyway because what choice did she have? Besides, she wanted the truth. She needed to know.

Did the CRF really try to kill me?

"Thomas," Issac greeted, opening the door.

"Where is she?" Tom demanded, the voice that of the commander, not her friend.

"By 'she,' I assume you mean Astasiya?" Issac used a taunting tone, one she suspected had Tom glowering at her demon.

"If you turned her, I swear to whatever god you believe in that I will kill you."

She stole a breath, the words a blunt confirmation of what she already knew, but to hear it so clear in his voice was an entirely different beast. It meant he really did send her to the Arcadia to witness Ichorians feeding. And what about the Conclave?

"With what?" Issac asked, sounding bored. "That CRF-modified pistol on your hip? That would imply you are able to see well enough to shoot. Or do you plan to use that fancy silver knife tucked into your boot? Again, requires sight, something I have no problem taking away if you threaten me again."

Silence met his words.

Stas's stomach churned, her palms clammy as she fisted them at her sides.

He knew.

He knew and he still sent me there.

How could he do that to me?

"Tell me she's okay," Tom finally said. "Please. Tell me she's okay."

Her heart stuttered at the worry in his tone, the first indication that he actually did care, that maybe he hadn't meant to do this to her. God, why did this have to be so confusing?

"She's fine," Issac replied, folding his arms. "What the bloody hell were you thinking, sending her to the Arcadia?"

Tom expelled a long breath, his relief palpable even through the door. "Fuck, I wasn't thinking. I let my emotions, my anger, take over. I just wanted her to catch you, you know, doing your thing."

"My thing?" Issac repeated, sounding bored. "What thing is that, Thomas? What exactly did you hope for her to see?"

"Feeding, asshole. I wanted her to see what you are."

"To what purpose, exactly? Other than endangering her life, of course."

"Goddammit, Wakefield. Just let me talk to her. I know she's here."

"Do you?" Issac arched a brow. "And how do you know that?"

"Her phone," Tom growled. "Come on, just… I need… I need to apologize. And I need to see for myself that she's okay."

"I'm fine," she said, moving to Issac's side, tired of hiding. "He hasn't turned me. You can go now." Because the headache brewing between her eyes didn't need more fodder, nor did she know what to say to him.

He sent her to the Arcadia to catch Issac feeding.

Well, hell. A conversation would have been a much safer alternative.

She frowned. *Wait, if Tom sent me to the Arcadia to find out about Issac, then that means he assumed she didn't know about Ichorians.*

Didn't that contradict the theory about the CRF being aware of her fledgling status? Unless they assumed her to be ignorant of the supernatural world?

"Stas." Tom started forward, but Issac blocked him by placing himself between them.

"Easy there, Sentinel. I didn't invite you into my home."

"I want to talk to her."

"About what?" she asked over his shoulder.

"Privately."

Issac folded his arms again. "Not going to happen."

"I'm not going to do anything to her," Tom said. "Come on, Stas, you've known me for almost seven years. I didn't know it was a Conclave. They don't happen often. I went to the club the minute I realized what was going on, but I was too late."

"For what it's worth, he's telling the truth about that last bit. He was waiting outside the Arcadia when we left. He even followed us back to your place, which is why I stayed the night." He stepped to the side, his shoulder braced against the doorjamb. "It's also worth noting that it is not only stupid but also extremely risky for a Sentinel to stand outside the Arcadia. Especially one who happens to be the son of the CRF's creator. The bounty on Thomas's head is quite high. Essentially, he did risk his life to check on you as he is also doing now."

Her brows rose. "And you didn't mention this earlier

because…?"

"Because his showing up didn't change the fact that he nearly got you killed."

"You still should have told me." Not that there'd been a lot of opportunity with all the other conversations.

"I'm telling you now."

She didn't have the energy or will to argue over something so trivial. He told her now, when it counted, even though he could have omitted the truth. "Okay," she said, stepping into his side to lay her head against his shoulder.

Tom observed the exchange without commenting, his expression artfully blank.

"Why didn't you just tell me what he was?" she asked.

"Would you have believed me, Stas?"

Another indication that he expected her to be ignorant of the supernatural world. *Something's not right.* If the CRF knew about her fledgling status, then so would Tom, as the CEO's son. Yet, he'd just suggested doubt over what she would believe.

Why would he suspect that if he thought she was part of that world already?

"You're probably right," she said slowly, the lie burning on her tongue.

"He's told you about the CRF, right?" Tom asked. "What we do?"

Issac seemed to still beside her, his hesitation something she understood. He didn't want her to mention his accusations against Jonathan. That, she could do.

Stas shrugged to keep it nonchalant. "No, not exactly. But some things were implied."

"Did he mention that we hunt down rogue supernaturals who are causing issues in the mortal world?"

That wasn't exactly how Issac described it, no. "He mentioned that the military unit is equipped to handle immortals," Stas offered instead.

"Is that why you're hiding here? You're afraid we'll hurt you for finding out?"

"Will you?" *Your organization already tried to kill me once.*

"Of course not. You know me better than that."

Do I? she wondered. "Maybe," she said after a beat, still deciding his intentions. "But you've known about this for how long without telling me?"

"You weren't cleared to know, Stas."

Meaning the CRF doesn't know what I am, or they would have killed me automatically. "So you sent me to a nightclub to clear me?"

He palmed the back of his neck. "It was a discreet way of telling you."

"A discreet way?" Issac repeated. "Thomas, she met Osiris as a result. Was that discreet enough for you?"

Tom's eyes widened. "She met Osiris?"

"Oh, yes. And what's worse, she bloody intrigued him. Why do you think she's here?"

"Shit." He began to pace, his hands in his hair. "Fuck, you have to let me take her, Wakefield. She'll be safer at headquarters and you know it."

Issac snorted. "I don't need to let you do anything." He gazed down at her. "It's not my choice."

She stared back at him. "It's an option?" *To go to the CRF?*

"Yes, but it takes you back to the city." *Where it would be unsafe,* he seemed to add with his eyes.

"How would the CRF keep me safe from Osiris?" she wondered out loud, her question more for Issac than Tom.

But Tom was the one who answered. "We have wards and other security protocols that will keep him out."

"So I would have to live there?" She didn't like the sound of that at all.

"Not necessarily." A vague answer. "How about you come back with me and I'll explain how we can protect you? It's the least I can do for getting you into this mess. Then, if you aren't interested, I'll drive you back here myself."

"You expect me to trust that?" she asked, incredulous.

"I expect you to trust *me*. How well do you know him, anyway? You really think he'll help you before he helps himself? A man who comes from a long line of fallen angels?"

"I prefer *demon*," Issac murmured, his lips twitching at the reference to the so-called pet name she'd given him. "But whatever works."

"Has he explained why he drinks blood yet? A curse from the gods, right, Wakefield?"

"Is that why you stopped by, Thomas? For a history lesson?"

"Stop." Stas needed a minute to process, to gather more information on this decision. It was one she shouldn't be considering at all, but something still felt wrong. She needed more details, proof, *something*, to validate all the allegations. "If I go with you, you tell me everything. If I don't like it, I get to leave," she reiterated. "Yes?"

Tom nodded.

"And does your dad know you're here?" she asked, trying to figure out where Doctor Fitzgerald fit with this inane idea.

"No, but he knows about the club. And, uh, he's kind of pissed at me. Like, livid." He looked decidedly uncomfortable. "He loves you, you know. Like a daughter. It's a little weird, but I get it. You're family, Stas. You know you can trust us. Just think about it. Give me a chance to make this right. Please."

Movement caught her attention, Mateo waving his hand. *Five minutes*, he mouthed. Until what, she had no idea.

But Issac must have understood the cryptic hand maneuver because he said, "Astasiya needs a few minutes to decide."

"I thought you didn't make choices for her?" Tom countered.

"He doesn't," Stas said quickly. "But he's right. I need a few minutes to think about everything. You owe me at least that much, Tom." *And it seems Mateo wants to say something.*

Tom expelled a long breath, his shoulders falling. "Fine. Yes. You're right. I'll just… I'll be in my car. But will you tell me either way?"

She nodded, her chest aching a little at the sadness in his expression. "I will."

"Okay." He swallowed and took a step back, turning toward his car, then stopped. "Stas?"

"Yeah?"

"For what it's worth, I'm sorry. And I'm glad you're okay." Sincere words that pierced her resolve.

That was the look and tone of the friend she'd known for years.

Contrite.

Desperate.

And heartbroken.

"I'll be in my car," he added softly.

Issac shut the door before she could reply, his jaw clenched. "What is it you're trying to show me, Mateo?" he demanded, the irritation in his tone surprising her.

The blond male took a step backward, his palms up in the air. "Okay, hear me out before you reject the idea."

~*~

Hear him out?

"Start talking. Quickly, mate." Because from what Issac had inferred from the images rolling through his mind, Mateo wanted to send Astasiya on some sort of reconnaissance mission through the CRF headquarters.

"What's going on?" she asked, glancing between them. "What did I miss?"

"Tell her," Issac encouraged, folding his arms.

Mateo cleared his throat, his already pale face losing color. "This presents us with an opportunity. Tom wants to take her back to CRF's headquarters, right? Where the servers are? If Stas can get close enough to them, I could hack into the system the old-fashioned way."

"What would that require?" Aidan asked, his stance casual beside Mateo.

"All she needs is a device—which I can procure relatively quickly—and to find either the server room or a proper host connection."

"Host connection?" Stas repeated, her brow furrowed. "What does that mean?"

"Like a master computer with access to all the files," Mateo explained. "I imagine Jonathan has one."

"With his controlling nature? It's an absolute certainty that he does." Aidan scratched his jaw. "So you're suggesting Stas go with Tom and help you access the files that are blocked via unknown means. How certain are you that this method will work?"

Mateo didn't hesitate. "About eighty percent, give or take."

"You want to risk Astasiya's life over a plan with less than a one hundred percent presumed success rate?" Issac snorted. "No."

"Hold on," she said, focusing on Mateo. "Tell me exactly what you would need so I understand what you're asking of me."

"Okay." Mateo pulled his wallet from his jeans pocket and found a nickel, handing it to her. "You'll need to hide something of this size in your purse or in your pocket and place it near Jonathan's computer. It should provide me with the access I need, assuming he has host files on his system. If not, then you'd need to find the server room, which I imagine is in the basement somewhere, in a temperature-controlled room—"

"And shrouded in security, no doubt," Issac added in a growl. "There's no bloody way she'll find the server room without being caught, Mateo."

"Your faith in me is inspiring," she muttered.

"It's not meant to be personal, love. Just stating the obvious. Jonathan is renowned for his security. Case in point, Mateo can't access certain files and he's a bloody Ichorian with supernatural technical skills."

She considered him and nodded. "Issac's right. I've been

down there once, and it's a maze of white halls littered with security cameras. Finding the server room would be next to impossible."

"But if Jonathan invites you to his office for a chat...?" Mateo prompted.

"I could place this near his laptop," she agreed, holding up the coin. "Assuming I can get it through security. They scan all personal items through the machine, and there are metal detectors, too."

"I can work with that, but I would need the evening to prepare. I might even be able to make it into a card of sorts. Hmm." His gaze turned inward, his voice taking on a dreamy quality. "Oh, I could add a camera to your wardrobe, take video of the underground." He smiled, taking back the nickel and putting his wallet away. "Yes, architectural design. Stas could provide us with brand-new details about the layout."

Issac just stared at him. "Have you lost your bloody mind?" He was asking an untrained operative—Astasiya— to go on a suicide mission. "If Jonathan even senses her intentions..." He couldn't finish the thought, the ideas too horrific for his mind. "Absolutely not."

"Do you think there's information on Owen in those files?" Astasiya asked, ignoring Issac. "Maybe even Amelia?"

"I think there's a reason Jonathan is using a magical encryption to hide certain documents, and I would bet they're related in some fashion, yes." Mateo glanced at Aidan. "Do you agree?"

The eldest among them stared off into space for a long moment, strategy and intelligence radiating from his ancient gaze. He slowly nodded. "Yes, it is the most logical of explanations. Whatever he is hiding via supernatural means is something he wants no one to see." He blinked, refocusing on Issac. "Mateo's idea is worth considering. This is a unique opportunity to gather intelligence from the inside, which is what you desired all along."

"He's right," Astasiya murmured. "You wanted to use me for revenge, and this proves I really am your perfect pawn."

His gut clenched at the words, his heart skipping a beat. "Aya…"

"No, it's okay," she continued, gazing at him with eyes that showed her very soul. "I know you've changed your mind, but Mateo's right. If Doctor Fitzgerald was working with Owen, I deserve to know. I *need* to know, Issac. And those files might just have the answers."

"And if they don't?" he countered. "Then what?"

"Then we're right back where we started," she replied, grabbing his hand. "But at least we'll know what's in those files."

He shook his head. "I'm not willing to risk you over a *what-if*, Aya. There has to be another way."

"It's not your decision, Issac," she said softly, stepping into him and catching his other palm with hers. "Tell me, do you trust Mateo?"

An unfair question, particularly when voiced in front of his progeny. Issac sighed, his shoulders falling. "Mateo has never failed me." True words, ones that brought pride to Mateo's features. "So yes, I trust him."

"Then I trust him, too," Astasiya replied, squeezing his hands. "I need to do this, Issac. Not just for me, but for Owen."

"You'll risk your life in search of answers?" He tilted his head to the side. "Think about what you're saying, Aya. Think about what Jonathan could do to you. The Nizari poison was just a preliminary measure. He's been experimenting on immortals for over a decade."

"It's true," Aidan said, the voice of reason. "We don't know exactly how he's doing it, but the technology he's given the Sentinels is too advanced for human invention. Not to mention the runes."

"And those details, are they hidden?" she asked, her attention going to Mateo. "Can you access them?"

He shook his head. "Only superficial details with vague names regarding assets."

"Meaning these research projects are likely part of the classified files you can't reach," Astasiya inferred.

"Yes," Mateo agreed. "That's my theory."

"Theory," Issac repeated, disgusted with the word. "Not proven. Not scientific. Not fact. You'd be risking your life on a *theory*, Aya."

She swallowed, her gaze returning to his. "I'd be risking my life on a lot more than a theory, Issac. You want me to believe all these accusations about Doctor Fitzgerald, but I can't without more proof. I need to see him again, to really know that it's true." She cupped his cheek. "You're asking me to criminalize my mentor, the man who helped me with my career path, the one who has treated me with the utmost respect since I met him nearly seven years ago. Yes, the information you've provided is damning, but I need to know with certainty that he's evil. It's the only way I can help you achieve your revenge."

"But I don't want to use you in that way, Aya. I don't want to lose you." Didn't she understand? This was no longer a game of chess. Real emotions were on the board, with Aya front and center, and he couldn't risk the pawn who had become his queen. "Astasiya, you're worth more to me than vengeance."

Fuck, he could hardly believe the words falling from his lips, but they were true. Revenge—a quest of the past. He couldn't lose Astasiya, not over this, not over something he recruited her into. Issac would never forgive himself.

"I know," she whispered, lifting to brush her mouth over his. "Which is why I have to do this. It's no longer about you, but about me. If everything in my life has been a lie these last few years, I *have* to know. Trust me to do this. Please."

"It's not about trust," he replied, his arms folding around her back. "It's…" *It's about fear.* He didn't want to lose her. *But she's not even mine.* Not really. Exclusivity was one thing, a future entirely another.

Still, in regard to Mateo's plan to infiltrate the CRF...

Fuck.

Logically, Issac understood the idea. It was the best chance they had at gaining insight into their enemy's inner fortress. But risking Astasiya had him shaking his head, doubt creeping in. "I can't lose you," he said again.

"I can do this," she urged. "But I need you to believe in me."

"Oh, Aya. It's not about faith. It's the matter of not being able to protect you in the CRF." The last time she went in there without him, she came out poisoned. That had bothered him. Now he feared it would destroy him.

What the hell is wrong with me? Issac didn't do this with anyone. He always lived by his own code, allowing others to do the same. But the idea of Astasiya entering that building alone, without him, unsettled him immensely. Only a few weeks of her acquaintance and he already felt as if she'd bonded to his soul.

How is that even possible?

A tender emotion brushed her features. "Have you forgotten that I know how to protect myself? All it takes are a few demands."

"That's assuming your gift works in the underground," he replied, his mouth thick with foreign sensations. "Ichorians and Hydraians are essentially made human inside those walls. What will they do to you?"

"She's already mortal," Aidan said. "The runes shouldn't apply, as they're designed for immortal bloodlines."

"Shouldn't or won't?" Issac asked, his grip on Astasiya's hands tightening.

"I'll be okay, Issac," she whispered. "Let me trust my instincts. Please? Can you trust me?"

His heart leapt into his throat.

There was only a handful of people he ever trusted, and two of them were dead. But a fragile part of him, one he hadn't known existed until he met Astasiya, already trusted her, too. It was the same part of him that cared for her.

"What about Osiris?" he asked, going for a different tactic. The ancient Ichorian harbored a variety of homes, but he frequented the city often.

"He scares the shit out of me," she admitted. "But, Issac, I can't let fear drive my decisions. This is the right move." Spoken like the strong woman he knew her to be. One of the many traits he admired about her. "I'm not naive. I know going with Luc is my safest option, but I'm not ready yet. Not until I know the truth. Not until I find out what really happened to Owen."

Resolve shone bright in her features.

Astasiya would go with or without his support.

Either he respected her decision or he fought it.

Issac sighed. He'd never allow her to put herself in a life-threatening situation while thinking he didn't have her back.

"Oh, Aya." He gripped the back of her neck and pulled her in for a kiss, etching every foreign emotion and unspoken thought into her mouth with his tongue. She gripped his arms, holding him closer, returning the favor and devastating him with her own feelings.

It was as if they'd bonded on a level not of this earth, his soul aligning magically with hers, dancing somewhere in space.

He couldn't define it.

Didn't understand it.

Refused to ponder it.

Just embraced it.

My Aya... He deepened the kiss, not caring at all that they had an audience, ignoring everyone and everything around them. They were creating a pact, one that required him to give where his instincts desired to take.

She would always be in charge of her own decisions.

He'd never take that away from her.

Even when he craved control and longed to keep her safe.

But she had to follow her heart, to learn for herself, and

he understood that more than he wanted to admit. Telling her wasn't enough. She needed to *see*.

"Come back to me, my Aya," he breathed against her lips. "Promise me you'll come back to me."

Her lashes fluttered open. "You're trusting me?"

"Yes," he whispered, nuzzling her. "Do what you need to do." It killed him to say it, but grounding her would be wrong. His Astasiya was born to fly.

CHAPTER TWENTY-SIX

Technical Mayhem

ISSAC STOOD OUTSIDE THE DOOR, GIVING Astasiya space as she spoke to Thomas in the driveway. From the Sentinel's expression, he wasn't crazy about her proposal. Too fucking bad for him because Issac wasn't budging on this stipulation.

Tristan joined him, hands in the pockets of his trousers, his shrewd gaze on Astasiya. "If I caused offense earlier, I apologize."

Issac snorted. "Lies do not become you." He faced the man he considered his best friend. "But while you're here, mind telling me what has your knickers in a twist? You never care about who I fuck. Why the sudden change?"

"Because she's more than a fuck," Tristan replied. "You

took her to a Conclave, Issac."

"Not by bloody choice, I didn't." Osiris had compelled him to bring Astasiya. There was no alternative.

"You risked your fucking life for her—all of our lives."

"Something you did not take issue with at the Arcadia," Issac pointed out. "If I recall, you assisted me rather willingly."

"As is my duty, even when my best lad is away with the fairies."

Issac narrowed his gaze, not at all appreciating the accusation regarding his mental state. "And what would you have had me do instead, hmm?" There'd been no other option. He couldn't just hand her over to the likes of Osiris. Tristan knew that.

"It's not so much the decision as it's your reactions," he said flatly. "The lass is in your head. Soon your heart. And she's nowhere near good enough for you."

"Not good enough?" Issac repeated, his brows lifting. "Under whose authority was that decision made?"

His progeny faced him, his expression emotionless. "What kind of future do you have with her? She's a fledgling."

"I'm very aware of what she is, Tristan." And also how it impacted their relationship. "Is that your basis for disliking her, then? That she's a future Hydraian?" Those types of issues never bothered Tristan in the past. Issac didn't understand why they should now.

"I don't give a flying fuck about that. What concerns me are your feelings for the lass. You're letting her change you, making decisions based on emotions, not sense, and all for a temporary fuck. This will not end well, Sire."

Ah, there it was, the underlying reason for Tristan's concern—that Astasiya would change Issac on an irrevocable level. Possibly, yes, she'd already begun the process. But it was for him to fret over, not Tristan. "It's my business to sort, not yours."

"Then sort it," Tristan replied. "Because from my

vantage point, you appear to be falling for the lass, and hard. And your relationship is an impossibility."

"What makes you think I'm unaware of that?" he countered, slightly irritated by the censure in Tristan's tone. "Do you truly think I'm ignorant of our predicament?"

"Being aware of the truth and accepting it are two very different sentiments, Sire." Tristan took a step back, his gaze flicking to an approaching Astasiya. "Enjoy her while you can, but guard yourself."

He left before Issac could reply.

Fortunately, Astasiya hadn't overheard a word of it.

He held open his arms for her, and she stepped into them on a sigh, her forehead falling to his chest as Thomas drove off.

"I take it he agreed, then?" Issac inferred, his lips in her hair.

"Yeah. He's going to set up a meeting for noon tomorrow."

"That should provide Mateo with enough time," he murmured, his grip tightening around her. He still couldn't believe he'd agreed to this. The logic and motive behind it were sound. The execution was what concerned him.

Fortunately, they had two of the best strategists in the world on the case. If anyone could develop a foolproof plan, it was Aidan and Lucian. With Mateo's technical expertise, there shouldn't be any issues.

Unless Jonathan threw a play none of them expected, which was entirely likely.

"I saw you talking to Tristan," Astasiya murmured, pulling back to meet his gaze. "He's not my biggest fan, hmm?"

Right. She would be wondering about this. "He's protective."

"And seems to think you're destined for another woman?" she prompted, eyebrow arched.

Issac sighed, his fingers teasing the ends of Astasiya's hair. "Clara is just a friend. But yes, Aidan created her as a gift—for me." He palmed the back of her neck before she could step away. "Don't, Aya. There's nothing between us, only a long friendship with no desire for an intimate future."

Her gaze narrowed. "What about an intimate past?" Of course she would go there.

"If you're asking if I've fucked her, the answer is yes. Only once. And neither of us was particularly fond of the outcome." He tightened his hold as she tried to move away. "I won't apologize for my history, love. All I can do is pledge fidelity going forward, which I've already done."

"You could have warned me."

"Perhaps, but that would imply I consider it an important topic. Which I do not." Unlike his progeny who decided to mention the issue—one Clara and Issac hadn't discussed in decades because neither of them perceived the other in a sexual manner. "She's a friend and nothing more. A fact Tristan knows but decided to disregard to provoke unwarranted strife." He tilted his head. "Don't let him win, Aya. Please."

She studied him for a long moment and shook her head. "Your best friend is an ass."

He snorted. "I'm well aware."

"Yet you're still friends."

"He has his moments." Issac loosened his hold and brushed his mouth over hers. "There's no one else, Aya. Only you. I swear it."

She relaxed against him, her lips lingering against his. "I think you should take me to bed and prove it." The taunt was a whispered invitation that heated his blood. "We have all night, right?"

"Mmm, yes, we do. And I know of just the right distraction to keep us both occupied." He smiled against her mouth. "Something to take our minds off all the heavy discussion."

He really just wanted to see her naked again. Perhaps in another shower, or just in his bed, or on the table in the kitchen. Hmm, all three appealed to him. It would give them a night of pleasure before having to head back into the city tomorrow morning.

Issac could do with a bout of passionate fun, maybe even a bite.

Otherwise, he would waste the evening worrying about something he couldn't control.

Yes, he'd much rather spend it living and cherishing every moment.

"Now you're just teasing me," she accused, her hands falling to his hips as she tilted her head back. "But let me guess, does it involve my birthmark? Because I'd still like to win that bet."

His lips curled. "Actually, I'd just thought to take you back to the pool house for a few hours of sensual treatment and food, but now that you've reminded me, I would like to declare a winner." Which would be him, naturally.

"Sensual treatment?" she repeated. "I think I prefer that now."

"Too late, love. You've already inspired the idea." He caught her hand and pulled her alongside him. "Let's put this bet to rest, then I can put you to bed."

She snorted. "What a line."

He paused, arching a brow at her. "Is that your way of requesting a demonstration, love?" He backed her into the door, his hands on her hips, his thigh sliding between hers. "Just because we're in the company of friends and family doesn't mean I won't ravish you right here and now." The words were against her parted lips, his grip tightening. "Say the words, Aya. I dare you."

She shivered, her fingers digging into his shirt. "I—"

The turning handle had Issac pulling her to him just as the doors parted, a grinning Balthazar on the other side.

"Professional tip, Wakefield. Feed her a proper meal first. Then ravage her again. Provides better energy and increases enthusiasm." He glanced down at her, a wicked glint in his gaze. "And from what I overheard last night, you are quite passionate, sweetheart. When you're ready for a real immortal, you know where to find me."

A glorious pink overcame her cheeks as Issac arched a brow. "Did you miss my performance last night? Because I believe I left her more than satisfied. Over and over again."

Astasiya gasped, her eyes widening.

"Oh, I heard it," he replied, his lips curling. "I rated it a nine until you failed to feed her prior to the shower."

"I was busy eating—"

"Okay, yeah, we're not having this conversation," Astasiya said, sliding between the two of them to enter the house. She paused just inside the door, her face turning an even deeper shade of red. "*Fuck.*"

"That is the topic at hand, yes," Balthazar murmured, walking past her to join their audience in the living area. Most were gazing at Astasiya with interest, which had been the cause of her stumbling to a halt.

Issac closed the door before circling his arms around her from behind, his lips at her ear. "Ignore, Balthazar, darling. The rest of us do."

When she didn't speak or move, he kissed her cheek.

Time for a subject change.

"Aidan, Lucian, do you have a moment?" he asked. They were deep in conversation with Mateo, his blond head bent over his tablet, as usual.

The father and son duo glanced up at the same time, their faces so similar, yet one slightly more aged than the other. Neither of them favored facial hair, which only aided in their resemblance.

"Yes?" Aidan prompted.

"The rune," Lucian said, fully in tune with Issac, as always. Not due to mind reading, just a habit of knowing him well. "He wants us to look now."

"Ah yes." Aidan blinked. "Show us, Issac."

He telegraphed the image with ease while resting his chin on Astasiya's shoulder. Heat radiated from her cheeks, suggesting she'd not yet forgiven him for bantering with Balthazar. Issac could have thought the words instead, but saying them out loud felt so much more refreshing. Particularly after the bastard's blatant proposition.

As if Issac would share.

"Not something you ever considered an issue in the past, Wakefield," the mind reader said, smirking. He'd taken the seat beside Eliza, his arm stretched out over the back of the couch, carefully not touching the woman.

Although, she seemed to be comfortable with the proximity because her body was angled toward him. Not in a sexual manner so much as a comforting one.

Balthazar's secondary ability to control emotion would come in handy in her situation. He also tended to be rather tenderhearted in these circumstances, marking him as the perfect confidant. Amelia always did adore him in a familial way.

Issac did not share that opinion. *Astasiya is mine. Fuck off.*

Balthazar chuckled, his too-handsome face causing several of the females in the room to take notice. Astasiya, thankfully, was too focused on Aidan and Lucian to notice.

The two omniscient beings were chattering in an old language, a dead one from the sounds of it. They tended to regress when lost in debate and theories.

Issac waited them out, knowing one of them would eventually return to the future with his findings. "I believe I'm winning, Aya," he whispered against her ear. "I hope you're ready to take another shower. That's where we'll start."

She quivered, her soft intake of air confirming she'd visualized his words. He longed to see in her mind, to manipulate her vision with just what he intended.

Her. Wet.

Soft.

Willing.

Palms against the wall.

His cock sliding into her from behind, his lips against her neck.

Mmm, yes, that was exactly how they would start. He

allowed her to feel the stirrings of his arousal around her ass, grazed his teeth against her pulse.

The clearing of a throat brought his head up, his attention falling upon an expectant Aidan. "We have follow-up questions," he said.

Of course they did. "Which are?" Issac prompted.

"Does the mark ever bother you, Stas?" Lucian asked, his green eyes holding a faraway gleam that matched his father's.

Both were lost to their gifts, sorting through thousands and thousands of years of knowledge and experience, all while maintaining a conversation in the present. That sort of power was what qualified Lucian to lead and what kept Ichorians from challenging Aidan. Playing against an omniscient strategist was a fool's errand, indeed.

"Uh, no, not really," she replied.

Aidan didn't appear to like that answer. "Issac, can you try to manipulate her vision for me?"

Seemed a waste of time, but he nodded anyway and gave it a go. Astasiya squirmed a little, likely uncomfortable with the idea of being a test subject. Then she stilled, her lips parting.

"Oh, shit..." She spun in his arms, her gaze widening. "Do it again."

He frowned. "All right." He came up against another black wall of nothing, her mind completely shut off to him.

Her eyebrows were in her hairline. "My back... it... it tingles."

Lucian and Aidan were nodding, their conversation flowing again in a foreign language no one in this room understood. After several minutes of suspense, Lucian tilted his head to the side, his focus on Astasiya. "Have you ever seen a Seraphim, Stas?"

"A Seraphim?" she repeated, moving to Issac's side. "Issac said they were rare."

"Extremely rare," Aidan agreed. "I haven't seen one in several thousand years. I started to suspect they were extinct, but that mark suggests otherwise. When did you first notice it?"

"Uh, as a kid? It's a birthmark." Frown lines marred her brow. "Are you suggesting a Seraphim put a rune on my back?"

"Yes," they both replied at once.

"Why?"

"First guess, to protect you from Ichorians." Aidan shifted focus. "Have we tested Hydraian gifts on her thoroughly?"

"Only mine," Balthazar replied.

Aidan scratched his chin, his gaze searching. "Where's Jacque?"

"'Sup?" the teleporter appeared, a piece of pizza in his hand. "Heard my name from the kitchen."

"Stas, would you mind letting Jacque teleport you across the room?" Aidan asked. "To test your mark?"

She gaped at him. "You want me to let some guy I don't know teleport me?"

Issac pressed his lips to her temple. "Jacque's harmless, darling. Trust me."

"I'm not sure whether to be offended or pleased by that," the teleporter said around a mouthful of food.

"His manners, however, leave much to be desired," Issac added.

Jacque shrugged. "You try teleporting people back and forth all day across the world and tell me if you're not feckin' starved, yeah?"

"Across the world?" Astasiya repeated. "Yeah, no. Nope. Find someone else."

"I can always try it." The deep voice came from the hallway as Alik entered with a bottle of beer in his hands.

Issac tensed. "That's not—"

"Did you just speak in my head?" Astasiya asked, her eyes wide.

"Not immune," Alik summarized, collapsing into a chair beside Balthazar. "I can try my other gift if you're not satisfied."

"No," Issac said flatly.

"What's his other gift?" Astasiya wondered out loud, then shook her head. "Never mind, I don't want anyone else in my head."

Considering Alik could cripple an army with a thought, that was a wise decision.

"Did your mark tingle at all when Alik telepathically spoke to you?" Aidan asked.

She stiffened and shook her head. "No, not then or now. Stop doing that."

Alik shrugged, sipping his bottle, completely unperturbed.

"And no, don't do that either," she added, shuddering. "No wonder you're so... *dark*."

"Keeps me alive," Alik replied. "As well as everyone else."

Well, he must have answered her question about his ability to mentally torture hundreds of minds at a time. Brilliant. That would certainly warm Astasiya to the Hydraians.

"The protection rune is specific to Ichorians, then," Lucian was saying, in English this time, to Aidan. "Why?"

"I'm more interested in the how of it," Aidan replied. "What do we know about her ancestry?" The question seemed to be directed toward Issac.

"Just the names of her birth parents. Are you thinking they knew a Seraphim?" Issac rubbed Astasiya's arms while he spoke, her skin pebbled with goose bumps.

"Yes. It's possible her father knew one and requested a protective marking to help keep her alive." Aidan crossed one ankle over his knee. "I'd love to know what he negotiated in trade for such a precious gift. The higher angels hate Ichorians."

"Why?" she asked.

"Because we're considered an abomination to the angelic race." Aidan said it so casually, as if everyone knew that. "Do you remember meeting anyone unique in your childhood? Someone with an otherworldly air or poor communication skills? Seraphim don't socialize much with mortals, or anyone really. *Stoic* and *abrupt* would be good descriptors."

"Uh." She swallowed. "Not ringing any bells."

"What about your parents? Do you remember anything about them, Stas? Anything unique?" Lucian asked.

She pinched her lips to the side. "My father could compel. My mother…" She trailed off, slowly shaking her head. "It's… My memories have always been unreliable, fuzzy in nature."

Lucian and Aidan shared a look. "Memory tampering?" the eldest suggested.

"Possible," Lucian agreed. "We'll need to dive into that more."

"Indeed." Aidan switched to their archaic words again, the two of them lost to their minds. Mateo sat blissfully beside them, working on his plans for tomorrow.

The others all seemed to be melting into their own conversations as well.

"Do you have any other questions?" Issac asked, his arm sliding around Astasiya's shoulders.

"Not yet," Aidan and Lucian said together before returning to their discussion.

The question had been for Astasiya. "And you?" Issac whispered, his lips against her ear.

"What language are they speaking?"

He chuckled. "Honestly, I have no idea. They revert back to dead languages when they get excited about something." He kissed her shoulder. "It's rare for them to be presented with a learning opportunity."

"Because they know everything."

"Not so much know everything as they remember everything they've ever learned."

She glanced up at him. "That's terrifying."

"And amazing," he added, drawing his finger across her

jaw. "In any case, they'll let us know if they figure anything out, but I'm guessing that rune of yours will remain a mystery."

"And why's that?"

"Because only the Seraphim who gave it to you can tell us why." The only thing they knew for certain was the marking protected her from Ichorian gifts.

Her expression fell, her lips curling down at the sides. "Oh."

He lifted her chin upward with his thumb, his lips brushing hers. "You look like you could use a distraction right about now."

"I just found out my birthmark isn't a birthmark at all," she whispered. "A distraction would be great."

"There's food in the pool house."

"I'm more interested in the bed." Soft words, confidently spoken.

She'd just revealed the seductress she kept hidden away deep inside. The one who favored lace and craved his bite.

And oh, how his demon side approved.

"Yes, and I do believe I won." He allowed his gaze to roam over her slowly. "Anywhere and however I want, yes?"

She visibly shuddered, her eyes taking on a bedroom quality he adored. "I think I'm going to enjoy this distraction."

"That's the idea." He pressed his lips to her ear, his words for her alone. "I'm going to start by fucking that delicious mouth of yours, then we'll make it more interesting. Now, follow me."

CHAPTER TWENTY-SEVEN

Testing Boundaries

THIS IS A BAD IDEA.

The thought reverberated in Stas's mind as they neared the CRF headquarters. She fought the urge to fiddle with the top button of her blouse—the one that Mateo had sewn on this morning.

A camera.

That would link back to his tablet.

She swallowed. He promised the metal detectors wouldn't catch anything, and the button looked real enough.

Just like the item in her pocket.

A business card with Issac's contact information as CEO of Wakefield Pharmaceuticals on the front and his masculine handwriting scrawled across the back.

But between the paper edges was something that would allow Mateo to hack into Doctor Fitzgerald's system, so long as she placed the item close enough to his computer.

Issac squeezed her leg, his palm resting against her upper thigh as he navigated the Manhattan streets. "You don't have to do this, Aya."

Oh, but she did. They were missing something, some key detail. Every fiber of her being vowed that Owen never meant her any harm, even when they first met.

Of course, she felt the same way about Doctor Fitzgerald despite the evidence to the contrary.

"It's the only option," she said softly, more to herself than to Issac. "I'm just nervous, is all."

That the card in her pocket might set off some alarms.

That someone might notice the button.

That she might get caught.

That I might not like the truth.

She shivered, goose bumps pebbling her arms despite the warm summer day.

The electricity dancing across her skin intensified as the looming glass towers of the CRF appeared before them, a variety of flags decorating the courtyard out front.

"Last chance, love," Issac murmured, his hand moving to the shifter between them.

"I have to do this." The conviction in her voice didn't match her churning insides.

He nodded, slowing as they approached the gated entrance. "When we pass the guard stand, my gift will no longer be viable."

"Issac, this—"

"I want you to test your gift on me when I park inside, Aya. We need to know that it works."

"This isn't the plan," she gritted out.

"Plans change." He uttered the words while steering into place in front of the gate. "Let me do the talking."

Her stomach twisted, the small breakfast she'd eaten this morning threatening to make a reappearance. She bit her lip to keep from demanding him not to do this, knowing it was too late when a guard tapped on the passenger window. Another approached the driver's side. Pistols strapped to their hips.

Issac rolled down the glass and removed his sunglasses to peer up at the security officer beside her side of the car. "Good morning," he greeted, his tone deceptively pleasant. "I'm dropping off a guest for Jonathan Fitzgerald. I think you'll find he's expecting us."

The robust man didn't even look up from his clipboard as he asked, "Name?"

He didn't hesitate. "Issac Wakefield."

Two almond-shaped eyes popped up, his dark eyebrows rising. "I— I need to phone this in."

"Of course," Issac replied. "We'll wait." He relaxed into his seat as if he hadn't just alerted CRF security that an Ichorian wanted entry.

She had so many questions.

So many concerns.

But the open windows kept her quiet.

While one soldier went into the booth to make the call, the other stroked his weapon, his focus on Issac.

Were his gifts already moot?

She glanced at the stone columns on either side of the entrance, roughly five feet before them. *Are there runes etched into the rock?* she wondered, searching for patterns that her eyes refused to identify.

"He's clear," the male called from the booth. "Fitzgerald will meet them in the parking lot."

By the casual use of the surname, Stas assumed he meant Tom.

"Cheers," Issac said as the gates opened. The windows closed around them as he shifted forward through the stone pillars, his shudder visible as they passed.

"Have you lost your fucking mind?" she demanded, furious.

"You're allowed to put your life at risk, while I'm not?"

345

he countered, his sideways glance one of admonishment and disbelief. "That is not how this will work between us, Aya."

"Damn it." Her fists clenched, her heart beating a mile a minute.

If something happens to him…

If they catch him…

God, she'd never forgive herself.

"Issac," she whispered. "You can't do this. Not for me."

"It's already done." He navigated into the parking lot off to the side of the building—an area reserved for diplomats and VIPs. Apparently, Issac qualified.

Unless this was a trap.

Would the Sentinels run out to grab him?

In broad daylight?

She glanced around the vacant lot, noting the normal afternoon air and the lack of movement.

Just a typical work day with a handful of empty cars.

"You asked me to trust you, Aya. Now it's your turn to do the same." His arm came around the back of her seat, his body angled toward her, the car humming beneath them. "Command me to do something, love."

She continued to survey their surroundings, while Issac appeared completely relaxed beside her.

No worries.

Not even a frown line in his forehead.

"How are you so calm right now?" she asked, her nerves straining her voice.

"Who says I am?" He tugged on a strand of her hair, forcing her to look at him. "Command me to do something," he repeated. "I need to know your gift is unimpacted by the wards. Please." A hint of emotion deepened his irises to an alluring sapphire, his expression otherwise blank.

He's concerned not for himself but for me.

She didn't know how to feel about that. No, that wasn't right. Of course she did. Because she felt the same way. They were surrounded by potentially dangerous elements, and all she cared about was his safety, not her own.

"I want you to do everything you can to leave the CRF grounds the second I shut the passenger door." Persuasion laced through her words, the demand as natural as speaking. She sensed it seep into his pores, his very being, saw the flash of recognition in his gaze, the acceptance in the flare of his pupils.

"Well played." He wrapped his palm around the back of her neck, pulling her closer. "Sexy as fuck, too." He kissed her hard, his tongue conveying some sort of hidden message, a secret she couldn't grasp. Not with her mind whirring, her body chilled from the very real possibility that Issac could be caught, or worse.

"You need to go," she whispered urgently. "It's not safe here."

"I could say the same to you, love."

"My gift is fine. I'll be okay. I promise."

He pressed his forehead to hers. "And now that I know that, I feel marginally better about leaving you here. There is one item I would like to request, if you'll entertain it?"

"Don't ask me to retract my demand." Because she wouldn't. Which proved she believed his accusations about the CRF. Otherwise, she wouldn't be so panicked.

And I'm about to waltz into the viper's den.

"No, it's something more personal." His thumb brushed her pulse. "You've healed from the Conclave. I want to re-mark you. It's a sign of devotion, one Jonathan will both understand and respect. It will also provide proof of our ongoing affair."

"You want him to know I'm yours," she translated.

"I do," he admitted softly. "Because it means if he hurts you, he'll have to contend with me. And considering the tenuous nature of our relationship, I don't see him wanting to draw more attention unto himself."

She understood what Issac truly desired—to protect her. This was a way to help him feel more confident about the situation, to know he'd done everything in his power to keep her safe aside from entering the building with her.

How had their charade melted into such intensity? Or had it been that way from the beginning? A part of her, some foreign sliver inside, had bonded to him on a level that superseded existence. That piece of her urged her to deepen the connection, to allow him this simple favor.

Because whatever he craved, she craved, too.

She nodded, understanding him in a manner that surpassed logic. "Can you make it quick?" she asked softly, aware of their location, but also knowing why he needed this.

"Not a statement most women say around me, but yes, I can." He nuzzled her jaw, his hand already pulling her hair to the side. "Just know I'll want more later."

"You could have fed last night," she reminded him, her voice huskier than she intended. They'd spent most of the evening hours lost between the sheets, even enjoyed dinner in bed—a dinner Issac had prepared.

But he never bit her. Even when she offered.

"Mmm, but I did." The words were spoken against her throat. "I licked every inch of you, Aya. And I intend to do it again tonight." His incisors pierced her skin, the sharp prick giving way to a sensation of euphoria that stole her breath.

She clutched the lapels of his jacket, her heart hammering in her chest.

Oh... This was inappropriate. Wrong. Not the right place. Yet the indecency of it only heightened the moment.

His name fell from her tongue, both a warning and a plea wrapped up in one. Stas couldn't decide if she wanted him to stop or keep going. But he made the decision for her, pulling away with a satisfied gleam in his eyes.

He cupped her cheek. "Jonathan would be a fool to touch you now."

A sharp rap on the window caused her to jump away from Issac, her gaze flying upward to Tom just outside her door.

Shit.

Issac rolled down the glass. "Thomas."

"Wakefield," he returned. "Brave of you to enter the grounds."

Her demon arched a brow. "I could say the same about you venturing into my estate."

"Touché." Tom stuffed his hands into the pockets of his jeans. "I appreciate you dropping her off. You've been noted as a nonthreat and will be permitted to leave without issue."

"Much appreciated." Issac reached over for her hand, giving it a gentle squeeze. "I just need one more minute with Astasiya."

Tom nodded, taking a step back. "I'll be on the sidewalk." He pointed to the path running alongside the building. Not waiting for confirmation, he left as the window slid upward.

"Your edict still stands," Issac murmured. "I'll leave as soon as you step outside."

She blinked. "You can feel it?" Odd that she couldn't. Except, she never really did. Would her control over it improve when she became a Hydraian?

"Mmm, it would seem your desire for me to escape unharmed is strong." He removed his hand, a smile on his lips. "I'm actually quite flattered, as it shows you care."

She unbuckled her seat belt. "Like you needed that to know."

"You're not the only one new to these emotions, Aya," he said softly. "Be safe. Please."

She paused with her hand on the handle, looking back at him.

What if I never see him again?

Don't think like that.

"Issac—"

"Don't, Aya. Don't say anything else. You're coming over this evening. No arguments."

She swallowed, nodding. "Yeah. After the meeting. I'll

be there."

"You'd better." He lifted his hand, his fingers light against her chin. "Be safe, my Aya."

"I'll see you soon," she promised.

"I know." He ran his thumb over her bottom lip, then pulled her in for a searing kiss that imprinted him on her soul. "Don't hide the mark." He gathered her hair over one shoulder while he spoke. "And remember what you can do."

"I will," she whispered, opening the door. "Now safely leave the grounds." That twinge of compulsion stirred inside her, punctuating her words on instinct alone.

"Call if you need a pickup, Aya."

"Okay." She grabbed her purse and shut the door, refusing to say goodbye. It felt like a bad omen.

Something tugged against her soul as he put the car in drive, her heart in her throat as she watched him exit the lot.

She needed him to be safe.

To leave without issue.

Walking quickly to the corner, she watched as he navigated the grounds, not a single person or object in his path.

Then he was at the exit.

The gates lifted.

Electricity hummed over her skin as he passed through the cement columns unscathed, her breath leaving her on a sigh.

"I'm a man of my word, Stas," Tom said, having joined her. "You know that about me."

She glanced up at the much taller man, taking in the sincerity and hurt lurking in his eyes. "It's hard to know who to trust right now," she admitted. "All the lies. The secrets. This secret world of immortals." She shook her head, tears pricking behind her eyes as the emotions of the last few weeks caught up to her at once. "I don't know right from wrong or up from down anymore."

"Ah, Stas." He wrapped his arms around her in a hug

filled with adoration, brotherly love, and affection. Such familiarity. Such warmth. "I'm so sorry." Soft words saturated with such heartbreaking honesty that she couldn't help but return the embrace.

"You're going to make me cry," she accused, knowing full well it wouldn't be him at all, but the stress of their situation. God, she couldn't decide if she wanted to weep or scream or run like hell.

But Tom was right. She *knew* him. He may have kept a huge, devastating secret from her, but hadn't she done the same? She hid her ability to compel from everyone, even her closest friends.

"Will you ever forgive me?" he asked, his heart in his voice. "For the other night?"

That all depended on what happened today, what she learned inside the walls of the CRF. "I can try," she said instead, unable to voice the truth. Another secret between them, joining the vault with countless others.

How could she be angry with him for hiding a world from her when she was guilty of the very same crime? Even now, she intended to help Mateo break into the CRF records.

It's the right thing to do.

Is it, though?

Maybe. Yes.

She sighed, stepping back, meeting his troubled gaze. "I'm ready to see your dad." To determine the truth once and for all.

He nodded. "He's waiting for you, too. Let's go." He gestured for her to follow, his much longer legs carrying him across the concrete in wide strides. She kept pace, gripping her purse as her breakfast churned in her stomach.

This is it.

Deep breaths.

The creepy black flag hanging over their heads seemed to taunt her entry. *Memento Mori.* White cross. A curse of death.

351

And not the omen she needed right now.

"You'll need to check your purse and your phone," Tom said conversationally, standing beside the metal detector just inside the entrance.

She nodded, placing her bag on the conveyor belt.

The card seemed to burn in her pocket, as did the tiny camera on her blouse—one she'd forgotten about until just now.

Mateo promised it would pass the scanners.

She hoped he was right.

Tom walked through, the system blaring loudly in response, mocking her.

Perspiration dotted her spine, her hands, her brow. *Oh God...*

The officers said nothing to Tom, completely aware of who he was and not caring at all that he'd set off the alarms. He wore a pistol on his hip, something no one seemed to mind.

Had he brought that outside because of Issac? Or did he always carry a firearm?

"Stas?" he prompted, his expression concerned.

"Sorry," she mumbled. "I, uh, just expected them to make you go back through."

He chuckled and scratched the days-old stubble dotting his jaw. "They're used to me setting it off, aren't you, boys?"

Two of them snorted. The third just looked bored.

Right.

So, he always kept a weapon on his person.

Good to know.

"You can go through," one of the security guards said, his shoulders twice the width of hers. Not because he was overweight. No. That was all muscle.

Noting all their younger ages and stature, she finally put something together.

They weren't security guards at all, but Sentinels. Like Tom. Hence, the easy camaraderie between them and militaristic features—short hair, clean-shaven, athletic forms.

How had she never noticed that before?

Because you didn't know the organization might be evil.

"Stas?" Tom gave her a look, one filled with curiosity and concern. Because she was acting like a crazy person, frozen beside the metal detector.

That doesn't make me look guilty at all.

She forced a laugh. "It's been a really long weekend."

His features softened a bit, understanding bright in his chocolate eyes.

A couple of employees entered behind her, likely returning from an early lunch break.

Now or never, she told herself. *I really hope you did your job, Mateo.*

She crossed the threshold.

CHAPTER TWENTY-EIGHT

Truth and Deception

THE RHYTHMIC DRUMMING IN STAS'S EARS drowned out all sound around her, including Tom's voice as he handed her a temporary badge from the security desk.

She slid the lanyard over her head.

Nothing happened.

No one tackled her.

They didn't request a pat-down.

Just a bunch of nodding Sentinels, two of which smiled at her warmly.

Mateo's devices hadn't set off the alarm.

I'm losing my mind over nothing, she realized, mentally shaking herself. What if all this was a complete misunderstanding? Yes, the CRF dabbled in the immortal world. But maybe Issac and the others had the wrong opinion on it.

"Ready?" Tom asked after securing her bag with the Sentinels.

She nodded. "Yes."

"Cool. Follow me." He led her to a bank of elevators on the other side of the three-story lobby and swiped his badge. "You went down here for your polygraph, yeah?"

Unfortunately. "And my medical exam."

His brow furrowed. "Medical exam?"

"Yeah, with Doctor Patel."

His expression darkened, almost to the point where she wanted to step backward. "Doctor Patel gave you a medical exam?"

The elevator dinged before she could reply, her throat suddenly dry.

Tension tightened his shoulders, his square jaw clenched as he scanned his badge to select the lower level. "What did she do during your exam?" he asked as the doors closed before them.

Stas swallowed. "Standard things, at least until the vaccines."

He muttered a curse, shaking his head. "*Fuck.*"

"Your dad said it's not common procedure."

"It's not," he growled. "Not at all."

Her pulse quickened as they stepped into the underground cavern of endless white hallways. A sensation of wrongness crept over her, similar to how she felt during the Conclave. Except Issac wasn't here to protect her this time.

She caressed the mark on her neck, the two pinpoints against her skin providing a false sense of comfort.

"This way," Tom muttered, his steps clipped.

They took a different path from her last visit down here, one that led them through a room of armed military men.

Oh, I hope you all are seeing this, she thought, remembering the camera against her blouse. *Because this can't be normal.*

There were so many guns and cameras and mirrors. Every wall. Covered in thick two-way glass.

Energy crawled over her skin. Not the good kind, but the bad kind.

"You're breaking protocol, Fitzgerald," a deep voice said from their left. Two brawny arms corded in muscle crossed a burly chest that left her gulping.

Not the kind of man you want to piss off.

"Bite me, Hawthorne." Tom swiped his badge against another door to lead her away from the hostile guards.

"They seemed friendly," she said as he took a left down a dimly lit hallway. No cameras this way. Interesting.

"They're assholes." He kept moving, his boots shuffling against the white tile until a familiar blond male turned the corner with a raised eyebrow. "Where is he?" Tom asked by way of greeting.

"Where do you think?" Light green eyes flickered her way. "Miss Davenport."

She swallowed, unnerved by that knowing gaze. *He* knew about her exam because he'd taken her to Doctor Patel. "Agent Stark."

Tom glanced between them. "You two know each other?"

She wiped her clammy palms against her black pants. "Yeah, he was my polygrapher."

Skepticism deepened the creases in Tom's brow. "I didn't know you moonlighted as a polygrapher, Stark."

"Only when requested," he replied, walking away.

Stas frowned after him. "If he's not a polygrapher, then what does he do?" Could he have been involved in her poisoning somehow?

"You don't want to know," Tom replied. He took an abrupt turn down another corridor void of surveillance and stopped at a door a few feet down, knocking twice. It cracked open, just enough for Doctor Fitzgerald to see them.

Tom cocked his head toward her. "I told you she was

356

fine." Flat words accompanied by a somewhat hostile stance.

Well, that's new. Every time the two men interacted, she caught only respect and admiration. However, the Tom standing beside her now radiated fury.

What gives?

"Thank God," Doctor Fitzgerald said, his relief palpable. "I just need to finish up this conversation, Stas. But I'm looking forward to catching up with you."

"Me, too," she lied, forcing a smile.

"Take her to my office" was all he said to Tom before shutting the door.

Wow. Okay. Definitely some tension here.

"It'll be my pleasure," Tom gritted out, his gaze narrowed at the letters etched into the wood.

A-7.

Stas wondered what they meant and whom Doctor Fitzgerald might be talking to in the room. Whoever it was, Tom didn't seem to approve.

He stalked off down the hall—still white with no cameras—and opened a door at the end of it. "He means his office down here," Tom explained.

Does that mean the computer Mateo needs is in here? she wondered, entering the reasonably sized space. An oversized oak desk took up a quarter of the space with a collection of chairs around it—two in front, one behind—and a table for four sat in the corner.

Two computer monitors.

One laptop between them.

That had to be what Mateo needed.

Tom palmed the back of his neck, noticing her inspection. "Yeah, it's not as swanky as the one upstairs, but no one really sees this one except the Sentinels."

"You mean the humanitarian military personnel who are not actually conducting humanitarian missions?" She couldn't help the sarcasm, particularly after seeing the army waiting underground for intruders.

What are they guarding in this area that requires that much firepower?

"There are still humanitarian missions, Stas. We've saved people from some pretty fucked-up situations. If you thought the Arcadia was bad, you should see some of the other Ichorian dens." He looked pointedly at her neck. "As you obviously know, they require blood to stay alive. Most of them call it a curse, but there are some who luxuriate in it more than others." Disdain tainted his tone.

"You don't seem to like them very much."

"I detest them."

After what she saw during the Conclave, she could understand why.

Tom sat in one of the chairs across from Dr. Fitzgerald's desk and waved at her to take the other, putting her closer to the laptop. Mateo said he needed the card within a foot of it. She estimated the current distance at just over two.

"What all did Issac tell you about the immortal world?" Tom asked, tucking his hands behind his head in a way that accentuated the strength in his arms.

"He explained the difference between Hydraians and Ichorians. And he mentioned the Blood Laws." As well as a lot of other shit she couldn't repeat.

"I assume he didn't paint the CRF in the kindest light."

"Not exactly, no."

He smirked. "Yeah. They don't care much for our technology."

"Why's that?" The immortals had mentioned something about it being beyond human invention, meaning the CRF had employed supernatural means of some sort.

"Because we develop instruments that can kill them." He brought up his ankle to rest on his opposite knee. "They're immortals with psychic gifts. All we have—as humans—is our strength and agility and, now, weapons."

Except you're a fledgling, she thought. *And not exactly human.*

Doctor Fitzgerald chose that moment to enter, a towel in his hands as if he'd just been drying them off. "Do you mind giving us a few minutes, Tom? I'd like to speak with Stas privately."

A chill settled across the room, Tom frozen for too long a moment as he glowered at his father. Doctor Fitzgerald returned the look with a steely gaze of his own, his dominance filling the office with an almost ominous air.

Stas wasn't so sure she wanted Tom to leave. Not with this version of her mentor in the room.

"Yes, *sir*," Tom said, standing. He left with a not-so-subtle slam of the door.

Um… This was not the father-son duo she knew.

"I can't tell you how relieved I am to see you here, Stas." Instead of taking the chair behind the desk, Doctor Fitzgerald leaned against it with his legs crossed at the ankles a few inches from her. His nearness didn't normally bother her, but it did today. She felt caged between him and the wall, like he feared she might run.

Do I have a reason to?

Dressed in black slacks and a pale blue dress shirt, he resembled the Doctor Fitzgerald she respected and adored. He even had the same genuine smile.

Why did he suddenly feel like a stranger to her?

"Tom tells me you had an eventful weekend," he continued, his soft brown eyes falling to the mark on her neck.

"That's one way to describe it." She preferred *intimidating* or *paralyzing* to *eventful*. "Honestly, I would rather get to the point and talk about the Sentinel program."

I want to talk about you.

And I also need to figure out how to place this card close enough to your laptop.

He chuckled and shook his head. "I've always enjoyed your directness, Stas." He pushed off the desk, walked around it, and settled into his chair. Lacing his long fingers together on the desk, he leaned forward.

"The CRF still does everything you've been told; it just also does a little more. There's a humanitarian wing that caters to those in need, helps with search and rescue missions, and delivers aid. That's all true. What the general public isn't aware of is we also have an elite group of Sentinels who dabble in supernatural affairs. Tom, as you now know, belongs to the latter. From your expression, I gather Issac already told you all of this?"

"He did."

"I see." He narrowed his gaze. "Did he also mention his involvement in your medical exam?"

Uh… "What?" *How much does he know? About my reaction to the Nizari venom? Does that mean he did try to poison me?* Ice drizzled through her veins. *Oh, I never should have come here. I never—*

"Hmm, I can see he didn't." Doctor Fitzgerald typed something into his keyboard and switched on one of his monitors. What appeared to be an interrogation video displayed across the screen. "After what you told me Friday night, Agent Stark and I had a long chat with Anita Patel. Needless to say, we learned who gave her the directive to administer the vaccinations." His gaze snagged hers for a moment, his lips tightening. "I'm sorry, Stas, but you're not going to like this."

She sat forward to better see the video. He hit Play.

Doctor Patel appeared in her lab coat, sitting across the table from two suit-clad men. Agent Stark appeared to be bored, while Doctor Fitzgerald wore a hostile expression—similar to the one he just gave his son.

"You recently administered a medical exam to Astasiya Caroline Davenport," Doctor Fitzgerald said, giving the dates and details of her security interview. They went over a few documents before he reached the heart of the matter. "You gave Miss Davenport inoculations meant only for paramilitary personnel when her file clearly indicated *civilian*. Further, it appears you dispensed vaccines that are not part of our paramilitary exam protocols. Nizari poison, if the surveillance feeds outside of the exam room are correct. Do you deny any of this?"

Apathy painted the woman's features in harsh shades, her lack of concern evident. "No."

Stark's expression remained unchanged, his gaze steady. "Who gave you the Nizari poison, Anita?"

"The man who hired me to give it to her."

"And who hired you?" he asked in the same monotone from Stas's polygraph. The man took stoic to a whole new level.

"Issac Wakefield." The answer was clear and concise and sent a shock down Stas's spine.

What?

No.

That wasn't possible.

He *saved* her.

Unless...

Unless saving her was the point. To poison her and then rescue her. To give her a reason to be wary of the organization he intended to get revenge against while simultaneously instilling a deep-rooted trust in him as her savior. An ingenious plan that had "Issac Wakefield" written all over it. She was a pawn to him, at least in the beginning. He would have had no problem toying with her life, and even admitted he might one day get her killed.

The video continued to play and she pretended to watch, her mind spinning with possibilities and adamant denials.

A brilliant plan, maybe, but Issac wouldn't do that to her. Never once did he insinuate it could be anyone other than the CRF who tried to poison her.

But the video was incriminating.

And he had been there when she arrived that afternoon. The Tuesday night date had been his idea as well. An odd choice.

Did he set it all up?

She recalled Doctor Fitzgerald's concern when she mentioned the shots after her medical exam. His shock was believable. That was not a man who ordered her assassination. She wondered at the time if Doctor Patel worked on her own and somehow knew about her fledgling status. Because Issac told her?

No. He wouldn't do that to me.

This had to be a scheme, a way to turn her against Issac. The man who dropped her off today was not someone who wished her ill will; he'd even advocated against all of this. He wanted her safe. Protected. His.

It may have been a charade in the beginning, but not anymore.

He cared about her.

And she cared about him.

"You asked me to trust you, Aya. Now it's your turn to do the same." His words from the car played through her thoughts, vibrating in her heart.

She couldn't fail him now.

He didn't do this.

"I'm sorry," Doctor Fitzgerald murmured. "Are you familiar with Nizari poison and why it's used?"

Her spine tingled.

The rune.

Someone nearby was using an Ichorian gift.

Was it Doctor Fitzgerald? She'd never asked Issac what he could do.

She frowned. "I'm sorry. Can you repeat that? I'm still a bit, uh, well, shocked."

He smiled gently. "Of course, dear. I understand. It's all a bit harsh to hear, and I'm very sorry to be the bearer of bad news."

I just bet you are, she thought back at him. Oh, he sounded genuine enough. Even looked apologetic. A master manipulator, the man behind the mask. *Who are you really?*

"I asked, 'Are you familiar with Nizari poison and why it's used?'"

More tingling.

She cleared her throat, focusing. Instinct told her to lie. "Uh, no, I'm not familiar with it."

"It's used to kill Ichorian offspring. Permanently. My

guess is Issac wanted to test your mortality. When you didn't react, he knew you were human and therefore a viable candidate for him to pursue."

"Viable candidate?" she repeated, her brow furrowing. *What the fuck is he talking about?*

"Yes. I think he intends to turn you." His gaze went to her neck again. "After he's done reaping the benefits of your mortality, anyway." A deliberately cold statement that made her shiver. He couldn't be more wrong on that assessment. Not that she could correct him. "He doesn't have any female progeny yet. It seems you've caught his fancy. He must sense something unusual about you that will benefit him."

"You seem to know a lot about him," she noted, uneasy with the turn in conversation. Issac told her his attentions would intrigue Doctor Fitzgerald, but now her mentor wanted to know more about *why* the renowned billionaire Ichorian had chosen her. She did not want to go down that path of speculation.

"I do. I've never seen him so interested in a woman. It's made me wonder if perhaps his interest is also tied to your employment, or maybe your relationship with me. Any ideas?"

She pretended to consider and shrugged. "He hasn't mentioned anything." *But it's fascinating that you would make that assumption. And also somewhat incriminating.*

"Interesting." He scratched his chin in a thoughtful manner. "You know, we've never had a female Sentinel. This could be a unique opportunity. As you're already aware of the world, it's an obvious next step. Of course, if you prefer to continue working in marketing, that's perfectly acceptable. The pay won't be as good, or the benefits, really, but I'll understand."

Wait... "Are you offering me a job?" Because that was not at all what she expected from this conversation. Hell, she still hadn't even called Human Resources back.

"It's a win-win in my book. You learn more about the

supernatural world, we keep you safe and train you how to defend yourself, and we groom our first female Sentinel. Of course, I'm just thinking on my feet here. I would have to run it by the team first."

Okay, uh, what? "But I'm not military."

"No, but you're young and in decent shape. Stark or Tom will handle the rest. It'll be a lot of hard work and long hours. You would also have to end whatever you have going on with Issac, though I doubt that'll be much of an issue after what I revealed today."

And that's the catch, what he desired. To take her away from Issac. "How—"

The door flew open with a bang. Tom stood just outside, his face contorted in rage.

"I need a minute with you. *Now.*" The words were spoken through clenched teeth and directed at his father.

Doctor Fitzgerald sighed, standing. "Stas, will you excuse me? My son seems to have lost his manners."

By the look on Tom's face, those were the wrong words to say. What the hell had gotten into him? He looked ready to commit murder. *And is that blood on his hand?*

"Yeah, sure," she murmured at the closing door.

What the fuck? Tom hadn't even looked at her. She wasn't used to seeing him angry, let alone disheveled.

The screen of the computer was still facing her with Doctor Patel's face frozen in a smile that made her stomach churn.

She nearly turned the screen off again when it dawned on her that she was alone in Doctor Fitzgerald's office.

The card. She stood and pretended to stretch while searching for any signs of surveillance. There weren't any, but that didn't mean there wasn't something obscure observing her.

Plucking the card from her pocket, she pretended to read the contact details and the note on the back. Then, acting as though she was annoyed, she flicked the card onto the desk, sending it across the space toward Doctor Fitzgerald's laptop.

Anyone watching would assume the item offended her.

And after that video, they'd know why. Because it had Issac's name and handwriting on it.

With a feigned huff, she stared up at the ceiling.

What the hell had set Tom off? she wondered. Clearly, there was something going on here.

She glanced at the still-closed door. Were they having a conversation in the hall? She stepped casually closer, hearing nothing.

Hmm.

Maybe she could open it and say she needed to use the restroom? Give her a chance to wander with the camera on her chest?

Seemed practical enough.

She cracked open the door, prepared to voice her excuse, except the hallway was vacant.

With a frown, she stepped into the corridor. No sign of life. Silent. But the entryway to the room Doctor Fitzgerald had occupied earlier was slightly ajar.

Had they ventured in there?

She could just wander and knock, right? Voice her excuse politely?

On impulse, or perhaps due to a moment of stupidity, she crept forward.

Curiosity killed the cat, her helpful conscious reminded.

Good thing I'm not a fucking cat.

She stopped outside the room, listening for voices. Nothing. Weird. Where did they go? Stas took a step, when a soft humming caught her attention, the sound hypnotizing.

"Do it again, Mommy!"

Her mother's laugh tickled the air around her as she reappeared, joy radiating in her features. "Oh, my darling, you are truly my little angel."

"Teasing our daughter again?" Daddy came up behind Mommy and wrapped her in his arms, his lips against her neck.

Astasiya scrunched up her nose. "Gross."

He chuckled. "One day, little angel, you may disagree."

Her mother snorted. "Are you kidding? You'll kill anyone who touches her."

"Well, that's true," he agreed, nuzzling her.

"Mist again," Astasiya said, pleading with her mom. "Please. Please mist again!"

Her mother smiled and disappeared, the sound of wings humming through the air as she fluttered her invisible feathers.

A tear rolled down Stas's cheek at the vivid memory, one she'd forgotten for nearly twenty years. Was it real? Did that actually happen? Or was it a dream?

That whisper of a sound drew her gaze back to the room, the soft purr forcing her forward.

She pushed open the door to find a woman crumpled in the corner, her face hidden beneath a curtain of brown hair.

Not her mother.

Not even close.

A whimper escaped the female, her pain palpable and visible from the metal cuff digging into her ankle.

Oh, fuck. Stas rushed forward and came to an abrupt stop when the frail woman lifted her head. Clear, sapphire eyes met hers.

"Well, this is new," she said, her voice stronger than Stas would have expected. "What game is Jonathan playing at now?"

Stas gaped at the woman, her striking features and British lilt familiar. But it was the eyes she recognized most. They were the spitting image of Issac's.

"Amelia," she breathed. "You're alive."

And, oh God, he can see this...

"For today, anyway." Amelia stretched an arm over her head and winced. Bruises and welts littered her skin, while her face remained unmarred. Someone had recently delivered a beating. A bad one. *Jonathan...*

"I've got to get you out of here." Stas checked the hallway for surveillance. No visible cameras anywhere in this area, unlike the others.

She frowned. Okay, but how would she be able to get Amelia past security?

And the elevator only moved for Tom's key card, not hers.

And that shackle around Amelia's very swollen ankle appeared to be locked on tightly.

Stas eyed the thin silver collar around the woman's neck, as well as the tiny blinking light at the center. *Definitely not your typical accessory.* Was it a remote-activated device? Would it sound an alarm if she left the building?

"That's rich, love." Amelia extended her legs, revealing more bruising that painted her skin in shades of purple and blue.

"*Jesus.*" She looked nothing like the beautiful woman in Owen's photos. "What the hell did he do to you?"

Her long, dark lashes blinked once. "He beat me, of course. Are you here to do the same?"

"No!" Realizing she yelled that, she glanced at the door again and waited to hear voices.

Still nothing.

Thank God.

She didn't have much time and she needed to think. Except she had no physical way to help Amelia escape.

Is Issac already on his way here?

He had to see the footage, right? Assuming the camera was working?

What if it's not? The thought chilled her. He'd never believe this without seeing it.

"Issac thinks you're dead." The words sort of spilled from her mouth unceremoniously.

"Oh, this again? Yes, as I told Jonathan months ago, or maybe that was years ago. Time is a weird thing here. But yes, I have finally come to that conclusion as well. Are we done?"

"No, I mean he might not believe me when I tell him you're alive." She really, really hoped the camera was working. Except that would also mean he'd just seen his sister in this state. "I need to give him something only you would know."

Those perceptive blue eyes that were too much like her brother's looked her up and down. "This is a terrible game. Obviously, I'm not going to fall for this." She rested her head against the wall and closed her eyes. "Can we get back to the healing bit now?"

An odd request, one Stas didn't have time to clarify. "Look, I don't know how much time I have."

Amelia appeared unfazed, simply rolling her forehead against the wall and groaning to herself. This woman was as stubborn as her brother.

Shit.

Okay.

She needed to give her proof. What had he told her about Amelia that not everyone would know? "Uh, you taught him to dance because it's the way to win a woman's heart, but he always told you he had no interest in it."

Amelia snapped upright and took Stas's measure again. "What have you done to my brother?"

"Nothing. He's, uh, we're sort of... No, that's not important." She glanced again at the door, terrified they would get caught. "Give me something to tell him."

Amelia's gaze flickered to the wall beside the door. "This is quite dull."

Stas grabbed the back of her neck, her limbs shaking from the possibility that someone may catch her here. And then what?

No.

She had to make this quick, get out, and tell Issac.

"I'm risking my life right now standing here. Give me something, Amelia. I'm begging you."

The first signs of uncertainty filtered through Amelia's features, her lips curling down as she tilted her head in an eerie way. "Issac sent you?"

"It's complicated and I don't have time to explain."

"Mmm, and he's all right?" she asked.

"Yes."

Amelia bit her cheek, her gaze falling to the floor before lifting again. "I miss his blue butterflies, you know." She traced indistinguishable designs on the wall with her finger, a tear licking a path down her cheek that she didn't seem to notice. "I dream of them sometimes. Maybe I'll dream of them again tonight." She sighed, closing her eyes. "I'm wary of this madness, you see. So very wary."

Fuck, what had Jonathan been doing to her all these years? She was so utterly broken. So... fragile.

Stas resisted the urge to console the woman and instead checked the hallway. Still clear. But she doubted it would be for long. The blue-butterfly line would have to be enough.

"I have to go," she told Amelia. "But he'll come for you. Even if it means burning this place to the ground."

"I used to believe that," Amelia murmured, still drawing aimlessly on the wall. "Then I learned hope only equates to pain."

CHAPTER TWENTY-NINE

The First Female Sentinel

STAS SPRINTED BACK TO THE OFFICE, Amelia's parting words a shadow on her soul. *Hope only equates to pain.* Stas had wanted proof of Issac's claims; now she more than had it.

Doctor Fitzgerald was a monster. She may not have seen him beat Amelia, but he'd clearly been the last one in her room.

Was that why Tom wanted a word? Why he'd been so furious?

The handle twisted, Doctor Fitzgerald entering with an apologetic smile. "Sorry about that. Minor issue regarding asset management." He softly closed the door, Tom nowhere to be seen.

"It's okay," Stas managed to say, her throat as dry as the Sahara.

He smoothed his hand down his dress shirt and sat across from her, his eyes deceptively kind. "Where were we?"

Her heart jumped, an entirely different question popping into her mind while he spoke. *Where were you?*

Does he know I just found Amelia?

Are there hidden cameras that caught me?

She swallowed, wiping her palms against her pant leg. He stared at her expectantly, waiting for a reply. What had he asked? *Where were we?* Right.

"Um." She cleared her throat, her voice slightly hoarse. "I, uh, you were talking about a job, I think."

She knew from his expression she'd given him the correct response. "Indeed I was. What do you think?"

I think you're a sociopath who likes to beat women.

"Well, it's a little overwhelming," she said instead, referring to the job.

Then an idea occurred to her.

One that could ensure he let her leave here alive while also potentially allowing her to return to save Amelia.

Hmm, it was a long shot, but if he agreed, it just might work. She just had to play this right, to stroke his ego and entice him into an arrangement he couldn't refuse. All while not revealing a single emotion or thought.

No pressure.

She cleared her throat again. "But"—Stas forced a smile—"it's also exciting."

Pride radiated from Doctor Fitzgerald's expression. "It is, isn't it?"

Such a masterful façade. Even now, despite everything she knew, a part of her wanted to beam with gratitude, as if he'd trained her to accept and adore his praise.

A larger part of her wanted to throw up all over his desk.

His desk.

Oh, fuck.

The card.

It still sat beside his laptop, Issac's name proudly displayed on the cardstock paper.

"Now, Tom just mentioned you met Osiris," Doctor Fitzgerald continued, curiosity coloring his tone. "I'm afraid that makes it a little more imperative for you to join us. If you become a Sentinel, I can give you certain resources that are not available to civilians—resources that can save your life."

Well, that was unexpected. "You can protect me from Osiris?"

"I can provide you with the ability to guard yourself, yes."

"Like weapons?" she guessed.

"Among other things." He laced his fingers together on the table again, leaning toward her conspiratorially. "I'm sure Issac has promised to keep you safe, but his way would involve taking on immortality. Am I right?"

Not in the way you think, she thought while nodding.

"That's a big decision. Are you ready to make it?"

Well, at least on this she could answer honestly. Because no, she absolutely was not ready for immortality. "No."

His head bobbed as if he expected that response. "Well, joining my team would grant you an opportunity to explore the supernatural world in its entirety before you decide whether or not to join it." He settled back in his chair. "With the added bonuses of learning how to defend yourself with weapons and via other supernatural means."

Runes, she realized. *He's talking about runes.*

"You know, since the first day I met you, I suspected you were destined for greatness," he added, his charisma on full display. "That's why I recommended you to Brandon down in marketing. But now, I'll admit, I'm keener to have you on my team. Assuming you're up for it, of course."

A clever way of pretending she had a choice in the matter when they both knew she didn't. Stas suspected refusing would result in something uncomfortable, such as her death.

Yet, looking at her mentor now, she'd never suspect it. He had an air of eagerness and sincerity to him that masked the evil lurking beneath his skin. Because only a sadistic bastard could leave Amelia in that condition down the hall.

"What do you think?" he prompted when she remained quiet for too long.

"When would I start?" she asked, needing time to work out her plan. It would take the right wording, a way for him to think it was his own idea all along.

"Well, given the Osiris situation, I would say as soon as possible. I can talk to the marketing team on your behalf, save you from any hard feelings."

Yes, her boss would be slightly disappointed. Not that she'd been an all-star employee this last week, what with forgetting to call Human Resources back and all that.

"I would appreciate that," she admitted. After everything she'd learned, she never wanted to work with the CRF again, but that didn't mean she disliked her boss. Chances were he had no clue of the company's sinister purpose.

"Then it's settled? I mean, assuming my team approves, but I don't see why they wouldn't agree."

She forced herself to hold his gaze. "There's just one thing."

"Oh?"

She pursed her lips, needing to phrase this the right way without sounding too eager or conniving. "I don't want to end things with Issac."

That sent both of Doctor Fitzgerald's eyebrows into his hairline. "You care about him more than this opportunity? Even after the video?"

"God no, nothing like that." A blatant lie. "But I think there might be an opportunity here."

He studied her for a long moment, his thumb stroking the stubble dotting his jaw. "What kind of opportunity?"

Curiosity piqued? Check.

"Well, he already took me to a Conclave, right? Imagine

what else he might show me. Unless you already have someone on the inside of Ichorian society feeding you information?"

"You want to be a double agent," he translated.

More like a triple agent. "Maybe. I don't think I'm phrasing this right." She pretended to consider, needing him to speak the idea for himself. "I'm just wondering if we could somehow recruit him, or if I could use my connection to him to somehow further the CRF. Honestly, I don't know what all you need, so feel free to tell me I'm way off base." *But I know I'm not.*

He continued rubbing his chin, his interest evident. "This could place you in a precarious situation."

She snorted. "I'm already in one, thanks to Issac."

He flashed her a knowing grin. "Thirsty for revenge?"

"You have no idea." Vengeance for Amelia, possibly for Owen. *Fuck, the card.* How was she going to get that back without Doctor Fitzgerald noticing?

He considered. "Do you really think he could be of use to us?"

"Issac?" she asked. "Yes. Yes, I do." Another idea formed, an impulsive one that she jumped on without considering the alternatives. "Look at that." She glanced pointedly at the card.

Doctor Fitzgerald frowned at the item, picking it up to study it. "Where did this come from?"

"Uh…" She feigned a sheepish look, twisting her lips to the side and clasping her hands in her lap. "Yeah, I may have tossed that at your desk while you were gone. He gave it to me earlier, telling me to use after our meeting. And, well, after seeing the video, I was a little annoyed. There wasn't anything else of his to throw, so…" She trailed off with a shrug.

He gave her a look before turning over the card to read Issac's scrawl. "What's the code for?"

"His security alarm." One Issac would need to change after today. "He wants me to meet him back at his condo."

Doctor Fitzgerald's eyebrows shot up again. "His personal residence off Chambers Street, or one of his guest suites on the same floor?"

"He has guest suites?" she asked, actually curious. "I think I've only stayed in his penthouse." As far as she knew, anyway. All his suits and books were there. That made it his personal space, right?

"Did it have a formal dining area? Balconies overlooking the Hudson?"

She nodded. "It's, uh, impressive, yes." Understatement.

"That's his condo, not one of the guest suites." He whistled and set the card down. "He really is quite taken with you, isn't he?"

"Sure. Enough to try to poison me, apparently."

Doctor Fitzgerald chuckled. "I'm guessing he just wanted to test your bloodline before investing the time." He shrugged, his entire demeanor changing. "Honestly, it's pretty common practice, if a bit archaic."

Uh-huh. "Well, regardless, I'm not all that pleased with him at the moment. Still, I think he could be useful." She dangled the bait and waited, hoping he would bite.

Stas couldn't save Amelia on her own, but Issac might be able to with access to the right resources. This would hopefully open the door he needed to proceed, or a way around the runes.

And she would help him every step of the way.

"Do you think he might be interested in working with us?" Doctor Fitzgerald asked, his voice sending a tingle down her spine.

Someone is using a gift.

She frowned, unnerved by the sensation. It had to be him. But what was he trying to do? *Why didn't I ask Issac about Jonathan's talent?*

Swallowing, she focused on his query and how to reply. "With the right motivation, I think we could convince him. But it won't be something he accepts overnight."

"And you think you can convince him?"

"I'd like to try," she replied. "When he explained the CRF to me, he wasn't negative. If anything, he sounded impressed." In a dark "I want to kill Jonathan" sort of way, but she didn't mention that part.

"Did he?" Doctor Fitzgerald sounded surprised. "I've just assumed him to be uninterested all these years."

"Perhaps he wasn't presented with the right opportunity," she suggested. *Such as the motive to kill you and free his sister.*

Her former mentor nodded, his gaze taking on a dreamlike quality. "He could bring a lot to the table."

Blood.

Torture.

Murder.

Death.

Yep.

"All right, Stas. You've intrigued me. The relationship can remain for now while you either siphon information from Issac or potentially recruit him." He smiled. "These things take time, so as long as you're up for the task, I see no problems with it."

"Oh, I'm up for it," she assured. And hopefully, Issac would be, too. Unless, of course, Mateo gathered everything he needed from the hard drive. Were the immortals on their way here now?

What if they want me to stall?

~*~

Several Minutes Earlier

"I'm in," Mateo announced, his fingers flying across the keyboard.

"Thank fuck for that," Issac replied, running his fingers through his hair. They were all standing in his study, where Mateo had set up shop about an hour ago.

Aidan stood beside the oversized desk, his hands tucked

into his pockets, gaze vibrant, while Tristan entertained Clara and Anya in the living area. Nadia lounged on a corner chaise, her long legs crossed at the ankles, her attention on her phone rather than the task at hand.

Rows of data scrolled before them, too fast for Issac to catch, but Aidan seemed to be reading it all with ease, his brow furrowing with each passing second.

"What is it?" Issac asked, recognizing the lines of concern etching a path into his maker's features.

"The files appear truncated." He continued reading, his brow furrowing. "It's like someone placed a bunch of file names with cover sheets in the system while removing the bulk. Do you see that, Mateo?"

"I'm still downloading," he replied, focused on the computer. "But yeah, it feels incomplete."

"Meaning your plan didn't work?" Issac couldn't help the note of censure in his tone, his concern for Astasiya's well-being fraying his nerves. However, their last glimpse from her camera showed her safe and sound. He took it as a good sign that Jonathan hadn't immediately apprehended her.

"Oh, my plan worked. The files just appear to be incomplete." Mateo frowned, shaking his head. "It's like someone keyed the names of all the projects, provided high-level detail, and erased all the metadata."

"There's no reference to additional files, either," Aidan added, his expression rivaling Mateo's. "The entire server is a smoke screen."

"So it would seem. Maybe they're saved to his local drive." Mateo flipped monitors, showing an interrogation room of sorts with three frozen expressions.

"What's that?" Issac peered over his shoulder for a better look. "Are they in another room? Where's Astasiya?"

"That's Jonathan's desktop," Mateo replied. "It's the video he showed Stas before leaving the room."

Ah yes. They'd not been able to hear it. "Can you play it?" Issac requested, curious about the contents. The visual was much clearer now, showing Jonathan, Agent Stark, and Doctor Patel.

"Sure." Mateo pushed a few keys and pulled the image to his other monitor, pressing Play.

Issac's lips thinned as he watched the footage. "Clever," he muttered as they neared the end. "And clearly rehearsed."

"Did you warn Stas about Jonathan's affinity for the truth?" Nadia asked, her ebony gaze on the screen.

"I didn't mention it," Issac admitted, regretting the oversight. "Fortunately, she's immune."

Jonathan's ability to compel the truth out of a person was why Agent Stark played the interrogator in that video. Had it been Jonathan, Doctor Patel would have been forced to answer truthfully, which would have defeated the purpose of the entire charade.

"Will Stas believe any of this?" Aidan scanned the words flowing over Mateo's other monitor while he spoke. "The video, I mean."

"She knows me better than that by now," Issac replied, certain. "Jonathan would have to do a lot better than that to convince her to distrust me at this point." If anything, the CRF's CEO had just proven Issac's accusations to be true.

Jonathan Fitzgerald was an evil son of a bitch.

"Where's Aya now?" Issac wondered, needing to see her again to confirm she was still all right.

Mateo touched a few keys to bring up her video feed.

Issac studied the viewpoint, his brow creasing. "What the hell are we looking at?" he demanded, his chest cracking. "What the fuck is that, Mateo?"

"The v-view from her blouse," Mateo breathed. "That can't be…" He enlarged the live stream on his bigger screen, Amelia's face bright beneath the harsh lighting of the room.

The image blurred as Astasiya moved, a white wall coming into view. And then Amelia's face appeared again.

Issac grabbed the monitor, his knees weak.

Amelia.

She sat crumpled in a corner, wearing a filthy shirt that hardly covered her thighs. Thick clumps of dark hair hung around her gaunt face, hiding her aristocratic features and the blue of her eyes.

But he'd recognize his sister anywhere.

Bruises littered her body, her ankle was twisted at the wrong angle, and a metal collar circled the thin column of her throat.

"Oh my God," Nadia whispered.

Clara, Anya and Tristan were at the doorway a second later, a gasp coming from one of them.

"Is this real?" Aidan sounded hoarse. "Is this *real?*"

Mateo started typing, the sound drifting into the background behind Issac's thundering heart. The video rewound to Jonathan's office, then crept forward as Astasiya stepped into the hallway.

And the room appeared again.

Fast-forwarded to the present, where Amelia remained on the floor.

Alive.

"Amelia," he whispered, his eyes glued to the screen, time ceasing to exist. "That bastard has Amelia."

He shook his head. "How is this possible?" They found records of a crematorium visit near the Hamptons estate. Eli had been found holding her ashes. "Is it a trick?" But no, it couldn't be. Astasiya wore the camera. She wouldn't allow Jonathan to play such a cruel joke, clearly didn't believe it herself by the way she kept moving around the room.

And she appeared to be speaking to Amelia.

Why wasn't there sound attached to the recording?

Would he hear the agony in her voice? Would it match her broken body?

"Can you zoom in on her neck?" Aidan asked, his tone one of reason and practicality and not at all similar to the voice rioting in Issac's head.

Amelia's battered face and neck appeared, black-and-blue marks marring her pale skin. Aidan said something about her collar, his words drowning behind a volcano of fury erupting inside Issac's head.

He couldn't concentrate on anything beyond the image on the screen.

Amelia is alive.

Fuck.

How is this possible?

Eli had been holding her ashes that day. Her rings were in the urn.

But Jonathan had staged it all.

The sick fuck had kept Amelia in the CRF underground for the last six years while Issac focused on his plans for revenge rather than saving his sister.

Because he thought she was dead the entire time.

Oh God, Amelia...

Would she ever forgive him?

"We need to get her out of there," he breathed, interrupting whatever the others were saying. "We need to go now."

He started moving, only to have Aidan step into his path, his hands landing on Issac's shoulders. More words were spoken, a whisper of sound that Issac couldn't understand over the water rushing through his ears.

"We need to go," he repeated, his hands fisting at his sides. "We need to get her the fuck out of there!"

She was alone.

Hurt.

Beaten.

"I'm going to kill that son of a bitch," he growled, picturing Jonathan's smug face. Fuck, he'd kept this from Issac for over six years. Kept his sister prisoner after killing Eli. And pretended to be his *friend*.

Lava poured through Issac's veins, fueling him to push against the wall blocking his way. He wanted to throttle Jonathan, rip him apart, burn the remains, and force the man to watch the entire time.

"…protective wards," someone said.

"…be smart about this."

"Issac, this isn't…"

"You're not… clearly."

"Stop."

The words hardly registered, only one thought driving him forward. *Save Amelia.*

Agony struck his chest, sending a blast of energy and pain through his limbs. His head spun, his hands still fisted at his sides.

The world trembled around him.

Darkness prickled his vision.

A cloud of thoughts all drenched in agony.

My sister is alive.

And I left her there…

Tortured.

Alone.

Scared.

I failed her.

He had to make amends, to fix—

A loud clap thundered through his mind, yanking him from his thoughts. The ceiling appeared above him, followed by Aidan's furrowed brow and a very concerned Tristan.

"Did it work?" Lucian's voice came from the left, startling Issac.

The Hydraians had all returned to Hydria this morning.

Yet all four Elders stood inside Issac's study. In his condo. In New York City.

What the hell…?

"He's back," Balthazar said, voice low, his expression concerned.

Back? Issac repeated. *Back from what?*

"We need a plan." Aidan's voice held a note of urgency in it. "I want her back as badly as you do, trust me. But if we go in there now with our emotions high, we'll die. Or worse."

Issac frowned as he sat up, his head throbbing. *How did I end up on the couch?* His desk sat several feet away, unoccupied. Everyone else stood around him.

"You were hell-bent on saving Amelia," Balthazar explained. "You wouldn't listen to reason."

"I don't..." Issac blinked at the now-black screen—the same one he'd held only moments ago. "Turn it back on."

"We need a plan," Aidan repeated.

"I get that," Issac replied shortly, having heard him the first time. "Now turn on the bloody computer."

"Stas already left." Lucian moved in front of the desk, his imposing body taking on an intimidating stance. "She's on her way here, hopefully with helpful information."

Issac shook his head as if to clear it. "On her way back? She was just in that bloody room with Amelia."

A room he needed to save her from.

He started to stand, only to have Balthazar push him back down. "Take a deep breath, Wakefield. We all want to get her back, but it has to be the right way."

"How are you even here?" Issac demanded, confused and irritated. "And where's Astasiya?"

Aidan handed him a bottle of water. "Drink that. It'll help."

Issac narrowed his gaze. "Tell me what happened." Because he'd clearly lost time somehow. It was the only explanation for the miraculous appearance of the Elders and for him waking up on the couch. He took a sip to appease his maker, demonstrating he was calm despite the insanity surrounding him.

Aidan blew out a breath, taking a step back. "You became fixated on Amelia and wouldn't listen to reason, so—"

"I subdued you," Nadia finished with a grimace. She stood just inside the doorway with Clara acting as a shield in front of her. Both women appeared wary of his reaction.

Understanding tightened Issac's shoulders. Nadia possessed the ability to knock a person out by delivering a psychic blow. The agony he felt hadn't been from emotions but from *her*.

"Why?" he demanded.

"To stop you from doing something stupid," she replied, sounding only slightly apologetic. "You can't just storm in there, Issac. You'll die, or worse."

"We all want her back, but we need to approach this strategically," Aidan added. "Now, we've already begun analyzing the device on her neck, as well as mapping out the underground from Stas's video surveillance."

"The artillery room will be an issue." Lucian folded his thick forearms. "We'll be at an extreme disadvantage, even if we enter armed."

Aidan nodded. "I agree. Have you found anything else that may be of use, Mateo?"

"Still searching for records on the device," Issac's progeny called from another room. "From what I've gathered so far, it's an explosive collar of some kind." He appeared in the doorway with his laptop, his uneasy gaze landing on Issac. "It'll detonate if she leaves the CRF by force."

Fuck.

Issac ran his fingers through his hair, his throat working as he tried to digest all the information. Saving her had been his only thought, his only priority. But now that his initial shock had dissipated, logic overrode his mind.

"Can the device be removed without detonation?" he asked, his voice hoarse.

Mateo shook his head. "The files are all truncated, even on Jonathan's hard drive. I can only find high-level details, like one-sentence or two-sentence summaries in each log. It's almost as if he's reporting the information to a superior—perhaps the benefactor—while keeping the full files on his own personal device. Not his laptop, because I checked that, but something else."

"I wonder—"

"Issac!" Astasiya's yell interrupted Aidan's reply, her

voice holding a touch of panic that pierced Issac's heart.

His legs were moving before he registered the action, heading down the hallway into the main room of his condo to find Astasiya panting in the living area. Her wild gaze met his, tears streaking down her cheeks. She dropped her bag and collapsed into his open arms. He held her tight, his lips brushing her forehead, her hair, her temple.

"W-when you didn't answer... I thought... Oh God, I thought you were on your way to the CRF. I tried to stall, but... I couldn't stay there. When he let me leave, I taxied straight here." She shuddered violently, her shoulders hunched over in a way that hurt his heart. "A-Amelia... Issac, she's alive. Jonathan i-is... *Fuck*."

"It's all right, love," Issac whispered, his palm sliding over her back. "You're all right." Just murmuring those words helped heal a part of him he hadn't realized was wounded. Despite the revelation about his sister, he felt oddly whole again, as if Astasiya's presence had soothed him somehow.

My other half.

"We have to get her out of there." Astasiya gripped the lapels of his jacket, tugging as she pulled back to meet his gaze. "You saw her, right? You saw her?"

Issac swallowed and nodded. "Yes. We saw her."

Astasiya sagged against him again. "I was so worried you might go after her, but the runes... the guns... the Sentinels..." She shook her head. "I couldn't help her, Issac. I wanted to, but I couldn't. I didn't know *how*."

"You did the right thing," Aidan replied, joining them in the living area. "Had you attempted to save her, Jonathan would have placed you in a similar predicament, or worse."

"He's right." Issac continued rubbing her back, his heart thudding in his chest. "We can't react emotionally." Even if all he wanted was to march into that building and rip Jonathan's head from his body.

I will kill him.

But it would be the right way.

With planning.

Because they needed to play this smart.

Once they had Amelia back, Issac would destroy Jonathan and everything the man had ever created. Starting with the CRF.

"I…" Astasiya cleared her throat. "I… I might have a suggestion."

CHAPTER THIRTY

What is Elizabeth Watkins?

ISSAC LISTENED INTENTLY WHILE ASTASIYA detailed her discussion with Jonathan, telling them everything from the video—which she didn't believe—to the job offer.

"So that's why I suggested we recruit Issac," she concluded from her seat beside him on the couch. "Because it might give him access to something that can help us free Amelia."

"I still vote we just storm the place and torch it to the ground," Alik said with a shrug. "Not many would consider it a loss."

"Too many innocent lives," Lucian replied casually. "It would also attract Osiris's attention, something I'd prefer to avoid."

Yes, and the only way to take on the CRF as a collective unit would be to involve the Hydraians. Which could be perceived as an attack since the Ichorians considered New York City to be their home.

Issac ran his palm over his face and blew out a breath. "It was a smart move, Aya," he admitted. "It'll grant me closer access to Jonathan and his organization, which we can use appropriately." Not only to free Amelia, but to demolish the CRF empire.

Aidan nodded from the chair across from him, his hands clasped in his lap. "If you can earn his trust, we might be able to locate the device with the missing files and find out more about his mysterious benefactor."

"It also serves as a way to protect Stas while she's undercover as a Sentinel," Lucian added. "Which I consider to be a requirement."

"A requirement?" she repeated.

"Yes. You are a future Hydraian, and if you're going to risk your very valuable life by playing double agent in a city full of Ichorians, then I am entitled to several requirements for your stay. The first being your protection."

Astasiya's eyebrows lifted. "I'm not property, Luc."

"No, but you are a powerful fledgling and a future asset to Hydria. I take that very seriously, as should you." The not-so-subtle reprimand in his voice had Astasiya's shoulders tensing.

"We can work through the semantics at a later point," Issac interjected, his arm tightening around her shoulders. "For now, let's review our options. How do we free Amelia?"

Lucian crossed his ankle over his opposite knee, the chair beneath him resembling a throne more than a recliner. "If we storm the CRF tonight, we have a thirty percent chance of saving Amelia. That's a success rate that does not account for the collar that may or may not detonate upon exit. Not to mention the external consequences involving the Conclave, as well as giving up a valuable playing card—Stas's double agent status."

"It's not the most strategic response," Aidan agreed. "We need additional information on the device, plus a more detailed layout of the CRF's underground. The video footage only accounts for maybe a tenth of the estimated square footage beneath the building."

"Meaning we require more surveillance to establish a better plan," Lucian translated. "As much as it pains me to say this, rescuing Amelia tonight would not be in her best interest or ours."

Issac's chest ached, his instincts warring with reason.

He'd left his sister there for too long already and continued to fail her every second he remained here. Yet, it would not help her if he were captured, or worse, killed.

I'm going to slaughter Jonathan for this.

Losing Amelia had been the worst experience of Issac's life.

Knowing that she was alive and he couldn't save her was worse.

Astasiya flinched beside him, reminding Issac that he held her hand.

"Sorry," he whispered.

"I understand," she replied. "I want revenge, too."

"Well, you're really going to want to kill him now," Mateo announced as he entered the room with his laptop, his expression grim. "I was sorting through the files, looking for anything that might be able to help us, and I found something you all need to see." He set his computer on the table, the image on his screen one Issac recognized immediately.

Astasiya's intake of breath confirmed she did as well. "That's Owen."

Mateo nodded and brought up a file with a handful of words on it, starting with the date of Owen's murder.

Order executed by JF at 00:00.

Assignment completed by GS at 04:00. Visual confirmation

attached.

"That confirms Jonathan ordered his death, but not why," Aidan said, studying the document.

"Yes." Mateo clicked another button. "But I found this, too. From about a week before."

JF: It's been brought to my attention that Owen Angelton is not only residing in New York City but has also befriended the roommate of a valuable CRF asset. We believe he is using her for access to information. Suggested action is termination.

GS: Assigned project to Sentinel Charlie.

CC: Suspicions confirmed. Owen Angelton is too close to the asset and requires termination.

GS: Task to be handled personally.

Astasiya's hand was at her mouth. "The date at the top is the day I mentioned inviting Owen to dinner after graduation."

"Which would imply they hadn't known of his existence in the city until then," Issac deduced. "Then who funded the bar?"

"An excellent query." Aidan stared thoughtfully at the screen. "It's potentially a bogus file, but I can't determine a purpose for it. Have you found anything else on him?"

Mateo shook his head. "These are the only two referencing his name. I also searched for the bar, dates corresponding to when Owen befriended Stas, anything on Stas and Elizabeth living together, and a variety of other items, and these are my only findings thus far."

"Confirming this to be a crime of circumstance and not related to a history of working together." Lucian's lips flattened. "That's both comforting and disappointing. What have you found on Elizabeth?"

"Nothing." Mateo sounded frustrated. "Not even a file name."

"Why would there be information on Lizzie?" Astasiya asked.

Right. Issac hadn't covered that topic with her yet. "We suspect Elizabeth is a product of the CRF. Likely a failed experiment, or perhaps a successful one. We don't actually know."

"A *what?*" She pulled away from him, her eyes wide. "You think my best friend is an experiment? And you didn't think to tell me that until *now?*"

"As Issac said, we don't know for certain." Aidan used a soothing tone that did nothing to dispel the fury radiating from Astasiya.

"I've had my plate full with explaining our world, and to be honest, this detail escaped me." Along with surely another dozen or so items. Alas, this particular one was something he should have told her. "For what it's worth, Elizabeth is completely unaware of everything. From the way she behaves, it's clear she considers herself human. And maybe she is. The only thing we know with certainty is she is in no way biologically related to Lillian and George Watkins. Until roughly seven years ago, they didn't have a daughter. She merely showed up one day."

Astasiya's mouth opened, then closed, then opened again, and she just shook her head. "I need a drink." She pushed away from him and headed toward the kitchen.

Issac sighed, standing. "I'll fix it."

"Allow me," Balthazar said with a look that had Issac pausing midstep. *Trust me*, his brown eyes implored. *Please.*

Issac studied him for a long moment before giving a nod. *I'll give you ten minutes.*

He returned the nod, his lips twitching in gratitude.

Balthazar could grate on even a saint's nerves, but when it came down to matters of the heart, he was a loyal friend. Issac trusted him. And most importantly, he trusted Astasiya.

~*~

Lizzie is a CRF experiment.

A simple statement, easily voiced, yet completely forgotten.

How?

Stas shook her head and started looking through cabinets for liquor. Preferably, something a hundred proof or higher. The stronger, the better.

"There's a wet bar in the living area, but as I imagine you need a few minutes to yourself, may I interest you in a glass of wine instead?" Balthazar's warm tones flowed through the kitchen, causing her to bolt upright from her crouched position by the island. "Or there might be some bourbon in one of the guest suites across the hall, if you prefer."

She frowned. "Guest suites?"

"Where Issac usually entertains his conquests," Balthazar murmured, a twinkle in his gaze. "Only family and close friends are allowed in his actual penthouse." He found a bottle in the fridge and showed it to her. "A white from Northern Italy? It's one of Issac's favorites."

"You know a lot about him," she observed, folding her arms. Yet, they bickered like rivals. Issac's distaste for the mind reader was palpable.

He chuckled as he found a corkscrew on his first try. "It's a brotherly relationship, I assure you. I care quite a bit about him, which is the reason I'm risking my life in his condo at present. Has he told you about my other gift yet?"

She shook her head.

"Can you grab two glasses from the cabinet behind you?" He nodded with his chin toward the wood door in question.

Stas plucked two crystal wineglasses from the shelf and set them on the island.

"I control emotion," he said while pouring her a small amount. "Taste this and let me know if it suits."

"You control emotion?" she repeated, taking the glass.

He nodded. "I do. The extent of it matches my ability to read minds, meaning I can hear and control for several miles."

That's overwhelming, she thought as she sipped the cold liquid. *Mmm, citrusy.*

"I hear approval," he murmured, smiling. He filled himself a glass before topping off hers and sliding it back across the marble. "And yes, it can be overwhelming, especially when someone I care about is distraught or conflicted." He glanced pointedly at her. "Would you like to know how Issac feels now?"

She wrinkled her nose. "Seems an invasion of privacy, doesn't it?" If Issac wanted her to know how he felt about something, he'd tell her.

"Sometimes we need a little nudge to express our emotions, Stas. Especially when we're not accustomed to them." Balthazar leaned on the island with one forearm resting across the marble countertop, his opposite hand swirling his wine. "I've known Wakefield for several centuries, and would you like to know how many women he's let into his personal quarters?"

She swallowed a healthy sip of her wine, unsure if she wanted the answer. Issac's reputation as a playboy didn't bother her, nor did it really thrill her. But she couldn't hold his past against him.

"One," Balthazar said, even though she never replied. "You, Stas. Which is why you can imagine my surprise when he took you to his bed, rather than to one of the other suites on this floor, after your Nizari poison incident. This relationship between the two of you has been unique from the beginning."

Stas set down her now-empty glass and leveled him with a look. "Why are you telling me all this?"

"Because I want you to understand how special this is, Stas. What you have with Issac is unlike anything he's ever experienced, and he's going to make mistakes, such as not telling you about Lizzie up front. But he's giving it his best effort and he adores you. Try not to be too angry with him for it. You've both had an emotionally draining day. I suggest you work it off in an active manner rather than a negatively reactive one." He finished his wine and collected their glasses, placing them in the sink.

Issac entered, his expression sheltered as he took in the bottle on the counter. "Aidan and Lucian are going through all the files Mateo downloaded to memorize and sort through the details."

"Yes, I hear them," Balthazar said, his lips curling down. "Some of the project names are disturbingly cryptic. Aidan is toying with anagrams in his head, which makes it worse."

"Most days, I do not envy your talent," Issac admitted, a hint of a grin glimmering in his sapphire eyes.

Balthazar shrugged. "No worse than seeing the fantasies of a million people at once, I imagine. Speaking of…" Sin danced through his features, causing Issac to growl low in his throat.

"Continue down that path and I'll turn it into a nightmare you won't soon forget." He glanced pointedly at a set of knives on the counter.

"That's just cruel."

"You thinking I'd ever let you top me is wicked, too."

Stas blinked, the image forming behind her eyes unbidden. The two of them in bed together would be—

"Explosive," Balthazar finished for her. "And next time I'll imagine you topping me, Wakefield. Just for fun." He winked before sauntering out of the kitchen, completely unfazed by the glower Issac sent after him.

"Is he, uh, serious?" Stas couldn't help asking.

"Balthazar never jokes about sex," Issac muttered. "So, unfortunately, yes. And he's been suggesting it for nearly three centuries now."

Her lips parted. "That long?" *And it's never happened?*

"He knows it's an impossibility, which only makes it more fun for him." Issac sighed and ran his fingers through his hair before meeting her gaze again. A beat passed between them, and a hint of wariness settled across his features. "I'm sorry, Aya. I should have told you about Elizabeth earlier. With everything else requiring an explanation, I didn't think about it. And now with Amelia…" Pain flickered in the depths of his gaze, sending an arrow through her heart.

His sister wasn't just alive, but was being held captive by the man he despised. Issac must feel so angry and guilty for not searching for her, for not saving his sister. And that was all made worse now by his inability to go after her.

Because as much as everyone hated to wait, Aidan and Luc were right. They needed a plan founded on strategy, not emotion.

"I'm sorry," Issac repeated softly. "I didn't mean to keep it from you."

Oh, Issac. He mistook her silence for anger. But she didn't have it in her to be mad at him. Not after everything they'd been through.

She moved past the counter and wrapped her arms around him, choosing actions over words. Because he looked like he needed a hug, and the way he clung to her in response proved it. His lips fell to her neck, his nose buried against her skin as he held her tightly.

"Aya," he breathed.

"I'm not upset," she whispered. "I understand."

"I should have told you."

"Yes," she agreed. "But I know now. And it only fuels my decision to go after Jonathan. He's taken too much from us. He won't take Lizzie, too." Her roommate might be an experiment, as they called her, but she was still Stas's best friend. "I won't let him hurt her."

Issac remained quiet for a long moment, his arms a protective band across her lower back, his mouth heated against her neck. "You want to take the job."

"I do." It was the only logical course. She would learn more about the CRF Sentinel program, the underground, and the experiments and feed all the details back to the others. "Those files are somewhere," she added. "If Jonathan lets me get close enough, I'll find them." And Mateo would equip her with the means necessary to do it. "We'll destroy him, Issac. And we'll find the information we need to save those we care about. It's our best move."

His exhale scattered goose bumps down her neck. It was long, low, and hot.

"You're so strong, my Aya." He kissed her pulse and lifted to press his forehead to hers. "This won't be easy."

"I know." It would be the hardest task of her life. Even harder than saying goodbye to her parents. "But we don't have a choice." She needed to do this for Owen, for Lizzie, and for Amelia. And she knew Issac felt the same. "It's the right decision."

"Yes," he whispered, his exhale a breath against her lips. "We're in this together."

"Always," she agreed.

"Always," he repeated, brushing his mouth against hers. Electricity hummed across her skin, his kiss sealing an unspoken promise between their souls. He repeated the action, sending a jolt through her bloodstream. And again, this one harsher, more urgent.

"*Issac.*" His name was part plea, part vow. She didn't know what she wanted, but it translated to a desperate sound in the back of her throat that he silenced with his tongue.

His fingers knotted in her hair to angle her head to where he desired, his kiss intense. Hard. Thorough. Possessive. He put everything he owned into their embrace, and she returned every emotion with one of her own.

Pain.

Sadness.

Heartache.

Confusion.

Joy.

Because while she'd experienced hell over the last few weeks, she'd also been introduced to a passion unlike any she'd ever known.

"I need you," he whispered, lifting her onto the counter and stepping between her legs. "Fuck, I need you, Aya." His hands were on her pants, his thumb on the button. "Distract me, please. I can't think anymore. It's driving me to insanity."

The beseeching quality in his voice said everything.

Issac wanted to lose himself in passion, to forget the present, to forget the hopelessness of Amelia's situation, to forget his inability to help his sister escape.

And he'd chosen Stas to help him through it.

To provide him with the release he needed from reality.

She would never deny him. Somehow, at some point, he'd become a part of her, adhering himself to her heart and soul and binding them for eternity. Their future didn't matter in the present.

All that mattered was the here and now, the heavy emotion flourishing between them, and the passion only he could unleash in her.

She kissed him again, her fingers threading through his hair as she answered him without words.

Take me.

Use me.

Love me.

I'm yours.

CHAPTER THIRTY-ONE

Blood Vows

ISSAC LOST HIMSELF IN ASTASIYA'S MOUTH, her tongue doing things to him that he could hardly comprehend, let alone describe.

He felt possessed.

Adored.

It was exactly the distraction he craved. She was his cure to the madness lurking in his thoughts. The only one keeping him grounded. His rock.

It terrified him.

Floored him.

Left him vulnerable in a way he'd never experienced.

Yet, she also strengthened him.

The convoluted combination drugged him, shadowing

his mind and soothing his soul. All he could do was enjoy the afterglow and take what she readily gave, to sink into her body and connect them on a level that shouldn't exist.

Mine.

The impossibility of their relationship no longer mattered. Issac adored a challenge. They would figure this out. Somehow, someway, they would make this work.

He led her to his room, not caring at all that they still had company in the living area, and ordered her to strip beside his bed. Her blouse and bra fell to the floor. Her boots, socks, and pants followed. Then her lace thong, an item he should have removed with his teeth, fell to the top of the pile, leaving her naked and flushed before him.

Perfection.

Curved in all the right places.

Confident.

Legs for days.

His ideal woman, his partner, his Aya.

"On the bed, darling," he murmured, his gaze running over her in a heated wave.

That she obeyed him thrilled him all the more. Her stiff nipples and quivering thighs said she returned the sentiment.

Her blonde hair spilled over Issac's pillows, her gaze hooded as she watched him loosen his tie. He considered binding her wrists to his headboard, knowing it would leave her open and exposed to his touch.

But he needed her hands on him tonight. Her lips. Her tongue. Everything she had to offer.

He tossed his tie onto the ground beside her clothes and began unfastening his cuff links. Astasiya's green eyes flared with desire as she watched, her tongue dampening her swollen lower lip.

"Spread your legs," he demanded, needing to see her aroused flesh.

She complied on a moan that went straight to his cock. He adored that sound, enjoyed even more the damp haven between her thighs.

Issac slowly unbuttoned his shirt, prolonging the anticipation and admiring the flush creeping over her skin. She'd not balked as he strode her past the others in the living area, fully trusting him to shield their presence from everyone in the room. He hadn't even needed to explain; she merely knew.

Their connection only intensified the intimacy flowing between them, her faith in him fueling his need to fuck her.

Mmm, no, not quite the right word. He was craving something slower, more thorough, and underlined in passion.

Her gorgeous eyes danced appreciatively over his chest and abdomen, his shirt falling to the floor behind him. Followed by his belt, pants, and boxer briefs. His shoes and socks were long forgotten, leaving him naked as he knelt on the bed.

Astasiya reached for him as he crawled over her. He took her mouth in a kiss meant to brand, to own, to possess, his tongue demanding reciprocation and devotion. She conceded on a groan, her nails digging into his shoulders, her legs wrapping around his waist. Slick, wet heat met his erection, her body more than ready to take him despite their minimal foreplay. And as much as he wanted to take his time, he also needed to feel her, to take her, to claim her.

She cried out as he slid into her on a harsh thrust, her back bowing off the bed. "Issac," she breathed, her body trembling beneath him. "*Fuck.*"

"Too much?" he murmured, his lips tracing her jaw.

"Not enough." She pressed into him, forcing him deeper, her heels digging into his ass. "More."

"Mmm." He drew his nose across her cheek, his mouth tasting her skin as he went. "What if I prefer slow?" He demonstrated with his hips.

She growled in response. "Don't hold back on me now."

"Maybe I want to worship you." He continued the unhurried motion, driving them both mad and loving every minute.

"Liar," she accused, breathless. "Gentle isn't in your nature."

"Care to test that theory?" he asked softly.

He swallowed her responding groan, his tongue parting her lips to engage her in a passionate dance between their mouths.

Fuck, he adored kissing this woman. It satisfied him on a level he didn't know existed until her. And the way her hand curled around the back of his neck, holding him in place, suggested she felt the same.

He palmed her cheek, his fingers sliding into her hair. She tasted like mint, her tongue determined against his. Her nails against his nape spurred him on, her hips rising and lowering to meet his measured movements.

No rushing.

No fucking.

Just adoration.

Every touch, nip, and lick was his way of cherishing her. He'd never done anything like this with a woman, had no idea he would enjoy it, but with Astasiya, it came to him naturally. She would be the only one he'd ever indulge in this manner—the only one he'd ever revere.

So thorough, tender, and mind-melting.

His heart pounded in time with hers, sweat trickling between them not from the physical strain but from the thriving emotional connection.

"What are you doing to me?" she whispered, her lips brushing his with each word. "God, Issac, I feel... I feel like I'm on fire."

"Mmm, it's addictive," he agreed, his cock throbbing for release inside her despite the leisurely penetration. "Kiss me."

"I am." Her tongue followed her words, entering his mouth and dueling once again with his, lighting him up from within. His fingers curled in her hair, tugging. She reciprocated in kind, competing with him and proving herself his equal even while submitting to his assault below.

My Aya.

He sank his teeth into her lower lip as she unleashed a delicious moan. He fucking loved that sound. His hips drove into hers, the pace deliberate and right, his lips curling as she moaned again.

Glorious.

He felt every quake, every squeeze, every groan as he brought her closer and closer to orgasm. The intensity nearly undid him, his skin slick with the force of their lovemaking.

"I'm close," she whispered.

"I know," he mouthed, keeping his movements steady and complete. "Say my name when you come."

Her nails scored his back, her slick walls tightening around his shaft. It felt amazing, perfect, exactly the way it should.

"Take me with you, love," he murmured, thrusting deep and hard. "Come with me."

"Issac…" She froze for one tantalizing second, her muscles cementing around him, and then released on a wave of quivers that shook him to his very being.

Her name left his lips on a guttural growl that rumbled between them as they dove headfirst into a cloud of ecstasy and wonder together.

The power of it shocked him, sending trembles through every limb as he spasmed inside her, marking Astasiya as his in the most masculine of ways. She clamped down around him, her body forbidding him to leave, her nails firmly embedded into his back, and everything about it felt *right*. A mutual claiming. Their bodies joining as one while their souls bonded on a plane of their own existence.

And Issac wouldn't have it any other way.

"You're mine," he whispered, his mouth tracing the words against her throat. "I'm never letting you go." His incisors pierced her skin, pulling her essence into his mouth and solidifying the pact on instinct alone.

She writhed beneath him, her lower half reacting to the endorphins pumping through her bloodstream and sending her into another orgasm. His name rent the air on waves of her passion, telling the world who owned her.

"More," she begged. "Everything, Issac. Give me everything."

He gave in to the urge to fuck her—hard—his cock seeking the heaven of her tight sheath and blissful warmth. Each stroke drove them to oblivion, her blood euphoric on his tongue. They were lost in each other, in the moment, in how they felt together.

Time became obsolete. Thought no longer processed. Only sensation and emotion ruled them now.

Rapture masked the pain of the past.

Agony melted into sensual bliss.

Their moans mingled intimately, their hearts beating as one.

And sometime, a long time later, they finally paused to breathe, his forehead touching hers, their bodies a tangled mess beneath the sheet. Somehow they'd ended up on their sides facing one another, Astasiya's leg strewn over his hip, his cock lodged deep inside. She panted against him, sweat glistening across them both, her lips pulled up into a drowsy smile.

The lack of sound and visuals in his condo said they had long been left alone, something he would thank his friends and family for later. Because he needed that—*this*—with Astasiya. She grounded him, healed him, strengthened him.

"What was my life before you?" he sighed, his arms going around her.

A laugh escaped her, the sound hoarse and tired. "I think I should be the one asking that. A month ago, graduation was all I cared about. Now…"

"Your life is forever changed," he finished for her, his fingers running through her hair and twisting the strands behind her ear. "How are you faring, darling?" he asked softly. So much had happened over the last few weeks between finding out her future path, Jonathan's intentions, the truth about Owen's murder. *My sister being alive.*

"I'm overwhelmed," she admitted, her green eyes glistening with sincerity. "I'm also furious, like I want to break something or someone." She studied him for a long moment, a serious quality overtaking her features. "I understand your desire for revenge, how you could justify using another for the sake of vengeance."

He ran his thumb over her bottom lip. "Mmm, yes, my perfect pawn." He met her gaze again. "But you know this relationship between us is no longer a charade, that these emotions run far deeper, yes?"

She nodded. "I do, but I'm still the right tool in this equation. Jonathan offered me the job, Issac. All I have to do is formally accept it, and I'm in. You wanted to destroy him from the inside. We now have the opportunity to do so, with you at my side."

His fingertips lightly traced her jaw, the shapely lines alluring and strong, just like her. "You're certain this is the path you prefer? Because it will be a dangerous one, especially with you residing in the city near Osiris."

"Is there another choice?" she asked, her voice low. "You felt the impact of the runes, Issac. And you saw the artillery room. That's only the beginning of our obstacles. To free Amelia, we need more reconnaissance. What better way to gather information than by playing alongside the enemy?"

"Not to mention the ability to destroy his organization from within," Issac added, his shoulders falling. "But it means leaving Amelia with him." Just saying the words battered his heart, sending an ache to his gut. "I don't know if I can do it, Aya." Even now, knowing the risk, part of him *needed* to rescue his sister.

She cupped his cheek. "We'll save her, Issac. I promise. But it has to be the right way. You will be of no use to her dead."

He swallowed, knowing she was right and hating it all

the same. Issac rolled to his back and Astasiya followed, her chin resting on his chest, her thigh draped over his. "How did she seem?" He wasn't sure he really wanted the answer, but needed it all the same. "Was she…?" He swallowed the rest of the words, his throat thick with emotion.

"She dreams of blue butterflies," Aya whispered. "And she seemed… strong."

He glanced down at her. "Strong?"

Astasiya nodded. "She thought I was another of Jonathan's games, whatever that meant. But she didn't feel like playing. She said a few odd things, but mostly, she came off as empowered."

His breath shuddered out of him, a weight lifting from his shoulders. "She's not broken."

"No," she replied. "But she was wounded."

"I saw the bruises." He'd memorized them as well so he could inflict the same ones on Jonathan, only with deeper coloring and blood. "I'm going to kill him."

"I know." She cupped his jaw, her gaze meeting his. "And I'll help you." Promise radiated from her irises. "We can do this, Issac. We'll save her. Together. And then Jonathan will pay for everything he's done to those we care about. To Amelia, to Lizzie, to Owen." Her voice cracked on the last name, but her expression never wavered. "I need to find out what he's done to Lizzie, to avenge Owen's death. Just as you need to destroy him for what he's done to your sister and everyone else. Let's beat him at his own game."

"You want to be the queen on my board," he murmured.

"An upgrade from a pawn."

"Indeed." He pushed her onto her back, hovering above her on his elbows. "Does that make me your king or a knight?"

She cupped his cheek. "It makes you my partner and fellow mastermind on the playing field. My very own demon." The latter was said with a twinkle in her gaze. "You're mine, too, you know."

"Am I?" he asked, amused.

She nodded. "You—"

An urgent knock on his bedroom door cut off her words, the unexpected intrusion causing Issac's gift to engage throughout the building.

Mateo.

Aidan.

Jacque.

"They've found something," Issac said, his jaw tightening. "That's the only reason they'd return." And from the image he was reading from Mateo's mind, he understood the urgency of their interruption. With Astasiya's assistance today with the card trick, Mateo had been able to build a back door into Jonathan's system through the hacking connection. Despite her taking the device home, his presence in the CRF network remained.

"What is it?" Aya asked, sitting up as Issac rolled off her.

Asset Seven. Based on Aidan's analysis, that classification applied to Amelia, something he conveyed with a series of images to Issac.

"My sister," he said, his tongue suddenly too thick for his mouth. "There's a new file with today's date."

The color drained from Aya's face, her hands automatically bringing the sheets up to cover her chest. "Oh no… What does it say?"

Issac swallowed thickly, his heart fracturing in his chest. "The orders are to move her."

"To where?"

"We don't know," Aidan said, entering the room. "Which means there's no other option. You need to accept the job. And Issac will be working with you."

EPILOGUE

Gabriel

"YOU REALIZE THIS would be easier if we just told her the truth, yes?" Ezekiel asked, a glass of amber liquid in his hand. He'd ordered a second for Gabriel that remained untouched on the bar countertop.

"Not yet," he replied. "Not until she's grown into her gifts."

"You Seraphim sure enjoy the long game, hmm?" Ezekiel took a sip, his leather jacket and long, dark hair drawing notice from the females at the bar. Not that he noticed or cared. The former Nizari assassin would sooner kill the gawkers than fuck them. "At least Issac will be helping us guard her with Owen's untimely retirement."

"I'll be assisting as well through the CRF," Gabriel

replied.

"Assuming she takes the job."

"She will." He was certain of it. "Jonathan just issued orders to move Amelia to somewhere remote."

"Why do I suspect that was your idea?"

"Actually, his son suggested it under the guise of hiding her from Stas." Gabriel had been impressed. It demonstrated that the younger Fitzgerald may have a future yet. "Jonathan wasn't too keen on it originally, so I may have urged him to reconsider."

"You always harbored a soft spot for Amelia," Ezekiel mused. "Not that I blame you. She's lovely, from what I recall. Pity what Jonathan has done to her."

"You're missing the point entirely. I didn't do this for Amelia." *Not directly, anyway.* Gabriel hid his grimace by taking a sip of his drink, allowing the burn to etch a path down his throat. *I've been around humans far too long.* He was losing his grip on practicality. "The reason I pushed the suggestion was because it will entice Stas to join the CRF, and it also frees me up to be more involved in her training."

"Providing additional security."

"Precisely." He finished the amber liquid in his glass and signaled for another. "But yes, I admit that it also gives Amelia a break from the torment." No one should endure the type of treatment Jonathan had inflicted on Amelia. If Gabriel didn't need the Ichorian alive, he'd have killed the bastard years ago.

"Who did Jonathan assign to babysitting duty?"

Gabriel's lips actually curled, a feat considering they rarely moved, aside from being used to speak. "Have I mentioned that being my favorite part of the whole plan?" He rarely deviated from the course, but this, well, *this* he rather enjoyed contriving.

Ezekiel cocked a brow. "Who did you set up?"

He met the assassin's gaze, brief amusement touching his chest. "Tom Fitzgerald." It served as a way for the CRF's CEO to punish his son for his recent "untoward" behavior and presented Tom with a unique opportunity. One Gabriel hoped he would accept. If Tom was the man Gabriel suspected him to be, then Amelia would be in far better hands.

Ezekiel chuckled, devious energy rolling off him in waves. "Oh, I bet he loved that."

"On the contrary, he's quite displeased. But of all the Sentinels, I trust him with her the most. He's the only one with a heart." And the only one with potential to prosper beyond the darkness. This would prove to be a test of sorts, to see how Tom handled it. Gabriel wished him luck. Because if he failed, Gabriel would have no choice but to kill the man.

"Brilliant," Ezekiel replied. "And I told you—you're soft on her."

Gabriel snorted. "I'm not soft." But, all right, maybe he wanted Amelia to escape. Just a little bit.

"Not even for Stas?"

A young girl flashed through his mind, one with big green eyes radiating pain and sorrow over the loss of her parents. Sethios and Caro.

Soon, he vowed, closing his eyes briefly. *I'll tell you everything soon.*

"Definitely soft," Ezekiel said, understanding darkening his gaze. He picked up one of the new drinks as they were delivered and raised it. "To fate."

Gabriel snorted. "Fuck fate." He clicked his glass against Ezekiel's. "To Skye's prophecy."

May it come to fruition, and soon.

THE STORY CONTINUES WITH FORBIDDEN BONDS...

Exile never felt so good...

Tom's a trained sniper, not a babysitter. He kills rogue immortals for a living, but after releasing classified information to a friend, he's banished to a remote location with the CRF's most prized asset.

Can two tortured souls find solace and love in one another?

Secrets unfold as Tom forms a forbidden relationship with his new charge. The immortal woman evokes memories and feelings long forgotten and forces him to question everything he's ever known.

Sacrifices must be made.

A rash decision sends them both running for their lives as immortal enemies vie for their heads.

Some bonds are meant to be broken...

IMMORTAL CURSE SERIES
WHAT'S NEXT

Dear Reader,

Thank you so much for reading *Blood Laws*. I hope you enjoyed meeting Issac and Stas. You might be wondering about some of their unresolved issues. Don't worry; I have huge plans for them. They are main characters throughout the series (appearing in all books) and will have more than one novel featuring them as the primary hero/heroine. This was the beginning of their story, and there is much more to come for them.

Up next is *Forbidden Bonds*, where Tom will question everything he's ever known as he gets to know Amelia in ways he never anticipated. As sexual tension and emotions flare between them, they will need to decide just how much they are willing to sacrifice for love. I've included the first two chapters next so you can get an idea of how this series will flow.

For sneak peeks, early chapter reveals, and special excerpts, please join my reader group on Facebook or sign up for my newsletter. Please keep in touch!

Cheers,

Lexi C. Foss

ABOUT THE AUTHOR

USA Today Bestselling Author Lexi C. Foss is a writer lost in the IT world. She lives in Atlanta, Georgia, with her husband and their furry children. When not writing, she's busy crossing items off her travel bucket list. Many of the places she's visited can be seen in her writing, including the mythical world of Hydria, which is based on Hydra in the Greek islands. She's quirky, consumes way too much coffee, and loves to swim.

www.LexiCFoss.com
https://www.facebook.com/LexiCFoss
https://www.twitter.com/LexiCFoss

ALSO BY LEXI C. FOSS

Immortal Curse Series
Blood Laws
Forbidden Bonds
Blood Heart
Elder Bonds
Blood Bonds
Angel Bonds

Blood Alliance Series
Chastely Bitten
Royally Bitten

Dark Provenance Series
Daughter of Death
Son of Chaos

Mershano Empire Series
The Prince's Game
The Charmer's Gambit

CPSIA information can be obtained
at www.ICGtesting.com
Printed in the USA
LVHW040239091120
671123LV00002B/11